HOME TRUTHS IN TUMBLE CREEK

Louise Forster

The best adventure is the one I'm on
with you.

~~~ Unknown
~~~

Home Truths in Tumble Creek

Louise Forster

Chapter 1

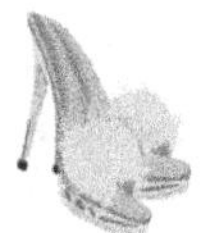

Well, this is interesting, Jennifer Dove thought. She stared at the misted windscreen from within her sister Sofie's old station wagon. Rain drummed on the roof. Every muscle in her body ached. Australian summer heat and the wild storm had turned the car into a sauna. A distinct aroma of sweaty sneakers in a gym locker wafted up from the threadbare carpet. And where the hell were Sofie and her niece, Claudia? How could they leave a dishevelled, jetlagged woman asleep in a parked car at night? At least leave a note: We've arrived at Uncle Bob's. Back soon with a double-shot latté. This could mean no more travelling. God, she hoped so. Hopping across Europe and Asia on a forty-hour flight from London to Sydney was bad enough, but on landing, Sofie and Claudia had whisked her into a car for a five-hour country road trip. She felt shattered and longed for a soft bed and lots of sleep with no —

'Hello!' a deep voice boomed. Jennifer jolted out of her daydream. 'Anyone there?'

Adrenaline shot through her. Nope. She hunkered deeper into the bench seat, fumbling for her phone, hoping he'd go away. A shadowy figure peered through the misted side window. Jennifer slid further down, her bum nearly on the floor. Streetlights glared through the windscreen, and pain hit the back of her eyes.

Damn, he'd seen her. Jennifer eased herself up and quickly checked the doors. Thank goodness Sofie had locked her in.

'You left your lights on!' the man called out.

Jennifer slid across the bench seat and reached around the steering column. Her fingers found the switch to turn off the lights. Opening the glove box, she pulled out a rag and wiped the side window. In that same moment, she noticed the frills, the frayed waistband and crotch—Sofie and her bloody recycling.

Her gaze trailed up from the undies to catch a man smiling at her through the rain. She clenched her teeth and smiled back, mortified; the cowboy was getting an eyeful of her sister's pink undies. *Bugger, bet he thinks they're mine.* Heat rushed to her cheeks.

Jennifer wound the window down. It cracked open, then jammed. 'Thank you,' she called out through the gap while squinting against the rain.

'You'd better…' the man started just as a truck thundered past, blue exhaust trailing behind, and she missed what else he had to say.

'Didn't hear you!' she yelled.

'Better make sure the battery isn't flat,' the man advised, his face obscured by the streaky window. 'I've got jumper leads.'

Jennifer copied what she'd seen her sister do and pumped the accelerator a few times, then turned the key in the ignition; thankfully, the engine started without a stutter. She squeezed her fingers into the window's tiny opening and tugged it down a few inches.

'Listen, I'm missing a sister and a niece. Have you seen a young woman, cherub face, blonde curly hair, about five-six, and a teenage girl, face like her mum, but trying to be Goth —black clothes, black hair, black eyes?' *Black mood. Who would've thought Goth would make a comeback?*

The man looked up and down the street, and as the lamplight touched his face, Jennifer craned her neck for a better look. Hmm, interesting. This bloke in his Akubra hat and oilskin raincoat could stop London traffic. His rugged features were likely etched by sun, wind…and possibly humour.

She followed his gaze but couldn't see past a few pedestrians sheltering from the rain.

'I reckon your family's coming this way. One of them's giving me the evil eye, ready to take me on.' He sent them a brief, it's okay wave and turned back to Jennifer. When their eyes connected, something—she wasn't sure what—happened to her stomach.

'Are you passing through?' he asked.

'I don't know,' she said, rubbing her face. Her jetlagged brain felt like fudge after forty hours on a dodgy plane. 'Is this Tumble Creek?'

He gave her a warm, easy smile. 'Yep.'

'Thank God,' Jennifer sighed with relief. 'No more travelling. We're here for our uncle's funeral tomorrow.'

'Bob Feldman's your uncle. My condolences, Bob was a good bloke.' The stranger gave Jennifer a solemn nod in recognition of her loss. Rain dribbled off his hat.

'You knew him?' Jennifer asked.

'It's a small town. I'll be seeing you then.' Turning up the collar on his long coat, he jogged to his car, boots sending water flying with every step.

With effort, Jennifer pulled the window down, stuck her head out the small gap, and yelled, 'Thanks again!' He turned and, like a mini salute, touched the brim of his hat. *Nice.* It was definitely worth getting wet for another look. He slid into the driver's seat of his Range Rover and merged into the traffic. With both hands flat on the glass, she pushed the window back up, muttering about Sofie and her clapped-out old car. She probably kept it to annoy their image-driven mother.

Huddled under a plastic raincoat, Jennifer's niece, Claudia, threw herself into the back. Sofie shoved Jennifer aside as she slid into the driver's seat, tossing Jennifer a takeaway bag. As the tempting smell of hot food filled the car, she felt her stomach grumble.

'What did that gorgeous-looking bloke want?' Sofie asked eagerly.

'He was hot!' Claudia blurted out from the back seat.

Jennifer raised an eyebrow at her sister. 'The cute cowboy kindly told me our car's headlights were on.'

'How thoughtful. He looked like Hugh Jackman in that movie *Australia,*' Sofie said, 'He waved and gave me a smile. I swear my legs went to jelly.'

'Mum's legs turn to jelly watching a GQ tank ad,' Claudia muttered.

Maybe I should've told him it was my ditsy sister who left the lights on, and that they weren't my frayed pink undies I used to clean the window.

'Oops.' Head down, Sofie busied herself opening a takeaway bag.

'Mum's *what?*' Claudia shrieked.

Jennifer realised her mistake and quickly changed the subject; there'd been enough tension between mother and daughter.

'I smell food,' she peeked in the bag. 'Or perhaps not?'

'Wait just a minute,' Claudia demanded, edging to a full-blown teenage rebellion. 'A strange guy got an eyeful of Mum's big, old undies.'

'Excuse me! They are *not* big. And that's recycling, sweetie. Everyone uses old undies to wash and polish things, and they're great for cars —'

'You mean to say,' Claudia cut in, her voice pitched too high, 'you washed this car and used...'

'Yes, on the front lawn. Your friend Skids wanted to polish his bike, so I gave him a pair.'

'Noooo!' Claudia yelled, arms crossed tightly over her budding chest. 'Next thing I know, it's on TikTok. Imagine it: me humiliated across the country—the whole bloody world! I can't believe it. *Aaagggh!'*

Jennifer shot her sister a look. Sofie was trying to hide a grin. 'I think your mum was kidding.'

'*Think—think!'* Claudia shrieked.

'Don't worry, Claudia, if the cowboy tells just one person what he saw, by morning, I'll be humiliated all over town. And I don't care.' Jennifer's conscience threw a little tantrum over her blatant lie. Her own self-image had been a work in progress from the time she'd left home.

'He's a stockman,' Sofie corrected.

'Beg your pardon, Stockman.' Jennifer rubbed her face, thinking this was just the beginning; she had another week of this banter. Despite her irritation, she couldn't help but smile.

'Sorry to break this to you, but you should see your hair,' Sofie giggled. 'All your curls are flat and up one side. Not that it matters, you were in the car the whole time.'

Jennifer dropped the bag on her lap and pulled the visor down to peer in the mirror. 'I look like a raccoon!' She raked her fingers through her dark curls. Her mother would be horrified— 'Fix your hair—Fix your face, You're not wearing that, are you?' Without thinking, she straightened her black linen pants and scarlet tunic.

'No, you look Goth, like Muggins.' Sofie hitched a thumb over her shoulder at Claudia.

'What happened?' Jennifer asked no one in particular. 'Somewhere between London and Sydney, I aged ten years.'

'Shut up, Jen, don't make me lean over and smack you. You're gorgeous. London-winter-pale, but gorgeous. Some women resort to surgery for that doe-eyed, green-eyed, gypsy look.'

'I'd love to have your skin, Aunty Jen,' Claudia said. 'White is so cool.'

Spending nights in the restaurant and sleeping during the day, how could she be anything but pale?

'Mum, how come Aunt Jen's a brunette and you're a blonde? She's tall, and you're short?'

'Short? Thanks, sweetie,' Sofie said dryly. 'Jen's a throwback from a past liaison?'

'Yeah right, Sofie. You're the throwback. I can't see Mother having an affair twelve months after you were born to fall pregnant with me. Hardly,' Jennifer put in.

With the same old discussions resurfacing, she wondered if they could've had different fathers. Sofie drove around in a battered car and dressed like a hippy, which was odd considering their parents' aim in life was to make the right impression.

'How long have I been asleep?'

'It's nine-thirty now; you had less than an hour.' Sofie patted Jennifer's knee.

'My brain's playing catch-up with my eyeballs. I can't move. My bloody body is still floating, and I had the weirdest dream.'

'Dream about what?' Sofie cracked open a can of Coke.

'Uncle Bob… dying.' Jennifer let go a heavy sigh. 'And why did he leave that strange message for us with his solicitor, saying he meant no harm? What he did was for himself, not anyone else. Who does that?'

If he meant for them not to investigate, it was the wrong way to go about it. In fact, Jennifer was already curious. Did it have something to do with her mother and the reason she'd turned her back on Bob, her own brother? When Jennifer was a teenager, her mother had tried to knock sense into her about doing the same. Like that was going to happen. She loved her uncle; he was never critical of others, especially not of their appearance.

She screwed her eyes shut and tried to picture her uncle's gentle face. Okay, he was dead. But that didn't mean he couldn't send her another message or sign. Then again, if anyone was going to get a sign, it would be Sofie. She could see signs in wisps of smoke.

'We'll work it out. Uncle Bob'll probably send me a sign,' Sofie said.

Jennifer resisted an eye-roll.

Claudia piped up with, 'Pity Mum didn't get a sign about a country town seeing her undies.'

Sofie's mouth popped open. Before she had a chance to say anything, Jennifer pulled a spring roll from her takeaway bag and shoved it into her sister's mouth, then took a bite of her dim-sim. The salty, deep-fried pastry and something resembling mincemeat made her reach for her Coke. She threw the remains of her dim-sim back into the bag and took a long swig to wash the greasy taste from her mouth. Then she rolled up Sofie's recycled undies, making sure they weren't recognisable, and wiped the side window to peer at the row of shops.

'You've parked outside Uncle Bob's pharmacy. Hey, why are the windows papered up?'

'Claudia and I discussed it earlier,' Sofie mumbled around a mouthful of spring roll, 'and we don't know.'

'I think we'd better get inside,' Jennifer suggested, taking another swipe at the window. 'Got the keys to the house?'

'Of course,' Sofie mumbled around the spring roll between her teeth. She started the engine and swung the car onto Grey Street. A few minutes later, they were in the back lane. She stopped in front of the double garage roller door that was part of the back fence.

'Got a brolly, Sofe?'

Sofie grabbed an umbrella from under the seat and tried to open it. 'It's a bit bent since I used it on Jett's head—and his car.'

'On ya, Mum!' In a flash, Claudia made the switch from undie-outrage to mother-daughter united. 'Wish I'd seen it.'

'Good for you.' Jennifer laughed until she noticed her sister's eyes had a glazed, mutinous look. 'Perhaps we should dump this in the rubbish.' She tugged the umbrella out of Sofie's grasp. 'I know you'd like to do it again, Sofe, but it's time to let go.'

Claudia leaned over and kissed her mum on the cheek, and a dreamy look softened Sofie's face. Watching the tender moment between her sister and niece brought on a pang of longing, as she remembered similar moments during their childhood when it was the two of them against their mother's wounding rule.

'Getting wet due to your brainless ex-husband's headache will be a pleasure.' Jennifer squeezed her sister's hand, then shouldered the car door open.

'Do you remember the code for the garage door?' Sofie asked.

'Uncle Bob used our birthdays, the sweetie,' Jennifer said wistfully.

She held Sofie's useless umbrella over her head and punched in the code. The roller door rumbled open. Jennifer guided Sofie into the garage and quickly threw the battered umbrella into a dark corner. She found the light switch, and a fluorescent tube flickered on, casting a blue-white glare over shapes and angles hidden under a dust cover. Whatever it was, it took up one side of the double garage.

'You're soaked through,' Sofie frowned, climbing out of her car. Claudia slid across the bench seat and followed.

'I'll be fine,' Jennifer said. 'I've just come from a London winter.'

Claudia peeked under the dust cover. 'Awesome!'

'Well, lift it up so we can all see,' Sofie urged.

But Claudia just stared with her hand over her mouth. Jennifer grasped one corner of the dust cover and pulled. It slithered onto the garage floor, revealing a shiny, yellow and white vintage model Cadillac with huge headlights, fins, and a mass of gleaming chrome.

'Uncle Bob, you eccentric old coot,' she whispered. 'He finally got his wish, and it's a convertible. It's so ugly it's beautiful. I wonder who the lucky relative will be who gets this.'

'Hope Mum doesn't get her hands on it,' Sofie muttered.

Jennifer leaned against the bonnet. 'Somehow, I don't think he'd leave Mum this amazing car. Besides, it'd be a terrible waste.'

'Yeah, you're right.' Sofie gently ran her hand over the car's duco. 'Uncle Bob had plenty of friends in Tumble Creek who are more deserving.'

Claudia draped herself across the shiny bonnet. 'No way! This is so me, don't you think?'

'Get off there before you scratch it with one of your belt buckles,' Sofie warned.

Claudia made a face and slid off.

'Uncle Bob may have left it to Claudia.' Jennifer patted the bonnet and raised an eyebrow at her sister, hoping she'd get the hint and ease up on her daughter.

'Honestly,' Sofie groaned. She helped Jennifer throw the dust cover back over the car.

'Let's go inside,' Jennifer grabbed her leather tote bag, moved to the door at the far end of the garage and pushed. The old door scraped heavily over the flagstones, but they managed to shove it open wide enough to squeeze through into the dark, damp courtyard garden. A broad flagstone path led from the garage to the patio and the back door.

Jennifer flicked a switch, illuminating the garden with soft sepia tones. 'It's always so pretty in here.'

'Yeah,' Sofie said. 'Uncle Bob loved his cottage garden, especially his snapdragons and roses.'

Jennifer hurried through the puddles, her sister and niece right behind her. They reached the back door and huddled under its narrow awning. Faced with the papered-up door and windows, Jennifer felt like a trespasser.

'Just like the front,' Claudia muttered.

Jennifer fumbled with her uncle's Marilyn Monroe doll key ring, chose the most frequently used key, and slipped it into the lock. She eased the door open. They stepped across the threshold. As they entered the dimly lit interior of the sunroom, an uneasy feeling stole through Jennifer.

She dropped her bag near the stairs. 'Uncle Bob only died a few days ago. The place seems empty — surely someone would've kept the pharmacy going?'

'Yes, people need their medications,' Sofie said. 'Uncle Bob's solicitor never mentioned any of this.'

Jennifer pulled a corner of the newspaper aside and scanned the courtyard through rain-spattered glass. A sense of unease settled inside her. Something was wrong. She felt the need to be with her sister and niece and moved to join them in the central hallway.

Claudia stepped out of the shop's kitchenette as Sofie appeared from the staffroom. Jennifer's shoes squeaked on the shiny floor tiles as she headed to the main area of the pharmacy. She suddenly stopped, unable to believe her tired eyes. Her uncle's impressive Edwardian shop was deserted. All that remained of his working life were the shop fittings and display cases.

'Where is everything?' her troubled voice echoed around the walls.

Sofie shrugged. 'Beats me. This is creepy.'

Underneath the grime and dust, it was clear there had been no change to the original cream and dark-blue mosaic tiles arranged in an intricate pattern of scrolls and flowers. Jennifer admired what could be an elegant room with its lofty ceiling and decorative plaster scrollwork. It gave the room an old-world charm. This stunning shop had been empty for a long time. Now Jennifer found herself reflecting on her uncle's life and sudden death.

'When was the last time you saw him, Sofe?'

'I think it was at school...' Sofie trailed off.

'The night of the school play,' Claudia prompted. 'I had a part in the chorus, and Uncle Bob came down to see.'

'Four weeks ago.' Sadness etched Sofie's face as she gripped Jennifer's arm. 'I wonder if he knew he was going to—you know, die?'

Jennifer would've preferred it if her uncle hadn't had imminent death hanging over him. She shook her head. 'Of course he didn't know. We're his favourite girls, he would've said something.'

'When did you last see him or hear from him?' Sofie's voice trembled.

'We had a regular date to Facetime every two weeks. The last time we spoke was a week ago. He looked great. We spent a week together last July, remember? I sent you photos from Paris. We met an acquaintance of Uncle Bob's.' Jennifer stopped to think. 'Can't remember his name, but he was from the Polish Embassy and invited us to a cocktail party. We had an amazing time, and the food was great. That's where I met Dobry and suggested he come to London sometime—and he did, damn it.' Jennifer's doubts about her Polish boyfriend were starting to grow.

'Claudia, never trust a man who yabbers poetry in a foreign language; he could be reciting his shopping list.'

'I'm off men,' Claudia voiced flatly. 'Boys are okay, especially Skids.'

'Uncle Bob was a man,' Jennifer said, 'and we could always rely on him.'

'Uncle Bob was—different,' Claudia said.

'True. He was a sweetheart that night at the embassy. After we left, he took me to a café and we talked until the early hours, reminiscing about the clothes and gaudy jewellery he used to buy for us behind our parents' backs.'

'I remember,' Sofie smiled. 'Mum didn't want you to get your ears pierced. She thought you'd end up with piercings all over your body.'

'Jeez, no wonder I get funny looks from Gran,' Claudia muttered.

Jennifer gave her niece a sympathetic smile. 'You're not a good look for wannabe socialites, and I wouldn't fret about it for a second.'

'Whatever,' Claudia said with just a hint of disappointment. 'I don't give a shit.'

Jennifer draped an arm around Claudia's shoulder and kissed her cheek. 'I like your attitude. I'm sure Uncle Bob would've told you that as well.'

'We spoke on the phone,' Claudia sniffed back a tear. 'But I didn't see him as often as I would've liked.'

'I quizzed him about why he moved away from Sydney,' Jennifer said. 'But he just gave me some lame excuse. He seemed uncomfortable about it, so I let it go.'

'He was the same with me,' Sofie added. 'I'm just grateful we all stayed in touch. Weird how Mum and Dad never let us visit him when we were young.'

Jennifer frowned. 'Really weird. But they couldn't stop us in our teens. I remember making a fuss.' Sorrow washed over her. 'What have we missed? What's been going on here?' She ran her fingers over the brass moulding surrounding the curved glass top of a display case. The shiny surface gleamed; thoughts of a new restaurant came to her mind, and how this beautiful display case would enhance its décor. Impossible to ship, she shook her head and refocused on her surroundings. 'I don't understand.'

'Maybe he was sick for a while but didn't let on,' Claudia said from the other side of the room. She held up a dusty packet of bobby pins she'd found on a shelf. 'Remnants of a country pharmacist's life?'

'I'm sure there's a lot more to our uncle,' Jennifer choked back tears.

They made their way up the creaking, dark timber stairs. In stark contrast to the shop, their uncle's home was clean and lived-in, immaculate, as if he'd only stepped out for milk and bread.

At the top of the landing, a timber floor gleamed on either side of a Persian carpet runner. At the end of the hallway, warm streetlight streamed through a tall window.

Jennifer opened the first door on her right. She found the switch and flicked the lights on. 'The living room hasn't changed at all.' A faint buzz shot through her fingers. She examined the old brass switch and curled her fingers protectively; perhaps her hands were a little damp. 'This heavy timber furniture must date back to Grandma's time,' she said, heading for the heavy, red brocade drapes. She pulled one aside to look out through the rain trickling down the window onto Grey Street below, so quiet compared with the constant hum of London traffic. A corrugated awning stretched over the footpath below, hiding it from view. Beyond that, Jennifer could see flowerbeds and glistening trees along the central nature strip that separated northbound and southbound traffic. Wet asphalt gleamed, slick with summer rain.

Across the street, she caught sight of a stout man as he walked under a streetlight. He looked straight up at her. A cold shiver ran down her spine. The man adjusted his collar, ducked his head, and quickly stepped back into the shadow of a shop doorway.

It's nothing, she told herself. *This is a country town, bugger-all happens here. Poor bloke is sheltering from the rain, that's all.*

Chapter 2

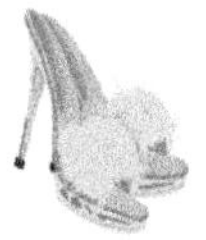

Jennifer closed the drapes and walked over to where Claudia sat slumped at the dining table, chin resting in her palm. She tugged at her niece's sleeve.

Dead tired but still floating as if on the plane, she ignored the leather sofa that beckoned her to lie down. 'Come on, let's see what else there is.'

They found Sofie in a room across the hall.

'Uncle Bob's bedroom,' Jennifer whispered.

'Great, Uncle Bob's bed?' Claudia whispered.

'Yep,' Sofie sighed.

'He died in his sleep...heart failure on that bed,' Jennifer said softly.

'I'm outa here.' Claudia shuddered.

Jennifer turned to leave. 'Let's go to our old room, Sofe.'

'This is creeping me out,' Claudia muttered, hooking one arm through her mother's, the other searching for her aunt's.

The three shuffled down the hall past a long oak sideboard, which had neatly arranged photographs in silver frames sitting on top. They caught Jennifer's eye, and she hesitated, but her sister and niece weren't in the mood to stop.

'Wait a minute,' Jennifer said, her tone hushed. 'Why are we sneaking around as if we might wake the dead or something? And why are we whispering?'

Wide-eyed, the other two answered with a shrug.

'Whatever, Aunt Jen, as long as I'm in the middle,' Claudia whispered.

'Okay, but we're being silly.'

Jennifer turned the lights on. The room softened into a gentle golden glow.

'Ahh, now that's more like it.' She smiled at memories of weekends laughing and dressing up in this very room. 'A bit over-the-top frilly, but hey, Uncle Bob did it all for us, God love him.'

'Funny lighting in this place,' Claudia said, eyeing the pink, smoky glass ball hanging from the ornate ceiling rose. 'It's like they have to warm up or something.'

The bedroom was the same size as her uncle's, with pink roses-and-vines wallpaper that Jennifer could never look at for long without feeling dizzy. Flouncy curtains hung over burgundy velvet drapes. Resembling a giant tutu, a pink bedspread covered the mattress of a gleaming antique brass bed.

'So Uncle Bob decorated this for you guys?' Claudia's nose wrinkled in distaste. 'Where's the black, or at least dark purple?'

Sofie rolled her eyes.

'It'll pass,' Jennifer whispered to Sofie. 'Pink will be the new black. Wait and see.'

'Poor, stuck-in-a-gay-closet Uncle Bob,' Claudia said, matter-of-factly.

'He was, wasn't he?' Jennifer stated.

'Yeah.' Sofie sighed sadly. 'He said he had girlfriends, but lately he only talked about someone called Veronica. He often bought her presents too. Thing is, I never met her.'

'Now that you mention it,' Jennifer said, 'he bought Veronica a bra and panty set in Paris.'

'Maybe,' Claudia put in with a shrug, 'his girlfriends were just that—girlfriends.'

'And they stayed here, in our old room,' Jennifer said as she scanned the excessively pink boudoir. 'I think he missed his calling. He would've made a brilliant decorator.'

'Yeah, look, someone threw a frog in a blender,' Claudia said, pointing at a large pink frilly cushion surrounded by green leaves.

'Claudia's right,' Jennifer said. 'Many frogs gave their lives so we could have a princess bedroom.'

'So many frogs.' Claudia dramatically swiped an imaginary tear from her cheek.

'Wait 'til you see the bathroom.' Reaching for the door, Jennifer opened it. 'Look, it's green with fluffy pink accessories.'

'Bless his cotton socks.' Sofie dabbed her face. 'He hasn't changed a thing.'

'This bath is awesome,' Claudia said, leaning over the claw-foot bathtub big enough for someone to lie down in.

'Ooh, a shiver just ran down my spine.' Jennifer rubbed her arms.

'Jen, you're soaked. Put something else on,' Sofie ordered.

'My suitcase is in the car,' Jennifer peered behind the bathroom door. 'This'll do for the moment.' She unhooked a large, pearl grey silk shift from a brass hook. 'And these,' she held up a pair of fluffy pink stiletto slip-ons. She stripped down to her underwear, hung her wet clothes over the tub, and slipped on the shift and stilettos. 'Can you see my bum?' Jennifer bent over with a hand on each cheek.

'No, and anyway, who cares?' Sofie said. 'It's just us.'

Jennifer straightened and turned around to face them.

Sofie gulped back a squeal. 'Look,' she said, pointing at Jennifer's chest.

'I know; my nipples are sticking out, I'm cold—well, I was cold. They just haven't caught up yet.' Jennifer placed her palms over the little buds and rubbed.

'I don't care about your nipples, look at what's written on the front of the slip.'

Claudia clapped her hands and laughed. 'It's Veronica's.'

Jennifer turned to look in the mirror above the basin. There it was: *Veronica*, printed in a sparkly pink curly font. 'Good grief, I hope she won't mind.' She looked down at the slip-ons. 'Aren't these just wonderfully frivolous? Every girl should have a pair.'

'There's heaps of great stuff here.' Claudia held up scented bath oils and Chanel toiletries.

'Veronica has expensive taste.' Jennifer turned on the hot water tap over the basin. The water spluttered then trickled out. 'I wonder if someone turned the hot water off. I'll find the fuse box and switch it back on. A cold shower is the last thing I want.'

'Damn,' Sofie complained, frowning. 'Getting hot water will take hours — but you can wash with the most expensive stuff in the country.'

'Yeah, and I will,' Jennifer laughed, wrapping an arm around Sofie's shoulder. 'Look, we're all dead on our feet—let's stick to the plan. Head to the motel, and I'll see you in the morning.'

'Okay,' Sofie cupped Jennifer's cheeks and caught her eyes with hers, 'I can't believe my sister is finally opening her own restaurant. I want to hear all about it in the morning.'

'I promise I'll fill you in on every detail. Right now, I need to sleep alone, and you two probably snore. I may have had a catnap, but I've been awake for over forty hours.'

'You poor thing.' Sofie kissed her cheek. 'We'll come back in the morning with breakfast.'

'Sounds good to me. Juice, strong coffee, and a bacon and egg roll.'

'Yay! Jeez, finally!' Claudia cried, swung around, quickly headed for the stairs and the back door.

Jennifer took Sofie's hand, and they followed Claudia to the car.

'Make sure you lock all the doors,' Sofie ordered before getting behind the wheel.

'Really, this isn't Sydney,' Jennifer huffed, fatigue making her sound grumpy.

'Yeah, yeah, do it anyway,' Sofie ordered.

Claudia muttered about creepy corners.

The old station wagon drove off. The roller door rumbled shut. Silence settled around Jennifer, and the sense of unease crept through her again. That's because I'm cold. And I'm cold because I'm tired. She dragged her case, its little wheels clattering over the flagstones, into the house and locked the back door. 'Don't let their wild imaginations scare you,' she told herself.

*　*　*

Gerek Laska hid in the shadows of an alcove doorway on Grey Street. After rubbing his eyes, he focused on the second-storey window of the building across the road. He nearly collapsed from fright when he saw the woman looking directly down at him. Thank goodness she had drawn the heavy drapes again.

Soft light still seeped out past the edges of the drapes. Gerek sighed and rubbed his neck, frustrated at waiting for the women to leave. Surely, they wouldn't stay in a dead man's house overnight? Maybe they were tougher than he'd thought.

Excitement fluttered in his chest at the thought of being so close to his goal. This was more his style and so different from sitting behind a computer in Canberra.

He chuckled. His belly jiggled, and the chuckle became a wheeze. He reached for his hip flask. A quick gulp of Anna's homemade Fruit Brandy would soothe the wheeze before it became a cough. Damn, he'd left it in the car. He peered up the street at the empty police car parked a short distance away. The car worried him; the officers had to be somewhere—hmmm. If they showed up, it would be a complication he didn't need.

He'd been tailing the three women since they left Sydney. Now he knew where Bob had lived, and with luck, this would lead him to the woman who called herself Veronica. His foolish friend and boss at the Polish Embassy in Canberra would be happy about that, and eventually, they would both get what they wanted.

He felt relieved that the rain had stopped. Heat trapped in the tarred roads, combined with the rain, caused a warm mist to rise across the town. Frowning, Gerek peeked out of the darkened doorway and risked a quick scan up and down the street. A grin spread across his face when he recognised the old station wagon as it turned the corner and drove away. Good, the women had left the house; one problem solved. That just left the police officers and their whereabouts; he'd have to move carefully. He dared to step out of his hiding spot and into the light. Then, walking up the road as if he belonged, he headed to find the back entrance to Bob's home.

Gerek reached what he hoped was the shop's back fence. With a herculean effort, he pulled himself up to get a good look over the top: yep, this was the right place. He let himself drop and rubbed his shoulders.

After a quick scout around, he found the keypad that would open the garage door. It took him no time to figure out the simple code and slide the roller door up. The sound of creaking, rumbling metal echoed out into the night. Panic caused the hair on the back of his neck to stand up. In a flash, Gerek grabbed the door to stop it from moving. He shot a glance up and down the alley to see if he'd disturbed anyone. Everything was quiet. He looked down at the gap beneath the roller door and figured he had about fifty centimetres. Could he make it?

He eyed his ample belly and, with a resigned grunt, eased down on all fours to the wet ground and almost cried out when a sharp piece of gravel bit into his knee. Clenching his teeth against the pain, he lifted his leg, pulled the stone out, and chucked it. It bounced off the fence on the other side of the lane and sent a dog into a fit of raucous barking. Gerek held his breath and, wasting no more time, sneaked a peek inside the garage. Soft light pooled through the grimy garage window. Silly women left upstairs lights on in the house. He sprawled down, his big belly flattened against the cold concrete. The pressure caused blood to pound in his ears as he began to squeeze under the door. His back hit the rubber seal along the bottom edge and stopped him cold. He tried to push through, but the metal door rumbled like a roll of thunder.

'*Idiota.*' *(idiot)* Gerek wheezed. Stuck, he let all the air out of his lungs, which gave him a few millimetres, and quickly wriggled, army style, until he was through. He lay inside the garage on the concrete floor, dragging air back into his lungs. That was close. He hauled himself up, dusted his hands off on his clothes, and scouted for the way out.

Gerek's arse vibrated, and his heart leapt. He fumbled for his phone in his back pocket. Quickly, he wrapped chubby fingers around the device and answered promptly.

'Antonin, later,' he grated and switched it off. He focused on the garage walls: surely the way out was opposite the roller door. *Ah-ha!* Found it.

The door was slightly open, and Gerek rubbed his hands, thinking this job was going to be easy. He checked to make sure the coast was clear before squeezing through the narrow space and venturing into the courtyard. He ducked down as low as he could and crept along the flagstones, avoiding the soft earth on either side of the path.

Gerek felt a mosquito sting on his neck and slapped it. He wiped the sweat off his face with his forearm and silently cursed the Australian heat. His thoughts turned to Warsaw, where the temperature would drop below zero. The image of his wife Anna and her last words, before he left the embassy in Canberra, kept haunting him.

'Why not send a younger man who is more agile, not so chubby?' she had said, worried eyes questioning him.

A grumble escaped Gerek's throat: he loved his 'wifey.' And despite a few slip-ups, he knew the drill. Still, he wished a thousand curses to his fool of a friend in the Warsaw political party for making him feel guilty if he didn't do this. So what if they were all sent to Suwalki, in Poland's freezing far north?

He stayed in the shadows as he crept towards the back of the house. He pressed his face against the glass to peek through a torn piece of paper covering the window: the coast was clear. He pulled the lockpick out of his pocket and started working on the old lock, opening the back door within seconds.

He carefully eased the door open. Cool air drifted out, soothing his sweaty skin. He noticed a bag and suitcase near the stairs and heard movement above.

Someone was still here.

*   *   *

A change of air fluttered across Jennifer's face. She looked around the cavernous shop to see where it might have come from, but there was no explanation for it. Goose bumps crept up her neck.

Ice ran through her veins. She stiffened and bolted for the stairs, stilettos clattering all the way.

Reaching the top, logic returned and Jennifer sighed with relief. There was nothing to worry about; she'd locked the doors. 'All that fear—for what?' she told herself. 'A headache?'

Her feet were blissfully silent on the carpet runner. She slowed her pace and stopped by the sideboard to check out the photos neatly arranged on top. One stood out from the rest, a silver, art deco-framed photo of Jennifer's grandmother, Polly Feldman.

'Hi, Gran, I miss you too.' She ran her index finger over Polly's long, white lace wedding gown and the matching veil that crowned her head. Something caught her eye. She stepped closer for a better look. It looked like someone had cut George, Polly's image-driven husband, out of the photo. *Did Uncle Bob do that? Why would he? He must have felt pissed off no end.*

Jennifer rested her elbows on the sideboard and cupped her chin in her hands. 'Gran, how come Mother often said Uncle Bob had strange habits? Maybe she thinks unconditional love is a strange habit.' She skewed her mouth in thought. There had to be a reason for her uncle to cut his father out of the wedding photo and for his sister, Jennifer and Sofie's mother to despise him so much that he left Sydney to avoid her altogether. How long had the photo been like this? Jennifer hadn't noticed it before. Maybe her uncle's solicitor had the answers. Perhaps in the will, if there was one.

'Anyway, Gran, I don't suppose you can tell me why there's no hot water, hmm? Maybe I should just fall into the cloud of ruffles.' She could almost hear her grandmother laugh, wag her arthritic finger, and touch the tip of Jennifer's nose, tut-tutting. 'Comfort overrules? Yes, you're probably right.'

She opened a door opposite the sideboard and stepped into the spacious walk-in closet, its shelves stacked with linens. The old familiar scent of lemon-fresh, sun-dried laundry and memories of weekends with Gran brought a smile to her face. She helped herself to sheets and pillowcases.

As Jennifer closed the closet door, she heard a clicking sound filter up the stairs. She flinched, held her breath, and paused to listen.

Nothing. She was alone in the house, just her and her imagination.

Come on, Jen, it could've been a car door. Or a neighbour putting the cat out.

She heard the faintest gritty scraping noise, and her heart lurched. It couldn't be Sofie and Claudia; there was no reason for them to come back. Jennifer waited, ears straining. The silent, empty house was creeping her out — London was never this quiet.

This is nonsense; old houses always creak.

Halfway down the hall, Jennifer heard a faint shuffle. She stopped and listened. There it was again: someone was moving around downstairs.

'Oh my God,' she whispered.

Clutching the bundle of linen to her chest, she tiptoed down the hall as fast as she could and hurried into the pink bedroom, tossing the sheets onto the bed. She needed to ring someone, but her phone was downstairs in her bag. Where had she seen the house phone— the living room?

Jennifer's mounting fear had her searching for a handy weapon. 'Christ! All I can do is scare someone,' she hissed.

She eased the bathroom door open and hoped there would be something in there besides a bottle of shampoo. That could work, right in the eyes. Nasty, though. She scanned the toiletries, grabbed the shampoo and a large, old-fashioned, wooden-handled toilet brush.

Yes, she could do some damage with these. Brain, whoever—or gross them out and run.

She tiptoed to the bedroom door and dared to peek out. If only she could make it down the stairs. She snuck across to turn the living room lights off. Her fingers sought the old light switch, easing it up. An electric shock zapped her. She clenched her teeth against a cry of pain and fright and tucked her hand in her armpit.

Nursing her hand, she headed for the desk and managed to find the phone. Should she ring Sofie?

Her sister in a panic? Not a good idea. Call triple O. Emergency?

She heard the sound of slow, creeping steps but wasn't sure where they were coming from.

Jennifer broke out in a cold sweat. Her breathing was short and shallow, and every nerve in her body prickled with alarm. Horror stories of axe murderers and rapists ran through her mind. Her dry mouth fell open and all bravado fled. An intruder was roaming the house. She needed to hide, but where? She scuttled behind the door and peered through a crack, fixing her eye on the landing. Oh God, she could see a faint light. Did intruders use torches? How brazen. She forced herself to take slow, even breaths, but adrenaline pumping through her body made it impossible to stop the trembling. She opened her eyes wider, as if that might help her brain come up with a safe exit plan, but her frightened mind drew a blank. Anger filtered through fear and exhaustion. Anyone with an emotional mix like that rushing through their system has to be a little insane.

Jennifer raised her weapon and crept out of her hiding place. She was about to yell, scream—anything to scare whoever it was—when a loud knocking came from the open back door.

Open door? But she had locked it.

A deep voice boomed, 'Hello! Anyone there?'

'Don't come any closer.' Her voice wobbled. She cleared her throat, determined to sound convincing. 'I've called the police and they're on their way!'

'We *are* the police,' the stranger rumbled. 'Is everything all right?'

Jennifer heard heavy boots stomping up the stairs. A pale blue torch beam flickered and moved towards her.

Brandishing the toilet brush in one hand and a shampoo bottle in the other, Jennifer sneaked a peek around the door and came face to face with a mountain of a man heading her way. His companion was much shorter and thinner. Badges and epaulettes on their pale blue shirts glinted in the faint light.

'What a relief,' she said, shoulders dropping.

'Nice toilet brush and shampoo,' the large officer said, shining the torch in her face. 'You can drop them now.'

Eyes squinting, she hadn't realised her hand was raised, toilet brush pointing at the ceiling. An image of herself as The Statue of Liberty flashed through her mind. Her arm came down faster than she could blink. She let go of the wooden handle. It bounced once, then drummed on the timber floor.

'Thank you, ma'am. Tony, find the light switch,' the deep voice ordered as he shone the torch at his partner.

Without looking, Jennifer reached for the table and placed the shampoo bottle down. Briefly blinded by the blue torchlight spots in her vision, she forgot to yell, 'Don't touch the switch.'

The light flickered on, and the officer cursed as he checked his fingers.

The large, muscle-bound officer had a look of surprise and irritation on his face. Maybe dealing with the younger bloke had been tough all night—all week.

Jennifer recovered from the shock of police officers in her uncle's living room, blinked and said, 'I'm so glad you're here.'

'Is something wrong?' the officer asked, his black, bushy eyebrows creased together.

'How did you get in?' Jennifer asked.

'We came through the roller door that was partly up, and then we found the back door unlocked,' No-neck said as he slowly inclined his head towards the stairs, a tricky manoeuvre for him. Meanwhile, the younger bloke was busy rubbing his electrocuted fingers.

'I'm sure I locked it,' Jennifer said urgently.

'Tony, go scout around and make sure everything's okay.'

'Thanks, I appreciate that.' Jennifer gave him a tired smile.

'You're family of Bob Feldman?' The officer asked as he rubbed the back of his head. At least, she thought it was the back of his head. Or was it his neck? Difficult to tell when head and neck were the same width and sat plonked on a pair of broad shoulders. It was a wonder he'd made it through the doorway.

'Yes, I'm Jennifer Dove, Bob Feldman's niece. My mother is Elizabeth Feldman, Uncle Bob's sister, before she married my dad, Henry Dove. That's why I'm a Dove, not a Feldman.'

'Right, good to know. We were expecting his nieces, a grandniece, and a nephew,' the big officer said with a smile.

'My sister and niece are at the motel, and our brother, well, he could be anywhere.'

'It's not that I doubt what you're telling me, but proof helps me sleep better at night.'

'In my bag downstairs. Uncle Bob's solicitor sent a letter and keys via courier to my sister Sofie. We had no idea our uncle was going to…um, die.' Her control began to waver. She could feel it in the back of her throat and in her eyes. Perhaps it was mental and physical exhaustion. She took a deep breath and clenched her teeth against the sob that threatened.

No-neck swept his hand across, signalling for her to go first. 'After you, ma'am.'

They trundled down the creaking stairs to where she had left her leather carryall.

She should've stayed in London. After all, her uncle wouldn't ever know she'd gone to all this bloody trouble. Guilt gave her a nudge. Sorry, Uncle Bob. She dug deep into her bag and, in one swift motion, pulled out her wallet. Randomly, she handed No-neck various cards. 'Visa, Chefs' Pastry Club, video store, licence…' she trailed off. The officer eyed her licence. 'It's a bad photo.' Jennifer leaned in, pointing at her picture. 'I've had my hair cut since then, plus I had a really bad head cold. So I look a little like a fugitive…doesn't mean I am one…' she quietly trailed off.

As the young officer came through the back door, a familiar voice called, 'Hey Tony, that you in there?'

Jennifer held her breath. The hot cowboy stood outside the front door of her uncle's shop.

'Yeah, Calum,' the younger officer yelled, and in passing said, 'Nothing out there, Sarge.'

'Everything alright? You hassling Bob's family?' Calum asked.

'Would we do such a thing?' No-neck bellowed, and scanned her licence. His face was hard to see, but Jennifer didn't miss the quirky grin.

'Ah, Brock, you too,' Calum said from behind the door.

'Miss, would you mind if we let Calum in?' Brock asked politely. 'He's a member of the neighbourhood watch. Because Bob's place is empty, we've all been keeping an eye on it.'

'Sure, go ahead—what's one more?' Jennifer handed the officer another photo.

With a sideways nod, the big man sent Tony off to open the front door. The sound of locks and bolts sliding echoed through the shop. The door slammed shut with a bang, making Jennifer flinch.

Tony and Calum chatted quietly as they headed back, their deep voices echoing around the empty shop.

'Ma'am.' Brock's tone turned serious. 'Who were you planning to clobber with that lethal, toilet-brush weapon?'

Jennifer's focus had turned to the man with Officer Tony. He walked with an easy, broad-shouldered swagger. Mesmerised, her brain switched to slow-mo as his long stride brought him closer. An urgent, far-away voice in her mind told her she looked like crap and demanded she run, but her legs weren't going anywhere.

Chapter 3

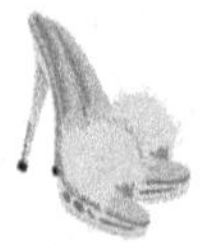

'Ma'am? *Ma'am!'*

Jennifer tore her eyes off Calum and tried to focus on the police sergeant.

'Apart from us, did you hear anything unusual?'

'At first I heard a sort of creeping, sliding noise—but that would've been the two of you, right?'

'No, we knocked and came straight up.'

Jennifer's mind reeled. She was so tired she could barely think straight. And Calum, the hot-hunk, broad-shouldered trouble in country boots, snug jeans and tan leather jacket, waited, hands in his pockets, with an aura of amused calm.

Her gaze drifted up to his face. Mischief sparkled in his soft hazel eyes—eyes that conveyed promises, as if he knew something she didn't, which was ridiculous. He grinned, and Jennifer's stomach did a tumble. Her brain geared up a notch and treated her to a litany of images: her sister's panties, boots, water splashing, and this guy jogging to his car.

Sigh.

Jennifer rubbed her face. She needed a shot of brandy, maybe even electric shock treatment. Come on, think! A draft of cool air brushed Veronica's shift. Her nipples peaked, and a cold shiver ran through her body. She wrapped her arms around her chest for comfort.

Calum stepped forward, shrugging off his leather jacket. 'Here, Veronica.' One corner of his mouth lifted, and his warm eyes conveyed something that made her belly melt. He swung his jacket around her shoulders and pulled it snugly under her chin.

Instantly, his body heat seeped through and settled on her skin. Her heart thudded. It had been forever since anyone had offered her such a thoughtful courtesy. Warm hands brushed her cheek as he adjusted the collar. She breathed in his warm male scent, infused with a hint of pine.

'Thank you,' she said with a sigh.

'You're welcome. Hey, love the shoes.'

'Thanks, but they're not mine.'

'Veronica's?' he asked, head tilted.

Jennifer wished he'd stop looking at her as if she was the best dessert on the menu: her knees couldn't stand much more. 'Must be,' she whispered, breaking his gaze to look down at the pink, fluffy stilettos.

'Brock, meet one of Bob's nieces,' Calum said with a quiet chuckle. 'Bob showed Gran and all of us at home some photos of his trip to Europe. There's no mistake.'

'Yeah, I know,' Brock studied the Paris photo. Tony peered over the other man's broad shoulder. 'Nice shot of Bob and you, Jennifer.' Brock turned the photo over to see the back and moved it out of his own shadow, then with a voice that rumbled around the room, he read the inscription. 'Hi Jen, remember our picnic near the Eiffel Tower? I had a wonderful day, thank you, Twinkles. All my love, Uncle Bob.' The letter and licence are proof enough. The photo is icing,' he said, handing it back. 'Despite the circumstances, I hope your sister, niece, and you have a pleasant stay.'

Their kindness was becoming overwhelming in her fragile state. 'I'm just glad I made it. There were times when I thought I wouldn't. It's a long way from Heathrow to Sydney on a tin-can plane with a couple of wings taped to the sides. I'm so not happy about all of this. For the shop to be empty, Uncle Bob must've been sick for a while and didn't tell us. He should've told us. I could've been on that tin-can-plane a hell of a lot sooner and been here for him. I'm not happy about a lot of things, mostly that he's gone, damn it! So, no wonder I...' A lump welled in Jennifer's throat. She had to stop before her emotions got the better of her.

She was babbling and making three blokes uncomfortable. Correction, two blokes were shuffling their feet and avoiding eye contact. Calum stood facing her, arms crossed, hip cocked, sympathetic but amused.

Tears pricked her eyes; she cleared her throat, determined to regain control. 'How long has my uncle's shop been empty?'

'About eight months.' Brock extended his hand. 'I'm Sergeant Stewart. Just call me Brock.' Her hand disappeared in his. 'And this is Officer Stone, or Tony.'

She offered her hand to Tony and whispered, 'Pleased to meet you, Tony. Sorry about the electric shock. And I'm sorry about the toilet brush. It was all I could find, but I certainly wouldn't have hit you with it.'

Tony gave her a shy smile and a quick nod.

Calum's throaty, sexy laugh echoed around the empty shop. She could hardly believe it, but there was no stopping it; his laugh sent a quiver straight to her belly and beyond, hitting the sweet spot between her thighs. She held her breath and crossed her legs, hoping no one noticed.

Thankfully, Brock broke the spell. 'If I hear a word of this outside these walls, I'll haunt you for the rest of your life,' he warned Calum.

'Yeah, there'll be no safe parking spot in town,' Tony added bravely.

'I wouldn't dream of offering our local paper the caption, "Police frighten woman with toilet brush."'

'We were the ones she threatened,' Brock said, fighting to suppress a smile but failing.

'And you've twisted it around!' Tony cut in, all puffed up and serious.

Introducing himself, Calum stepped forward and offered his hand to Jennifer. 'Hi, Jennifer, I'm Calum McGregor, by the way. We met earlier.'

The cowboy had a good sense of humour. Jennifer took his hand firmly. His warm, strong fingers wrapped around hers, steady and powerful. Oh my.

'Anyone hungry?' Calum asked, amusement dancing in his eyes.

'Maybe a little,' Jennifer's voice came out like a grated whisper; she quickly pulled herself together. 'But I'm much too tired to eat. I've had no sleep the past couple of days.'

'How about take-away?' Calum suggested, reaching for the back pocket of his jeans.

Jennifer zeroed in on Calum's hip-wriggle as he tugged at his phone. She momentarily forgot where she was until the words take-away filtered through her brain. A top London chef having food ordered over the phone was shocking, wasn't it?

'Is something wrong?' Calum pulled a puzzled but comical expression. 'Maybe something light? Meryl makes great soup.'

Jennifer looked for confirmation, but Brock and Tony had moved a few yards away and were muttering into a shoulder mic. Then, with heads inclined, they listened to a crackly-voiced reply.

She wished they'd all disappear so she could collapse in a heap among the flowers in the girlie bedroom. She heard herself whisper, 'Sounds like heaven.' *Idiot!* She hadn't meant to say that out loud. 'I was thinking out loud about the bed.' She blinked, pointing upstairs.

Calum simply smiled, and Jennifer thought, *he does that a lot.*

'Forget everything I've said,' she waved, palms out. 'Soup sounds great.'

In a flash, Calum was on his phone ordering food.

'I'll have a hamburger with the lot!' Brock rumbled.

'And I'll have a hamburger with the lot and double chips—and a chicken roll,' Tony added.

'Mate, your appetite astounds me,' Calum stated. 'But don't you have to, you know, be somewhere—like on patrol?'

Jennifer peeked at Calum. She thought he looked a little desperate, as if somebody was about to pinch his lollipop.

'It's all right, we're off duty,' Brock replied.

'Really,' Calum nodded sideways with his head. 'What, no overtime, crims to find, people to book? And what about the...um...the football club?'

The two officers gave him a blank look. 'What?' Brock asked, confused.

Jennifer thought, *I've got dibs on confusion.*

Then the penny dropped, and she almost laughed out loud. Men are dense. Even in her tired state, she finally caught on: Calum wanted to be alone with her, which was more than a little exciting as well as sweet.

A voice blared from Calum's phone. He looked at it before tentatively holding it to his ear. 'Yeah, I know, Meryl. I know you're busy,' he said. He then went on with the order, closed off, and slipped the phone back into his pocket. 'Ten, fifteen minutes tops,' he added, glancing at Jennifer again. The warmth in his smile made her stomach flip, but she was determined to fight that feeling — damn right she was.

'Now,' Brock said, rubbing his hands together, 'while we're waiting, is there anything we can do for you?'

'Please, could someone check the hot water system in the attic? I think it's turned off or something. Maybe it's off at the fuse box, and I can't remember where that is.'

'Have you been up in the attic to have a look?' Calum asked.

'Last time I was up there, I was about twelve, and a big, hairy huntsman spider, about the size of your hand, fell on me.'

'I kept them as pets,' Calum chuckled.

'You don't still do that...right?' Jennifer shuddered.

'No, I moved on,' he stated in a deep, matter-of-fact tone, his wicked grin leaving no doubt about what he had moved on to.

Brock's broad shoulders swivelled as he looked for a place to start searching for a fuse box. 'Take a look through the rooms, Tony. When you're done, check outside and in the garage. I'll help Calum check that there aren't any ghosts.'

'Can I help? Hold the ladder or something?' Jennifer asked.

'No thanks, I do this all the time,' Calum said. 'You'll have hot water.'

'Otherwise, cold showers never hurt anyone.' Brock turned to follow. 'I have one every morning.'

Calum shook his head and smiled. 'Of course you do, Brock.'

*   *   *

Gerek listened as the voices and thumping footsteps faded. It seemed the people were moving further away from him to go upstairs. This might be his only chance to escape. He quickly scanned the small kitchen, in case there was another exit. Glupie! (Stupid), he muttered. He'd cornered himself. He turned the door handle, hoping it wouldn't squeak, and eased it open. Glancing over his shoulder, he hurried silently out, shut the door, and made a stomach-wobbling, hasty retreat back to the garage, where he made himself comfortable.

'Bloody Australians!' Gerek peered through the grimy garage window facing the backyard. 'They never sit still! In and out, in and out,' he muttered against the glass. 'They make me do this too, up the garden, back in the shed, waiting, waiting.' Maybe this was a sign to start his search in the garage?

Movement caught his eye. Stressed, he pressed his lips together when he saw a uniformed man appear at the shop's back door, his torch beam flicking across the backyard.

Policja! (Police), his brain roared.

For a split second, he toyed with the idea of letting the Australian police catch him. They might let him trade a stash of juicy info for mercy. But the consequences of that spun around in his head, and knowing he couldn't betray his friend back in Canberra, he frowned with disappointment. All this political, secretive fuss could also spell trouble for him and his dear Anna. A shiver ran down his spine, and it had nothing to do with his friend Antonin's knowledge of a government threat of forced retirement in the distant Polish city of Bialystok, working in a dusty library updating files, which at the moment was worth considering.

Anything to escape this brain-frying Australian heat. Maybe he'd try again to convince Antonin to forget about the whole thing. It was pointless anyway. If the secret ever slipped out, **whatever** that was, Gerek could just deny it, say it was propaganda. After all, that's what all politicians did. Eventually, Gerek returned to the same question: What does a Polish attaché have to do with a country town pharmacist in Australia of all places?

The police officer headed straight for the garage, and Gerek could hear his pulse thumping in his ears. He crouched behind the covered car as the officer entered through the garage door, whistling tunelessly. His torch beam swept the walls and flashed over the cars. Trembling, Gerek raised the hem of the dust cover and hid under it, pressing his cheek against the car's cold metal. Enough light shone through the cover for Gerek to see the officer's shadow. His torch made one last sweep around the garage, then he turned and left.

Gerek crept out of his hiding place and watched the officer stroll to the back of the building to check a small alcove where the adjoining shops met briefly, then moved on. Knees creaking, he hauled himself up using a shelf for leverage. He waited a second to let the blood flow back into his legs. Despite his bulk, he had learnt long ago to move quietly when installing microphones and electronics. But this roller door was a challenge. He went through the same agony of stuffing himself through the narrow gap. He hauled himself up and walked on the balls of his feet, fighting the urge to run as long as he could before breaking into a big man's shuffle-jog.

Some distance behind him, he heard swift footsteps, and he knew they were after him. Damn. Adrenaline shot through him. He had no other choice but to hit Grey Street, which was flooded with light. He rounded the corner and, not wanting to attract attention by running, walked casually, hands in pockets, towards the safety of his car. Breathing hard, Gerek sucked in his gut, eased his belly under the steering wheel, and gently shut the door.

He suppressed the urge to cough as his chest heaved and sweat trickled down the sides of his face. He'd only just escaped in time. Now it was a matter of staying inconspicuous. He chuckled. At five-foot-eight and over a hundred and ten kilos, it was difficult to be inconspicuous, especially when he opened his mouth to speak. But tonight wasn't the night he would get caught; he could feel it in his bones.

Up ahead, Gerek saw a police officer peering into shop alcoves, looking left and right, up and down, as he made his way along the street, occasionally speaking into his shoulder mic. The officer came closer, and Gerek's heart pounded; sweat trickled down his back, making him stick to the seat. He had picked a good parking spot away from the streetlights and between two other cars. And he wasn't a complete idiot: he'd hired an old ute instead of a sedan or something fancy. Trouble was, his bulk made it difficult to find comfort as the seat wouldn't go back any further to allow room for his ample belly.

Gerek ducked down as far as he could. The steering wheel pressing into his stomach made it difficult for him to breathe. Squished like a big, soft-boiled egg, he watched the police officer turn and walk back the way he came.

He waited another five minutes before squeezing out from behind the steering wheel and heaving himself over to the passenger side. He could breathe at last. With effort, he bent down, pulled his carry bag from under the seat, and rummaged for his hip flask. A drink first before ringing his friend. He took a long swig of Anna's homemade Fruit Brandy to steady himself and enjoyed the rush as the alcohol hit his stomach. He screwed the top back on his hip flask and placed it on the seat next to him. No doubt he'd need more soon enough. He pulled the phone out of his back pocket; not a single number was listed, not even his wife's; and dialled the familiar number.

'*Witam.*' *(Hello)*.

'Gerek here.'

'Have you got it?'

'*Nie.* (no)Too many peoples and police.'

'Why do you wait? Why don't you go in earlier, you fool! What can three women do to you? Get in. Get stuff. Get out. Is easy.'

'Don't be imbecile, do you know how much noises three women can make? And they stick together like gloop. One see me out window, she would know me straight away, and then what? Or should I go wearing mask?' He growled. 'I could wear sack and she would know me.'

'You should have tried harder. These nieces must know something. You go in, make friends, talk to them. Have few drinks.'

'You are, *idiota,* (idiot) I tell you,' Gerek scolded, and hit his forehead with the heel of his hand. 'I should make friends with police too?'

'*Nie!* (No)

'Good. Have brandy, clear your brains. In this house, I am looking at people, in and out, in and out, busy like bureau. They know something, these police here. Have people watching the house all the time.'

'You stay there until she leave, or get her alone. Do what you have to do. Or else.'

Gerek ended his call and shoved it in his pocket. He grabbed the hip flask. Warm brandy gurgled down his throat. When it was all gone, he cursed.

*　*　*

From somewhere along the upstairs hallway, Brock and Calum's raised voices drifted down to Jennifer. They were having a heated discussion. It had something to do with Uncle Bob. Jennifer moved closer, straining to make out what they were saying, but she couldn't catch enough words to make even a wild guess. When they appeared at the top of the stairs, she asked, 'Everything all right?'

Brock clomped down the old, creaking stairs. Calum, brushing cobwebs out of his hair, followed close behind. Tony was yet to surface.

'No sign of rats or mice, nothing's chewed through the wires. The rest of the wiring up there is scary.' Calum pointed his finger towards the ceiling. 'Bob had planned to do something about it, but...' he pressed his lips together and shrugged. 'I strongly advise you don't venture up there; it's dangerous. You need an electrician damn quick. As for hot water, you probably didn't wait long enough for it to heat up. But I'll check the fuse box, just in case.' He strode off to the back of the shop and into the kitchen.

'How was your flight from London?' Brock asked politely. 'Sticky-taped wings sound a bit rough.'

'Yeah, that and the ride to the airport on a Kawasaki with a maniac madder than a cut snake in charge of the bike.'

'*Scary.*' Brock tried not to smile. 'I noticed Bob got rid of the Volvo, but kept his Caddie. If you need a car but don't want to drive the beast, come and see me. I've got a dual-cab you can borrow any time.'

'Thank you, that's very kind. I'll keep it in mind.' Scraping noises, and what sounded like tins being stacked, drifted in from somewhere at the back. Jennifer turned towards the kitchen and waited; everything was quiet again. Worried about Calum's safety, she asked, 'Do you think he's okay?'

'Sure,' Brock nodded. 'Besides running a great cattle stud, Cal's the best electrician in town.'

'Oh.' She relaxed, feeling a little better about Calum poking around with live wires.

Calum strode in and stood beside them, hands loosely on his hips, eyes shifting from Brock to Jennifer. He pursed his lips, seemed to suck up whatever he wanted to ask, and said, 'Yep, the hot water's on.'

Jennifer glanced at the ceiling and then back at Calum. 'What was the work you did for Uncle Bob in the attic?'

'Electrical,' Calum replied. 'Bob wanted a connection for his computer, one that wouldn't make it crash. As I said, be extra careful and don't venture up there.'

Jennifer massaged her neck, hoping to ease the headache threatening at the back of her skull. Her shoulders ached all the way up to her eyebrows.

'I promise not to touch any wires. Anyway, we're only here a few days.'

'Ma'am,' Brock said, dusting his hands off, 'that'd be a shame.'

'Thank you, Brock. Just one thing, could you please cut the *ma'am* stuff? Every time you say that, I age ten years. At this rate I'll be dead soon.'

'Miss Dove?' Brock deadpanned.

Jennifer groaned and rolled her eyes. A loud knock on the front door drew her attention away from Brock and his teasing and focused on Calum as he moved to answer it. She could watch him walk anywhere: his confident and relaxed stride made her breath hitch in her throat.

Hot!

His worn leather boots squeaked across the dusty mosaic tiles; moments later, he returned with a container and a bulging plastic bag.

When the smell of hot food hit Jennifer's nose, she wished she hadn't been such a snob and had ordered a hamburger with the lot—grease, sauce, and all.

'Shall we head upstairs to the living room?' she asked, grabbing her bag on the way. 'Where's Tony?'

'Don't worry,' Brock said. 'He'll turn up.'

'Shouldn't you go look for him?' Calum asked, doing the sideways nod again.

'What is it with you? You got a cricked neck or something? I can fix that.' For his size, Brock moved remarkably fast as his big hands reached for Calum.

Calum stepped back. 'Knock it off. I'm fine.'

They settled on the leather lounge, and Calum handed out parcels of food. He gave Jennifer a small carton that served as a tray. Inside, there was a large, lidded paper cup filled with pumpkin soup, a plastic soup spoon, and a buttered wholemeal roll.

Jennifer lifted the lid and took a deep breath through her nose. 'This smells delicious.'

'I remember seeing you as a kid,' Calum said as he peeled the paper off his hamburger. 'You're the one living in London.'

'That's me,' she said, tilting her head. 'Why are you grinning?'

'It's your posh accent; not all the time, just some words. Are there any more relatives coming to the funeral?'

'We're all the family our uncle kept in touch with — my sister Sofie and her daughter Claudia, who are at the motel. And God only knows where my brother is, but he's supposed to be here too,' she sighed. 'Before I forget, thanks for keeping such a vigilant eye on Uncle Bob's place.'

'Bob was a top bloke,' Brock said, 'always willing to lend a hand in the community. It's fair we look after his shop now that he's gone.'

'We're all gonna miss the old...' Calum looked a bit sheepish and took a big bite of his hamburger.

'Pharmacist?' Keeping an eye on Calum, Jennifer blew across the hot soup before tasting it.

Calum took a long drink of water and set the bottle down again. 'Let's just say he was quite a character and we'll miss him.'

'I adored my uncle,' Jennifer's voice trembled with a flood of tender memories.

Brace yourselves. Once people find out Bob's nieces are in town, they'll be lining up to ask you all sorts of questions.

Chewing on a mouthful of burger, Brock rumbled and nodded eagerly.

'What would they possibly want to ask me?' Jennifer bit into her roll.

Calum ran his fingers through his hair. 'What I'm trying to say is, talking about happy memories makes people feel good, especially at a time like this. Memories they'd like to share with you. And you, in turn, can do the same for them. Bit like an Irish wake.'

'Right, I see what you mean...' Jennifer's thoughts drifted. 'I'm so tired I can't string a sentence together.'

'Yeah, you look ready to drop,' Calum smiled. 'We'll take off.'

Jennifer waved a weary hand. 'That's okay. Finish your burgers. I haven't finished my soup yet anyway.'

Calum and Brock settled back into the lounge chairs, chatting about an upcoming wine festival. Jennifer felt comforted by the low murmur of their deep voices. Gradually, their words drifted into a distant place. It became impossible to keep her tired eyes focused. She didn't have the strength to fight off sleep any longer. She snuggled into the corner of the couch and barely noticed someone gently taking the paper tray from her hands. Nestled into Calum's warm jacket, her chin dropped. Her shoulder and head eased sideways onto the arm of the sofa.

Her last thought was, *God, I hope I don't drool. No one in the Dove family drools. Mother would not allow it.*

She was vaguely aware of someone covering her with a blanket, then that person took off her shoes.

'G'night, Twinkles,' Calum whispered.

Jennifer caught the smile behind his words. A moment later, sleep claimed her weary body.

Chapter 4

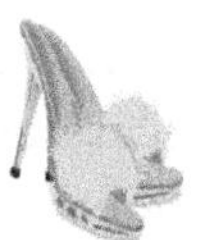

Jennifer sat bolt upright and blinked at her surroundings. Her fingers played with the tea-rose quilt cover as she tried to focus on the snippet of a thought that had woken her with a pounding heart. Holy crap, she was with a man last night. No, make that three men. Images of a living room, soft couch, hot soup, hot bloke, and falling asleep crystallised in her mind, and a flush of heat burned her cheeks.

He had covered her with a blanket. Fingertips in her hair, Jennifer rubbed her scalp hard, hoping it would stimulate her brain to remember his name. A manly scent mixed with pine hit her senses. She pulled his soft leather jacket closer around her shoulders.

'Calum.' She lifted the lapels; folds of gold satin lining gleamed. She buried her nose in the warm, dark hollow and inhaled deeply. 'Damn, no one should smell this good.'

Then she remembered more. Had she nuzzled his shirt, or was that a dream?

'Christ, what if I was dribbling?' Horrified, she felt around the corners of her mouth and her chin. No sign of any drool. Jennifer ran her tongue around her teeth. 'Ugh.' She swung her legs off the couch, found the fancy pink stilettos, and slipped them on.

A faint knock echoed somewhere. Downstairs? Listening, Jennifer tilted her head, and a sharp twinge ran up her neck. She stretched her neck and hauled herself off the couch, then padded down the hall to the girlie bedroom. She pushed the drapes aside, yanked the sash window up, and yelled, 'Keep your shirt on, Sofe, I'll be there in a sec.'

Quickly, she splashed her face with cold water and rinsed her mouth. She couldn't find a towel, so used her Veronica shift, leaving dark wet patches around the hem. As she hurried out of the bathroom, a dishevelled image caught her eye. She did a double-take at the full-length mirror on the massive old closet. 'That's not me.' Her skin was tight and pale, her cheekbones more prominent than usual, which may have had something to do with the shadows under her green, bloodshot eyes.

More knocking at the front door, and Jennifer called out, 'Oh crap, I'm coming, Sofe!' She mussed her hair with her fingers and clattered down the creaking stairs. Two shadows, like a couple of long-armed aliens, stood outlined on the newspaper covering the glass front door. She wondered why Sofie hadn't come around the back through the garage.

Jennifer hurried across the tiled floor, her stilettos resounding like a hammer striking an anvil in the empty shop, making her flinch with every step. 'Hope you've got coffee!' she yelled, sliding the bolts across to fling the door open. Early morning sun smacked her in the eyes. 'Ooh, that's a bitch!' She clapped a hand over her forehead and peered at two silhouettes. 'Get in here, Sofe!'

No response.

Oh-oh, Jennifer forced her eyes to focus.

'Hello, dear. Didn't mean to wake you,' said a sympathetic, aged voice.

Jennifer stared, surprised to see two elderly women at her door. The taller woman had weathered skin that spoke of years in the hot sun and dry, cold winds. But none of the lines and wrinkles detracted from her natural elegance. Her soft grey hair curled out from under a straw hat and wisped around her face. Hazel eyes, enhanced by a lilac blouse, crinkled as her warm smile widened.

A younger, stockier woman, probably in her mid-fifties, stood next to her. Glossy brown hair, cut in a severe bob, suited her round face. She seemed sad and tired, her tentative smile worried.

Jennifer turned back to the taller woman and thought, I've seen those hazel eyes before. She frowned, trying to recollect where. Out on the street, a four-wheel drive crawled past. I've seen that car before.

The driver poked his head out the window and waved.

I've seen that face before...Calum! Hot hunk — big trouble — killer smile.

'Who —?' Jennifer asked, blinking at the elderly woman.

'Connie McGregor,' the woman said, extending her hand, her voice direct and friendly. Strong bony fingers clasped Jennifer's in a no-nonsense greeting.

Her thoughts slowly came together. 'Oh, you're...' she found herself looking and pointing at the empty street.

'I'm Calum's grandmother, dear.' She looked at Jennifer with a perceptive eye. 'His leather jacket suits you.'

'We...' Jennifer began. 'I should return it. But he's...' she looked down the street, 'gone.'

Connie's smile deepened. 'Not to worry, dear. I'd like you to meet Shirley Jarvis, your uncle's housekeeper.'

Mrs Jarvis had a firm grip. Her bright, grey eyes sparkled from a round, rosy-cheeked, freckled face. 'Bob Feldman was a pleasure to work for.'

'We are so sorry about your uncle.' Tears glistened in Connie's bright eyes. The depth of her emotions made her voice thick and unsteady. 'You've come a long way to be here for him. Bob was a *wonderful* man.'

Jennifer rubbed her face, hoping her brain would catch up with time zones, a drastic change in climate, and cultural differences of a magnitude she hadn't experienced since arriving in London.

'We've caught you at an awkward time,' Connie continued. 'We just came by to give you this.' She handed over a large basket.

The mouth-watering aromas of freshly baked bread and warm scones drifted into Jennifer's nose. Among the food was a jar of Vegemite, a tub of butter, a pot of strawberry jam, a jug of cream, and a thermos.

'This smells so good, thank you. I never imagined...'

'Compliments of the Country Women's Association; we like to help the immediate family cope with their bereavement.' Connie's chin began to crinkle, and her eyes glistened again. She turned away and fumbled for a handkerchief hiding somewhere down her blouse.

Shirley put a comforting arm around Connie's shoulder. 'We'd better be off. We're arranging flowers at the chapel.'

'We heard Father Thomas is looking after things — but a chapel?' Jennifer asked, surprised.

'Oh dear girl, I know your uncle was strongly against all religions, but Bob, being Bob, threw himself into fundraising. As a result, he spent time with all the clergy in town. But Father Thomas and your uncle became great friends. They'd have rip-roaring debates about all sorts of things, but always with a laugh. Didn't they, Shirley?'

Shirley smiled. 'They were great friends.'

Connie chuckled. 'Bob once said no one was going to stomp around in his head and make him feel guilty for the harmless things he did. I hope that's helped you understand why it will be at St Mary's, dear?'

The harmless things he did? Was that the same as his comment to us that he meant no harm?

Jennifer patted Connie's arm. 'What about a suit for Uncle Bob? He was a dapper dresser. There must be some lovely ones in his room.'

Connie fluttered her hand in an animated fashion. 'Oh no-no-no, his clothes are taken care of. But thank you anyway, dear.'

'Can I help with the flowers? Perhaps I could take them to the chapel for you?'

'I understand your need to be involved and I don't want to disappoint you, but as it is, we have so many willing hands, the hall will be like a chook pen with a fox let loose. A lot of clucking and flapping arms.'

The image that formed in her mind made Jennifer laugh. 'What about after the service? I've had no time to prepare anything.'

'Your uncle took care of the catering some time ago. There'll be plates of sandwiches, little pies, cakes, lamingtons, coffee, and tea set up in the town hall.' Connie took a deep breath and dabbed her eyes again.

Jennifer's heart went out to them. 'I'm so sorry, I'm forgetting my manners. Would you both like to come in for a glass of cold water?' she said, moving back from the doorway with a sharp clack-clack of stiletto slip-ons.

Shirley peered down at Jennifer's feet. All colour drained from her face.

Connie clutched Shirley's arm. 'N-no thanks, dear, we won't bother you,' she said breathlessly.

Jennifer reached for Connie's hand. 'Are you all right? Is there anything I can do?'

'I'm fine, dear, thank you.' Connie smiled and dragged her gaze away from the stilettos. She patted Jennifer's hand. 'Will you be saying a few words at the service?'

Jennifer sneaked a peek at her feet. The pink stilettos were frivolous, but otherwise there was nothing about them that should cause a reaction. She met Connie's steady gaze. 'A few words? I had planned to. Perhaps my sister Sofie will as well. My parents won't be coming. At least, they bloody better not,' Jennifer said lightly, but irritation flared.

Connie gave her a sympathetic smile. 'I'm so glad you understand about Bob's wish regarding his siblings. *You* were his family; he adored all of you. We must go. Enjoy your breakfast, dear.'

'Yes, we must run,' Shirley said, flustered.

Jennifer glanced down at the jacket around her shoulders. 'Wait, you'll probably see Calum before I do, would you mind taking it? And please tell him thank you from me.' She put the basket down and muttered, 'Hope Veronica doesn't mind me borrowing her clothes, but I was wet through last night and my suitcase was in the car.'

Connie's eyes sparkled. 'Of course she wouldn't.'

'Veronica and Uncle Bob must have been close. No doubt she'll be at the funeral. We've never met. Would you mind introducing us? We should pass on our condolences.'

The two women seemed taken aback. Jennifer regarded them closely. 'Is everything all right?'

Ignoring the Veronica question, Connie reached forward to pull the jacket back over Jennifer's shoulders; drawing it together at the front, she prattled on. 'You know what men are like, best not confuse matters. Calum left his card in the basket. He said to call him when you're ready and he'll drop by for his jacket.'

'Okay.' She could do that. The flutter of anticipation at seeing Calum again wasn't a problem. No *siree*. 'Thank you both, it's very much appreciated, Connie, Shirley,' Jennifer smiled. 'I'll ring Calum later this morning.'

'Lovely, dear. We'll see you at St Mary's.'

Jennifer watched them as they walked arm in arm down the footpath, and the old classic movie *Arsenic and Old Lace* came to mind. Connie wore a sensible straw hat, pale lilac slacks, and darker lilac blouse and Shirley wore a beige T-shirt and serviceable baggy brown cotton slacks. They both looked genteel — on the surface, but something was going on, and Jennifer didn't have a clue what it might be.

With a clack-clack of stilettos, Jennifer moved back to close the door. She peered at her feet one more time, shrugged and made her way to the upstairs kitchen. She set the basket down on the scrubbed pine table and gazed around the room. Memories flooded back of times when she and her sister had huddled around the black combustion stove while their uncle flipped pancakes for them. He hadn't changed any of the décor. The stove still sat in the cream tiled alcove with its green border and chimney above. All dated, but not tatty. The cupboards, with sturdy brass hinges, hadn't been updated either, except for a coat of paint. Through the tall windows, she could see the neglected courtyard below. She looked up and beyond the outskirts of town; grapevine-covered hills stretched into the distance until they reached the dark-green foothills of the blue-tinged mountains.

What a view. No wonder her uncle had loved living here.

Jennifer sniffed the air. She could almost smell apple pie and cinnamon, herbs and spices imbedded in the old timbers and paintwork. She unhooked a mug hanging from a bench-top stand and peered into it, making sure there weren't any spiders; finding one in her mouth with a swig of coffee did not bear thinking about.

Jennifer pulled a chair out and sat at the old table. Drawing the basket closer, she grabbed the thermos and opened it. *Real* coffee. She poured herself a cup, enjoying the quietness, and wondered when Sofie and Claudia would turn up. Perhaps she should ring.

She glanced at her watch, still on London time. She'd never been good at maths but tried to work it out anyway. 'Shit, it must be around seven-thirty.' Her forehead hit the kitchen table. 'I can forget about ringing Sofie. I'll be here talking to myself for hours.'

She finished her coffee and headed back to her room to unpack her clothes and hang them in the enormous, antique mirrored wardrobe that somehow gave her the heebie-jeebies. 'Silly goose,' she muttered. But what if her uncle's clothes were in this closet, would seeing them bring her undone?

Uncle Bob had been a powerful ally and a shoulder to lean on when her family tried to undermine her for wanting to move to London to study haute cuisine. He gave her the confidence to go for it, he was so proud of her when she did. Now, her champion was gone.

'I have to fight my own battles now,' she told the closet.

Steeling herself, she swung open the doors. Her uncle's winter clothes hung under plastic covers as if they'd just come back from the dry cleaners. She shoved them aside to make room for her things. Strange scents wafted out, dry-cleaning fluid, cedarwood, and something she couldn't quite identify. Lavender for Veronica?

'So much better than mothballs, Uncle Bob,' Jennifer muttered into the dark, cave-like interior.

She hung all her clothes up and shut the door. With a backward glance, she strode out of the room and into the kitchen to have breakfast.

Jennifer poked about in the cupboards and found an old flip-downs toaster. She cut two slices of bread from Connie's basket of goodies, popped them in the toaster, and switched it on. No sooner had she turned her back when loud crackling noises erupted, and instinctively, Jennifer ducked for cover. A pungent smell of burning bread and electrical fumes filled the room. When she finally looked over her shoulder, she saw blue smoke billowing out of the socket.

'Shit-shit-shit!' Jennifer searched the room for a broom, anything to extend her reach and flip the switch off from a safe distance. 'Help!' came out as a pathetic squeak. Yanking drawers open, she found a wooden spoon and a pair of red, polka-dot oven mitts. She ran to the toaster. Leaning back, Jennifer held the spoon end under the archaic brass switch and flicked it off. But what if that wasn't good enough? She grabbed the cord and yanked it out of the socket, causing a small explosion. Sparks flew, and she flung her hands out as if that would magically stop everything. 'The toaster was on fire!' Jennifer squealed into the empty room. A room that quickly filled with acrid blue smoke. 'Bloody hell!' Wrestling with one of the tall sash windows, she used all her strength to tug it open. Cool, fresh air wafted in. She turned back to the toaster and smacked it with the polka-dotted mitts, again and again, which had no effect. She needed something to smother the flames and spotted an old tea towel hanging on the oven door. She grabbed it and threw it over the burning toaster. Holding the lot at arm's length, she chucked it out the window. As the wind caught the towel, it ignited, releasing tiny embers that drifted away until they became ash. 'Shit!' Jennifer cursed, wiping perspiration from her forehead with a mitt as the toaster clattered onto the flagstones below. Filled with burning holes, the tea towel floated after it. She watched as it smouldered out of harm's way, a wisp of blue smoke trailing up.

Jennifer slumped down on a chair to catch her breath. With her hands still wedged in the oven mitts, she plonked her elbows on the table and rested her head in her hands. Big mistake. 'Phew!' She wrinkled her nose. The acrid stench of blackened fabric and melted stuffing was horrible. Without looking, she threw the gloves into the sink.

'I need more caffeine,' she told herself. 'Once I've had caffeine, everything will be alright.' She poured another coffee and gulped down a mouthful. Shit! She'd nearly burnt the place down. Jennifer let out a long, drawn-out sigh of relief and reached for the basket. She removed the scones, cream, and jam. 'Who needs a toaster when you've got the Country Women's Association?' she quipped and glanced up to see a cloud of blue smoke floating above her head before it trailed out the window. Good. She'd be able to stand up soon and breathe without passing out from toxic fumes.

As her nerves gradually settled, she heard sirens wail in the distance.

Was the day about to become even more interesting?

Chapter 5

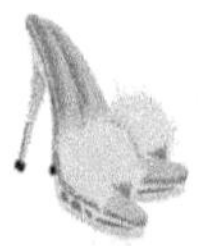

Jennifer glared at the blackened socket. What could that be—ambulance? Police? She could never work out which was which. 'Fire!' The truck was coming closer with every second. The siren was deafening. Thankfully, the noise wound down like a dying beast as the truck stopped in the back lane. Jennifer watched in fascination as its flashing red light reflected around the walls of her uncle's kitchen.

Hands on the table, she pushed her chair back and moved to the window. 'It's got to be next door.' She leant out to see who the unfortunate neighbour was; perhaps she could help. Immediately, she knew that was an irrational thought.

Yes, the morning was about to get a whole lot crazier.

A half-dozen firemen, all wearing protective gear, wrestled an enormous hose through the gate. Their boots clomped over the flagstones in her uncle's courtyard. Two more firefighters arrived, carrying large, bright red extinguishers with nozzles at the ready. They aimed them at her smouldering toaster and shot it. The old toaster disappeared under a pile of white foam.

The man holding an enormous fireman's hose aimed it up at her window. 'Oh my God!' Jennifer leaned out as far as she dared and frantically waved ceasefire-style. The rest of her made ready to duck in case he decided to blast her with the hose, which had a brass nozzle the size of a cannon.

'No-no!' she yelled. 'It's all right, trust me, there's no fire!'

As if they hadn't heard a word she'd said, one of them yelled up, 'Don't panic, lady — we're here!' Seconds later, a fireman with an extendable ladder appeared. He lunged forward, aiming for the window. It landed with a thump against the wall directly under the window ledge.

In a matter of seconds, a burly fireman, his weather-beaten face grinning with expectant heroism, clambered up the rattling ladder.

'I can sling ya over me shoulder, no worries,' he said, arms reaching for her.

Someone shouted from below, 'You did that in record time, Bruce. Only five seconds!'

Bruce looked down and gave the shouter the thumbs up. He turned back to the open window and Jennifer, patting his broad shoulder.

'Okay, luv. C'mon.'

Horrified, Jennifer stepped back, hands out, palms up. 'Hold on just a minute! I'm quite capable of going down the stairs by myself.' She hitched a mitted hand behind her, indicating the door leading out.

Disappointment flashed across his features. 'It's a ladder, luv. I can still help ya.' His hopeful expression returned. 'Don't look down, just climb out the window backwards. I'll be right behind ya to make sure your feet are on the rung.'

'Not the ladder, the stairs!' Jennifer tried to explain. A flash went off from somewhere below. She glanced in the direction it had come from and saw a tall, thin man with a comb-over and an enormous camera pressed to his face. It looked like the local paper's newsman-slash-photographer had arrived. He stood apart from the crowd to get a clear shot with his telephoto, wide-angle lens.

'C'mon darl, let him carry ya down,' the photojournalist yelled up. 'Treat it like a fire drill. Great practice for Bruce.'

'There *is* no fire. The toaster blew up, that's all!' Jennifer yelled back.

'Are you sure?' the fireman on the ladder asked with a friendly but awkward grin, a grin that didn't reach his gentle brown eyes. Damn, he was disappointed; could she live with that? 'Ya face is all black, luv, and I can smell burning wires.'

'Face? Black?' Jennifer rubbed at her cheeks, smearing the soot she'd put there with the oven mitts.

'Can't be too careful with these old buildings, they're heritage listed, ya know. That means *old,*' he added, peering past her into the kitchen. 'I've heard you're Bob Feldman's niece, is that right?'

Jennifer nodded.

'Great to have you here, Jennifer. Bruce Stiles,' the fireman said. She took his extended hand, thinking this was the weirdest introduction she'd ever had. 'This is a great old building, isn't it? It's one of the best examples of Edwardian architecture in the area. I s'pose ya know it used to be a pharmacy,' Bruce informed her, elbows resting on the sill, chin in his hands. 'You're not a pharmacist, are ya?'

'No. Is that a problem?'

'Nah, just curious.'

'Bruce!' a fellow fireman called up. 'Stop flapping ya gums. Do we have a fire or not?'

'Nah, false alarm!' Bruce called down. He turned back to Jennifer. 'You should get yourself a small fire extinguisher and smoke alarms,' he told her earnestly.

'I won't be here for long, but I promise to keep it in mind for the future.'

'Aw, c'mon darl,' the journo yelled encouragingly. 'Let Bruce carry ya down; at least their trip here will be worth their while. It's ya duty to the community!'

'That's not fair!' Jennifer shouted angrily. She pointed her finger at the journalist just as a flash went off. 'Damn!' she muttered, guilt-ridden as well as embarrassed.

'Pay no mind, Jennifer luv,' Bruce advised. 'He's just spoil'n for a bit of fun.'

From the hopeful look on Bruce's face, Jennifer could see that he would love this opportunity to put his fireman's skills into practice. She scanned the scene below. Neighbours had started to arrive. People were hanging over fences and out of upper-storey windows for a better look. She'd better do something quick before the whole town showed up.

The sea of faces below looked up with eager anticipation. They were Bob's friends and neighbours. How could she let them and her uncle down?

'Oh hell, Bruce, I'm community-minded enough to give it a go.'

Bruce's face beamed. '*Yeah?*'

Jennifer nodded. 'Don't drop me, it's a long way down to the flagstones,' she said, peering over the sill and checking out the ladder. The graphic mental picture of Bruce rattling up the ladder mushroomed. *Shit!* There'd be extra weight going down. She didn't want to be here. She didn't want to do this.

'Just relax,' Bruce told her. 'Let yourself flop over me shoulder.'

Jennifer pulled back, eyes wide as she stared into his face. 'Flop! Oh, sure, Bruce,' she covered her sarcastic tone with a smile. 'I'm an expert at flopping out of second-storey windows!'

Bruce chuckled and corrected, 'First storey.' Pointing down, he said, 'Ground.' Tapping the windowsill, he said, 'First.'

'Bruce, it's a very high first storey!'

'Sure it is, luv. But don't you worry; you're in safe hands.'

'*Oh?*' Jennifer leant forward, grabbing hold of Bruce's broad shoulder. 'That makes me feel a whole lot better.' Shouts and applause erupted from below. A surge of butterflies exploded in her stomach as suddenly the distant ground below swayed before her eyes. 'How often,' her voice strained with the pressure of his shoulder digging into her stomach, 'have you done this?'

'First time for me. How about you?' Bruce replied, relishing the moment.

A strangled cry escaped Jennifer's mouth at that bit of frightening news. 'They sent up a first timer,' her voice squeezed out, 'not a veteran!?'

* * *

Sirens continued to blare on the outskirts of town. Carrying a box of switches and circuit breakers from the hardware store, Calum stopped to listen. The klaxon sounded urgent, different from the times when they were on a drill. His blood went cold and goose bumps broke out on his arms. The blaring came closer as he threw the rest of his equipment into the back of his ute.

He looked down the street and saw Tumble Creek's fire engine pass through the intersection. Calum jumped into his work ute and followed the sirens. He caught up with them at the roundabout and followed until it parked out the back of Bob's old chemist shop.

'Shit—the wiring!' Apprehension gripped him, and every muscle in his body tensed. Calum knew the fire chief wouldn't let him get near the place right now, but he had to get in and see what was happening. Gravel flying, he let them do what they do best and drove around to the front of the building.

'Don't be locked, don't be locked,' he muttered to himself, nearing the papered windows and door.

He grabbed the shop's front doorknob, twisting it open, relieved when it swung wide. He stumbled inside and flung the door closed behind him, the glass rattling in the frame. His eyes searched as he strode through to the back of the empty shop. He sniffed the air for the familiar pungent smell of burning electrics, but there was nothing. He scouted around the shop's kitchen and storage room. Still nothing.

'Fuck,' he growled quietly, yet his voice echoed through the shop anyway. He went to the stairs; a draft filtered down, and he caught that telltale smell he guessed was coming from the upstairs kitchen.

Calum took the stairs two at a time, then hurried along the carpet to the kitchen door and came to an abrupt stop. The tension in his body eased, and he relaxed, crossing his arms, leaning against the doorjamb, smiling as he watched Jennifer's arse disappear through the window. Not wanting to risk her precarious state, he waited until she was safely out.

He moved to the window and looked out. 'G'day, Bruce, you lucky bastard, you've finally got a live one?'

Jennifer let out a strangled cry, and in a flash, her hand whipped around to cover her lovely arse.

Calum chuckled.

The ladder bounced, and Bruce grabbed her thighs. 'Keep still,' he told Jennifer, 'pretend you're unconscious.'

*   *   *

'Calum McGregor?' Jennifer yelled.

'Yeah!'

'Go away!'

Bruce stopped moving down the ladder, looked up, and called out, 'G'day, Cal. You might wanna check the socket above the bench over there.' She felt him wiggle his head sideways, probably pointing in the direction Calum should look. Jennifer was thinking, he's an electrician; he's hardly going to miss a blackened hole in the wall.

'Yeah,' Calum replied, then called out to Jennifer. 'Jen, don't use any plugs.'

Firemen below yelled, 'Mornin', Cal!'

'G'day. Be back later,' Calum told them.

Jennifer tried to twist around, and asked, 'Is he gone?'

'Er…yep…relax!' Bruce said, sounding a bit confused.

'Pretend I'm unconscious? Seriously?' she squeezed out through a constricted diaphragm.

But that wasn't her only problem. Mindful of the fluffy, pink stiletto slip-ons, she scrunched up her toes, clinging to them, fearing that if they were flung loose, they'd hit Bruce on the head. Not a good idea, at this point, at least not until they hit solid ground.

And what was everyone laughing at? She'd like to see one of them try this and think it's funny.

As he resumed their descent, Bruce's firm grip tightened around her thighs.

The Veronica shift crept up. Jennifer's desperate attempts to yank her top down past her bum proved futile. Her immediate thoughts were, how much of an eyeful did Calum get? She'd never be able to look him in the face again. And Christ, which undies was she wearing? And thank God, her mother couldn't see her now.

Jennifer's world rocked. Her head bobbed, and blood rushed to her face as she clutched Bruce's protective jacket with its bright yellow reflector strips. She squealed as the ladder bounced with their combined weight. What if it broke? That frightened her more than anything. Mouth open, eyes wide, face flushing crimson, she had to be the perfect picture of sheer terror. Thinking it must be easier if you couldn't see what might befall you, she screwed her eyes shut and prayed for it all to be over.

'Stop right there, Bruce, and give me a wave!' the journalist called out.

'Bruce, if you value your life,' Jennifer wheezed, 'don't you dare let go of me or the ladder to wave at that idiot.'

Bruce stopped his descent. 'I wouldn't do that, luv.' He used the arm wrapped around her thighs to hook through the ladder. With his free hand, he waved and grinned at the photojournalist.

Jennifer thumped him on the shoulder. 'Bruce! My eyes feel like they're about to pop and my head's about to explode!'

'Oops, sorry, luv.' He continued down. It took forever before the swaying stopped.

Applause erupted around her. With a sigh of relief, Jennifer felt solid ground beneath her feet. Feeling light-headed, her legs buckled. In the blink of an eye, half a dozen firemen lunged forward, eager to be the one to come to her aid.

'You all right, luv?' Bruce asked.

'Sure…think my blood's stopped flowing to my legs.'

'Everyone,' Bruce called out, 'I'd like ya to meet Bob's niece, Miss Jennifer Dove.'

'Miss Dove,' the photojournalist called out. 'You've been a terrific sport. Could we have a photo of you in Bruce's arms and the rest of the fire crew in the background?'

'Oh sure,' Jennifer smiled feebly, still shaken by the episode.

Ten minutes later, she watched the clean-up start. Hoses scraped, brass nozzles clanged and bounced over the flagstones. The ladder clattered down to less than half its size. Talking and laughing among themselves, the men gathered their gear.

'Nice meet'n ya, Jennifer. We're all volunteers, so we don't often get the chance to practice.' The firemen sauntered out of the courtyard; Bruce stayed back and took Jennifer's hand. He leant in and quietly said, 'I'll see ya later at the church.' She gave him a slight nod. He gave her a peck on the cheek. 'For Bob.' He smiled and took off.

Jennifer swiped at a couple of stray tears, smearing more soot across her cheeks. She headed towards the secluded kitchen for some quiet reflection.

How long had she been here? Not even twenty-four hours.

Chapter 6

Jennifer sat at the kitchen table with her feet up on the chair opposite. 'Shit.' She wiggled her toes and eyed the pink, fluffy stilettos. *'Great, I can see it already, front page news: "Woman rescued from burning building. Still needs rescuing from poor fashion sense." Or: "Woman burns heritage building, but saves fluffy pink stilettos." '*

On autopilot, Jennifer buttered herself a scone, adding lashing of jam and cream. Bugger the hips, she thought, biting into the spongy little cake. It had been an action-packed couple of days, and she'd only just survived—arrived. She peered at her watch, quickly did the maths: nope, Sofie wouldn't be up yet. She thought about changing her watch from London to Tumble Creek time, but what was the point? She'd be heading home soon.

'Ah, London,' she sighed, thinking about her quaint flat that had never threatened to electrocute her or set her alight. The Tate Gallery, where she could spend days gazing at old masters, like Turner. Being able to go shopping down Oxford Street and pop into Harrods, just because you could. Marble Arch, Buckingham Palace, Hyde Park…Jennifer smiled. Yes, she missed the place already. But a little flame of doubt burned in her mind, and that inherent feeling of belonging, normally associated with home, escaped her.

Ah, but Europe had everything.

Not a bunch of firemen who made her smile.

Or a countryman whose expressive eyes suggested he knew everything about her, but of course, that was impossible.

The words, you're in deep trouble, fluttered through her mind. Jennifer didn't allow herself dwell on what they meant.

Instead, she polished off another scone and, taking Calum's card, wandered down the long hall. She stopped to admire another black and white glamour photo, this one of the stunning Audrey Hepburn. What would become of these photos? What would become of all her uncle's personal things?

Sighing, Jennifer walked into the girlie pink bathroom. She turned the taps on in the shower cubicle and put her hand under the water to check that it was warm. However, turning the taps on full bore didn't improve the flow. She let it run while undressing, just in case it decided to adjust its performance. She shrugged out of Calum's soft leather jacket and placed it on her bed along with his business card. She stripped off Veronica's shift, turned around, and saw her face in the mirror. 'Oh my God!' What will everyone think? Rubbing the soot smudges with her fingers, she hurried to the pathetic dribble called a shower, having to move her body like a belly dancer to get wet.

A shower usually took her about five minutes—ten minutes at most if she had to shave her legs, but this was ridiculous. Shampooing her hair wasn't too bad, but rinsing the lather out was a nightmare. She glared at the old showerhead, gave up, and towelled herself dry before slipping into her undies and bra and giving her hair a quick brush. Without thinking, Jennifer plugged in the dryer—BANG. She yelped and threw the dryer onto the vanity.

Smoke curled out of the power point.

'Shit! Calum said don't use the plugs — shit! Hurry-hurry-hurry!' She danced around, arms flapping, knowing what she needed to do. She scanned the bathroom for something she could use. 'What'll I do, what'll I do? Toilet brush, shit! Left it—can't remember where.' One fire rescue per day was quite enough, thank you very much. Edging forward with her hand outstretched, she quickly grabbed the cord and yanked it free from the plug.

With a sigh, Jennifer let her body sag against the wall. She rubbed one shoulder and then the other, digging her fingers in, trying to drive out the tension. A week's worth of excitement in one day had worn her out. She eyed the bed, beckoning her to fall into its flowery, pink ruffles and just lie there while the world sorted itself out. Instead, she forced herself to stay in the ensuite. No matter what happens, you can't neglect your skin. She slapped moisturiser on her face. 'Relax, stay calm. Breathe in, breathe out. Ah,' she soothed, though her fingers trembled. 'Feeling better already.' No crackling, smoking electrical gremlins were going to stop her from moisturising her skin against the summer's dry heat.

She moved into the bedroom and grabbed her phone to call Calum. When she heard his voice, the English language vanished from her mind. If she tried to say anything, it would've come out as gibberish.

'Hello…hello…speak,' his voice a deep purr.

'Sorry, Calum, my mind was on something else.' And that was not a lie. 'Um…I'm ringing about your jacket.'

'I was coming back; I'll be there in about half an hour, if that's alright?'

'Great, see you then.' She waited, her hand gripping the phone like a lifeline.

'Jen?' Calum asked.

'Um…yeah?'

'Do not touch any power points!' he ordered.

'Um…No, of course not.' She heard him softly chuckle and disconnect.

In a dream, Jennifer stood there for a bit longer, phone to her ear.

'Jen, breakfast!' Sofie sang out.

Quickly, she dropped her phone on the bed as if it had scorched her fingers. 'I'm up here, Sofie!' She took a deep breath and hurried into the hall.

Sofie, wearing a flowing, tie-dyed caftan and carrying a Go-Green Planet Ark supermarket bag full of food, laboured up the stairs. Claudia was close behind, dressed in her favourite colour— black hipsters and a singlet top. Jennifer ran down the hallway in her white lace knickers and matching bra, arms wide open, ready for a hug.

'We're a bit early. Did sirens wake you?' Sofie asked.

'Not exactly,' Jennifer mumbled. 'Hope you've got my bacon and egg roll. Let me put something on and I'll tell you all about last night—and this morning.'

Sofie turned and headed for the kitchen. 'No ghost stories, I hope.'

When Jennifer walked into the bedroom, her phone was buzzing on the bed. She eyed the number and groaned. Damn, why had she hoped it was Calum? She'd only just spoken to him.

'Hello, Mother.' She sounded flat and knew it. Damn it again, that wasn't her intention. *Be bright and bubbly, so she can't hang shit.*

'Jennifer, darling.' Her mother's hoity-toity accent was such a sham. 'We've missed you terribly. Why didn't you drop by on your way?'

'We had no time, Mother. Have you heard from Bret?'

'Not recently. I expect he's terribly busy. Last time we spoke, he was organising a new business partnership. He's investing with them; it all sounds so exciting. He'll make time to call me soon. Unlike you, who never does.'

Jennifer rubbed her face. 'Mother, I've only just arrived and finally had a good night's sleep.' Thanks for asking. Why did she always feel she had to justify herself? Especially since this wasn't a 'Hello, darling daughter' call. It was a pump-for-information call.

'Yes, London's a long way. But now Bob has left you some money, you can buy us two first-class tickets as an anniversary gift. All our friends at the bowls club will be so jealous.'

Jennifer almost choked. 'Are you serious?' Just when she thought her mother couldn't shock her anymore, she did it again. But there was no point arguing, so she cut to the chase. 'Why are you ringing, as if I need to ask?'

'Well, there must be some way we can attend Bob's funeral. He was my only brother. I've got to be there. How would it look if I weren't? Goodness, that's just unheard of.'

'I'm not going against Uncle Bob's strict instructions, and neither is anyone else. He didn't want you there, especially after the way you treated him — and about that, I'd like to know exactly what happened. Why did you wipe Uncle Bob all those years ago? Now he's gone, you owe all of us an explanation.'

'Oh honestly. Do you have to bring that up now? Bob's dead and no one needs to know,' her mother said, sounding put out and irritated.

'Was it so terrible?' Jennifer hardly dared ask, but needed to know. 'Was whatever he did…criminal?'

'Good heavens no! But it should be.'

'That's just typical of you, Mother. If it doesn't look good, make it illegal. Uncle Bob was your brother.' Annoyed, Jennifer absentmindedly plucked at a loose thread on her lace undies. 'Well, one way or another, I'm going to find out.'

'Bob was always an embarrassment to us. And you're not much better, always saying what you please, wearing what you please, and looking like something the cat dragged in. I suppose you've gone and cut your lovely long hair too.'

'Thank you so much, Mother. Yes, it's so short I look like a boy, and I don't have to bother with a comb or brush. I've always aspired to be just like my Uncle Bob.'

Jennifer flinched at her mother's mocking laugh. 'You'll never be that, I can assure you.'

Their conversation was rapidly declining. Jennifer pushed her fingers into her curls and massaged her scalp. She thought she'd better end it before she said something she'd regret.

'I have to go, we'll talk later.'

'The motel was full in Tumble Creek. We're in the next town, Parrot Rock or something…' Jennifer's mother trailed off, clearly unimpressed. 'Darling, see what you can do about us attending the funeral. Talk to Father Thomas.'

'Bye, Mother.'

Jennifer threw her phone onto the bed and turned to pace up and down the bedroom. It didn't help much. She paused and told herself to breathe. 'Calm,' she sighed, which helped, sort of. She yanked on a pair of Capri pants, a white T-shirt, and a pair of strappy sandals. She looked in the mirror to fix her hair. 'God no,' she muttered and tried to smile, but it was more like a grimace. 'Stop this right now. You do not look or act like your mother!' She turned and headed down the hall to the kitchen.

Sofie looked up from buttering a scone. 'What's up? Why are your nostrils flaring?'

'I just had Mother on the phone.'

'*Ooh,*' Claudia said. 'Aunty Jen needs a chill pill.'

'*Aah,*' Sofie nodded. 'I had my call last night.'

With a look they'd shared for years, Jennifer knew she didn't need to say more.

'Don't fill me in either, I know that look,' Claudia said, wagging her finger at them.

'Anyway,' Sofie flicked the air with a butter knife, signalling they should start fresh. 'Wow!' she exclaimed and pointed at Jennifer's pants. 'Did someone pour you into those?'

'They're stretch.' Jennifer plucked her pants away from her leg and then let go. The fabric sprang back with a soft thud. 'See?'

'I want a pair.'

'Yeah, Mum, get out of those hippy caftan things.' Claudia waved her arms out wide.

'Leave me alone. They're cool on a hot day.'

'Aunt Jennifer looks *cool*.'

Sofie made a face. 'Let's get back to Jen telling us all about last night—sleep well?'

'Yes, once the police and Calum left, I slept like a log.'

'Whoa, Jen, police!' Sofie's worried eyes widened. 'What's happened? Why were the police here? And who's Calum?'

Jennifer spent some time explaining what had happened to her earlier, including the burning toaster, fireman Bruce, and the ladder incident. And that Calum probably saw a good deal of her arse.

'*Hectic!*' Claudia giggled. 'Damn, I probably missed the best part of this trip.'

'Crikey, Jen,' Sofie said, 'I can't date a bloke who can string a sentence together that doesn't include the words football, cricket, or cars. But you, half comatose, have a conversation with three blokes, then one puts you to bed! Plus, a neighbourly chat with a fireman, up a ladder no less. I hope Calum did see your arse, and lots of it,' she giggled.

'Sofie!' Jennifer yelled, horrified.

'You'll be married within a year; I can feel it in my bones,' Sofie added.

Jennifer laughed. 'No, and as soon as I'm back in London, Dobry's gone, so I'm definitely not marrying anyone. I'm going to focus on my restaurant.' She eyed her sister. 'There's no room in my life for boyfriends or marriage.'

'Ha!' Sofie scoffed.

Jennifer exaggerated a long, suffering sigh before changing the subject. 'Remember the bloke who saw your undies when I was wiping your car window? That was Calum. Shit, he's probably seen mine as well now.' She rubbed her face, pushed her hair back, looked at her sister, and continued. 'His grandmother, Connie McGregor, and Shirley came by earlier with coffee and scones. I asked them about Veronica. They didn't say much; hopefully they'll introduce us.'

'I can't wait to meet her. But when?' Sofie asked.

'She'll probably be at the funeral or the wake,' Jennifer answered. 'Sofe, do you want to say a few words?'

Sofie nearly choked on her coffee. She coughed until her face turned bright red. 'No, thank you,' she wheezed. 'It's all yours. I'll be a blubbering mess.'

'I will.' Claudia's voice was soft, but certain.

Sofie's chin dropped as she stared at her daughter.

'Why are you giving me that bug-eyed look?' Claudia asked her.

'You hardly knew him,' Sofie said.

'Yes, I did. Every time he came down to visit, he spent time with me. We talked a lot while you were busy arguing with Dad. So can I?'

'Sure you can. Want to write something down?' Jennifer asked.

'No, that's okay. I've already written something.'

'Good on you,' Jennifer said. She reached across the table to hug her niece. She had considered writing down a few words herself, but decided against it, wanting her eulogy to sound natural and not as if she were reading from a script. 'Got any ideas about the flowers?'

'He loved purple irises,' Sofie whispered, eyes welling.

'Yes, he did.' Jennifer patted her sister's hand. 'I'll go get some. Before I forget, don't use any electricity. Don't plug anything into the power points unless you want to risk getting fried or meeting the fire brigade. With all that noise, you can expect the rest of the town will arrive with cameras.'

'I might give that a try,' Sofie giggled.

Jennifer left them eating scones and wandered through the house. She tried to get a sense of the connection her uncle had had as the local pharmacist in this small town. Downstairs, in the large, empty shop, a few odds and ends remained on dusty shelves. Jennifer touched them with her fingertips: a packet of bobby pins, packets of grey hairnets, a small box of deteriorated rubber teats, and a tube of Golden Eye ointment. Was this all that was left of a person's working life? She shook her head. Surely not. Memories were a wonderful thing. But right now, she needed to do something positive for Uncle Bob. She called up the stairs. 'Sofie, I'm going out for the flowers now.'

Sofie peered over the banister. 'Take your sunnies and a hat, or you'll fry out there.'

'If a man called Calum turns up, I'll be back in a few minutes.'

'Sure, I'll entertain him,' Sofie winked.

'Go have another scone.' Jennifer, waving a dismissive hand, headed for the front door. She grabbed the old brass bolt, metal scraping on metal as it slid across, and pulled the heavy door open. The heat outside was like a baker's oven as she stepped out backwards and pulled the door shut behind her.

To her surprise, she collided with a solid mass of muscle.

* * *

Calum had no time to step aside before Jennifer's back bumped into his chest. 'Whoa. Sorry, Jen.' Instinctively, Calum's arms wrapped around her waist. His hands found warm, bare skin. A rush of heat surged through him. Man, she was silky soft. She could collide, fall, stumble into him anytime she wanted.

Jennifer gasped, and he felt her stomach tighten. She wriggled her hips. He wasn't sure why she did that, but fuck that was nice too.

He took a deep breath. 'You good…steady?' he asked, not letting go of her soft curves. She looked at him over her shoulder, and his hazel eyes fixed on her brilliant green ones.

'Erm…yes thank you.' Her husky voice, with the lilt of her London accent, hit him straight in the guts and made him smile.

She squirmed just a little. He really should get his hands off her. Reluctantly, he let go.

'You okay?' he asked, intending to look at her feet, but his eyes stopped at her snug-fitting pants curving over her peachy bum and the bare, creamy sway of her back.

Jennifer self-consciously straightened her top, which wouldn't meet the pants. 'Sorry, my fault.'

Calum's heart hammered so hard he felt his body vibrate. She looked amazing in cut-off pants that sat just below her navel. Damn fine navel. He wanted to take his time and just gaze, but steadfastly brought his eyes up and fixed them on her pale face and those incredible eyes squinting against the bright sunlight. Her crown of dark curls ruffled in the hot, dry breeze.

Vulnerable or self-confident? He decided both applied to Jennifer. Calum suddenly realised he was still holding her arm and stroking her skin with his thumb. He thought he'd better stop before she slapped him.

Jennifer tugged at her hair.

Self-conscious around him? Yeah, just a little. He felt a deeper smile coming on.

'No, my fault.' His voice broke. Christ, he sounded like a sick bull. 'I should've been more careful.'

'Oh no, it was me. I wasn't watching. Did I tread on your toes?' she asked, looking down at his feet.

His eyes followed her gaze. He knew she was waiting for his answer, but the words wouldn't come right now. He was enjoying the sight of her slender legs, right down to her dainty toes lacquered in some pearly colour. Her perfect feet looked tantalising in a pair of strappy sandals. His gaze drifted up her legs to her midriff. *I want to kiss her navel. Christ, forget her navel—I want to kiss her mouth—for a very long time.*

'No,' he finally managed a word. 'Steel-capped boots,' he said, tapping a foot on the pavement. 'Work safety.' He caught her eyes with his and smiled. 'How're you this morning? Hope we didn't keep you up last night?'

'Nothing could've kept me up last night, I apologise for being such a boring hostess.'

'Nobody felt bored.' Least of all him. 'Blind Freddy could see you were out of it.' He'd had the urge to kiss her last night as he tucked her up on the couch. Looking at her now, he wished he had. With an effort, he hauled his brain away from her mouth and breathed in her scent, which he hadn't a hope in hell of describing. It was intoxicating; he knew that much.

She raised her eyes to his and said, 'Thank you, and thanks for tucking me in. Your jacket kept me warm last night. Um…come up, and I'll return it.'

Jacket? She can have my jacket — she can have me and my jacket.

'You can hang on to it if you like?'

'No, I'll get it.' Jennifer opened the door and stepped inside. 'Every time I come in from outside, I'm amazed at how cool these old, solid brick buildings are. Come on through and meet my sister and niece.'

'Thanks, but I'm covered in crap, been working in the roof cavity at the pub. How are the power points?'

'Well…' She turned to face him; she looked guilty as sin…and adorable. 'Without thinking, I used one in the bathroom, and it blew up. I think it killed my hairdryer.'

'I'll disconnect all the power points, you don't want the fire brigade running over here every time you plug something in. Though I'm sure the boys wouldn't mind a bit, you're quite a hit with them.' Calum tried to keep the humour out of his voice but it wasn't easy. 'The paper should be an interesting read on Tuesday.' His eyes focused on her bottom, admiring the rhythmic way her cheeks moved in the tight hipster pants as she made her way up the stairs. 'The boys at the fire station want to know if you've got lingerie to match those fluffy pink things you had on your feet.' *Fuck, I want to know.*

Hand on the rail, Jennifer stopped, one foot poised on the next tread, she looked down over her shoulder. Her unconscious pose reminded him of a Hollywood glamour girl, but one that was trying not to smile.

'I'm sure you got an eyeful.' He didn't respond, but his mouth twitched as he tried to hold back a grin, easily giving him away. 'Yeah,' she nodded, with a look that said she'd caught him out. 'And you can tell Bruce and your firemen friends the perky, pink slip-ons aren't mine, nor are they my style.'

Was that a purr in her voice, or simply something he wanted to hear?

'Pity,' Calum murmured quietly.

'What was that?' In a flash, Jennifer's sultry Hollywood pin-up pose evaporated.

It didn't matter. He loved what she did. 'Pity about the shoes, they looked good.'

She stopped on the landing. 'Did you leave when I asked you to?'

'Of course,' but he couldn't help himself and pressed his lips together to hold back a grin.

She rolled her eyes and muttered, 'I thought as much.'

Calum heard voices coming from the kitchen and saw a blonde head pop around the doorway.

'Hi!' Her eyes sparkled with amusement and interest as the rest of her came into view. A teenager, with black hair and dressed in black, closely followed her. A Goth? She had the same cherub features as the blonde. Calum assumed she was her daughter.

'Calum,' Jennifer said, 'I'd like you to meet my sister Sofie and my niece Claudia.'

'Hi, ladies!' His deep voice rumbled down the long hallway. The three women looked just as surprised as he was. He added in a softer tone, 'Welcome to beautiful Tumble Creek.'

Silence.

He hadn't said anything wrong, had he?

Sofie kept staring at him, while an embarrassed-looking Claudia peered at her mother.

Calum looked from one to the other, wondering if he had something crawling on his shoulder or the top of his head, courtesy of the pub's roof cavity. Nah, they'd be squealing, flapping their hands, and pointing. He shrugged it off and carried on as if nothing was wrong. 'Sorry your visit isn't under more pleasant circumstances. My condolences for your loss. Bob was a good bloke.'

Claudia nudged her mother to speak.

'Um… yes, well, if Uncle Bob hadn't passed away,' she stammered, 'it wouldn't have entered our heads to come this far out of the city unless we were on holidays. But then, this town is hardly a place for a holiday and…' He could see she realised she was babbling. Her cheeks went red and the rest of her face soon followed.

He turned to face Jennifer, who gave her sister an intense look.

Shame, he thought. Sofie was digging such a nice hole for herself. These women fascinated him. The sister must've forgotten what she was about to say next because her mouth parted, but nothing came out. Calum felt that grin creeping up and held it back as best he could.

'I'll just pour some more caffeine into Mum,' Claudia said, tugging at her mother's arm.

'It doesn't run in the family,' Jennifer asserted. She raised a what-the-hell eyebrow before turning to walk down the hall.

Head tilted, Calum enjoyed the sway of Jennifer's hips and jiggle of her bum cheeks until they disappeared into a room. He didn't follow but waited outside the door, leaning against the wall, arms folded, ankles crossed.

Jennifer came back with his jacket dangling from her index finger. She handed it to him and said, 'Don't move.'

Ah, there *was* something crawling on him. Casually, he ran his fingers through his hair. Couldn't be much, she wasn't squealing.

Jennifer walked straight past him into the kitchen, and Calum felt like a goofy teenager hoping he was the centre of her attention, only to find he wasn't. Moments later, she came out of the kitchen clutching his grandmother's basket.

'You're welcome to keep the jacket a while longer,' he told her, taking the basket.

'Thank you, I'll be fine. And thanks again for tucking me in last night,' she said, head tilted to the side, waiting. She arched an eyebrow, clearly expecting a reply.

But Calum was lost in a hot little fantasy that involved the curves of her neck. Idiot, say something. 'Hope you enjoyed breakfast?' he cringed inside. That was pathetic, but he could hardly say what he was thinking—and he was thinking a lot.

'I did, and the coffee was divine. I really must remember to thank your grandmother again. She's doing so much for—'

Emotions were overwhelming Jennifer. Calum raised his hand to stop her, yet it was hard not to move closer and touch her soft, trembling mouth with his fingers; instead, he reached out and gently rested his hand on her shoulder. 'It's okay, both Gran and Shirley were very close friends of Bob's. She'll do anything to help.'

'Thank you, yes. Uncle Bob always spoke lovingly of them both.' She glanced at his hand still resting on her shoulder, then asked, 'By the way, where can I get some flowers?'

'Give me a minute and I'll take you to meet Trudy, the florist. But first I'll disconnect the power points, then it won't matter if you plug something in by mistake.' Calum strode off, happy that he was going to be in her company a little longer.

When he re-entered the room, he paused to watch as muted morning sunlight filtered through the newspaper-covered shop window, illuminating Jennifer's skin, so beautiful she seemed to glow. She had no idea how stunning and radiant she was amidst dusty shelves and an old display case in an empty space.

She must have sensed he was there; she turned to face him. 'You don't have to lead the way, just point me in the right direction.'

Oh no, now that he had the chance, he wasn't leaving her alone. He intended to stay by her side for as long as possible. 'It's okay, I'm headed for the bank and the flower shop is on the way.' Not quite the truth, but he'd walk the extra mile to enjoy her company a little longer.

* * *

As they strolled along the footpath, Jennifer felt Calum's solid presence beside her. It gave her an indefinable feeling, and it frustrated her that she couldn't quite put a label on it. It felt nice, only better. Like an itch—no, more a tickle—in her stomach that reached up through her chest and sat at the hollow of her throat. Similar to butterflies, but more like bats. She took a deep breath and sighed.

Calum glanced at her. 'What was that for?'

'I don't really know.' *Ain't that the truth?* 'It's such a beautiful day.'

'It'll be a scorcher. Round lunchtime you'll be able to fry eggs on the road.'

'*Yum.*' Jennifer pulled a face.

She felt relieved that Australian shop awnings stretched across the footpath, providing pedestrians with welcome shade from the blazing sun. Jennifer caught the scent of steamy hot tar from the previous night's rain. All that remained from that summer storm were a few puddles. The raindrop prisms on trees and flowers from earlier that morning had long since evaporated.

'I s'pose you wouldn't find anything like Tumble Creek in Europe?' Calum asked.

'Not even close. But what Europe lacks in space, it makes up for with history and charm.'

'Charm, hey?' Calum nodded.

'Yeah, charm.' She emphasised her words with a look. 'For instance, I live in a beautiful eighteenth-century building. Fortunately, the electrics and plumbing work.'

'Yeah, Bob, let that go. Something will need to be done about it soon.'

'How could he live like that?'

'Don't know. We tried,' Calum shrugged. 'Here we are.' Calum stopped in front of a purple shop with painted vines and flowers over the picture window. 'Trudy will look after you.' He paused, eyes penetrating hers with…she wasn't sure, except for one thing—it was deep and it was hot. 'Got to go.' A muscle above his jaw twitched. 'See you later, Jen.'

He took her hand in both of his and leaned in towards her. For just a moment, his gentle expression shifted to a frown, then gone in a flash. Had she blinked, she would've missed it.

'Later,' he said, smiling warmly, and jogged down the street towards what she assumed was the bank.

Jennifer's knees felt weird. What on earth was going on? Then she realised, as she walked into the flower shop, muttering to herself, 'Aha, of course. It's jetlag, that's it.'

'Isn't he a doll,' the ponytailed, doe-eyed young woman behind the counter said with a smile. 'He's not married, you know. Every single woman within two hundred miles has tried to get him to the altar.'

Something about this chat unsettled Jennifer enough to ask, 'He's dated plenty of times, though?'

'He did for years and then…' Trudy brushed leaves and twigs off the counter into a small bin.

'And then what?'

'Never mind. What can I get for you?'

Okay, not a gossiper. That's good, Jennifer thought. 'We're in town for Bob Feldman's funeral; he's our uncle.'

'My condolences, Bob was a top bloke, the best.'

'Yes, he was a gentle man, so caring.' Feeling emotional, Jennifer turned away to study Trudy's arrangements. 'Do you have any purple irises? They were his favourite.'

'I ordered some in for Mrs McGregor and Mrs Jarvis, and they took all I had. I'm sorry,' Trudy shrugged. 'But he loved roses, too. In fact, he used to put yellow roses and blue irises together, a perfect combination.'

'Okay, could I please have four long-stemmed, yellow roses, thanks.'

Trudy selected four beautiful roses, the best from a large bunch. 'A lovely choice. They have a pink tinge along the edge of the petals. Is that okay? And would you like them together or individually wrapped?'

Jennifer leaned over the counter to have a look. 'They're perfect, wrapped individually, please, that would be lovely.'

A lump in her throat, Jennifer blinked away her tears as Trudy wrapped the roses in cellophane and purple tissue paper. Jennifer cradled them back to Uncle Bob's. Their delicate scent and lovely petals nearly brought her to tears. This was it, the reality of her Uncle Bob's death, flowers for his coffin.

Chapter 7

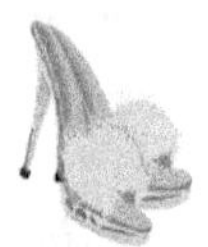

After the sweltering heat outside, it was a pleasure to be back inside her uncle's home and feel the cool air on her skin. Never mind the goosebumps, Jennifer thought. She hurried upstairs into the kitchen and put the roses in the sink with a little water.

Sofie had left a note on the kitchen table. *'Didn't know how long you'd be, wink-wink. Gone for a walk and then back to the motel to get ready. See you later. Hugs, Sofie.'*

There is no wink-wink. 'Well, maybe just a little,' Jennifer muttered. She went into Bob's den, hoping to find something that would tell her more about her uncle and why he had sent them that mysterious message about meaning no harm. She made herself comfortable in his studded leather chair and opened drawers, looking for papers or a personal journal. She found handwritten notes in his daily schedule. Her uncle had helped raise funds for the high school hockey team, for hospital equipment, and other local charities. He had done so much for the community, much more than he'd ever let on. Jennifer felt a surge of pride, but with that came a sense of pressure to do the right thing by him.

Engrossed in the papers around her, she didn't realise how much time had slipped by. She glanced at her watch: it was three in the afternoon. 'Shit!' She had less than half an hour to get ready for the funeral. She ran across the hall into the pink bedroom, peeled off her clothes, aimed a few squirts of deodorant at her armpits, and wriggled into her slightly wrinkled black dress. She slapped on a little makeup and grabbed her matching black shoes, then hurried down the hall to the kitchen. Yanking the dripping roses out of the sink, she rewrapped them. Barefoot, she headed downstairs, slipping her shoes on when she reached the bottom.

As she ran through the shop, a teasing little voice in her head said, someone should fill this space with drapes and furniture. Someone like you. Bugger off! She yanked the front door open and waited on the footpath for her sister and niece. The dry afternoon heat made it almost impossible to breathe. She pulled out her phone to ring Sofie and say she'd be waiting inside when she noticed the text message. We tried to do the right thing and attend this funeral, but we've been let down again by Bob and you, Jennifer. I'm so disappointed in you. Mother.

Anger built up inside her until she felt like screaming. She looked up from her phone and saw her sister's battered green station wagon barrelling down Grey Street, and the sting of her mother's crap message vanished. Almost.

Sofie brought the car to a stop at the kerb in front of the shop, its doors opened, and her sister and niece piled out. 'But you always wear black,' Sofie was saying to Claudia, making hand gestures an Italian would envy. She was wearing her simple black dress cinched in at the waist with a wide belt. 'Now all of a sudden you want to wear a kaleidoscope of colours to Uncle Bob's funeral?' Jennifer met her sister's eyes with a meaningful gaze of her own. 'What, Jen? You don't think I'm right?'

'Think about it, Sofie,' Jennifer said, slipping an arm around her sister's shoulder. 'What does it really matter?'

'Our argument was on a roll.' Sofie shrugged and turned to face her daughter. 'I just wish you'd wear colour at home occasionally.'

'Well, she's wearing it today,' Jennifer smiled at her niece.

Claudia was wearing a red and green tartan mini skirt, a red figure-hugging T-shirt, red and green striped socks long enough to cover her knees, and ankle boots. She had her hair tied up in a messy ponytail with red spiky bits sticking out from the top.

'Claudia's outfit is quite appropriate considering we're in Celtic country. But maybe your mum's right, a little colour now and then?' Claudia's eyes narrowed in on Jennifer. 'Then again, maybe not. Come on, let's go, I'm melting. And I'd like to get to the chapel before everyone else.'

*   *   *

It was twenty to four when they walked into St Mary's. The scent of incense and burning candles took Jennifer back to her childhood, when she and Sofie, under duress, had to attend Sunday Mass without fail. Nonetheless, today she felt comforted as she gazed at the sunlight streaming through tall stained-glass windows. A kaleidoscope of vibrant colours fell on arrangements of purple irises and the dazzling white lace-trimmed altar cloth. Her uncle would have loved the atmosphere surrounding them.

Although they stepped lightly, their footfalls echoed on the rich, timber floors. Talking in whispers, Jennifer asked, 'You both okay?' She got their nod and led Sofie and Claudia to the front pew.

'Why are we here so early?' Sofie asked, nervously fidgeting with the strap of her handbag.

'I'm hoping Father Thomas will be here. I'd like to have a quick word with him.'

A flurry of white vestments caught Jennifer's eye, and she turned to see a priest stride in through a side door. He carried a vase of penny gum sprigs and looked to be in his late sixties, a stout man with a bald pate gleaming under rays of amber light. Mesmerised, Jennifer's thoughts strayed. *He's got a halo.* He placed the vase in front of the organ, then walked towards them.

'Hello there.' His round, freckled face lit up with a warm smile. 'You're Jennifer, Sofie, and Claudia,' he said. 'It's lovely to finally meet you all. In case you're wondering, it's not a divine connection; Bob was always showing me photos of you.'

Jennifer extended her hand: Father Thomas led a soft life; tending his flock hadn't caused any calluses. For her uncle to have befriended him said a lot about the priest.

'My condolences. I know Bob loved each of you dearly and felt loved in return. I'm sure you'll miss him; I certainly will.' He smiled again, his bright blue eyes disappearing into folds and wrinkles. 'I understand Connie informed you about your parents as well?'

'Yes,' Jennifer replied.

'I must say your parents are quite persistent.'

'They've called you?' Sofie asked.

'No, they came by yesterday, insisting they would attend the funeral, despite Bob's request that they not come anywhere near him—dead or alive.'

There was a long, awkward pause as Father Thomas looked at each of them in turn. His gaze lingered on Jennifer; being the tallest, she guessed he'd decided she was their spokesperson.

'And?' Claudia asked impatiently.

'As I told your parents, I will stand by Bob's request to the letter. He had me swear on the Bible and, in his words, promise not to deviate or be bullied by them. So, are any of you planning to give a eulogy? I hope so; otherwise, we'll all have to put up with Sean, who calls out raffles and bingo at the local bowls club. And none of us have planned for a picnic dinner, if you get my drift.'

'I am,' Jennifer said. 'And so is Claudia.'

'That would make Bob very proud. You look worried—is there something else?'

'Well yes, but I don't know whether I should talk to you or his doctor?'

'You can start with me if you want.'

'Okay, what was wrong with Uncle Bob? And how long had he been sick? The police officer, Brock, told me the shop's been empty for about eight months.'

Father Thomas tucked his hands into his sleeves and raised his eyes to the chapel ceiling. Perhaps he was hoping for divine guidance as he paused in thought. His eyes shifted back to her, and he said, 'That would be about right.'

'What!' Jennifer's voice echoed through the chapel. Guilt flashed through her. Mother would not have approved of her raising her voice in church—unless she was singing.

'It's all right,' Father Thomas chuckled. 'St Mary's is used to a bit of noise.'

'But he was with me in Paris last July, why didn't he tell me he was sick? We could've been here for him. He needn't have been alone.'

'Oh, he was never alone.' Father Thomas shook his head. Was that a wicked grin? He looked like a cheeky cherub. 'And, I might add, quite active until the very end.'

Jennifer blinked in confusion. 'But the pharmacy,' she asked. 'And how could he live in a house that tried to electrocute me *twice?*'

'Bob knew the wiring needed replacing, but...' Father Thomas shrugged. 'When he found out his time was limited, he didn't want the fuss or mess. The townspeople insisted on helping. Bob complained, of course, but we wouldn't take no for an answer. The other chemist in town bought his stock, and Bob was finally able to relax. We played golf every Thursday until the week before he died.'

'Still, he should've told us. The trip to Paris…he was…' Jennifer's mouth trembled; she pressed her lips together and, with a deep breath, pulled herself back in control. 'He came to say goodbye.'

'Don't be angry with him. He loved you too much to have you drop everything to nurse him.'

'*That* should have been our choice,' Jennifer insisted, hot tears welling, threatening to tumble down her cheeks. 'Stubborn old fool,' she muttered, pulling a wad of tissues out of her bag, she dabbed her eyes and blew her nose.

'Ah, he was that. Forgive him for shielding you from the pain of seeing his decline.'

'It's going to be hard,' Jennifer told him. 'I'll be angry for a bit first.'

'You're entitled, I'd be miffed too.' Father Thomas pressed his lips together and nodded.

Claudia said, 'I think he lived and died the way he wanted to. You can't be upset about that, Aunt Jen.'

Jeenifer kissed Claudia's cheek. Sofie looked so proud; she sniffled and kissed her too.

'Good, good, we're all settled then,' Father Thomas said, then added, 'Please don't worry about the service, it'll be quite simple, but a little unusual.'

A whisper of voices and a shuffling of feet signalled that it was time.

'That's my cue,' Father Thomas said softly with a comforting smile.

*   *   *

Gerek paced in the country air terminal twenty minutes from Tumble Creek. He glanced at his watch; if the plane didn't arrive soon, they would miss the funeral. He scanned the runway and distant hills. A flash of reflected sunlight signalled that a plane was coming. A young woman's voice announced over the speakers that the flight from Sydney was about to land. He pulled out a handkerchief and wiped sweat from his brow, thanking God the building had air-conditioning.

Gerek watched as eight passengers stepped out of the small plane. Antonin, sharply dressed in a dark suit, a crisp shirt, and a stylish blue silk tie, was the last to descend the narrow steps. Gerek greeted his friend with a firm handshake and a warm hug.

'Come-come, or funeral will be over,' Gerek said as he escorted Antonin to his car. 'I park in shade, but inside will still be hot.' He stopped at his Ute and rammed the key into the lock.

'What is this?' Antonin asked.

'My tin-can car. You wait until you are inside my-you-beaut-ute.'

Antonin looked around. 'Where is the car hire place? We will get real car.'

'Don't be wimp. There is no car hire here at little airport,' Gerek grumbled.

Antonin's lip twitched as he curled his long frame into the passenger seat. 'Quick, drive so we get air in here, I am suffocating.'

'Look,' Gerek began, 'you want to slide in with crowd and not be like two blobs of cream on plate of zupa, then we go to

funeral in this lovely Australian oven, good thing it has wheels.'
He backed out of the parking spot and turned the Ute onto the road
that would take them into town.

Antonin groaned and mopped his brow.

Gerek tried to keep his irritation under control, but it wasn't
easy. 'I have baked in this car too many times—you only have to
do it once.' He sent his friend a mean side eye.

Antonin pressed his lips together and nodded gravely.

Gerek parked his Ute in the shade of a tall gum tree beside
the chapel. Antonin hurriedly swung open the car door and climbed
out into the afternoon heat.

'Here.' Gerek rounded the hood and shoved his silver
Brandy flask at his friend. 'Take drink, but leave bit for me.'

Antonin gulped down several mouthfuls and handed the
flask back. Gerek turned away from the crowd, emptied the flask,
and shoved it in his back pocket.

'We are nearly only ones in suit and tie.' Antonin fretted,
'We look like *jlupi* penguins.'

Gerek studied the people around them. 'Okay, we can fix.'
He shrugged off his jacket, its red lining flashing in the sun. The
high-pitched sound of silk sliding against silk followed as he
slipped his tie from under his shirt collar.

Antonin followed suit, tossing his jacket and tie into the
Ute. 'This is better.'

'Come, we should join, mix with the people going to the
doors,' Gerek urged.

Antonin still thought they looked out of place. The large
gathering of locals heading for the chapel mingled and appeared
reluctant to enter. Most mourners wore black, but in a casual,
practical style. A few women wore floral summer frocks, while
others had snatched a few moments away from work, waiting in
their overalls or uniforms.

'I cannot believe we are waiting here in hot sun,' Gerek
grumbled. 'But now you see what I have to do here.'

'Bob was very close friend,' Antonin whispered and pulled his stiff shirt collar away from the back of his neck. 'This is for me. I want to pay respect to a very good man.'

'I know this,' Gerek said, resignation in his voice. 'They close doors soon, stay with me,' he ordered. 'Look around, find Veronica. She must be here too.'

Gerek cast a quick glance at Antonin. Aside from his eyes, he kept his emotions tightly controlled and stood stiff and silent. Gerek wondered what this was really about. He tiptoed through the chapel doors with Antonin close behind him, into the cool, dim interior. With all seats taken, they moved away from the aisle to join others standing at the back. Gerek thought that wasn't a bad move. At least now they could remain unnoticed while looking over everyone's heads to see exactly what was happening.

*   *   *

But for the occasional cough or low murmur from mourners, the chapel remained silent. Then a lone Highland piper, dressed in a kilt and gold braided jacket, entered and stood at the open door. Though he was silhouetted against the sunlight, Jennifer recognised from his stance that it was Bruce, the fireman who had carried her down the ladder.

Tall and proud, he started playing Mull of Kintyre.

A rustling of clothes and a shuffling of feet rippled through the congregation as they stood. Back straight, Bruce slow-stepped down the aisle, followed by pallbearers shouldering the coffin that held their darling Uncle Bob. A lump in Jennifer's throat thickened, and quietly weeping, she manoeuvred Claudia between herself and Sofie. Arms interlocked, they watched the six pallbearers, all dressed in the same black trousers and white dress-shirts, carry the simple pine coffin towards the altar. A wreath of purple irises, delicate petals fluttering, lay on top. Upon reaching the bier, they carefully placed the coffin down and moved away to sit with friends and family.

Jennifer, Sofie, and Claudia placed their yellow roses on the coffin, along with an extra rose for Bret.

'Sorry, Uncle Bob,' Jennifer whispered. 'The little shit should be here.' Turning, she caught Calum's tender smile, then he gave her a slight nod in understanding.

'We are gathered here, friends and family…' Father Thomas's warm gaze shifted to Jennifer, her sister, and her niece, then settled back on his congregation, 'to pay tribute to a wonderful, generous man. But before I begin, I am under Bob's strict instructions to honour his wishes for, as Bob would say, his last hoorah. So, you may find his requests for the music a bit unusual.'

Jennifer smiled.

'Odd?' Sofie whispered.

Father Thomas, eyes brimming with tears, smiled, cleared his throat, and carried on.

Throughout the service, Jennifer kept glancing down the aisle to see if Bret had somehow made it, but no, he hadn't. Typical. She heard her name and looked up. Father Thomas smiled at her with his hand out, inviting her to come forward.

'Bob's niece Jennifer Dove would like to say a few words.'

Nerves fluttered in Jennifer's stomach. She had to do this and keep her emotions in check. Taking a deep breath, she stepped up to the microphone and looked out over the sea of expectant faces. Among them all, one stood out: Calum; his direct gaze and hint of a smile gave her the strength to carry on. What she had to say was from her heart and Sofie's. She got through, keeping her voice steady, with Calum's help. She concluded with, 'I can see how many friends Uncle Bob had—has, and how well you all looked after him. On behalf of my sister, my niece, and myself, thank you.'

Holding hands, Jennifer and Sofie watched as Claudia stepped up to the microphone. She took a moment to survey the crowd. Then slowly, and with a surprising amount of dignity, she began her eulogy.

'My great-uncle Bob taught me that it was okay to be different. He told me, *'Nothing matters more than caring for others, especially those who are different and unaccepted by family and community.'* I know great-uncle Bob was loved and accepted, and I can't thank you all enough for making the years he spent here truly happy ones.'

Looking at the coffin, Claudia finished off loud and clear: 'I love you, Uncle Bob, you're my special.'

A few tissues and hankies fluttered out of pockets and handbags.

But no, Claudia wasn't done yet.'

'He always made me feel special. A few months ago, he said —' Claudia paused, fighting for control. 'He said, *'You'd better not be wearing black at my funeral.'* And then he laughed.'

Claudia waited for the chuckles to fade before she continued.

'That's why I love him. He was always honest, kind, and the dearest man I have ever met. What he gave us was unconditional love.' She stepped down from the lectern and sat between Sofie and Jennifer, who both put their arms around her as she bowed her head and quietly sobbed.

'Honey, that was so beautiful.' Sofie kissed Claudia's cheek. 'Friends and local people here understood your connection with Uncle Bob; all of them were smiling and dabbing their eyes.'

'Yes, so true, Sofe. You are amazing,' Jennifer told her. 'And your eulogy was beautiful; Uncle Bob would've been so proud.'

'Please stand, and we'll all try to sing Bob's requested songs,' Father Thomas said, urging his flock with a palms-up hand signal. 'You'll find the words in that folded piece of paper tucked into the hymn books.' A rustle of paper, a wave of muttering, and chuckles rippled through the congregation as he continued. 'Right, now everybody put your hearts into it so Bob can hear you up there in God's own garden.'

The music kicked off from a stereo. Jennifer unfolded the piece of paper, then burst out laughing and crying all at once.

Uncle Bob's request that they sing Stayin' Alive by the Bee Gees had everyone cracking up. It was nearly impossible to sing and laugh at the same time.

'That's it!' Father Thomas raised his voice over the crescendo, a broad smile spreading across his face. 'That's exactly what Bob had in mind. Now, sing it loud!' And the rafters vibrated with Wham's song, 'Wake Me Up Before You Go Go.'

Jennifer, Sofie, and Claudia stepped into the aisle to follow Bruce and the pallbearers as they slowly made their way outside. The glare was blinding, and Jennifer shielded her eyes to get a better look at the shiny gold Cadillac hearse with fins so big they looked like they could take off. All it needed was a runway.

'Hectic!' Claudia exclaimed, sniffing back her tears.

Sofie leaned into Jennifer and asked, 'What *is* that?'

Jennifer laughed softly, 'That's a Cadillac Deville, hearse.' Despite her grief, she reminded herself this was what their Uncle Bob wanted, what he hoped for in his usual joyful approach to life. She didn't hold back and, arms around Sofie and Claudia, giggled, saying, 'You're a cheeky boy, Uncle Bob, and we love you for it.'

The driver, dressed in 1940s livery, was a perfect match for the Caddie. He tipped his hat and slid behind the wheel, closing his door with a hushed click. Engine rumbling, the hearse, carrying Uncle Bob, moved forward with a flourish of purple flowers trembling on the roof. A second, classy black car followed closely, with speakers blaring music hidden among more flowers. The crunch of tyres signalled the slow-moving cortege as it left the churchyard and headed down Grey Street. Jennifer tore her eyes away from the many people lining the street to glance at Sofie; her lips trembled as she surveyed the scene. The town had come out to pay their respects as the cars headed to the cemetery and Uncle Bob's final resting place. But Jennifer thought her uncle had outdone himself with the last song. She stood between Sofie and Claudia as their uncle's coffin was lowered into the ground, while the Pointer Sisters belted out, "Jump (For My Love)."

* * *

Gerek put a tragically miserable Antonin into his Ute and watched the traffic flow away from the chapel. Without explaining why this man, Bob, was so important, Gerek drove him back to the airport and left him to catch the late afternoon flight to Canberra. He didn't mention that this was the perfect opportunity to get inside Bob's house and search. Perhaps if he found the information Antonin needed, he wouldn't be so depressed and anxious. Gerek reached the shop's backyard and waited in the shadows. He scanned the windows and kept an ear out for any sounds coming from within the house. This was not the time to be careless. When the coast seemed clear, he crouched and crept to the back door, put an ear to it, and listened.

Nothing.

His mind and body were alert, with tension tightening every muscle as sweat trickled down his face, arms, and back. It had to be cooler inside.

He slipped on a pair of latex gloves, pulled out his lock pick, and with a quick twist, he was inside, closing the door behind him but leaving it unlocked. He slapped a hand over his thumping heart, while the other rubbed his stomach: nervous indigestion was getting the better of him. Should send younger man. And no more pies with tamaat sauce, he thought. He peeked through a torn piece of newspaper, surveying the backyard to see if anyone had followed him.

No one, not a soul.

This was his moment; he could feel it, taste it. He rubbed his hands and allowed himself a restrained wheeze-laugh while waiting for his eyes to adjust to the dark interior. He scanned the empty shop and quickly checked all the cupboards and drawers: nothing. He headed along the hall to the stairs, taking them two at a time. This took fortitude, which he'd had in abundance in his prime. At sixty, things were a bit different; with a sudden adrenaline rush, Gerak realised he'd lost his edge, his nerve was gone. His initial confidence dissolved, like a hot-air balloon collapsing in on itself. Hand on his chest, he looked around.

Shiiit!

So many doors; he didn't know where to start. Where would he find the computer and USB sticks? They could be anywhere. Gerek started in the kitchen and worked his way from room to room, checking drawers as well as any other place this Bob person could have hidden them. Always careful not to leave any trace, he moved on to explore the walk-in linen cupboard, searching and feeling his way through sheets and towels. He went through an open door at the end of the hallway and gasped. Hands to his cheeks, he whispered, 'Wifey would love this room, all pink and sweet.' He ran his hands over the ruffled bedspread and admired the wallpaper. He desperately wanted to take a photo with his phone but worried someone might see and ask too many questions. He hunkered down and shoved his arms under the mattress, lifted the pillows, and looked under the quilt. Nothing. Gerek opened the enormous closet and found winter coats and suits neatly covered with plastic. He quickly checked all the pockets— still nothing.

There was one room left; he hurried across the hall and opened the last door. Gerek smiled: he'd found the den. Maybe this was it. But seeing the hundreds of books tightly packed along the walls, his smile faded. Any one of them could hide the all-important tiny USB sticks inside their covers.

His heart sank.

*   *   *

People had gathered for the wake at the Edwardian town hall. It was buzzing with the low murmur of many voices coming together for the wake, and Jennifer decided it was a good time to thank everyone. She put her cup of tea down on the nearest table, clasped Sofie's hand, and pulled her toward the stage while keeping an eye out for Claudia.

'Where are we going?' Sofie asked, eyes wide with panic.

Jennifer glanced at her reluctant sister and said, 'Up on stage to thank everyone!' There was a tug on Jennifer's hand, but she kept pulling Sofie along.

'I'm not good at that sort of thing,' Sofie complained.

'Are you sure you're a teacher?'

'Yeah, a damn good one too. But you're dragging me out of my comfort zone.'

Jennifer noticed Claudia wasn't about to be left alone among a crowd of strangers. She hurried to catch up. The three of them stepped onto the old boards that creaked under their weight.

Jennifer had hoped someone would notice them and tell everyone to shut up, but no. She cleared her throat. 'Ahem,' she tried, but her voice didn't penetrate the general hubbub.

Calum emerged from the crowd, placed both hands on the edge of the stage, and vaulted up to join them. Gorgeously athletic, popped into Jennifer's mind and lingered.

He whispered into her ear. 'You want their attention?' His voice and warm breath sent a rush of delicious goosebumps up and down her neck.

You've got mine, Jennifer thought. She reluctantly pulled away and managed to give him a nod.

'Listen up!' Calum bellowed. A hush swept over the crowd as a sea of faces turned to look at them. 'These lovely ladies would like your attention.'

'Thank you, Calum,' Jennifer smiled. 'On behalf of my sister and niece, I would sincerely like to thank everyone, especially Connie McGregor, Shirley Jarvis, and Father Thomas, for organising this wake and—'

'Oi, that'll do, luv,' a farmer called out. 'Ted here's about t'cry and you really don't want to see that.' Ted thumped the man speaking on the arm.

'There's no need for thanks when it comes to Bob,' someone else called out, shaking his head. 'Cal, get 'em off there.'

Calum put his hands up. 'Hey, I know. But it's only fair they have the opportunity.'

Though Calum had her hand, she grabbed hold of the mic with the other and quickly said: 'Thank you all so very much!'

He wrapped his arm around her waist and carried her across the stage with a sideways nod to Sofie and Claudia to follow. Jennifer demanded he put her down, which didn't work, and set her down at the top of the stairs. He vaulted off the stage to help them safely reach the floor.

'I tried,' Jennifer told Sofie and Claudia.

Sofie gave a little shrug. 'Don't worry about it, Jen. They know we appreciate it, and that's what matters. I'm hungry.' She wandered off to get some food.

'I hate being the centre of attention,' Claudia muttered and trailed after her mother.

Calum said, 'Hope you're not offended by us locals? We're not real big on showing our emotions. It's been a tough day for you—for the three of you.' The tenderness in his gaze unsettled her.

'Uh huh.' Jennifer reached for a cup of tea. She took a slow sip and hid behind her cup until the flush in her cheeks eased. Her attraction to Calum was awkward, and she wished he'd stop giving her that quirky half-smile and stop looking all protective and hunky. The look in his eyes threatened to pull her in. Forget it, she told herself firmly, London was waiting with exciting opportunities.

'You could probably do with something to eat. Want a sandwich or something else?' Calum asked.

Jennifer's phone rang. *Oh bugger.* 'Excuse me.' She recognised the number. 'Sorry, it's my brother, I won't be a minute.' She moved to a quiet corner of the hall.

'Bret!' she hissed.

'At fucking last,' a man snarled. 'Your dumb-arsed brother has been giving us the runaround with all sorts of funny numbers— thought for a minute we'd have to rough him up some more, but nah, the little twerp coughed up his phone.' Ugly, raucous laughter came through the earpiece.

'What?' Jennifer's shock quickly turned to disbelief. Someone was pulling a cruel and stupid prank. 'This is not fun—'

'It's not meant to be,' the man yelled, sounding pissed off.

'Don't you shout at me!' Jennifer yelled back. 'Who the bloody hell are you and what the bloody hell are you talking about—where's Bret?'

'Listen, babe—'

'I am not your babe!' she screeched, glancing over her shoulder to see if anyone overheard. Sofie shot her a wide-eyed look while someone animatedly chatted at her. Wait a minute, a bloke was talking to Calum while trying to show him something on his phone. But Calum turned away, and with a furrowed brow, a face like thunder, he looked straight at her. Shit!

'Don't get the smarts with me—right! Your brother owes us ten grand. He says he doesn't have it. If someone doesn't cough up soon, we're gonna break both his legs and then his neck. Got that, babe?! You'd better have the cash damn quick! Don't even think about telling anyone else, because if we get so much as a whiff that youse involved the cops, youse can kiss your brother's arse goodbye—you got that?'

'How dare you threaten me or my brother,' Jennifer hissed. 'You—you just put him on,' she snapped.

'We'll call back in a coupla hours with instructions. Ye'brother's gonna say a few words and that's it.'

'Sorry, Jen, I need five grand real quick,' Bret said in a rush.

'Bret! Bret!' she yelled. Shocked, frightened and outraged, Jennifer stared at her silent phone.

*   *   *

Gerek muttered a few positive Polish wishes, sighed, and stepped into the study. His eyes landed on the silver laptop, and he smiled. He was a desperate man, but experience told him this would be too easy. Still, he squeezed behind the desk, placed his hands on the chair's armrests, and eased himself down, eyeing the laptop as if it were an unexploded bomb. He flexed his fingers and hacked in within seconds. Gerek began a meticulous search, checking his watch now and then and listening for any sounds of the women returning. He went through every file. Nothing. He barely knew what he was looking for, possibly some photos.

Half an hour later, Gerek still hadn't found anything of interest. But just in case, he wiped all of Bob's personal files clean.

If anyone opened the computer, it would look as if no one had ever used it.

The hair on the back of his neck pricked. 'Shiiit.' Maybe this laptop was a decoy with a homing device, and someone wanted him to take it. Sweat broke out on his forehead. 'Fool,' he whispered. What if they had bugged it? Sweat pooled in his latex gloves. As soon as he touched it, they'd have known. Feeling paranoid, he slowly pulled his hands back and cast his eyes around the room.

With the utmost care, Gerek shut the laptop and leaned back to peek through the curtains behind him. For a split second, he thought how silly Australians were to have these awnings stretching over the footpaths. But then, maybe Australians didn't need to worry about who was at the front door. Frustrated, he edged to the doorway and listened: the coast was clear. He started systematically searching every book for a USB stick or note, taking care to put each book back exactly as he'd found it.

Chapter 8

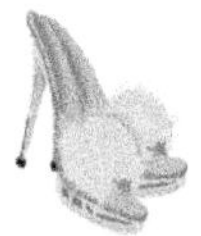

'Bret!' Jennifer knew, as soon as her brother's name echoed around the hall, that she was in trouble. In that same instant, the steady low murmur of voices and occasional laughter stopped. She became aware of the heavy silence behind her. 'Oh, bugger! She spun around to face the crowd of surprised faces, mouths open, delicate tuna sandwiches or scones poised, all staring at her. Their sudden focus on her was overwhelming. The hall was so quiet she could hear her heart pounding, and no wonder. She'd just been told her brother's life was in her hands.

With a forced smile, she sent a frantic glance at her sister. After Sofie and Claudia's initial stunned silence, they managed to get their feet moving. Their faces a mask of questions as they hurried to Jennifer's side. Quickly followed by a worried Calum and Sergeant Brock. Like a mini stampede on the old hardwood floor, four people thundered towards her.

Panic-stricken, Jennifer gave them a nervous grin. She zeroed in on Sofie, hoping her sister would read her wide-eyed, desperate look and, just this once, get the hint. Stop Calum and the cop! But no, Sofie kept coming, and so did the men. Jennifer forced her grin into a smile and didn't care that she probably looked freaked out. Her mouth was dry, her lips stuck to her teeth, and her brain was devoid of a single rational thought. A blank slate.

'What's happening with Bret?' Sofie asked breathlessly. 'Is he in trouble again?'

A brittle laugh escaped Jennifer. 'Trouble? Not at all.' She sounded hysterical. Where the hell did that come from? She was good at handling stress. Damn right she was. 'I um—I yelled at him because, well, because he didn't turn up in time for the funeral. You'd think that at least this once he'd make an effort, wouldn't you? And I think I can safely say he isn't going to make it at all. So I got a little angry.'

'Just angry, Aunt Jen?' Claudia asked. 'You know those animals caught in headlights?'

'Did I look like that? No, it's just that he hung up before I had a real chance to let him have it. You know what he's like.' Jennifer glanced toward Sofie and waited a couple of blinks to see if her sister understood that she was softening her story. No light bulb moment there. My sister is a featherbrain. There was no point dragging Sofie to the ladies' loo to tell her everything. She'd fall apart at the seams, and then what?

Jennifer felt a surge of hysterical sobs rising in her throat. She told herself to get a grip; Bret would be fine. But fear for her brother deepened, and her stomach twisted in a ball of knots. Bret would never truly be okay. Clenching her fists, she took control and changed the subject. 'Calum? Um…' Now what? There's a crisis, and she has a headache? Her thoughts on what else to say dried up, but her babbling continued. 'Anyway, where's your gran? I'd like to thank Connie personally. I know she helped a lot with organising everything. I'm hoping she can introduce us to Veronica. We've heard so much about her, but we've never met…' Too many people were focused on her rambling words, and she blurted out, 'I'm starving,' a bit too brightly. 'I think I'll try one of those delicious curried egg sandwiches.'

Calum craned his neck and scanned the crowd. 'Gran's over by the tea urn with Shirley.'

He clasped her hand, ready to take off, but stopped midstride and turned to study her, his face worried and questioning. Jennifer, lips trembling, nearly lost all control, but with steely determination, she fought it back. He said nothing, but gave her hand a squeeze, then let go and pulled her into his side, wrapping his arm around her shoulder with a tight, reassuring grip; he led her over to his grandmother.

Connie placed her cup down and smiled as they approached. Jennifer slipped out of Calum's hold to wrap her arms around the elderly woman. She was grateful for the wonderful turnout for her uncle, so saddened that he was gone, and then on top of everything, Bret's life might be in danger. Overwhelmed with emotion, she found it difficult to let go of Connie.

'Goodness, is everything alright, love?' Connie asked.

Jennifer forced herself to step back and wiped away her tears. She thanked Connie and Shirley for making the day easier for her, Sofie, and Claudia.

Connie's gaze flicked between Jennifer and Calum, and her tentative knowing smile grew. 'We loved Bob, and this day was our tribute to a truly wonderful, caring man.' She scanned Jennifer's face. 'Is everything alright? Is there anything I can do?'

'I hope so. Is Veronica here somewhere?' Jennifer asked.

'Oh dear.' Connie blushed *and* looked sad. 'What a pity you missed her. She was at St Mary's, but unfortunately, she couldn't make it here.'

'Shirl, got any, you know?' Calum asked, eyebrows raised.

'How…?' she started.

'Gran told me.' Calum reached for an empty teacup and held it out.

Jennifer had no idea what was going on, but was thankful Calum had put his arm around her again and tucked her into his side.

Shirley opened her enormous bag, pulled out a silver flask, unscrewed the lid, and poured a generous amount into the cup.

Calum handed Jennifer the cup. 'Drink,' his tone gentle but firm, as he studied her with concern.

Jennifer nodded, sniffed the contents, which made her eyes water, and took a gulp. Through coughing, she managed to squeak, 'Whiskey.'

Before Jennifer could ask any more questions, a couple of friends caught Connie and Shirley's attention.

'Take another sip,' Calum whispered in her ear, his warm breath and deep voice sending a delicious tingle through her. She brought the cup to her trembling mouth and drank.

Calum didn't leave her side all afternoon. How was she going to shake him off so she and Sofie could get home and answer the bloody call?

By early evening, Jennifer started to worry that people thought she had an obsessive-compulsive disorder about time and watches. She felt relieved when guests started leaving, and she could stand by the door next to Sofie, shaking hands and thanking everyone as they passed.

'Sergeant Stewart, thanks for coming.' Fearing he wanted to chat, Jennifer had to hold back the urge to hurry him along.

'Evening, ma'am. Some of us are heading to the pub. Would you like to come along?'

'Sounds like a lovely idea,' Sofie bubbled with enthusiasm, gazing up at Brock.

Jennifer blinked at Sofie. Could this be a way out, a way to avoid burdening Sofie more than necessary?

'That's a lovely idea, Brock,' Jennifer said, charm in top gear, 'Um…I tell you what, Sofe, you go ahead with Brock and everyone. I'll walk up to the pub as soon as I've had a chat with Connie and Shirley.' God, she hoped her sister wouldn't ask awkward questions.

'But didn't I see you talking to them earlier?'

Bugger! 'Um…yes, but then we, um, friends distracted them. It's all right, Sofe,' Jennifer urged, 'I'll be right behind you.'

'Okay.' Sofie agreed, but gave her a suspicious look. Then, eyes dancing between Jennifer and Calum, she gave them a knowing smile, wiggled her fingers, and said, 'See you in a few minutes…or not.'

Jennifer gave her sister a wide-eyed, teeth-gnashing smile, but she didn't take any notice.

'Hold on, Sofie,' Calum said. 'My sister Michelle's going to the movies; she wants to know if Claudia would like to come along.'

Michelle stood to one side, her clear blue-grey eyes smiling over a small nose dotted with freckles and full pink lips. Her glossy, auburn hair hung loosely to her shoulders. She wore a short, dark skirt and a T-shirt with the word Lost? written across her chest in sparkling silver.

'What a great idea. Thank you, Michelle. Claudia's leaning on our car; go ask her—I'm sure she'd enjoy the distraction.'

'Cool. See you.' With a cheery wave, Michelle jogged over to join Claudia.

Jennifer watched her sister and niece leave and sighed with relief that she could spare them this terrifying drama.

Once out of sight, Calum wrapped a hand around her shoulder and turned her to face him, his head bowed slightly, his concerned hazel eyes fixed on hers. 'There isn't anything more you want to say to Gran, is there?' She shook her head. 'You don't want to go to the pub, do you?' She shook her head again. 'I'm taking you home,' was his final, firm statement.

Calum took her hand, and a flutter sparked low in her belly. She couldn't remember the last time she'd felt a hand like his, big, strong, and calloused from hard work. He made her feel safe. He led her straight to his Range Rover, popped the doors, and helped her in. In a daze, she watched him move around the bonnet and slide in behind the wheel. He paused to glance over his shoulder at her. When she didn't move, he leaned over, grabbed her seatbelt, and God help her, he was right there, his face just inches from hers. She inhaled his masculine scent mixed with fresh pine and longed to bury her face in his neck and forget everything.

'You've got to buckle up,' he murmured and clicked the belt into place.

He shifted back into his seat, strapped himself in, turned on the ignition, and swung the car onto Grey Street. He'd rolled up his long-sleeved white shirt just below his elbows, and the relaxed, confident way he handled the wheel sent a shiver through Jennifer. Calum was in control, and she liked that…a lot.

Without a word, he stopped at the pub's bottle shop, jack-knifed out, strode in, and came back with bottles of wine wrapped in paper bags. He slid behind the wheel, turned around, and placed the bottles on the floor behind him, then headed for her uncle's place.

*   *   *

Calum wasn't going to beat around the bush; he wanted to know why a phone call from her brother would send Jennifer into a spin.

'You want to talk about why you were shaking like a leaf after your brother's phone call?'

He could almost feel her body stiffen. 'Bret's always been a worry, seems nothing's changed.'

'You can talk to me. I won't tell anyone, not Sofie, not anyone. I promise. But I think you need to tell someone what's going on.' He glanced her way. 'Come on, it can't be that bad.'

From the corner of his eye, he could see she was studying him.

'How can I believe you? People make promises and never keep them. I'm sorry, but what makes you so spe…any different?'

'You'll have to trust me. I won't tell a soul.' He shrugged and hoped that would cut it.

'He's been kidnapped by some-dude-who sounds as if he's escaped from maximum security,' she blurted out in a rush. 'I don't know, but I think they want either five or ten thousand.'

'Shit...that's heavy! Why didn't you say something to Brock? He was right there?'

'They said, involve the cops and we can kiss Bret's arse goodbye.'

Fuck! He hadn't expected that kind of problem.

'I'm really scared,' Jennifer muttered. 'My brother's constantly getting into strife, but never anything as bad as this. And I don't know whether to involve Sofie. She's been through so much already, and she's far worse at worrying than I am. I'll get the money together somehow.'

'What about your parents?'

'I'm the fool he called, not Mother and Father. Honestly, I don't know what their reaction would be. Not even sure they would believe me,' she shook her head. 'I'm not setting myself up for disappointment by ringing them to find out.'

'I see. I suppose that ties in with the fact Bob banned them from attending the funeral?'

'Pretty much,' she mumbled.

But Calum got the distinct impression that was as far as Jennifer was prepared to go. 'I gather the kidnappers will get in touch again, tell you when and how?'

'Yes, tonight sometime. Typical. I think they've been watching too many gangster movies, the idiots,' Jennifer muttered, twisting and untwisting her hands.

Calum reached across, took her hand, and rested it on his lap; holding it gently, he softly stroked it back and forth, trying to soothe her nerves. Neither spoke for a while, and the silence grew heavy inside the confines of his car.

He had to take his hand away from hers to indicate and manoeuvre the car through a roundabout. To his surprise and immense pleasure, she didn't pull her hand away from his thigh. A tiny smile tweaked the corners of his mouth.

I won't ditch our little pain-in-the-arse brother. But he's involved with who knows what sort of miscreants,' she clenched her fists. 'And I'm furious. I mean, shit, they know my phone number! What else do they know about me?'

'I'm sure your brother wouldn't have handed his phone over without a fight, Jen.'

'Huh! You don't know him. And now I don't know him anymore either,' she stopped and took a deep breath. 'No, you're right, it wouldn't be hard to wrestle him for his phone.' He saw her shudder. 'But why choose me?'

Although he wanted to pull her closer and hold her tight, he couldn't stop a soft chuckle deep in his chest. 'Keep venting, Jen, it's good for your health.' Calum patted her hand, still resting on his thigh.

'Yeah, but I'm terrified.' Calum felt her fingers flex and glanced across to see her staring out the windscreen, transfixed. Focused on inner demons, unaware she'd squeezed his thigh.

They drove in silence, the air inside the car thick with questions no one had answers to, and suddenly they were in the back lane in front of the garage doors.

'Thanks for dropping me off,' Jennifer said, unbuckling her seatbelt.

'I'm not leaving you out here, open the garage, please.' Okay, so she looked a bit stunned, but hopped out and punched in the code.

Calum pulled into the garage. He turned off the headlights, grabbed the wine, and slid out from behind the wheel as the roller door rumbled closed behind him.

He smiled when Jennifer took his outstretched hand and led him to the back door.

Calum noticed a faint glow drifting past the upstairs kitchen window. It was too dim to be from the light inside the room. Instincts told him something was wrong, a chill slithered down his spine, prickling his skin.

'Did you leave a light on?' Calum asked as they crossed the courtyard.

'I haven't been here since this morning, and after what you said, I didn't touch *anything* electrical.'

'Get behind me,' Calum ordered, not waiting; his hands went around her waist and lifted her out of the way. He took her keys, touched the door, and it swung open.

'Bloody hell,' she whispered over his shoulder. He felt her shudder of fear against his back. 'I locked this door after my sister left last night, and I haven't been out this way since.'

'Stay behind me,' Calum whispered as he peered through the doorway and crept in.

Hands on his hips, Jennifer followed. Nice, he thought, enjoying the feel of her touch.

They entered the sunroom and waited, listening. He couldn't hear anything; his gut didn't give him any vibes, so he placed the bottles of wine on the floor next to the stairs.

Jennifer shivered and rubbed her arms. Calum glanced over his shoulder, then reached out and pulled her into his side to keep her warm.

'You okay now?' she nodded. 'Stay here,' Calum ordered. Crouching low, he took off to search the shop and its rooms. A couple of metres along, he could feel a presence behind him. Fists clenched, he turned ready to swing a punch, stopping just in time. 'Jesus,' he hissed. Heart pounding, he relaxed his stance. 'I nearly smacked you in the jaw. Why aren't you back at the stairs?'

Eyes wide, she whispered, 'I'm not waiting anywhere alone until I know there's no one here.'

Still trembling, arms tight to her chest, she peered through the darkness at him.

'Come here,' he whispered, concerned. She moved closer to his side. Wrapping an arm around her shoulder, they moved forward and checked every corner.

Satisfied downstairs was clear, Calum locked the back door and said, 'I'll go upstairs, have a look around.'

'I'm not staying alone down here either,' Jennifer hissed.

He gave her a look, said nothing, and turned to climb the stairs.

Each tread creaked the moment Calum put his foot down. He started to take off his shoes and gestured for Jennifer to do the same. Her hands trembled so much he worried she might drop one, and she did. Calum grimaced as it hit the floor with a loud thud.

Jennifer's worried eyes met Calum's; on seeing her apologetic expression, he grinned.

'*Sorreee*,' Jennifer mouthed.

They reached the dark hallway. Calum pressed his back against the wall. He swung an arm out toward Jennifer, and his hand landed on her breast. She let out a faint gasp, and he quickly moved his hand to hold hers. He sidled into the living room, edging around the doorway. She leaned around his shoulder and peered in: no one was inside. They crept towards the bedrooms and found them empty. She hadn't let go of his hand, which he thought was sweet. They moved on to the kitchen, where a dim globe hanging from the centre of the high ceiling looked like it was about to cut out.

'Maybe you didn't switch the light off last night,' Calum whispered, and brought the back of her hand to his abs.

'You could be right,' Jennifer said, her voice barely a whisper as she stared up at the bulb. Calum smiled to himself when she subconsciously slid the back of her hand over his flat stomach, or so it seemed, and he hoped he was right.

'But that doesn't account for the unlocked back door,' he added.

Jennifer gasped. 'No,' she answered with a soft, worried sigh. 'Maybe there's a simple explanation, like it's an old lock and sometimes it happens?'

'Nuh, that's bullshit. Anyway, there's no one here,' Calum shrugged. 'May as well make ourselves comfortable and wait for the phone call.'

'Huh…you're waiting with me? I'm a big girl, you don't have to,' she told him, brow raised for emphasis.

'It's not a matter of having to. Christ, I just crept all over the shop and house with you trembling into my side, and now you're okay with being alone—well, I'm not.' His gaze softened, and he touched her cheek with the back of his hand. 'I want to stay.'

Oh my, that was sweet. Jennifer's belly did a little flutter.

* * *

Voices drifted down the hall, and Gerek quickly hid behind the study door. He managed to steady his breathing, but there was nothing he could do about his thumping heart. They were almost level with him now. He didn't want to scare either one of them, but he might not have a choice.

'I need to use the bathroom,' a woman said. 'Drank too much tea at the wake.'

Gerek nodded. *Go pee—go pee!*

Through a crack in the door, he watched and waited. And as he'd already seen, both entered the beautiful pink room opposite him. A few minutes later, the man came out and said, 'I'll wait in the kitchen.' And he disappeared.

Gerek's heavy shoulders sagged as he let out a breath, not realising he'd been holding it.

Though his gut tightened, he gathered enough nerve to creep out. He could hear the woman; it sounded like she was using her phone and leaving an angry message. Well, it was now or never. He slipped through the doorway and tiptoed down the hall. Despite his bulk, he moved quietly and with surprising grace. It worked—until he hit the stairs. He cursed as each tread creaked under his weight. He had no choice but to hurry; any loud noise would alert them to his presence. He scooted into the shop's kitchenette and quickly looked for the best place to hide. There was a door at the opposite end. It could be the pantry, he thought hopefully, and hurried through it.

*   *   *

Jennifer hurried down the hall just as Calum came back up the stairs with the bottles of wine.

'I heard something, was that you?' She threw herself at him. His strong arms instinctively went around her, and she felt safe.

'Not sure which noise you mean,' he chuckled. 'I heard something too and went down, but I couldn't find anything.' Calum pressed his hand to the small of Jennifer's back and guided her into the living room. 'Come on.' He placed the bottles of wine on the dining table, went to her uncle's crystal cabinet, and pulled out two glasses. 'We could use a drink after all the excitement. Red or white?'

'White, thanks.'

He waited for her to settle on the couch, then poured them both a glass of wine.

'Here's to Bret, the little shit,' Jennifer said, raising her glass.

'To Bret…because of him, I'm spending the night with Jennifer Dove.' Gazing at her, his smile and dark hazel eyes full of meaning.

Jennifer didn't know what to say or think about that, so left it well alone. She never felt nervous around people. Heck, being a chef at one of London's top restaurants meant you had to handle all sorts, especially hot-blooded, highly-strung head chefs. Yet, Calum made her fidget, and her belly melt every time he looked at her. As the only other person in the room, she couldn't mistake the messages he was sending. No one could.

She took a sip of fine wine, then swirled her glass a little before raising it to her nose for a sniff. 'Nice.' He didn't say much, just smiled as she babbled on about her uncle's unusual funeral. When Jennifer was on her second glass, she told Calum about Sofie and why she didn't want to burden her sister and niece with Bret's latest scheme, which must have gone terribly wrong.

'You see, Mother and Father never forgave Sofie for becoming an art teacher and marrying what's-his-name, Jett the surfer. Jett, the two-timing surfer-bum-father who broke his daughter's heart.'

Sure, she was tipsy; it never took more than two or three glasses of wine. Nevertheless, she could tell he was holding back. 'What're you thinking…hmm?'

'Surfer-Jett,' Calum said, fighting a grin.

Jennifer forgot her problems and burst out laughing.

'It's not that funny,' Calum chuckled.

She came down from her merriment and sighed. 'It was for me. He's an arse. I asked Sofie what happened to my cute, dimple-faced niece. You wouldn't know, Calum, but the change in Claudia is…dramatic. I was warned, but something went missing during our transcontinental chats. You know, the delays as satellites cross paths in the night?' Calum slowly shook his head. 'Anyway, Sofie said, how would you feel if your father screwed a barely-twenties-something girl? Then again, maybe our mother was a cold fish who…' she would be the one to say.' She stopped and shrugged.

Calum made no comment but seemed to concentrate on her every word while sipping his wine. Jennifer vaguely wondered if that was still his first glass. The thought popped out of her head as smartly as it had popped in. 'Here's a little snippet of what surfer Jett tried on with Claudia. Her father had asked her to babysit his twins, who were barely fourteen days old. My sweet niece told him to go fuck himself. Oh God, I just dropped the F-bomb.'

'Hey, do you think I care? Calum said. 'I've heard far worse. There's a Dutch friend of mine who translated a few of his country's colourful phrases. There's nothing that beats theirs.'

Jennifer was about to ask what they were, when her phone tinkled, making her jump. Adrenaline shot through her. She quickly fumbled for her phone, pulled it out of her bag, and studied the screen; it was Bret's number again.

She took a deep breath, got off the couch, turned her back on Calum, strode towards the windows, and with determination answered as calmly as she could. 'Hello.'

'Pay attention 'cos this is what we want youse to do. Youse better get the money or youse'll be…' The caller covered the mouthpiece. Jennifer pressed the phone to her ear, closed her eyes, and stuck a finger in the other ear; frowning, she concentrated hard on the background noise. Something was going on, something the caller was not happy about.

She could feel Calum's body heat close to her back—protective.

The thug came back. 'Um…we want the money now, or…'

'I can't get that kind of money from—'

'Don't tell me what youse can't do, bitch—ten grand—do it! King's Cross station tomorra, be there, five-thirty.'

'But—' The line went dead. Jennifer shook with rage, staring at the phone, hardly believing this was happening. It felt like she was watching her brother in a bad movie, only she was in it too. Muttering, she paced the room, checked received calls, and called them back. Tension filled the room, and it wasn't just hers. In her peripheral vision, she noticed Calum keeping a close eye on her every move. She redialled and held the phone to her ear, waiting. But there was nothing—no voicemail. Just silence. Fist clenched around her phone, she glared at it and growled.

Calum took her phone and, without looking, tossed it onto the couch. Then, he wrapped his arms around her and, voice steady, he gently asked, 'What did they say?'

She tilted her head back to see his face. 'Youse better get the money. His command of the English language is astounding. And he called me a bitch.' Jennifer frowned, thinking about what had just happened. She tried not to, but, body coiled tight, she began to shake. 'Oh, bloody hell.'

'Christ, Jen,' Calum murmured softly as he held her close. 'What else?'

'Something was going on in the background while I was on the phone; I don't know what, but it threw Scarface off his script, and he had to think on his feet. A tub of yoghurt has a better thought process.'

'A tub of yoghurt, hey?' Calum chuckled, which didn't last long; in a blink, he turned deadly serious, adding, 'You should talk to Brock; he's ex-SAS. He'll know what to do.'

'No—and you mustn't either.' She clenched her fists into his shirt and pulled him in close to her face. 'Promise me you won't?'

'Okay, I won't.' His hands slipped around her waist.

Jennifer leaned against him. 'God, I'm so tired of Bret's never-ending crap; now scary crap. Thanks for staying with me. I'm okay now, you can head home. The thugs think we're in Sydney.'

'Nah, not leaving,' his tone deadly serious.

She let her forehead drop to his chest and mumbled into his shirt, 'You're a grown man, do whatever you want. I need sleep…lots of sleep.' She took a deep breath. 'Did anyone tell you, you smell amazing?'

'Not for a while,' and no mistake, she heard the smile in his voice.

She sighed, 'Well, you do. I could take your shirt to bed and sleep with…oh God, please ignore me, I'm delirious.'

Chuckling, Calum scooped her up and cradled her in his arms, holding her close; exhausted, she rested her head on his shoulder.

* * *

Calum carried Jennifer down the hall and into her room. He laid her on the ruffled pink bed, took off her shoes, and covered her with the quilt. 'This is becoming a habit,' he murmured. 'I like it, and I'm not going to miss out on kissing you this time, Jennifer.' He bent down and kissed her soft mouth.

'Thank you. You know what this place needs?' she said drowsily.

'No, what does it need?' he softly murmured.

'People, lots of friendly people,' she said, then drifted off.

Calum brushed stray curls from her forehead and left the room. He went to grab her phone and, just in case, placed it on the bedside table within her easy reach. Then he sent his grandmother a message before heading back down the hall to collect bedding from Bob's room and laid it out on the floor at the foot of Jennifer's bed. He yanked off his boots, dress pants, and shirt, then stretched out. Arms folded behind his head, he mulled over what Jennifer Dove was doing to his mind, his body, and his life.

Christ, he hadn't felt this way about a woman—ever. His body ached to have her lying naked on top of him, under him, beside him. Whatever she wanted, he was ready to give it all.

He closed his eyes and replayed all the moments he'd seen her over the past few days, and he realised he cherished every single second.

Sleep was a long time coming.

* * *

It was still dark when, in a sleepy daze, Jennifer woke up, her mind replaying the day's events, then her brain started on the what-ifs. The chit-chat and scenes swirling in her head wouldn't stop. That wasn't nearly as bad as a drunken idiot singing somewhere. If he just kept at it, it'd be fine, but he'd pause, and Jennifer's whole system, already wound tight, would sag with relief, only for the bloke to start up again. And when out of the blue the wailing began, she flinched and cursed him under her breath. His mournful tones, his accent, sounded familiar, but of course that was impossible. She told herself his singing didn't matter, and instead of wanting to kill the bastard, she should relax into it. Eventually, exhaustion took over; she felt her body grow heavy and drifted off when…

Her phone buzzed.

Heart pounding, she fumbled in the dark and found it on the bedside table.

'What!?' she yelled, getting up on her knees.

'Fuck!' Calum roared, vaulting off the floor from behind the bed end, his body tense, ready for action.

Eyes wide, Jennifer squealed and stared at Calum, the only light coming from her phone. 'What're you doing here?!'

'Sis, it's Bret,' her brother hissed, breathing hard into the receiver. 'It's all right, it's me, Bret.'

Hand on her racing heart, she stared at Calum. 'Not you, Bret,' Jennifer snapped into her phone. She watched Calum's shock fade and his body unwind as he gazed back at her, a warm grin easing onto his face. 'Well, thank God! They're letting you use the phone?' Jennifer muttered, her mind distracted by Calum's presence moving closer.

'I got away,' he laughed. 'I got out while one of them was talking to you. Man, are they stupid or what?

After relief, anger quickly took over. Jennifer rubbed her eyes and looked at the fuzzy numbers on the bedside clock. 'It's two in the morning. And you think this is funny!'

'Jen—they're a couple of amateurs.'

Yeah, she thought, and you're practically bouncing with excitement about slipping away without them noticing. And he believed that made him cleverer.

Bret continued, 'They're little thugs with big ideas.'

Movement caught her eye: Calum had come around from behind the bed. Feet planted, arms crossed, he stood in front of her, wearing nothing but a pair of snug black hipster jocks that stretched snugly over his man bits. 'If…if…' She forced herself to look away and quickly gathered her thoughts. 'If they're such amateurs,' Jennifer seethed, 'why didn't you escape before they rang me and why wait until now to tell me you had escaped! Bloody hell, Bret, I've been frantic!'

'Hey, I've only just stopped running. I'm at a service station outside Blacktown, half an hour from Sydney.'

'Dare I ask where your phone is?'

'Jen, I'm really sorry. Just get yourself another number.'

'What a good idea, then you can't ring me either!' she yelled.

Silence.

'Um, Jen, I'm headed for Darwin, don't get any money out. If they ring, tell them from me to go to hell.'

'*You* tell them! And what if they decide to come for the money anyway? *Huh?* Do they know where we are? Bret!'

My ride's starting; the semi's engine's running. Bye, sis, call you soon.

'Bret! Don't you dare hang up. Bret!' Jennifer hollered. 'Shit!' The line went dead. She yanked the phone away from her ear and stared at it, as if by some miracle she could make Bret materialise. In a rage, she thumped the phone down on the mattress again and again, cursing with every downward thrust. 'Bloody-fucking-little-shit!' She knew Calum was watching and didn't care. She lifted her arm, ready to throw her phone at the wall, when a strong hand clasped around her wrist.

'You'd only have to buy a new one,' Calum whispered softly in her ear, and despite her rage, a small part of her sighed as a sensuous ripple flowed down her neck and into her breast. Her breath hitched a couple of times as she inhaled his amazing scent.

Throw your phone, Jennifer!

'Th-that isn't such a bad idea. A new phone and number, the thugs wouldn't be able to ring.'

He let her go. 'Okay, go ahead, you'll feel better.'

She raised her hand and pulled her arm back, ready to throw it, but hesitated and decided against smashing her phone. Besides, she couldn't do it to Bret. Instead, she pummelled her frustration out on the pillows. 'You bloody little—Aaarghghg!'

As if on cue, the drunken idiot started singing again. She couldn't get upset with one of Bob's friends tying one on today. Whoever it was, he sounded as if he was in a massive cave. 'Please, please, don't let there be a chorus of them,' she let herself drop, knees bent, back arched, face planted in the pillow, she muttered. 'And please, as a sort of tribute, don't come here to sing under Bob's window.'

'Shush, a minute,' Calum urged, resting his hand on her back. Jennifer stilled as heat from his palm seeped through her dress onto her skin. 'No, wherever he is, perhaps with friends,' he shrugged, 'they're not moving to sing under your window.'

Hair everywhere, Jennifer shifted her head on the pillow to look at Calum. 'Why are you here, in my room?' she quietly demanded, her voice shaky.

'Thugs?'

'Bret's always getting involved with the wrong crowd—on the wrong side of the worst scam yet. But they're in Sydney and they think we're in Sydney.' Jennifer straightened and knelt on the bed.

'You can't be certain about that. They haven't given you a location other than Kings Cross station, which covers a big area.

The moment your brother bolts, they'll be looking for you, assuming Bret will head this way. And Sydney's only two hours from here.'

Jennifer felt the blood drain from her face. What had her brother done? Not only had he brought thugs into her life, along with Sofie's and Claudia's, but maybe into this quiet, friendly town as well. The repercussions raced through her mind; the fallout made her tremble with fear—not for herself, but for everyone else.

'Jen,' Calum murmured softly, his deep voice gently caressing her skin. 'What I said was meant to alert you; I wasn't expecting you to react like that. I'm sorry.' He pulled her off the bed and held her close.

'Let me go, please, Calum,' Jennifer muttered against his bare chest, but made no attempt to push him away. Instead, her hands rose and gripped his muscly biceps like a lifeline.

'I'm not letting you go until you stop shaking.'

'Crikey… that might take a while.'

'Yeah? I don't mind—not going anywhere. You've had to deal with a lot of shit, and it's all catching up. Nervous energy on top of that, and you're drained. You need to sleep. Take your clothes off, get comfortable, and get into bed.' He let her go and moved away, and Jennifer suddenly felt very lonely.

'Where are you going?'

'Nowhere. Go change in the bathroom; I'll be here on the floor when you get back.'

'That's insane, why not use Uncle Bob's room or the couch?' She didn't want him to do that, but asking him to stay in her room seemed wimpy, and she wasn't a wimp.

She watched him scan her body. She tried to stop the shakes by tightening her muscles, but that only made it worse. Bloody hell!

'Sorry, I'm not leaving.'

She gulped, feeling nervous but needing his touch at the same time. A hug would be just what she needed right now.

'Okay, well, the bed's a queen, I'm sure we can share without…' she stopped and, with a backward wave of her hand, gestured towards the bed. 'Just get in…please.' Satisfied she'd made her point, Jennifer turned and headed for the bathroom. Her uncle had handpicked his pallbearers. Calum wouldn't have been one of them if he hadn't been an honourable and solid good bloke. She stripped, washed her face, pulled on the Veronica slip, and went back. Calum lay on his side on top of the bed, elbow in the pillow, head in his hand, and a loose cover that stopped at his waist, leaving his magnificent, broad, muscled chest bare. Then he reached forward and pulled the quilt aside, an invitation to join him. Her belly dropped. His eyes dipped to her mouth, then slowly trailed up with a warm, inviting smile. Crikey!

Were circumstances not fraught with Bret's problems, she could easily take things further, and judging by the look on his face, he'd be happy to oblige. Anyway, she couldn't risk it without getting involved, and getting involved was an emotional investment she wasn't able to make.

'Thank you.' She lay down, her back to him and closed her eyes; now so far from sleep, it wasn't funny.

'Night, Jen.' Calum's voice had that deep rumble she was beginning to crave.

She brought her legs up, pushed them down again, thumped her pillow, fidgeted until, exasperated, she rolled onto her back and looked at the ceiling. 'I can't sleep—damn it—I'm exhausted.' She let out a long, frustrated sigh.

Calum quietly chuckled, propped himself up with his jaw resting on his hand, and said, 'I can help with that.'

'Oh sure…how?' she asked hopefully.

'I'll give you a massage.'

'You're going to touch me?' Had she just said that out loud? He raised an eyebrow. Oh God, he was serious.

'It won't hurt, I promise,' he said with a cheeky grin. 'And you'll feel relaxed enough to fall asleep.'

Jennifer couldn't believe she was doing this, but when she looked at him, his grin softened, and his smile became achingly tender. Her reaction was to roll onto her stomach.

God help me.

She felt the bed move, then his knee slipped between her thighs. She forced herself not to react, but the tiniest whimper escaped. Calum lifted her Veronica slip, and she held her breath, but nothing happened.

'Calum?'

'Uh…yeah,' he sounded breathy, 'I just realised, my hands are pretty rough.'

Was she expecting too much, thinking he could do this without getting aroused? And for that matter, could she? Well, she was here on her stomach; might as well make the most of it.

'There's moisturiser in the bathroom, that should be alright,' she mumbled into the pillow.

The bed shifted with his weight. He left, then came back to settle in the same spot between her legs.

She heard him squeeze cream on his hands, then, after what felt like forever, he gently placed them on her back, and Jennifer gasped.

'Sorry, cream's a bit cold.' Calum rubbed his hands together and started kneading the muscles at her waist just above the elastic waistband of her undies. Face buried in the pillow, she let out a soft moan. Thumbs in the band of muscles on either side of her spine, he slid up to under her ribs, then further between her shoulder blades, then finally her shoulders and neck. With every push and circling of his thumbs, Jennifer whimpered. Then he worked back down again.

'Relax,' Calum ordered. 'I'm not going to hurt you or take advantage. Trust me. Let yourself go.'

Jennifer closed her eyes and focused on relaxing her muscles and easing the tension. She felt her body sink into the mattress, and that's all she remembered.

* * *

Calum's hands, coated in moisturiser, hovered over her skin. Christ, what was he thinking when he offered to do this? He took a deep breath, placed his palms on her lower back, and began to gently knead, bringing his fingers and thumb into play on her muscles. Working on her, he was glad he'd offered. Jennifer was far too tense.

With each downward pressure, Jennifer made soft noises into her pillow, which made Calum hard; something he had no control over. Despite his discomfort, he continued working on her back and shoulders. After a while, she was so relaxed that her jaw and mouth softened. Jennifer was asleep. He eased onto his side, set his phone to alert him at six am, and shoved it under his pillow, then made himself comfortable, closed his eyes, and smiled. Yep, he was in deep trouble and loved every moment.

It felt like no time had passed when his phone rang. He looked down to see that during the night, Jennifer's cheek rested on his chest. Her leg was draped over his hip, and she had her arm around his waist. He was trapped and loved the feeling so much that his grin became a chuckle. He slipped his free hand under the pillow and turned off his phone. Now, he had to carefully untangle himself from Jennifer. He started by gently easing out from under her, then carefully laid her head on the pillow, softly lifted her arm and leg, and slipped out of bed.

Chapter 9

A sliver of early morning sunlight hit Jennifer's face. She screwed her eyes shut and arched her body under the flowery quilt. She yawned and stretched her arms up and out to the sides. She froze, realising she'd told Calum to sleep next to her. Heart pounding, she lifted herself up to check. There was no Calum. Maybe, once she'd fallen asleep, he'd gone back to sleep on the floor. She threw back the quilt, crawled to the foot of the bed, and saw that all his clothes and bedding were gone. Okay, it was safe to say, Calum had taken off before she woke.

Jennifer told herself it was a good thing that nothing had happened; maybe, therefore, there was no emotional attachment on her part, or was it already too late? Damn, she had to stop overthinking everything. At least she'd had a decent sleep and felt much better for it. And Bret had escaped, and there had been no more phone calls. That had to be a good sign, right?

She rolled out of bed, showered, and dressed, hoping cargo pants and an embroidered cotton top would be suitable for a visit to the solicitor with Sofie. Once that was done, she could head home. And suddenly, that didn't seem like such a good idea. An anxious feeling burst in her chest. But why? She was eager to head back to London. Yes, of course, that was it. And really, Sofie and Claudia needed to leave as well. That way, they'd keep the quiet country town of Tumble Creek safe from a visit by city thugs.

She slipped into her favourite sandals, muttering about Bret and the extortionists.

'As if life doesn't have enough problems—honestly?' she muttered to Marilyn's black-and-white glam photo. On her way to the kitchen, she realised that, apart from some stale scones and coffee made from hot tap water, food was pretty scarce. She noticed a note propped against a thermos, with a paper bag beside it on the table.

She moved closer and picked up the note. *Back later, Twinkles. Calum.*

Her heart fluttered. Her breath quickened. Her mind was in a muddle. Calum had gone to the trouble of making sure she had breakfast. Jennifer dared not read anything into that.

She poured herself a coffee, opened the bag, peered in to find an assortment of sweet buns, and plucked out a cinnamon scroll. She wandered around the kitchen, munching and sipping her coffee. Jennifer imagined sitting around the kitchen table with Sofie and Claudia. And during winter, the old stove would keep them warm. Jennifer opened an overhead cupboard, found the most exquisite set of dinnerware, and took a cup down to look underneath. 'Wow, Royal Doulton, Rose Buds. Uncle Bob, you're a mystery.' She shook her head and put the cup back. Were they all wrong about his sexual preferences? Perhaps he had a female soul, and Veronica loved his gentle side. But where was this elusive woman?

A quick glance at her watch showed she had a couple of hours to spare before Sofie and Claudia arrived for their appointment with the solicitor. Jennifer went downstairs to the shop's kitchenette. Ideas for restoration flooded her mind, but she quickly brushed them off as silly fantasies and opened the cellar door. Cool air rose up and touched her face, and the smell that wafted up reminded her of visits to old vineyard cellars in France, Germany, and Italy. She'd only been down her uncle's cellar once, under his strict supervision. Drawn to the flagstone steps that plunged into inky darkness, she felt compelled to investigate, and now, she had to do it without their sweet Uncle Bob.

Her fingers search along the wall, feeling for the light switch, found it, and without thinking, flicked it on. A sickly yellow glow illuminated the way. Taking a deep breath, Jennifer headed down the worn steps. Then, with a snap, the lights went off, plunging her into total darkness. 'Crap!' She slowly fumbled back to the door and hurried to the upstairs kitchen. 'Torch, candles—pantry?' She found an assortment of both and headed back to the cellar.

Torch in hand, with a candle and matches in her pocket, Jennifer peered down the dark, gaping hole. There might be nothing more than damp cobwebs down there now, but somehow, she doubted that. She directed the torchlight at the sandstone wall. The faint glow was barely enough to see by. 'Great, it's a conspiracy.'

Ducking the spider webs, Jennifer carefully navigated the narrow steps heading down. The air felt cooler with each step. A nagging little voice inside her said, It's every chef's dream to have their own cellar. She replied, Sure, but not this chef and not this cellar.

The air was damp and chilly at the bottom of the stairs, and Jennifer rubbed her bare arms. Every move she made echoed around the cellar walls; the vast space felt like a big cave. The darkness almost sucked the light right out of the torch. She moved forward and shone the faint beam across the stone walls and floor. She did a double-take as her light passed over what looked like a pile of old clothes and quickly went to check. 'Oh my God, a hand!' Frozen with fear, her throat closed on a scream. Her whole body shook. She dropped the torch. It clattered onto the flagstones and went out.

Jennifer widened her eyes, but darkness surrounded her, as dense as an impenetrable cloak. Her breath came in short gasps, and strange, squeaky noises escaped her mouth.

RUN!

*   *   *

Calum left the hardware shop with a carton of smoke alarms to install at Bob's place as soon as possible. He stood at the front door of the empty chemist, hand raised, about to knock when a blood-curdling scream erupted from inside. The hairs on the back of his neck prickled. More screams echoed through the shop. It was hard to tell where they came from, but he knew one thing: it was Jennifer.

'Shit!' He had to get in there, fast. He hammered on the door, then thumped it with his shoulder—any harder and he'd shatter the glass. It crossed his mind to go around the back, but that would've taken too long. By the time he got there, she'd be at the front with her hair on fire because she hadn't listened to his warnings, or worse, she was fighting off thugs.

'Jen!' he shouted. Ignoring the few pedestrians who slowed their pace for a better look, he ran back to his work Ute and grabbed a mallet from his toolbox. 'I'm coming, Jen!' He raised his mallet, ready to deliver the first blow to the shop's glass front door.

'Cal! Ya can't use a mallet!' a passer-by yelled from across the street, 'the place is heritage-listed!'

Calum glared over his shoulder at the bloke and hesitated, then heard the brass bolts slide with frantic speed and turned to see the door fly open.

'Calum!' Jennifer shouted. The colour had drained from her face, but at least there weren't any scorch marks in her hair…or anywhere else. Calum breathed a sigh of relief.

Needing to hold her, he dropped his mallet. Before he could step in and wrap his arms around her, she grabbed a handful of his T-shirt near his throat and hauled him in.

'Get in here!' she yanked him across the shop floor. 'Quick, hurry, there's a dead bloke in the cellar!'

She pushed him through the cellar door and pulled a candle out of her pocket, shoving it at him.

'What's this?' Calum took it and peered down the dark stairs. 'What am I supposed to do with a candle?'

'That's a cellar, there's a horrible, dead body down there, and—' she pointed a trembling finger at the black hole.

'I take it you've tried the lights?'

'They were on for less than a minute and—bang! They went out. Look, will you please hurry up!'

'There's no hurry. If he's dead, he's not going anywhere.'

She eyed him with suspicion. 'You don't believe me.'

'I do! But a candle, Jen—come on. I'll wait here; you go grab a torch from my Ute. It's in the toolbox on the back tray. Unless you'd rather wait here while I get it?'

Green-eyed and panicked, she clung to the front of his shirt. 'Don't go anywhere, I'll grab the torches.' She hurried off.

'Dead bodies in the cellar. What next?' Calum muttered.

A strange, heavy scraping noise approached him, not from the cellar but from the shop. Adrenaline shot through Calum, and with clenched fists, he adopted a defensive stance. Then Jennifer burst through the door, a torch in one hand and dragging his mallet in the other.

'Christ, Jen,' he let his hands fall to his sides. 'Why did you bring that? All I wanted was the torch.'

'You might need it down there.'

'Give me that.' Calum took the heavy mallet from Jennifer's hands and leaned it against the wall. 'It's okay, he's dead,' Calum said with a raised eyebrow. Jennifer looked ready to crack, so he softened his tone. 'You don't look too good. Why don't you stay up here and call the police?'

'I'm not going to fall apart; I want to see for myself—you know? I'm not a sicko. I just need to know what I saw wasn't a figment of my imagination.'

'Okay, but stick close,' Calum said as he took her hand and placed it on his shoulder. The torchlight cast a ring of yellow light over the steps.

'Like a shadow.' Her trembling hands gripped Calum as they edged down the stone steps to the floor.

He shone the torch beam to the left, then back a bit to the right. The light passed over something shiny. He inched forward and stopped at a puddle on the floor.

Jennifer gasped. 'Look at all that blood!'

'What blood? And where's the body?'

'He could be hiding.'

'I thought he was dead?'

'He looked dead. I'm not silly enough to stop and check for a pulse! Would you?' Brow furrowed, she sent him a look. 'Of course you would.'

'What do you mean by that?' he swung the torch, carefully searching into the corners, then moved closer to the pool of 'blood.'

Jennifer shuffled behind him, peering over his shoulder, warm breath near his ear. 'You've got more muscle, in case we get jumped.'

'Right—' he tilted his head a little further, secretly enjoying the moment even though staying focused was tough. 'Glad to hear it.' Without thinking, Calum tipped his head to give Jennifer better access to his neck. Then he tried to breathe like a normal human being, but no way that was happening. 'There's no one here.'

'Bugger! He must've taken off when I ran up and opened the door for you. Yep—eewh, look, wet footprints heading towards the stairs.'

'Not very dead then,' Calum said with a wry grin. 'Damn big prints though.' He could feel the tension making the muscle just above his jaw twitch. 'Let's have a closer look.' Calum dipped a finger into the wet patch, rubbed it between his thumb and index finger, and sniffed it. 'What a waste.'

Jennifer looked down. 'It's not blood, is it. It's wine.'

'Yep.' Calum grabbed a bottle sitting on its side against the wall and handed it to her.

'He's been drinking wine down here. Oh my God! I don't believe it—Grange Hermitage! The bastard's been swigging the most expensive wine in the country—he was drunk on a one-thousand-dollar red!' Jennifer turned to Calum. 'He's been in here all night—all night! That's what I heard. He was singing.' She began to pace. 'I thought it was a pissed local. Damn it, what was he singing? I couldn't understand the words, but I'm sure it was familiar.'

'He left something,' Calum said as he picked up the photo and dusted it off.

'It's a woman.' Jennifer turned the photo over. 'Nothing on the back. There's something vaguely familiar about it, but I can't think straight. What's he doing in my uncle's cellar?'

Calum swung the torch around. 'What's this?' he asked as he peered deeper into the cellar.

Crouching, ready for anything, they faced at least ten racks of wine, five feet high and stretching across the floor. Silently and carefully, they searched between each rack but found nothing.

'Like you said, he's gone.' Calum rubbed his scalp. 'Maybe he knew about the cellar, and thought he'd try some before it all disappeared.'

'Are you being completely honest with me? On my first night here, you and Sergeant Stewart were having a heated discussion about Uncle Bob as you were coming down the stairs. What was that about then?' Jennifer waited.

Calum didn't want to sound insensitive. 'You're a woman of the world…' he began. Jennifer rolled her eyes. 'Okay, I'll get to the point. We'd only just met you, and the argument was whether or not to ask you if Bob was gay.'

'Is that all?' Jennifer frowned. 'We thought he was, but now I'm not so sure. It could be that he was a warm and gentle man with a feminine side. Uncle Bob bought his girlfriend Veronica frilly underwear in Paris. You wouldn't know where I could find her, would you?'

Calum shrugged. 'Nope. No idea.'

'Can I have the torch, please?' she asked, and holding it steady, she swung it towards the racks. 'This is unbelievable,' she said quietly, looking around. 'I knew Uncle Bob had been collecting wine for years, but this is…' she trailed off.

'One hell of a lot of wine,' Calum murmured, impressed. He quickly estimated that the cellar was huge, at least half the size of the shop above. Racks of wine filled most of the space. He watched Jennifer move towards the rack closest to them. She ran her fingers over some of the bottles, brushing away cobwebs and dust to reveal the labels.

'Oh my God,' she gasped. 'There's more Grange Hermitage. All these Australian wines are top labels.'

'That's not bad, I suppose.'

'Not bad? It's fantastic! What's in this cellar is worth serious money.' She moved to the last rack and studied the labels with Calum peering over her shoulder. 'They date back to the early fifties. I'm lost for words.'

'C'mon,' Calum took her hand. 'Enough exploring. We'd better let Brock and Tony know about the body and how it disappeared.'

His aim was to glance at her, but her stunned expression pulled him in. His gaze lingered, and his gut tightened. He tried to hold back a grin but didn't quite succeed. 'Hmm,' he heard himself think out loud, hoping it sounded casual, when his heart was anything but. So, keeping it cool, he led her to the stairs and followed her back to the shop's kitchenette. Calum rang the police station and briefly filled them in on the break-in.

'Yeah, we'll wait. Come around the back.' He closed off and opened the back door, letting sunlight flood inside. 'You've got stuff—' he said, pointing at her hair.

'What is it? What's in my hair?' Jennifer danced, head tilted down, fingers frantically ruffling through her curls.

'Take it easy. It's nothing. Just a lot of web,' Calum chuckled.

'You sure there aren't any spiders?' she asked, leaning her head towards his chest. 'Hurry, have a look.'

Calum peered into her hair, plucking at a few cobwebs. He ran his fingertips along her scalp from front to back; done, Jennifer straightened to examine his fingers.

Breath shallow, she licked her lips and said, 'Better do that again…just to be sure.'

'Yeah, I should,' he murmured. Her silky curls slipped through his fingers. Her beautiful face tilted back, and his eyes searched hers. They had darkened to a deeper green, blazing with desire. She was receptive to him, trusting. Her lips parted. Like a craving, he needed to feel her mouth on his, longed to dip his tongue between her lips. Heat coiled through his body. His fingers grasped the curls at the back of her head, and he brought his mouth down on hers.

Leaning into him, she moaned. This only made him hungrier. His hands traced down her neck and her back to the small of her waist, itching to go further and cup her squeezable arse, so he did. Her cheeks were firm, and he dared to tuck her into him. She moaned again, and he joined her. Her soft, plump lips pressed against his, playful and arousing. He shifted down, tucking his arms under her to lift her and move them both back inside.

*　*　*

The back gate creaked as it swung open.

Jennifer's eyes snapped open to see Calum looking the same, wide and sheepish with a hint of a smile, as if saying, Oops, caught out. With a final kiss, he gently lowered her until her feet touched the ground.

'We've got visitors,' he whispered.

'Damn,' she muttered.

He gave her a slow, wicked grin. Adding quietly, 'Later.'

She stepped back and straightened her clothes just as Brock and Tony strode into the courtyard, their serious faces turning quietly amused.

'G'day, Brock, Tony,' Calum said.

'Sorry to interrupt,' Brock, big and powerful, tried to hide a grin but failed miserably.

Tony chuckled, and Brock jabbed him in the ribs. Tony stumbled sideways, which shut him up quick smart.

'What've you got down the cellar?' Brock asked.

Jennifer invited them inside to escape the sun's relentless heat. Brock asked the questions, and Tony took notes. Half an hour later, they had all the facts, checked out the cellar, and removed the wine bottle to dust for fingerprints.

'So, I gather you have no idea who the drunk might be?' Jennifer asked.

'Er—no,' Brock said, 'but the photo will help. And if you can remember what he was singing, it'll help the investigation. Between us, we should be able to find out if this woman is a local. We'll let you know if anything turns up.' Brock shoved his notepad in his shirt pocket and sauntered back up the path to the gate.

'We'll keep you in the loop,' Tony called out over his shoulder.

With a loud creak and a clang, the gate swung shut.

Jennifer's pulse quickened.

'Where were we?' Calum's asked, a sensuous look back in his eyes.

Jennifer had taken time to cool down and think. 'Um…' Oh God, it would be so easy to drift back into that heavenly daze. His fingers in her hair, his hands on her body felt so good.
'Thanks for helping me out,' she said, catching his gentle smile. She quickly busied herself brushing dust off her hands and clothes. Every time she saw him, she was a complete mess, but what did that matter? she asked herself. It wasn't as if she was trying to impress. Ha.

'My pleasure,' he said, while kissing her cheek. 'Any time you want someone to check your hair for spiders, I'm your man.'

Jennifer laughed, 'Oh, that phrase died with dinosaurs.' However, she thought it was cute and only added to his warm charm.

'Yeah, okay, you can stop laughing now, but I meant every word,' he said, chuckling to himself.

'But listen,' Jennifer said, shifting away from the topic of spiders. 'I'm not happy about having slept with a drunk in the cellar all night. I'll have to install safety chains. Or do you have a better idea?' Yeah, like moving in and guarding my door, just like you did last night.

'Safety chains would be a good start. Under normal circumstances, I'd suggest alarms, but the wiring in this place couldn't handle it. Battery-powered alarms are available, but I'd have to order them in. There's no call for them here.'

'No, of course not. Sorry.'

'Don't be sorry or feel guilty; none of this is your or Sofie's doing,' he said softly. Moving closer, he focused on his fingers twirling a curl of her hair; he pulled it straight, then let it go. It bounced up, landing on her forehead. 'Great hair.'

'More spider webs?' she asked, her belly feeling like it was in free-fall.

'No... I could search?' he suggested hopefully.

'That's okay, but thanks for offering.' The urge to start over was tempting. She stepped back, and, worried they might stray, she tucked her hands into her armpits.

Calum nodded in understanding and changed the subject. 'I'd keep the wine to yourself if I were you. Once the locals get a whiff, you'll be a very popular woman. Not that you aren't already,' he grinned. 'Meanwhile, I'll install a few smoke alarms and safety chains for the front and back.'

'That's very kind, but I can do that, can't I?'

Calum shook his head. 'Don't—and I mean don't—touch anything. I won't be long.'

Jennifer hurried to the pink bathroom, peered into the mirror, and fiddled with her hair to no avail. Her hair did whatever it wanted, and nothing short of electrical devices could get it to behave. 'What's the point anyway? A couple of days and I'll be gone.' She shrugged at her reflection and dusted herself off.

Waiting upstairs in the hall, she passed the time by checking out the sideboard. Still wondering why her grandfather was neatly cut out of his own wedding photo, nothing came to mind that would clear up that mystery. She opened one of the top drawers. Among postcards and letters, she found half a dozen hair clips and lifted them out. As she ran her fingers over the fancy diamantes, she thought they were delicate and pretty. Veronica had left little traces of herself throughout the house. She had little time left, but she would try to find her. Her uncle's solicitor would know. Calum's footsteps pounded through the shop and up the stairs as he came closer.

She turned to watch him stride down the hall, effortlessly balancing a ladder on his shoulder. Tools jingled from a broad leather tool belt slung low on his hips, swinging with each step. The movement was hypnotising. She averted her gaze, lowering it to his washed-out jeans, which fit snugly around his thighs, flexing with every step. Then, back up to his white T-shirt, stretched taut across his broad, muscular chest and biceps. Jennifer was captivated. Without thinking, she dropped the hair clips on the sideboard.

'Jen?' Calum held up a couple of plastic carry bags.

'Huh?' she said dreamily.

'Smoke alarms.'

'Oh.' She snapped out of her daydream and met his gaze. 'Great.'

'I'll start in the kitchen,' Calum said and headed down the hall as Jennifer followed. He propped his ladder against the wall near the door and climbed up.

Jennifer placed the bags on a bench and lost herself in his supple, big-cat-like movements, with strained forearms and biceps, and jeans that hugged his backside and thighs. She tilted her head, gazing, content to observe him work.

''Scuse me, Jen?'

'Hmmm?'

'Could you pass me the cordless drill?'

'Drill? You want to drill something?'

'I want to drill these screws into the wall; otherwise, the alarm will fall off. Have you been wine tasting in the cellar?' he grinned.

'Course not. Sorry.' She mentally slapped herself, which had little effect. She stretched up, handed him the drill, and said, 'Thanks for the coffee and sweet buns. Breakfast was delicious.'

'You're welcome,' he grinned down at her.

Jennifer's enjoyment lasted for over an hour while Calum installed smoke alarms. Then he rechecked the old fuse box inside a cupboard in the laundry.

'Okay, I've turned off the mains power. I should've done it yesterday. Sorry, Jen, but I'd like a good night's sleep. Even though I've switched the power off, don't touch power points or switches. I can leave the hot water service on, as it's on a separate line and seems safe enough. The doors have chains, and I'm sure Brock and Tony are busy looking for the intruder.' He picked up the ladder and his tools. 'Where did you put the bag I gave you?'

'On the kitchen bench.'

'There's a pile of batteries in it. You'll need to swap them out for the old ones in all the torches so you're never left in the dark.'

Jennifer gazed at him, stunned; there was so much to think about.

Calum inclined his head and looked back. There was a long pause where neither spoke. Jennifer could hear her heartbeat thumping in her ears.

'Jen?'

'Yes, I'll do that. How much do I owe you?'

'Uh-uh. Call it community service, should've done it ages ago, I had no idea it was this bad.'

'No, I insist on paying you.'

'It's a small amount. Don't embarrass me. It could save your life and the lives of others up and down the street, okay?'

'Okay, have it your way.' On impulse, she reached up and kissed his cheek. 'Thank you,' she breathed, lingering for just a moment to take in his warm male scent tinged with a hint of pine. She stepped back and immediately felt a sense of loneliness. How did he get that smell? She could nuzzle his neck all day. His eyes slowly drifted to her mouth, and in a blink, the atmosphere shifted to something far more sensuous.

Calum's gaze fixed on hers, then a smile softened his features. It wasn't just any smile; in the depths of his eyes, she saw something—a knowing look, as if he could read her innermost thoughts. Jennifer took a deep breath and tried to settle the butterflies in her stomach. She felt as if she'd just gone down the big dipper at Luna Park. Oh, help, what have I done? We nearly had sex! Would've, if not for Brock and Tony.

'My pleasure.' Calum's grin widened; taking a step forward, he wrapped a big hand around her waist and drew her in. Tilting his head, he pressed his soft mouth on hers for a brief but very hot, deep kiss. 'Be seeing you, Twinkles.' He walked out the door just as Sofie and Claudia came in. He gave them a nod as he passed. 'Morning, ladies.'

'Morning,' they chorused, their voices tinged with surprise and curiosity.

Sofie strode up to Jennifer and whispered, 'Rearrange your AO face before Claudia sees you. She's not eighteen yet.'

In a dream, Jennifer watched Calum's athletic back, arms, and butt. 'Right,' she said with a sigh, and turned on her heel. 'Right!' she said more firmly this time.

'You look like you could do with a coffee,' Sofie said, raising her basket. 'I brought a thermos.'

'You've got real coffee in there?'

'No, instant, this will have to do. At least it's hot and tastes a bit like coffee.'

Jennifer kissed her sister's cheek. 'Come through to the kitchen, I've got a few things to tell you.'

'It's Bret, isn't it?' Sofie sounded on edge. 'I knew I shouldn't have left with Brock and the crew to go to the pub.'

Jennifer gathered cups and plates, then poured everyone a coffee before sitting down with them at the old, scrubbed pine kitchen table. Claudia raised her hand to rest her chin on her palm. Sofie clasped her fingers tightly, turning her knuckles white in anticipation that what they were about to hear was not good.

'The call yesterday wasn't from Bret,' Jennifer began. She told them the whole story, often having to calm Sofie down and explain that it was all right—that Bret had escaped and was on his way to Darwin. Claudia had no patience for her uncle; Jennifer knew she'd seen her mum worry about him too often and bail him out of trouble. She'd had enough and told them Shit-for-brains needed teaching a lesson.

'Obviously, they think we're worth a few quid. Maybe Bret told them we're inheriting everything from Uncle Bob. Boy, are they in for a shock,' Jennifer shrugged. 'I don't know!'

'What if they find us to get the money?' eyes wide, Sofie covered her mouth.

'Sofe, you can't go on about scenarios and what-ifs, okay?' Though Calum had said as much, but they didn't need to know that. 'You can't anticipate.' Jennifer clasped her sister's shoulder. Sofie's hand fell away from her mouth. Jennifer continued, 'We'll get the money. The thing is, you start something like this, and where does it end?'

'You call the police. That's where it ends,' Claudia thumped the table.

Jennifer sighed. 'Yeah, you're right, Claudia. I'm so bloody pissed off; that's exactly what I might do.'

'*Might!*' Claudia screeched.

'Oh bugger!' Sofie cried out. 'Do Mum and Dad know?'

'Are you kidding? I'm not involving them! Bret called us. If he wants them to know what's going on, he can tell them. They'd interrogate me, and I have no answers,' Jennifer flung her hands out, 'but they'd keep pushing, going way beyond Bret, and start on me, then you and Claudia.' She shook her head. 'Not happening—no way!'

'Okay—okay.' Sofie held Jennifer's hand and gave it a reassuring squeeze, emphasising her feelings. 'Really, it's okay.'

She wasn't happy about her outburst, but discussing her parents always got her fired up.

It was Sofie's turn to soothe and change the subject. 'What was Calum doing here?'

Jennifer looked up from her hands. 'He installed smoke alarms, but there's more.'

Sofie and Claudia edged closer.

'Calum was here when the thugs called…he stayed all night. Don't look at me like that. Nothing happened. It nearly did, but then the police came.'

'What…again?!' Sofie cried out, eyes wide, hands covering her face.

Jennifer was grateful that Sofie latched onto the word 'police' rather than what she nearly did with Calum. She finished by telling them about the comatose local and their uncle's cellar full of wine.

'Jeez,' Claudia complained, 'I missed all the fun—again!'

*　*　*

People went about their business in the street while Gerek tried to stay inconspicuous, but panting like a large, unfit jogger didn't make him look like an athlete. Plus, he was still recovering from the close call of getting caught. Squeals like a baby piglet had woken him. He'd felt the adrenaline surge so strong it made him belch. He'd tried to figure out where he was while a massive bass drum pounded in his head. He'd staggered up the cellar stairs and stumbled out the back door, then winced as the back gate creaked open, but felt relieved the coast was clear as he moved into the shadows. The sickening hangover combined with the midday heat had his head pounding so fiercely his eyes felt ready to pop.

Sweat dripped down Gerek's face as he leaned against his you-beaut ute. Yesterday, he'd parked the car in the shade; now it was baking in the blazing sun. Barely able to touch the door handle, he looked up at the sky, hoping for an answer—none came; angry, he muttered a curse, his knuckles black and blue. 'Do Diabla.' To hell with it. He squeezed his belly behind the steering wheel, turned the ignition on, and took off, winding his window down and leaving it that way for the entire fifty kilometres to his motel. It didn't cool him down at all. The hot, northerly breeze made it hard to breathe. Sweat dripped off his chin and elbow, and his shirt stuck to his armpits. He could almost smell the red wine coming out of every pore.

Marinated, steam-baked Polish.

He wondered how the locals managed to survive this unbearable, energy-draining heat.

He drove into the small town of Parrot Rock, parked the Ute outside his motel room, and staggered inside. Shutting the door, he slumped back onto the bed, panting. He was going to die—definitely—no one could survive this much pain. His hand reached for the remote to turn on the air-conditioner. It slowly whirred into life and burbled along with a rattle and hum.

'*Idiota!* Drinking wine is not good. Anna's Brandy, not do this,' he groaned.

With his breath nearly back to normal, Gerek eased off the bed to grab a flannel from the en-suite bathroom and soaked it under the cold tap. Then took himself back to bed and pressed the cold flannel to his face.

Maybe she hadn't seen him clearly, but thankfully, a snippet of logic kicked in. No! Cover blown. Fool. It was time for Plan B—whatever that was. He grabbed his phone and dialled.

'*Witam.* Hello, Gerek,' a familiar voice answered.

'Cover blown, Antonin. I'm coming home,' Gerek stated, leaving no room for doubt.

'Where are you?' Antonin demanded.

'Motel, you moron,' Gerek muttered quietly into the phone, knowing Antonin wouldn't have a clue what moron meant. He tried to stay calm, but the wine and the heat were wearing him down. He rubbed his thick neck muscles, knowing Antonin, sitting in his fancy office, would try to make him stay and tell him how to do his job.

'You let them see you! That's your problem. You go back and get stuff!'

'*Nie!* I have no way to find anything. I come home now. Forget about stuff. Stupid to get close to idiots. Bunch of smelly pig farts.'

'Who you calling pig farts? I am your superior, your friend. This trouble comes out, we both go to Suwalki; you know where it's freezing all the time. Or are you having a good time in Australia and have forgotten your country, Poland!' Antonin yelled.

Gerek dabbed at the sweat around his neck. 'Good. Nice and cool in Suwalki—*like* your office,' he grumbled. 'I was in shop. Man said, "Hot, is not it? You can fry eggs on bonnet of car!" and he meant it.'

'Listen Gerek, they'll humiliate me, then you…quietly! We will no longer work for the embassy. They will send us to Suwalki to sweep streets! Think about what could happen to you and Anna! They will cut you dead.'

'What for all this drama! *Heh?*' Gerek waited.

A long sigh drifted down the line, then with a soft, sad voice, Antonin replied, 'I cannot say over the phone. Stay for me and watch for a little while longer. Something might happen.'

Gerek disconnected and threw the phone down, then picked it up again to ring his wife. Hearing her lovely voice, he sighed, barely able to stand the heartache.

'Kichanie (darling) Anna,' he said, sending kisses down the line. 'I am to stay a little longer. Tak. (yes) I be missing you too, kichanie, (darling).' After talking for a while about family and friends, Gerek told his wife, 'I come home soon. Will ring tomorrow. Prashaitye (goodbye).' He sent Anna another kiss. 'Wybacz mi kochanie,' (forgive me darling) and regretfully closed off.

He might be grasping at autumn leaves in a high wind, but he had to try. While waiting for the line to connect him to his man in London, he rummaged in his bag for some headache tablets. He dropped four into his mouth, twice the prescribed dose, grabbed the brandy bottle sitting on the bedside table, and took a few swigs to wash them down. Using his shoulder to hold the phone to his ear, he filled his hip flask with the remaining drink.

'*Tak?*' *(yes)* a grating voice asked.

'Dobry! You pay attention—you have to get in girlfriend's flat,' Gerek demanded. 'Bob could give photos or something to his niece.'

'Of course there are photos,' Dolby told him with certainty, yet again. 'I've seen them, just Bob, in London, Paris and Italy.'

'No, they are Bob with Antonin. And they are very different.'

'How do you mean, *different?*'

'I do not know! Antonin will not say.'

'Stupid man,' Dobry grouched. 'Anyway, it's no good, do not have key. And caretaker would not let me in.'

'You use prune for brain and do it!' Gerek hung up, knowing Dobry's chances of finding anything useful in the flat were slim but worth a try.

Chapter 10

Jennifer thought her uncle's solicitor, Robert Spaulding, looked more like a balding vicar than a lawyer. His sharp, brown eyes flicked between the three of them, searching their faces for sins that needed exorcising.

Jennifer watched him steeple his fingers. Here we go. She braced herself for a sermon. On the other hand, she thought a sermon might be worthwhile if it meant they'd find out who Veronica was. She would surely benefit from his estate.

'Your uncle, Bob Feldman, was a remarkable man in the community. He left strict instructions that I, as his friend and solicitor, agreed to uphold his will, no matter who tried to contest it. I have ensured that his last will is ironclad. You may think it strange, but he trusted me. I knew this was exactly what Bob wanted. I made absolutely sure that no other person or company would get a cent of his money. Bob had an excellent sense of judgment.

Before continuing, Robert Spaulding waited for his words to sink in. Satisfied, he carried on. 'Jennifer, Sofie, your Uncle Bob Feldman left all his properties and investments equally to both of you.'

A hush fell over the room.

Robert Spaulding looked at Jennifer and Sofie in turn. 'This includes his pharmacies in Point Piper and Kings Cross, his vineyards—you can see some of them from his kitchen—and, of course, his property here in town, which brings me to Bob's pharmacy and home, where you are staying at the moment. Under your uncle's instructions, I held the building in trust for you both until his death.'

Jennifer's chin dropped. The room, with its bookshelves, dark furniture, and university degrees, faded away. Her eyes fixed on the man opposite her, while her ears caught Sofie's heavy breathing.

Claudia laughed, eyes wide. 'Get outa here.'

Sofie didn't respond to a gentle nudge in the ribs, so Jennifer shifted her gaze back to Mr Spaulding. 'What did you say?' she whispered, trying to come to grips with the news.

He tapped a pen on the documents in front of him. 'It's all here in the paperwork. You are now both wealthy young women.'

Jennifer couldn't stop a strangled squeak from escaping her mouth. She cleared her throat. 'We never dreamt—I mean, at least I thought some of it would go to someone else, like Veronica. Why us?'

'Bob confided in me, in his words: You are his only family.' 'He often spoke of you, with deep appreciation, but most of all, unconditional love.' The next moment, he was serious again. 'We know nothing of this woman Veronica.' Mr Spaulding had a sense of humour. Was that a cheeky little smile?

Sofie blinked, turning pale now. 'I need a paper bag,' she mumbled.

'Mum, get a grip,' Claudia urged, rubbing Sofie's back.

'What if our parents decide to contest the will?' Jennifer asked.

They can try. In fact, their lawyer has already contacted me. As I explained to him, they can spend a lot of money contesting Bob's will, but they will fail. Bob Feldman was clear—he didn't want his properties to fall into their hands. I am under strict instructions. Your uncle also had concerns about your brother, Bret. Bob decided not to leave anything to your brother, fearing it would be wasted on harebrained schemes and gambling. However, he did make provisions for Bret: it's a small boutique vineyard, twenty kilometres north of town. But you, Jennifer, and you, Sofie, hold it in trust until you believe Bret is responsible. Until then, you will both look after Bret as you see fit; Bob was adamant about that, too. There is a copy of a statement from your uncle in the file. Please read it carefully.

Jennifer's mind reeled at this news. If she couldn't cope, how must Sofie feel? She glanced across at her sister, who stared wide-eyed at Robert Spaulding.

'Probate will take a few months,' he continued. 'It's a formality that everyone has to endure. You needn't worry, your uncle made sure his properties were well managed, and he kept a close eye on all his accounts.'

Jennifer found her voice. 'I don't understand. We were close. He mentioned pharmacies, but we never thought to ask about his financial situation. Why would we? We also never took him up on his offer to help us financially. And he did offer. Thinking back, he used to buy us gifts he thought we needed.' She couldn't stop herself and babbled on. 'Are you sure Uncle Bob had no female friend, local people who helped him, the odd fireman, clergyman, or Country Women's Association members?'

'You are the only ones. Though he had many friends and often worked with local charities, his contributions were always generous.' He nodded for emphasis as he continued, 'Yes, many charities. Perhaps one of them could have been a special lady. I wouldn't know, nor is it any of my business.' He opened a drawer in his desk, took out two fat envelopes, and handed one to Jennifer and one to Sofie. 'Bob kept his financial affairs close to his chest; he wasn't one to boast. There's something he said to me once that might help you. "People behave differently towards you if they believe you have money. They want a piece of what you've got." Having said that, your uncle was a very generous man.'

'He certainly was,' Jennifer admitted. 'Unfortunately, the family image thing runs deep. Our sweet Uncle Bob had no connection with his sister for many years.'

'Bob knew you'd both be strapped for cash, as he would say. He left some with me to pass on to you. Take this folder too; all the legal documents are inside. Read them carefully and don't feel overwhelmed. It's all quite straightforward.'

He buzzed his secretary. 'Barbara, could you come into my office, please?"

Barbara, a statuesque grey-blonde, wearing a crisp white blouse under a navy-blue suit, came in and stood beside Mr Spaulding.

'Barbara, I need you to witness these young ladies signing the trustee papers and counting the money. Jennifer, make sure you have two thousand dollars. Sofie, you should have three thousand dollars, one extra for Claudia.'

'I've never seen this much cash,' Jennifer mumbled to herself.

'Me either,' Sofie whispered.

Claudia stared at the envelope. 'A thousand for me. Yay!'

'All there? Good. Sign here, please,' the solicitor indicated to the dotted lines on several sets of documents. An unexpected softness appeared on his serious face. Eyes fixed on Claudia, he paused. 'My dear girl, let me just say that your eulogy was exactly what Bob would've liked and, ahem, your outfit too.'

Claudia beamed. Jennifer took Mr. Spaulding's hand and shook it, thanking him. Sofie stood up but didn't move.

'I'm sure my sister thanks you as well.' Sofie hugged her envelope and nodded.

Out on the footpath, arms flapping, Claudia jumped up and down with excitement.

'Wow! Seriously awesome. Mum, we're rich! We can move from Manly into something huge. We can get the biggest wide-angle screen TV with surround sound. Oh, oh, I was so not looking forward to working as a checkout chick to save up for a car, and now I don't have to. This is fantastic, I can't wait to tell Skids!'

'Holy crap—we own vineyards!' Jennifer blinked at her sister, hoping it would help her understand.

'I can't get my head around this,' Sofie mumbled. She frowned at her daughter. 'You are not to tell Skids or *anyone*. I want you to be crystal clear on this, Claudia.'

'Mum! Jeez.'

'We own vineyards,' Jennifer whispered to herself.

'Jen! Help me out here, what do you think?'

'Well... there are responsibilities that come with this,' Jennifer nodded at Claudia. 'People's jobs, mostly. And I think what your mum is saying is, if the wrong people find out, like whatsisface your dad, then—I don't know, he might try something like demand half. And your mum wouldn't want to deal with that.' And there was Bret and his thugs. 'If Bret happens to ring,' she eyed them both. 'Do not say a word about this to him either.'

Claudia rolled her eyes. 'Skids wouldn't tell anybody.' Jennifer shot her a stern look. 'Okay, I won't say anything to anyone.' Another look from Jennifer. 'I promise. Anyway, listen to both of you, waffling on about negative stuff.'

'I need a double-shot latté,' Jennifer announced, looking around for a café.

All three squinted against the bright sun as they searched up and down the street, but couldn't see a coffee shop among the many signs hanging under the wide awnings.

'There's Trudy, the florist. Stay here, I'll go ask her.' Stepping out of the shade and into the sun, Jennifer instantly felt the sting of its rays. As heat rose from the bitumen straight through the soles of her shoes, she picked up her pace and jogged across the street, calling, 'Trudy!'

The young woman, dressed in a T-shirt, shorts, and Crocs, turned around.

'Oh, g'day, you bought the yellow roses yesterday. Bob Feldman's niece.'

'Yeah, that's me,' Jennifer smiled. 'I just wanted to ask, is there a café nearby?'

'Sure, there's the bakery and the teashop. Or the roadhouse, they make a great cappuccino with instant and lots of froth.'

Jennifer felt her shoulders slump. 'I'll try the bakery.'

'Good choice.' Trudy tilted her head and gave Jennifer the, I-smell-gossip, eye. 'I heard Mrs Jarvis say, Calum's been around Bob's Pharmacy a fair bit?'

'Has he?' Jennifer questioned. On reflection, Calum hadn't come around just for the sake of it. He always had good reason, hadn't he? She wondered where this was heading: part of her wanted, needed, to know, while another part was yelling, run!

'You can't keep anything quiet in this town. Though Mrs Jarvis is no gossip,' Trudy shook her head. 'She said Cal was installing smoke alarms to keep the shops next door safe. Others reckon there's more to it than that, especially after Cal nearly smashed the front door trying to get in, you know.' She gave Jennifer a quirky little shrug.

'He was…that's because he happened to be…um,' Jennifer stuttered.

'Anyway, don't listen to blabbermouths or any other rumours about Cal.'

Jennifer stiffened. 'What rumours?'

'It's nothing really. A local girl got herself pregnant and pointed her belly at Cal.' Trudy shrugged. 'One day he's every mother's dream son-in-law, and the next he's off their Christmas list. I don't care about that sort of crap; he's a top bloke. And he would never do such a thing. Never.'

It was totally irrational. Nevertheless, Jennifer couldn't ignore the sharp pang in her chest. 'I think we'll head off and find that coffee now. Thanks, Trudy.' Frowning, she jogged back to where Sofie and Claudia waited.

'What, no coffee to be had?' Sofie brushed away stray hair from around Jennifer's face.

'Sure there is.' Jennifer strode off, shoulders back, thoughts racing. What did it matter to her what Calum was accused of? She barely knew him. Come to think of it, she barely knew Dobry, waiting fruitlessly back in London. He was definitely off her Christmas list; he just didn't know it yet. A relationship is built on trust, and he'd lost hers when he took money from her purse. Borrowed money she never saw again. Booked her on a cheap, dodgy plane and kept the change.

Strike three—you're out.

*　*　*

Jennifer placed a small cardboard tray of coffees and fresh lamingtons on the low breakfast bar in her sister's motel room.

She sipped her espresso and sighed. *'Hmm…*this is good, and just in time, I was starting to hallucinate.'

'You probably drink too much of the stuff,' Sofie said, joining her while holding a folder of legal papers.

'What am I supposed to do while you sit there reading?' Claudia asked, biting into a lamington; desiccated coconut and chocolate stuck to her lips.

'We won't be long,' Sofie said. 'Watch an in-house movie.'

'Great,' Claudia moaned and flopped onto the bed. 'You should've let me bring my phone, Mum. Please, can I use yours?'

'We had a deal.'

'Mum!' Claudia whined. 'At least let me text Skids?'

Sofie handed Claudia her phone. 'Don't say anything about the will,' she warned.

Jennifer opened the folder to find several large photos of their uncle's vineyards. 'Have you got these?' she asked, waving them under her sister's nose.

Sofie looked at them. 'Yes, I've got duplicates,' she whispered in awe.

Jennifer spread the photos out in front of her. 'Stunning, simply stunning. I never dreamt they were like this. The buildings and home look like a small Tuscan castle.'

'There's a lot we didn't know about our uncle,' Sofie said. 'He took us there for my eighteenth, remember?' She pointed to a photo of a beautiful sandstone mansion with terraces overlooking rolling hills covered in lush vines. 'I didn't know it was his.'

By early evening, Jennifer couldn't take any more of the mumbo-jumbo legal jargon. 'I need an interpreter for most of this. C'mon, let's go for a walk and find somewhere to eat.'

Jennifer stepped out of her sister's motel room and stopped for a moment to enjoy the setting sun, which cast a warm orange glow over the countryside. If she ignored the Edwardian architecture and focused on the rolling hills covered with vineyards, she could almost be in Tuscany.

Jennifer tossed a coin. 'Okay, heads for the RSL, tails for the pub.' She peered down at her hand. 'It's the pub then. Come on, I'm starving.' She hooked Sofie with one arm and Claudia with the other, with them doing a little skip-step to match her pace as they headed for the hotel.

The gentle twang of country tunes drifted from inside. The glass panels in the double doors announced they were about to enter the 'Blue Sapphire Dining Room', with ornate scrollwork etched into the glass.

Together, Sofie and Claudia pushed open the heavy doors, with Jennifer following behind.

Familiar and delicious aromas of herbs, garlic, and char-grilled meat hit her nose, and her stomach started to rumble. They moved into a rustic timber dining room, where they were greeted with soft lighting and large candles burning on every table. The battered timber tables looked as if they'd seen a few steel-capped boots, belt buckles, and various other sharp objects, perhaps pocketknives. Clive had carved a love note to Betty: Clive loves Betty, Jan 1962. How sweet.

But something else, far more important, caught Jennifer's eye. The man had his back to her, but she knew instantly who he was. Calum sat with a group of men and women. Jennifer's heart did a little flip, her knees turned to jelly, and her appetite disappeared.

Sofie nudged her out of her daze.

Knees, stomach, body—hello! Jennifer told herself to get a grip; this was just plain silly.

Sofie nudged her again. She leaned in close to Jennifer and whispered, 'He's perfect.'

Jennifer's mouth went dry. She turned to Sofie and whispered in her ear, 'Shut up, Sofe, you're not helping.' Then, looking straight ahead with purpose, Jennifer walked casually— without bumping into furniture—across what felt like a football field filled with a sea of people. The local pub hummed with life;

the air thick with laughter and chatter. Clinking glasses, plates, and cutlery added to the noise. Claudia stood at the far end, choosing a meal from the chalkboard menu behind the salad bar, her figure glowing as a landmark they headed towards through the tables, chairs, and waiters delivering mouthwatering food.

A short, bald, clean-shaven cook, wearing an apron over his shorts, a T-shirt stretched across bodybuilder muscles, and crocodile-skin boots, came out through a set of swinging saloon doors and waited as they studied the menu.

'I'll have grilled fish, chips, salad and orange juice, thanks,' Claudia said.

'Charred shark, woodies and OJ,' he called out over his shoulder.

'I'll have a small prime steak and roast vegetables,' Sofie added.

'Prime moo and char veg,' he called again.

Jennifer sighed. 'I'll have a salad. Or soup—got any soup?'

The cook's heavy brows knit together in a frown; with an insane look in his eyes, he crossed his muscular arms and stared at Jennifer.

'For God's sake, Jen,' Sofie sounded impatient. 'You were hungry a moment ago.'

'Oh, all right.' Jennifer rolled her eyes. 'I'll have the prime moo and char greens, but make it small. Please don't give me half a cow. And could we have two glasses of your house red? Thank you.'

They sat in a quiet corner and discussed their legacy, while Jennifer did her best to focus on what Sofie was saying and ignore Calum's handsome back. He was leaning on the table, his white T-shirt stretched tight across his muscles.

Calum moved as if to get up, and Jennifer sighed with relief when he turned around to grab the serviettes. Mesmerised by his easy-going manner, Jennifer lost all focus.

'Jen—Jen!' Sofie prompted.

'Hmm?'

'As Mr Spaulding said, all Uncle Bob's businesses are running smoothly.' Sofie stopped talking when the waiter placed the food and wine in front of them. She took a sip from her glass. 'We need to figure out what to do with the shop and Uncle Bob's home soonish. And we also need to go through his personal belongings.'

'We've got two options,' Jennifer said with a mouthful of roast pumpkin. 'Sell or lease.'

'There's a third,' Sofie's eyes sparkled, her voice enthusiastic. 'We can run the pharmacy ourselves, you know, turn it into something great.'

Jennifer choked. She coughed into her serviette until her eyes watered and her face went red. Once her breathing was back under control, she managed to squeak, 'You can. I've got plans in London, remember? I'm about to sign a lease.'

Out of the corner of her eye, Jennifer saw Calum pivot on the bench seat, swing his long legs over, and head their way. A young redhead in a green smock approached him.

Smock! Was this the pregnant girl? It sure as hell looked like it. She was making a very public statement with her hand on his arm. It was better than an advert in the local paper.

Calum looked at her hand. Without a smile, he slowly raised his eyes to meet hers. She pouted and let her hand drop to her side. Jennifer couldn't make out what they were saying, but if their expressions were anything to go by, neither was happy. The redhead looked annoyed as she flounced off, but Jennifer didn't care, nope, not a bit. So what if they'd shared a hot, to-die-for kiss that didn't mean she was emotionally involved. Certainly not.

'I doubt whether you need to work anymore,' Sofie prattled on. 'And remember how, after we picked you up at the airport, you raved about Sydney Harbour, the bridge, and sailboats on the water. The space we had, all the green trees, and the azure, blue sky. Jen? Jen!'

Jennifer snapped out of her 'Calum daze' and managed to recall a few fragments of her sister's rambling. 'I enjoy working and London's where I do it best.' Sudden doubts about London gave her an uneasy feeling that constricted her chest, but she ignored it and pressed on. 'I've made it my home.' Jennifer paused as images of England flickered through her mind, but none of them were of a bright sunny day.

There must have been sun in London, but having left in the dead of winter, all she could remember were grey skies, grey buildings, bare grey trees, and grey streets. Grey people, including Dobry, who had stolen hundreds of pounds from her. *Oh fuck!*

'Why that funny look?' Sofie asked, squinty-eyed. 'I bet you're thinking about London and how drab it is.'

Her sister was uncanny sometimes.

'Definitely not,' Jennifer said quietly, brushing off any suggestion that she wasn't happy. 'Now, if you're both finished, I need an early night.' She started to sidle off the bench seat.

'Going already?' Calum held out his hand to Jennifer. Ignoring it would have been rude. His firm grip—the kind only a bloke who works with his hands would have—made her breath catch in her throat. Of course, it didn't help that she immediately imagined those hands running through her hair again and, with a bit of luck, all over her naked body. She tried to rein in her wayward thoughts, but it wasn't easy. This classic Aussie bloke, sporting a wicked grin, could fix anything with a pair of pliers and a bit of fencing wire. He would protect his woman and his family at any cost—and succeed.

'Hi Calum, where did you spring from?' Oh, very cool, Jennifer. She wondered how she'd managed to pull it off—or had she? She tugged her hand free and folded her arms.

Sofie did a dramatic eye roll behind Calum. Claudia let her chin drop, and her eyes widened in a what-a-great-big-fat-lie expression.

'I was with the wine festival committee,' Calum answered. 'It's our first meeting of the year. Can I buy you all a glass of wine or a coffee?'

'No thanks,' Sofie said cheerily as she slid off the bench. 'We're just heading off. But you're welcome to stay, Jen; we'll catch you in the morning.'

'No coffee for me either…' Jennifer glared at her sister, so annoyed she could hardly get her words out.

Sofie turned on her art teacher voice. 'Jen, sit. Stay. Relax. Have a brandy, they say it's medicinal.' She added a quirky smile that said, I know what you're getting later, then hooked Claudia's arm in hers and moved towards the door. 'And if Bret rings again—' she began over her shoulder.

'Unless they've caught up with him and cut an ear off, or he's dying, I won't ring you,' Jennifer promised. 'Maybe I'll turn my phone off before I go to sleep.'

'Ooh,' Sofie cringed. 'Maybe that's taking it a bit too far.' Without looking back, she waved as they hurried out the door.

'You heard from your brother?' Calum asked.

Jennifer's reserve started to crack. Damn, bloody damn, talk about a screwed-up family. Would Calum judge her for her brother's stupid choices? Wait a minute; she's not supposed to care. But his warm sincerity and gentle gaze were impossible to ignore.

'There's nothing else. You know it all,' Jennifer told him.

'I still think you should tell Brock.'

'What would I say? A couple of rough thugs had my brother, but the latest news is, he's heading to Darwin without them.'

'I see your point.' Calum gave her hand a gentle squeeze.

'He's not a bad kid brother. Sofie and I had Gran to give us time and love. She taught me how to cook, and Sofie how to garden and teach. But Gran died before she had a chance to show Bret anything, especially how much she would have valued and loved him. Our parents were only ever interested in money and image, and that's what Bret has to overcome. And if I didn't keep warning Sofie not to, she'd give him all her energy and have nothing left for herself or Claudia.' Jennifer downed the rest of her wine.

'He sounds like a survivor,' Calum said kindly. 'He'll either keep doing what he's doing, or with help—not necessarily yours—make better choices.'

'That's so fatalistic,' Jennifer said, running her fingers through her curls.

'What else have you got? You can't keep beating yourself up over something you have no control over.'

'No, but try and stop me, it's in the genes.'

Calum chuckled. 'Given half the chance, hmm, never mind…' he left his statement hanging.

Jennifer couldn't help but giggle. 'You seem to have a solid background; I've met your grandmother and your younger sister. Where are your parents?'

They're on their second honeymoon in Paris. They've never been anywhere, and when Michelle proved to be a responsible teenager, they took off before they lost their nerve. They're happily touring Europe in a motorhome, having the best time of their lives.

His warm, smiling eyes met hers, revealing a depth she'd never experienced before. Jennifer's heart melted, and her breath caught. Not wanting to face her emotions, his inviting gaze stirred within her; she pulled herself together and looked away. Besides, the man must feel confused, and who could blame him, the chaos in her family was enough to baffle anyone.

Jennifer rubbed her face, but it didn't help sort out her problems.

Leaning in close, Calum murmured tenderly, 'Come on, you're tired, I'll take you home.'

'Yeah, thanks…home sounds good.' *Oops*. Home was in London.

*   *   *

Calum parked his Range Rover outside the old pharmacy. After getting out, he rounded the bonnet and opened the door for Jennifer.

'Thank you,' she smiled up at him. 'I thought opening doors for women was a lost art.'

'You have met my grandmother?' The beginnings of a smile tipped the corners of his mouth.

'I get your point.' Jennifer pulled the key from her back pocket. 'Thanks for driving me home,' she said, facing the door. 'I'd ask you in, but…'

His broad hands gently squeezed her shoulders. Calum turned her to face him.

Oh my, he's going to do it again, isn't he? Her heart thudded. The hot, intense, slightly mystified look he gave her, as if she'd been missing all his life, and now here she was. He drew her in closer until they were almost touching, and his eyes locked with hers. Then she felt the warmth of his strong hands slowly caressing all the way up her neck to cup her face.

Kiss me quick before I melt.

Calum lowered his head, his lips a feather-light touch on her mouth as he whispered, 'I'm going to kiss you again, Jennifer. Any objections, take it up with me tomorrow…over breakfast.'

His deep voice resonated straight through her. Oh! Her body's immediate reaction caught her off guard. Then, achingly slowly, his mouth covered hers, firm and assured. Jennifer's long sigh turned into a sensuous moan. Calum responded with a hungry growl from deep within his chest. His warm mouth, tasting of wine, eagerly explored and teased hers. His hands slid down around her back, and arms wrapped firmly around her, Calum pulled her in close against his rugged body.

'Oh my!' she moaned softly as she pressed against him.

Damn it, she wanted to feel more of him. But with the front door key in one hand and purse in the other, there wasn't much she could do. She longed to feel him. 'Hang on a min—' she mumbled against his lips.

He kissed his way to her ear and gently sucked on the lobe, then nibbled her neck while taking the key and purse from her hands. Like magic, they disappeared behind his back.

The smooth way he helped her was like poetry in motion.

She was free to explore, and all her plans, not to invest her emotions and get involved, evaporated.

Streetlights caught his hooded, dark eyes as he searched her face. Mesmerised by his open, raw emotions meant for her alone, sent a bone-melting flush through her body.

Don't stop. Don't stop. She unconsciously licked her lips.

Calum's gaze zeroed in on her tongue, a teasing smile playing at the corners of his mouth. 'That was unfair,' his tone deep, longing. Then his mouth found hers again, and the world around her slipped away.

She slid her hands up his back, feeling the valleys and ridges of his strong muscles beneath her fingertips. He guided her into the dark alcove, away from the streetlights. Oh my, what was happening to her legs? The intense sensation in her stomach flooded her limbs. He pressed her against the door. His body hummed with power; best of all, he fit perfectly against her.

He felt like a dream come true.

A car horn blared, and a bloke yelled, 'Get a room!'

Jennifer jumped, but somehow Calum held her head protectively against his chest and covered her with his body. No one would have been able to see her. She heard the jangle of keys, and a second later, the door swung open. Mouth on hers, feet apart, Calum lifted her, shuffled forward, and kicked the door shut behind them.

Body trembling with need, Jennifer had never met anyone as sexy as Calum. Craving him, she deepened their kiss.

'I want you…I need you,' he whispered against her mouth, '…be with you, feel you all around me. Say it now, you don't want this? I'll stop. I'll go home and have a cold shower.'

'Stop?' Jennifer squeaked, her body tense at the very thought that he might. Alarmed, she cleared her throat, clinging to him, then whispered urgently, 'There's no stopping. No-no.'

He pressed her against the nearest wall as Jennifer kicked off her pants. Then, hands trembling, she tugged at his T-shirt and unbuttoned his jeans. Before his jeans hit the floor, he pulled out a foil packet from his pocket. He slipped on the protection, then wrapped her up with strong hands, holding her tightly against him. His mouth came down on hers, possessive, hungry, and a massive turn on. Her legs went around his hips and her arms around his neck.

'You're here,' he whispered, amazed, as if she were a treasured gift.

While kissing his neck, she pulled back and murmured, 'Calum, stop teasing.'

He gave her more, and arching her back, she cried out, 'Oh, yes.' Digging her fingers into his shoulders, Jennifer's body trembled with each pulse that surged through her, softly moaning her pleasure with every outward breath.

Calum locked eyes with hers and, in a breathy whisper, said, 'Jen, I'll never be the same again.' He nuzzled her neck, holding and squeezing her to him as if she were his lifeline. 'You okay?' he asked tenderly.

Jennifer rested her forehead on his shoulder. 'And I've never felt better.' And that wasn't a lie; she tingled with satisfaction and longed for more of the same, more of Calum.

He lifted his face from her neck and, with one hand, supported her while the other slowly caressed her hip, waist, breast, up to her shoulder and neck. His fingers swept into her hair, bunching it at her crown. He gently tilted her head back and kissed her deeply. Jennifer absorbed everything Calum offered—his passionate attention was entirely devoted to her needs. She had never met anyone like him; he was an extraordinary man.

When he paused, Jennifer whispered, 'Wow.'

His beautiful eyes searched hers, his mouth curved into his unique, quirky grin, reserved just for her. 'Yeah, there it is,' he murmured, his hand moving from her hair to cup her jaw, thumb gently sliding over her lips.

She wanted to ask what he was referring to, although she had a pretty good idea it was because he'd experienced the unrestrained, unshackled Jennifer.

'Just to clarify,' Jennifer began, 'I haven't been with anyone for over a year. I've lived a nun's life in my own homemade cloister.'

His face lit up, then he chuckled, 'I'm a very lucky bloke, then.'

'Most definitely. I reserved my wild side just for you—only you. The first day I was here, you remembered, saying you'd seen photos Uncle Bob was so proud to share. Visiting him could only happen once Sofie and I had our licence, because our mother couldn't hold us back, though she did try. So, together, we drove up to visit Uncle Bob. He was a breath of fresh air for us. Those days are gone now, our champion…' A sob threatened, and words caught in her throat.

Calum nodded, and his face showed he remembered everything and understood.

He moved his hand down to hook his arm around her back, and with his free hand, held her close as silent tears streamed down her face. They stood wrapped in each other's embrace until Jennifer stopped and wiped her tears away.

'Sorry, I'm a softie for Uncle Bob.'

'Don't be sorry, he was one of the best. The whole town thought so.'

Jennifer let out a strained squeak as he lifted her over his shoulder. He pulled his jeans up and squatted a few times to gather discarded clothes, then headed for the stairs and went up two at a time.

Laughing through her tears, Jennifer pressed her hands to his back and pushed up to ease the pressure on her stomach and catch her breath. She managed to reach his ear with her mouth, licking around the edge and grazing it with her teeth. She sucked the lobe; it popped out of her mouth as he carefully set her down in the pink bedroom.

Calum grabbed the back of his T-shirt and pulled it over his head, then stripped off.

Jennifer watched as his intense gaze slowly scanned her body.

'Fuck, you're beautiful.' He stepped in, wrapped his arms around her, and rested his forehead against hers. With a determined look in his eyes, he whispered, 'I'm staying the night.'

'Why?'

'Thugs.'

She let out a throaty laugh. 'That'll do it,' she murmured, enjoying the feel of his skin under her hands.

*   *   *

Jennifer awoke to the sound of her phone drumming on the old timber floor. Calum's heavy arm felt comfortable wrapped around her waist; her bottom, tucked into his groin. Nice. She didn't want to move, but to avoid waking him, she carefully wrapped her finger and thumb around his wrist and started to lift his arm. He gave a low grumble and tightened his hold.

'Sorry,' she whispered. 'Want to get to my phone and use the bathroom.' He gave her a squeeze, and like a gentle caress, he slid his arm off her waist and let her go. Jennifer swung her legs over the side of the bed, grabbed her cargo pants, and picked up her phone. As soon as she had it in her hands, it stopped ringing. She headed for the bathroom, checked her missed calls, but didn't recognise the number. Just in case it was Bret, she called back.

'Well, if it isn't the sister.'

'Shit!' she hissed.

'Don't hang up, bitch. Your brother won't get very far; you hear from him, tell him we're comin' for you and the money.'

Jennifer's throat tightened, and she struggled to breathe, but it sounded just like air squeezing past the neck of a balloon. Muttering curses, she jabbed the end call button several times and sensed a presence behind her. She swung around, catching her pale and terrified face in the mirror. It was hard to speak; her mouth was so dry.

Calum pulled her into his arms and held her close. 'Talk to me,' he said, his tone gentle yet firm and impossible to ignore.

'Thugs,' she dug her fingers into his back. 'They're coming for me.'

He eased his hold and steadfastly held her gaze. 'Talk to Brock.'

'I can't. I don't want anyone to be hassled by our problems.'

'What are you saying?' Frowning, Calum leaned back and added, 'Brock is there for you, and the town, that's his job.'

'No, no. We have to go. Save everyone from having to deal with city gangsters coming to Tumble Creek. I don't know how nasty these goons are, and I don't want them here. It's bloody scary.' She pushed out of his hold and turned, but Calum hooked an arm around her waist and tucked her back into his body.

'We're not a bunch of country bumpkins who can't handle a couple of dickheads. They don't know you're here.' His voice rumbled deep, caring, understanding, giving. 'The only way they'd find this town is if they followed Bret, and they don't know where he is; otherwise, they wouldn't be hassling you.' He kissed the back of her neck, slowly moving around to the side and up to her ear. 'I hope with everything I have that what we had last night wasn't a one-off.' His hands dipped past her ribs down to her belly, where, palm flat, he made lazy circles on her skin. God, his touch felt so good; she sank back into him.

Then out of nowhere, she was hit by a distressing thought. *Belly! A pregnant woman's belly!* Jennifer tried to ignore his caresses. Damn it, she shouldn't have lost herself last night and shouldn't be doing this now. No-no-no. Pregnant woman! Not staying! She lived in London, where there were no thugs about to descend—London where her dream restaurant waited!

A heartbreaking groan escaped Jennifer's throat as she lunged out of Calum's arms. What was she thinking? This was a small town packed with gossip, rumours, thugs, and a pregnant woman with her belly pointed at Calum. Rash judgments and self-doubts overpowered her heart. She decided it was best to avoid causing embarrassment and to leave immediately.

'Jen, what the fuck?' he said, voice tense, eyes dark, questioning.

'I've got to go,' she gasped, then pointed her finger at him, saying, 'No—you've got to go!'

'Jen, I didn't mean to rush you, but this is bullshit. You were enjoying 'Us' just as much as I was.' Frowning, he shook his head and paused. In that brief moment, it seemed he reached an understanding. His expression softened. Jennifer braced herself for his gentle attempt at coaxing, and she was right. Leaning forward, he softly told her what he believed to be true. 'I know that you know we have something great happening here. Something special and strong to explore together.'

'I'm in way over my head. I'm not a one-night stand kind of woman either, but I have…long-standing commitments in London. I'm sorry. I shouldn't have…' she pleaded.

Calum's hands dropped to his sides. Aside from his heavy breathing and eyes that revealed she'd hurt him deeply, he stood still, unable to hide his grief. Too bad, Jennifer tried to tell herself as her heart broke in two. She couldn't shake the thought of the pregnant woman and how she'd made a public claim on Calum. For goodness' sake, who else could she have been?

'There's a rumour around town that you made a girl pregnant. Are you the father?' She might as well have punched him in the stomach. The hurt and devastation on his face clenched her heart; the pain was almost too much to bear. She immediately regretted the words that shot out of her mouth. Staring at him, she wished the floor would swallow her up.

Understanding flashed in Calum's eyes. 'I see.' Hand on his chest, he gave her a brief nod and, slowly shaking his head, backed away. Deep sadness, and if possible, even deeper disappointment, marked his face. With one last devastated look, he turned, strode out of the bathroom, dressed, and without a backward glance, he was gone.

Trying to stifle the sobs tearing through her, Jennifer clamped a trembling hand over her mouth. What had she done? No one had ever made her feel such a profound mix of regret and sorrow. And she'd never seen a man tremble for her either. Her mind spun, and on the verge of collapse, she stumbled into the bedroom, fell onto the bed, and sobbed her heart out into her pillow.

She had to leave!

The only thing she was good at was being a chef. She had a business partner, a lease to sign, and a restaurant to open in glamorous London.

Chapter 11

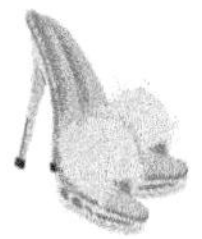

'I'm ready to go home,' Jennifer announced while having breakfast with her sister and niece. She didn't want to think about Calum's mouth, his hands, his lovemaking, and how it had made her lose her sanity.

And she wasn't going to scare them with the thug phone call. Bret was still on the run, and all they had was Jennifer's phone number. She wasn't worried about herself—head chefs were far scarier, and she dealt with them every day. No, for once, she was going to protect her sister and niece as best she could. She was leaving, and this was just another reason. As soon as she was back in London, she'd ring the thugs and tell them to give her a bit more time to gather the cash they demanded.

'We're not ready,' Sofie stated flatly.

'Mum!' Claudia wailed.

Sofie chased a cornflake around her bowl. 'It's school holidays. What's the hurry?'

'You know what this is, Aunt Jen? Mum met this bloke, a cop, who looks like Arni Swartse-whatever after she ran into a pole, and now they're making goo-goo eyes at each other.'

'*Ran into* what pole?' Jennifer raised her eyebrows. 'You don't look hurt—any bruising?'

'His name is Brock. We're both fine,' Sofie reassured her. 'I happened to nudge a pole, that's all. My brain curdled after Muggins here told me that she and Skids were in love.'

Jennifer turned to look at her niece. 'That'd do it.'

'Don't you start, Aunt Jen.'

Jennifer raised both hands and shook her head. 'I think it's time we all left.'

'And what about Bret?' Sofie asked, her voice shaky.

'What can any of us do? He's on the road to Darwin,' she hoped to God he was. 'I refuse to put my life on hold for him, and neither should you. He has my phone number, and probably yours, which means, so do they. Better get a new number. If he or they ring me, I'll be safe in London… okay?' And she'd deal with them herself.

'He's never had Claudia's and he doesn't have mine,' Sofie pointed out, looking a bit sheepish.

'Yeah,' Claudia said, 'A brat of a kid threw Mum's into the loo at school. No one's going to fish it out and use it after that.'

'His punishment was to buy me a new one. Trouble is, it came with a new number, and I haven't had the chance to pass it on to Bret.'

'You're safe then,' Jennifer sighed, feeling relieved, sort of. 'I've got to get back; probate will take a while, and life goes on. Bills have to be paid—that's just how it is.'

'Uncle Bob gave us money to get us by until…' Sofie shrugged, hopefully.

'Yes, and it will help get the shop's rewiring started. It's a massive hazard—huge,' Jennifer flung her arms out. 'To stop the whole street from going up in flames, it needs doing straight away. Calum's the obvious choice; he knows the building well. And I'm sure he can recommend a good plumber. Give Calum the keys; I trust him to do the right thing.' Jennifer's heart flipped. A big word, trust. Then why was she running? Because she had commitments—a restaurant that was set to be the go-to spot for the well-heeled to dine in London. It had been her dream for the past ten years.

'And who's going to supervise the work?' Sofie asked.

Jennifer rubbed the back of her neck. She was letting Sofie down by leaving. 'Calum will be there; I'm sure he's up to it. I'm sorry to rush off like this, Sofe, but I'd like a couple of days to recover from the flight. I don't want to be throwing knives around when I'm jetlagged. And probate will give us time to decide what we want to do.'

'What about the wine in the cellar?' Sofie asked.

'Get ready, Aunt Jen,' Claudia said, looking up from texting on her mother's phone. 'Mum's going to tell you again she wants to do something with the shop.'

'Sofie? What were you thinking—a bottle shop? A good quality one, of course.'

Sofie shook her head. 'I don't think that'll work; the locals will keep getting their wine at the pub. I haven't figured it out yet, but my brain's grabbed a few ideas and won't let go.'

'Sofie, if there's anything you want to create with the shop, go right ahead and do it!'

Claudia pulled a pissed-off face. 'Mum can. I'm staying near Manly and Skids.'

* * *

Gerek arrived in Canberra hot, tired, mean and cranky. After enduring the baking Ute for nearly two days, he was ready to make mincemeat of anyone who crossed his path. First, he would kiss his wifey and swap this old bone-crusher oven-on-wheels for his air-conditioned embassy sedan.

Every time he remembered his last chat with Antonin, frustration flared like heartburn. Wifey might have to wait. Better to blow off some steam and get friend sorted first. He parked in a reserved spot under the building that wasn't his and didn't care. Luckily for Gerek, an empty lift was waiting. He stepped in, jabbed at the fourth-floor button, and with growing irritation, waited for the doors to shut.

Exiting the lift, he glared at the luxurious surroundings; he'd been working in a shithole while everyone else enjoyed air-conditioned comfort. Gerek's anger spiked, and with a dismissive wave, he strode past the receptionist, hitching his pants up, and stomped down the hall. When he reached Antonin's office, his blonde secretary, Katya, surged out of her chair and stuck her hand to stop him from entering.

'You cannot go in,' she ordered. 'Go sit, wait in chair.'

'He has person in office?' Gerek asked, nostrils flared, mouth pulled in a hard line.

'*Nie (no)*. He asked not to be disturbed.'

'That is bullshiiit.' Gerek clipped Katya's hand away and ignored her protests. He was in no mood to be nice. He turned the brass handle, pushed the heavy timber door open, and slammed it shut on the advancing Katya.

Antonin looked up. 'Gerek.' He smiled, genuinely happy to see him. 'Have you good news?'

'No, I fry in bloody car, and drink bad, bloody wine, then fry in bloody car, watching bloody police and fry in bloody car. You okay, sit here in cool office while I fry on bloody pavement.'

Katya swung the door open, fire in her eyes. She held one hand to the bump on her head, while her other had a death grip on a long silver envelope opener. Just as she was about to speak, Antonin waved her off with a quick flick of his hand.

'Katya, bring cold drinks,' Antonin ordered.

Katya glared at Gerek, turned sharply on her black patent leather stilettos, and disappeared, closing the door firmly behind her.

Gerek moved closer to the gleaming desk with its silver-framed photographs and ornate desk set. He took a chair by the picture window overlooking the beautiful, lush garden.

'You are my only hope, Gerek,' Antonin pleaded.

'I have done everything to find these photos and USB sticks you talk about.' Sweat had dried on Gerek's face but left stains on his shirt, especially under his arms. He flexed his shoulders in an attempt to get some relief. 'There is nothing. Nothing, I tell you. He destroyed them before he kicked the bucket.'

Antonin gasped, eyes wide, tears gathering. He looked ready to say something but changed his mind, closed his mouth, and sucked on his bottom lip. Gerek wondered what the hell was going on. There was no doubt his friend was in some kind of pain. Alright, he conceded, emotional pain. It must have something to do with that woman. Veronica.

Antonin slumped back in his chair, which suddenly looked too big for him. He swung around to face the window. Gerek moved to the side of the desk and watched him silently. After a long pause, Antonin pulled a monogrammed handkerchief from his pocket, wiped his eyes, and blew his nose. Gerek had never seen such an emotional display over someone who had died and a missing woman, neither of whom were relatives.

'What is with you?' Gerek asked. He had to stop himself from grabbing his friend by the shoulders and shaking sense into him.

Antonin's fingers trembled as he meticulously folded his handkerchief, and that's when Gerek noticed the gold embroidered letter "V."

'This woman...' Gerek made a slow va-va-voom hand gesture, indicating Veronica must be every man's dream. 'I have not found anything of her. She vanished.'

Antonin stood and grabbed Gerek by the shirt. 'You and I, we know each other thirty years. You have not tried hard enough. If found out, my whole life will be in ruins. My wife and children will be persecuted for the rest of their lives. No job opportunities for them.'

'You don't have wife and children.'

'Not yet,' Antonin began, 'but one day there will be and, because of me, our wives will not talk to each other. I will lose job and so will you!'

The gravity of Antonin's dilemma sank in. Gerek draped his arm around his friend's shoulder and patted his back in a there-there fashion. 'How can affair do such damage—huh?'

Katya sashayed in with a tray and stopped in her tracks. Antonin shot her a fierce look.

'His dog died,' was all Gerek could think of.

'Nyet,' Katya said. 'Antonin has no dog.'

'No-no, his doc died.' Gerek slapped Antonin on the back a few times, his way of saying, get a grip, while he gave Katya the hard stare. 'You need to get English lesson.'

Katya put the tray on the desk, raised her chin, and eyed them both. 'You weirdos,' she muttered, and left.

'Let go of me,' Gerek ordered Antonin, who hastily uncurled his fingers from Gerek's shirt. 'Come sit, have cold drink. Pull self together. You look like fool. Not good image for diplomat in foreign country—not good in Warsaw,' he nodded, wiry eyebrows raised. 'You will have to tell me what is on disc and USB. What are these photos? Was Bob working on chemicals, bacteria—what?'

Antonin looked troubled but managed to say, 'Bob would never do such a thing. Never.'

*   *   *

Jennifer trudged up four flights of ancient timber stairs to her London flat, dragging a grocery bag filled with essentials to restock her fridge. She felt drained after a stressful night at her boss's restaurant, where every presentation had to be perfect and on time.

She sighed and stepped inside. Her home was bright, thanks to the south-facing dormer windows overlooking a park that, come spring, would be lush and green. Right now, though, she wondered if she'd ever come to terms with the gloomy winter grey. Jennifer shut the old door with a sharp thump of her hips. She ambled to the tiny kitchen. Every wall lined with cupboards, hooks, or shelves was designed for easy reach. A window above the deep granite sink let in some much-needed natural light. Dropping her shopping bags on the bench, Jennifer dug out her perishables and stored them in the fridge. Moving back into her living room, Jennifer went through the familiar ritual of shedding heavy winter clothes layer by layer.

She slipped on a pair of thick socks to warm her cold feet, grabbed a few tissues, and blew her nose. The cold air always made her nose turn pink and drip. 'Here I am,' she sniffed, 'on my own, working long hours and too tired to enjoy life unless I'm on holidays, when I'm alone again,' she told the walls.

Jennifer grabbed her phone, turned it on, and listened to Calum. 'G'day Jen. I wished you'd ring. Just ring, say hi. Tell me you're okay.' Tears burned. She pressed her lips together, forcing the emotions back, but her chin crinkled and the lump in her throat thickened. She should delete all his messages and texts, but she just couldn't bring herself to cut that last link. She took a few deep breaths and turned her attention to some of her travel photos of Paris, Venice, and Rome. A weak smile tugged at the corners of her mouth. Next time she would head for Greece and Athens.

Her flat was a real find. For a single person. The four walls were barely four metres apart, and lately they seemed to be closing in on her. Hoping to stop that feeling with a distraction, she threw her arms in the air and, standing on tiptoes, stretched to get the kinks out of her body. Her fingertips brushed a beam. So what if the place was small? It had never bothered her before. So what if it only took three strides to cross the room, they were big strides. She was on her feet all night, and it was a lovely thing to come home to her cosy flat, where she didn't have to move far to reach anything.

But none of it helped. Long minutes passed as Jennifer felt the fabric of her life unravel a little more. Suddenly, her pulse quickened and a horrible tightness in her chest squeezed the air from her lungs. She slumped onto her blue mini-sofa and broke out in a cold sweat. She pressed her hand against her chest and tried calming herself with logic.

'It's a panic attack, that's what it is. You'll be alright, just take it slow and steady, nice easy breaths.' She sat for a while, cleared her mind, and focused on relaxing.

She sat in quiet desperation, listening to the tic-tic-tic of the clock, almost in sync with her heartbeat now. It took time, but the moment passed. Relief made her feel weak. She was glad to be sitting down.

As normality returned, Jennifer grabbed her stuffed hippo cushion and hugged it to her chest. 'What's happening to me?' She felt her forehead: it was cool but clammy. No fever. This could *not* be happening, to Sofie, maybe, but not to Jennifer Dove, who could handle anything, even a crazy knife-waving Head Chef. She threw the hippo aside, headed for the kitchen, and poured herself a glass of cold water. It helped her dry throat, but it didn't change how she felt. Cut adrift. Aimless and empty.

She needed to take control and pursue her lifelong dream of owning her own restaurant.

* * *

On a hilltop lookout twenty kilometres south of Tumble Creek, Calum opened his truck's glove compartment and pulled out the small leather purse he'd never managed to return to Jennifer. Or was it that he didn't want to remember? He held it to his nose and took a deep breath. It still carried her distinctive scent that was out of this world and filled him with a longing he'd never felt before. It tore him apart that she hadn't stayed, hadn't given him a chance to tell her the truth. He had to stop beating himself up, dammit. The pain of wanting her so badly almost crushed his chest. God, he missed watching her quirky ways and the smile that lit up her face. It messed with his head so badly he'd nearly electrocuted himself—twice.

He thumped his fists against the steering wheel, stopped, and dropped his forehead onto his knuckles, muttering, 'Gotta switch the mains off or you'll die, you fuckwit-idiot'

Why didn't Jennifer answer his calls or at least text him back? Her accusation about him fathering a child cut him deep. On reflection, he realised that her doubts and his pride had led her to flee the country. Though at the time, he thought explaining shouldn't be necessary. Not one person who knew him would even consider the rumour to be true. Not one man pointed the finger at him and told him he should grow some, man up and admit he'd fucked up. But Jennifer hadn't known him since childhood, as most honest folk in town had. He should've taken what she'd said on the chin and explained, all of it.

Calum put the tiny purse back in the glove compartment, stepped out of his truck, and roared at the surrounding hills.

'Ahhhggggg! You're driving me nuts, woman!' Then he took the path along the ridge and jogged hard until he could barely breathe.

Chest heaving, he looked out over the stunning escarpment. It was time to organise a passport. And as soon as it arrived, nothing was going to stop him from heading off to London. Nothing, damn it!

*   *   *

Jennifer lay under a bulky feather quilt, staring at the ceiling, hoping it wouldn't drop on her head. A mindless, clog-wearing idiot in the flat above didn't understand the meaning of quiet. She closed her eyes and willed herself to sleep. It didn't work. Frustrated, she turned from side to side. She pummelled the pillow, stuffed earbuds in her ears, and thumped her CD player until her favourite soothing music clicked on, hoping it would lull her to sleep.

During the early hours of the morning, she dreamt of being with Sofie and Claudia, sharing jokes and laughing in the Tumble Creek pub. Calum sat beside her. She could almost feel his warmth and the heaviness of his arm around her shoulder. Then her dream jumped to when he installed the smoke alarms. It jumped again to the quirky electricity in her uncle's home, to the toaster on fire, the hairdryer on fire. With each jump, her dream darkened and became more worrying, until she was outside watching the building burn. She was yelling at a fireman who looked just like Bruce, but he wasn't helpful at all. When she begged him to please put the flames out, he shook his head and said it was too late, it was all too late. Jennifer thrashed under the quilt, her breathing heavy. Adrenaline surged through her, and her heart pounded. She woke with a start, hot and sweaty, the horror of her nightmare still fresh. She had ignored the wiring in her uncle's heritage-listed home, and now the flames threatened nearby buildings. She clutched the quilt under her chin. 'Holy crap!' Cold air seeped into the flat through her Betty Boop T-shirt. In the dim light, she looked at her bedside clock. Should she ring? Who would she call — the Tumble Creek police? What could she say? 'Oh hi, Brock, I was having a nightmare and wondered if there've been any fires lately.' Sofie said she would check on the wiring, so maybe she didn't need to worry.

By late morning, Jennifer couldn't take it anymore. Not only did she feel shattered, but the overwhelming sense of loneliness was worsening. She was so frustrated by her own inability to make something of her life that she decided to head out. A bit of retail therapy would do her a world of good. She began her wrapping ritual, starting with her boots, winter coat, beanie, and scarf. Rugged up, she was ready for the great outdoors of London's winter.

She opened the door and…

Chapter 12

'Hello, darlingk,' Dobry's smarmy voice purred. Arms outstretched, he stepped over the threshold, forcing her back into her flat. Sleet, sprinkled over his Polish fur hat, was already starting to melt.

'Hold it right there! I told you it was over and I meant it. I'm not in the mood for your Machiavellian ways.' To make her point clear, Jennifer struck Dobry squarely on the chest with both hands. She thumped him again, harder. Caught off guard, he teetered. A stunned expression flickered across his granite-like features. How quickly he recovered. The seductive look returned in a blink, and she immediately thought he'd missed his calling. He should've been an actor.

Jennifer was now fully aware of his tricks; it was all a joke. How could this idiot have ever fooled her? Had she really been that desperate?

'I've missed you, darling,' he said, chin down, peering at Jennifer through his lashes. Cold grey eyes zeroed in on her, with just enough of a hangdog look to the seduction. In a flash, he shrugged off his coat and tossed it aside. In her crowded, tiny flat, his coat was bound to land on a piece of furniture. 'You have missed me too, I see.' He raised one eyebrow for effect.

'Huh?' Jennifer stepped back until her backside hit the mini-sofa.

'You're hot for me. You want me to talk dirty Polish,' his voice rumbled, dark and thick like molasses, sticky. 'We can have so much fun, Jennifer.'

Disbelief and a healthy bash of cringe became a storm inside her. How could she have let this gigolo into her life? Hang on, gigolos were more honest than this blatant lounge lizard. She'd mistaken charm for sincerity, and now the truth stung: he'd never cared for her. Only what she could give him. He moved closer, leaning over her. Jennifer's back arched, trying to move away. With a speed she hadn't seen before, he grabbed the end of her scarf and, with a couple of twists, pulled it off her face. His other hand yanked her beanie off; her hair crackled and stood up with static electricity. He moved in closer until Jennifer flipped over the back of the couch and fell, head and shoulders onto the seat, her legs in the air. In a flash, Dobry was around to the front of the couch, gathering her upper body in his arms.

'You want to play games, heh? I like games.' His hand slid under her neck, his face above hers reminding Jennifer of the cartoon character Pepé Le Pew. She snort-giggled. Dobry looked both confused and amused, but that didn't stop him. He was on a mission. He brought his face in closer and stroked her hair while murmuring his Polish grocery list, which Jennifer interpreted as: I want money, sex, food, freedom, and the key to your flat.

Jennifer shoved him aside and rolled off the sofa.

'Dobry, you're a liar and a cheat. Leave now, you really don't want to be around when I lose my shit!'

And then he dared to laugh.

'Oh really? Over the past couple of weeks, I've had a taste of genuine honesty, which just makes you look even more like a bloody arsehole.' Jennifer's sudden realisation that Calum was her ideal bloke hit her like a whack upside the head—*doof.*

'You-you're kicking me out into ze cold?' His incredulous, arrogant expression didn't surprise her. She knew that Dobry wouldn't give up his meal ticket easily.

'Yes. Again.' She slipped her index finger under the collar of his jacket. Handing it to him, Jennifer was momentarily transported to another place, another time, another jacket— Calum's.

What was she doing here? Sofie and Claudia wanted her home. Calum was in her thoughts day and night.

'Get out before you make me cry for all the time, energy, and trust I wasted on you!' she yelled at Dobry. 'You snivelling rat!'

'Ah, I see, you all confused,' Dobry smiled. 'I will stay and make you happy.'

'No, you won't.' Jennifer shoved him towards the door. 'Now go before I get nasty, because after that horror flight,' she shoved him again, 'on an old rickety plane.' Shove. 'Taking my hard-earned money.' Thump. 'I did promise myself that if I saw you again, I'd put out a warning on all my social media, about who and what you are.'

Dobry backed up as far as the open door, shot her a filthy look, and spat out, 'Fook you!' He cursed, stumbling backwards and hitting the railing. 'You crazy old woman!'

'*OLD!?* How can thirty-two be old? You *idiota!*' A little Polish came in handy. Jennifer slammed the door. Windowpanes rattled throughout her flat.

She shrugged off her winter gear and waited for half an hour, flicking through a magazine without paying attention to the glossy pages. Occasionally, she peered out her window at the pavement below to check that Dobry wasn't lurking about before she dared to step outside. This was a fine way to live, reluctant to leave your own home.

Home! She ran her fingers through her hair and massaged her scalp, hoping to get a grip on what she had to do and make a mental list.

Dressed in her winter coat, hat, scarf, gloves, and fleecy boots against the bitter cold, she trudged downstairs, poked her head outside, and scanned the street. No sign of Dobry. Relief washed through her like warm wine. She took the shortcut for a brisk walk through the park to the restaurant where she worked to confront her business partner, Phillip.

She told Phillip her circumstances had changed, and their partnership plans to open a restaurant were over; he'd need to find someone else. Maybe she shouldn't have said anything until he'd put the cleaver down. With an angry glare, he hacked through a large pumpkin as if he were chopping off her head. She apologised profusely. Phillip didn't say a word in response. He didn't need to; instead, he kept hammering the cleaver down until the pumpkin looked like baby food. She hurried out, with all her limbs and digits still attached.

Out on the street, the icy wind pushed against her back as she headed for Hyde Park. Squirrels darted from trees to the path and back again, scurrying for scraps in rubbish bins or leftovers from some kind person who fed the pigeons. Shrugging deeper into her coat, she crossed the bridge over the Serpentine and headed back. Unfortunately, facing into the wind, the biting cold felt like needles pricking her face and sliced right through to her core. She told herself a new coat would fix that.

She bought a couple of almond croissants at her favourite patisserie and headed home. With her head bowed low, she barely noticed other pedestrians as she hurried along the footpath, clutching her scarf tightly under her chin, while the bag with her croissants swung back and forth against her side.

She pushed her way into the small tiled foyer of her building. On a wall opposite the stairs were ten gleaming brass letterboxes. Hers had a thick, brown paper parcel shoved into it. Jennifer pulled it out and gathered the rest of her mail.

She juggled her parcels upstairs and dug deep into her coat pocket for her keys. They weren't there. 'Crap!' she muttered, searching all her pockets and her purse, but no keys. Something silvery caught her eye—her key sat in the lock. She hadn't done that. Her key ring was always in her coat pocket; all she needed to do was pull the door shut to lock it.

Not knowing what to expect, Jennifer cautiously opened her door. She peered inside and immediately felt icy fear crawl over her skin. She stood staring at the carnage, paralysed with shock. The contents of her drawers and cupboards were scattered all over the living room. Carefully moving through her flat, she discovered someone had ransacked every room.

'I've been burgled,' came out in a dry whisper. Her knees buckled, and she sank onto the mini-sofa. Outraged, she clenched her fists, and her body shook. She was convinced Dobry had done this out of spite. 'The bastard,' she growled. He'd picked her pockets while trying to seduce her and let himself in.

A car horn blared down the street and snapped her back to her battered flat. She wondered whether to involve the police. What could she tell them—my ex-boyfriend threw a fit? She could say his visa was nearly expired. They'd look at her as if she was just being a bitch, and crap would start flying. No, she decided. Unless something really valuable was missing, she wouldn't bother the authorities.

With a heavy sigh, Jennifer pushed herself off the sofa and started gathering paperwork. Four hours later, she could almost smile again. The mess had given her the chance to sort through the accumulated stuff she'd been saving, and didn't know why.

She made a hot chocolate and sat at her coffee table with her croissant. Between sips and a tasty bite, she sorted through her mail. Hoping it was a treat and not something else to worry about, she left the long parcel covered in brown paper until last. Before opening it, she checked the back to see who had sent it, but there was no return address. She ripped it open.

Someone had sent her the Tumble Creek Gazette. A photo slipped from the pages onto her lap. Her breath caught, and her stomach clenched. 'Calum,' she whispered. His charming, wicked smile looked back at her. She wanted to laugh, cry, and scream all at once. She turned the photo over to see if he'd written anything. Flowery, feminine handwriting on the back said, 'He's missing you.' Jennifer dropped the photo on the coffee table and grabbed a handful of tissues to dab her eyes and blow her nose. Calum's smiling eyes looked at her from the photo on the table, and she wept a little louder. She turned his photo over, only to turn it back again. God, she missed him so much.

Through a blur of tears, she studied the Tumble Creek Gazette. Maybe there was something about Calum. She grabbed another tissue, dabbed her eyes, and tried to focus.

A full-colour photo of her slung over Bruce's shoulder as he carried her down the ladder graced the front page. Her mouth and eyes were wide open, and she had a death grip on his jacket. The headline read: Bob Feldman's Niece Follows In Her Uncle's Footsteps. Then, underneath in smaller print, a caption stated, In more ways than one.

Jennifer slumped back, laughing and crying at the same time.

Turning back to the Gazette, another photo caught her eye. A couple outside the church on their wedding day. She recognised the groom, fireman Bruce, and his heavily pregnant bride. It was the same woman who, at the Tumble Creek's Blue Sapphire Pub, had put her hand on Calum's arm. Was she carrying his baby but marrying Bruce, the fireman? No, that was absurd. Neither man would go for that.

Looking more closely, it was clear. Bruce and Kathleen's love for each other shone brightly.

Jennifer dried her eyes so she could read the official announcement.

Kathleen Gregory married Bruce Winter on Saturday.

The article also noted that many locals from Tumble Creek attended the wedding reception at Sapphire Winery, which was once owned by the late Bob Feldman.

Congratulations to the happy couple, who finally took a united stand and married.

Like Trudy said, all that talk about Calum being the baby's father was just a silly rumour. An image flashed into her thoughts: her last day in Tumble Creek; after an incredible night with a very hot Calum, the thugs called, and Calum held her. Needing to get away, she'd mentioned the paternity rumour. Deep down, she knew Calum would never do such a thing. What she did to him was ugly. His devastated expression broke her heart. It was too late now; she couldn't take back her accusation. And she would never be able to erase the sadness she'd seen in his eyes that day. But it did the trick; she got away. Got away from the worry those thugs would find her and the chaos that would cause in the small peaceful town. But Calum was right; the thugs would never find her in Tumble Creek unless they followed Bret. And even he wouldn't be stupid enough to lead them to his big sister. She bit into her croissant and munched away her sorrows, sipping her cocoa… thinking. A plan was forming. She straightened up and, without worrying about the time in Sydney, she picked up her phone.

Sofie answered, her voice croaky. 'Jen, is that you?'

'Sorry, did I wake you?'

'Sort of. I've got a virus and fell asleep watching telly. It's nearly nine-thirty in the morning. Are you okay? You sound terrible. Did you hear from Bret—is something wrong?'

'Gosh Sofe, take a breath. Bret's okay for now. He rang yesterday and said he's in Broome, but who really knows. I gave him your new number, just like you said.'

'Good, he'll ring soon then…maybe, the little shit.'

'Listen, Sofe, I've decided to come home.'

Deafening squeals blared through the phone. Jennifer quickly pulled it away from her ear.

'Bloody hell, Sofe!'

'Oh Jen, I'm so happy. *Whoohoo! Yesss!*'

'Who would have guessed,' Jennifer quipped.

'So, when will you be here?'

'I've got stuff to sort out, you know, my flat, my packing, and the scary one, my job.'

'See? I told you, your home is here. Have you thought about what you want to do when you get here?' Sofie asked cautiously. 'The rewiring is underway at the shop,' she prompted. 'Calum's been doing a great job, plus overseeing the plumber. He's locked the cellar until we decide what we want to do with the wine. But I think it should be put to good use and…'

As Sofie talked on, Jennifer tried to find a way to broach the subject of opening a restaurant. She hoped Sofie wouldn't object. After all, it was originally Sofie's idea to do something with the shop; she just didn't know what.

When Sofie paused to catch her breath, Jennifer jumped in. 'I was thinking of opening a restaurant.'

Silence.

'Sofe! Sofie!' But all Jennifer could hear were wailing sobs. 'For God's sake, Sofe, if you had your own plans, that's fine too. Did you want to open an art gallery?'

'No—no plans.' Sniff. 'Hang on a mo.' *Pthpthpthpth.*

'What the hell was that?' Jennifer held the phone away from her ear.

'I blew my nose.'

'Oh Christ! Don't do that without warning me, I thought you were choking or something.'

Sorry. Look, honestly, I don't know exactly what I want, except I want to move to Tumble Creek and live there for the rest of my life. I love the place. It feels like home. And now that you'll be there, I'm over the moon.

'But how will Claudia feel about this?'

'Claudia,' Sofie let out a long sigh. 'She's broken-hearted. It seems Skids is over his Goth phase and into cheerleaders.'

'Oh, poor kid, she'll be scarred for life.' Jennifer's heart ached for her.

'No. She's taken up a new hobby—voodoo and sticking pins in Ken Mattel.'

There was total silence as Jennifer tried to come to grips with her sweet niece's attraction to the darker side.

'Lighten up, Jen,' Sofie giggled. 'I'm kidding!'

'Oh.' Jennifer let go a breath she hadn't even realised she was holding. 'Don't do that to me, Sofe. Is Claudia all right?'

'Sure, she's buried her nose deep in her schoolbooks, determined that her life is entirely under her control and it's up to her to make the most of it. Hope it lasts.'

'I have a feeling it will.'

'Anyway, Claudia's been ranting about how much she hates Sydney. I know it's just a phase and that she wants to run away from all the crap that's been happening to her lately, but the interesting thing is, she's become friends with Calum's young sister, Michelle. They're Facetiming or texting every night after school. Michelle's a lovely girl. Not once did she ask Claudia why she was trying to be a Goth. I think my girl will be quite happy to make a move.'

Jennifer realised that Calum and Michelle were very alike, always laid-back and non-judgemental.

'Wow. I don't know what to say. I'm just so happy I'm speechless,' Sofie said. 'Tumble Creek's given us all a real sense of belonging. I think a restaurant is perfect; it's a fabulous idea. I'm so excited.'

'Sofe, how do you feel about getting involved in the planning and refurbishing? I imagine Calum will need a hand with style and, I don't know, all kinds of things?'

'I'd love to, but the courtyard's mine. Plans are already forming for alfresco dining. I'm getting butterflies just thinking about it. I can help on weekends and over the school holidays. Aside from that, I'm committed until the end of the school year. I can't leave my Year 12 students floundering with a new teacher. That wouldn't be fair.'

'No, of course not. Do me a favour: ask Calum if he'll oversee the renovations, especially the chef's kitchen.'

'Ask him yourself. Do it now, it's not too late.'

'I doubt whether he's talking to me.'

'What a load of crap,' Sofie said, sounding frustrated. 'He's so hot for you, he's sizzling. And you're just as bad…or good,' she giggled. 'You need his phone number?'

'No… he's been calling and texting; I just need to stop acting like a guilt-ridden muppet and ring.' She told Sofie about finding a copy of the Tumble Creek Gazette in her mailbox, along with the photo of Calum that fell out from between the pages. 'I know it wasn't you, not your handwriting. And it's not Calum's.'

'Ooh, that's heavy. Anyway, you need to sort it out with Calum directly about the renovations and shit. And you know what shit I'm talking about.'

'Okay, I will. I need to apologise. There was something else in the paper. Bruce and Kathleen got married. It's not Calum's baby; it's Bruce's.'

'Really?' Sofie said dryly. 'I told you so.'

'Thank you for reminding me what an idiot I've been,' Jennifer said, amused. 'I'd better go. I'll see you soon, sis.' She blew her sister a kiss.

'Can't wait!' Just before hanging up, Sofie said, 'Ring him—and for God's sake, for once in your life, don't doubt, don't hedge your bets, just be honest about yourself.'

*   *   *

Jennifer took a deep breath, but it didn't ease the flutter of nerves in her stomach. 'You're being ridiculous,' she told herself. 'For goodness' sake, just bloody do it.' Heart pounding, she stared at her phone, dialled Calum's number and waited, listening to the ringing tones.

'Calum's phone,' a young woman answered.

Jennifer's heart lurched. She hadn't anticipated that. 'S-sorry to intrude, I was after Calum.'

'Everyone's after Cal, just a sec,' she giggled. 'I'll pass him the phone.'

Ears straining, Jennifer tried to work out what the girl was doing. It sounded horribly like the rustle of sheets, then it sounded as if the girl had heaved herself out of bed. Was that a toilet flushing or a shower going? Oh God, she'd interrupted them. Jennifer tried to stop the images forming in her mind of Calum and this girl having hot, sweaty sex among a tangle of arms, legs and sheets.

NO! Just hang up—hang up now!

'Hello, Jen,' he said, voice husky. Yeah, definitely sleepy-husky. Doubt nudged her mind, and Jennifer lost the power of speech.

'Jen. Can't hear you, speak up.'

'Um, hi.' She mentally kicked herself. 'I didn't mean to interrupt anything or wake you.' *Oh, great start, Jen.* She slapped a hand to her forehead.

Deadly silence, except for the pulse pounding in her ear, her breathing short and loud in all the emptiness surrounding her.

Freaking out, she gripped her phone and waited.

Then his voice came through, rumbling softly, 'You didn't. It's ten in the morning,' he murmured. Then something shifted; thousands of miles away, she could feel the atmosphere change, could sense his smile. 'What did you think I was doing, lying around in bed, having a sleep-in?' After a pause, he continued. 'Not without you, Jen. Never without you.'

Shit! Oh-my-God! He just said he wanted me to sleep in with him. He did, I heard him. Her heart pounded so hard it hurt. She took a deep breath, filling her lungs, and hoped oxygen would head straight to her brain. 'Oh…crikey,' came out in a whisper.

'Yeah…' Calum murmured, his tone warm and inviting, making it clear he needed her with him.

'Um…' God, what could she say to that?

'Jen?' his deep voice rumbled, and it went straight to her heart, sending a trail of passion and longing from her chest to all the sensitive parts of her body.

Then a young impatient voice yelled, 'Gran wants to know do you want a coffee and a slice of pie before you go?'

She let herself fall face down into the hippo cushion. Thank God, she hadn't asked him who that was. She heard Calum call back to his sister, 'Sure.' Then his deep voice in her ear said, 'You finally decided to return my calls.'

'Um…I'm sorry, that was very rude of me, but…' Come on, Jennifer, be honest, tell him. 'I had stuff to sort out.' Damn and blast, that was lame.

'Stuff? Okay, doesn't matter; you called. It's good to hear your voice, Jen…' Calum trailed off.

Shit! Why couldn't she open up to him and be herself?

'It's good to hear yours as well…' She leant over her knees and held her forehead. Go too far now would just make it look like she called because she wanted him to oversee her refit at her uncle's shop. Not saying anything would be too harsh. 'Shit, I'm such a mess.' She just said that out loud, didn't she?

'Why don't you come out with…' he said, starting to sound a little impatient. 'Jen, take a deep breath and spit it out. The whole lot. Don't leave anything out.'

She did her best to keep her breathing steady and stay calm, but her words came out in a rush.

Okay, here goes. 'Calum, I'm coming back. I want to open a restaurant in my uncle's shop, and since you're already busy rewiring, I was wondering if you know someone who can project manage it for me?'

There was a long pause. Jennifer wondered if he was still there. Then she heard it—he'd covered his phone and growled, 'Fuck yes!'

He came back, though his voice sounded a bit shaky. He cleared his throat. 'Why don't you let me handle it?'

'I thought, with the farm and electrical work, you wouldn't have time.'

'I'd be happy to sort it out for you. I know enough local tradies who'll do a good job. Leave it with me. When do you plan on being back?'

'I'm not sure yet. There's a lot I need to organise. If we communicate via email, I can send you kitchen plans, paint colours, and furnishings. Would that be okay with you? And if you have any problems with deliveries or need to know something immediately, because the chef doesn't allow phones in the kitchen, you can always ring Sofie—she's great with style and colour.'

'Sure. I can send photos and run anything by you for approval. Don't see how it could be a problem. Got a pen?' They exchanged email addresses. 'Jen, you don't know how much I look forward to working with you,' he said with feeling. Or was he trying to seduce her over the phone with coffee and pie?

She was so on edge that the thought made her giggle.

'Something funny, Jen, hmmm?' his tone playful.

Hearing Calum's sense of fun made Jennifer burst into happy tears. 'I-I, it's great to hear your voice. I've missed you.'

'Um…well, that's good to know. I hate to be the only one,' he said quietly, but she caught the smile in his voice as it rippled through his words.

'I'll wait to hear from you. Bye, Calum. I can't wait to get back. I can't wait to see you and talk to you.'

Visibly shaken, Jennifer dropped her phone on the floor and, hand over her heart, took a moment to slow her breathing. He said he'd sleep in, but only with me. Well, she shouldn't have thought that, because it didn't help at all. She paced her tiny living room and focused on what she had to do to make this change happen—and quickly, for herself, Sofie and Claudia, for their future. And Bret, too, the little shit.

But, more importantly, with Calum.

*   *   *

Halfway through Europe's beautiful spring, Jennifer finally managed to leave London. Nerves fluttered in her stomach as the taxi took her from the small Tumble Creek airport into town. Lining the streets and scattered across the rolling hills, poplars, oaks, and maples blazed with autumn colours. Like beacons, they stood out sharply against the blue-green eucalypts. Neat rows of grapevines turned yellow and gold. All of it was a stunning sight that made her heart sing. The driver manoeuvred his cab down the lane to her late uncle's shop and stopped at the double roller door. Jennifer paid him, hopped out, and turned her face to the sun.

'Ah, heaven,' she whispered.

'Yeah, you Poms could do with a bit of sun,' the cabbie chuckled, pulling his cap down as he strode to the boot of his cab. He heaved her suitcases out and, grunting, hefted them over to the back fence of the old pharmacy shop, dropping them by the gate. Then he slid back behind the wheel. 'Be seein' ya,' he waved and took off. The taxi disappeared in a little cloud of dust and exhaust fumes.

Jennifer faced the gate that would lead to the start of her new life. Excitement and a good dose of: can I pull this off? caused havoc inside her. It's going to be great, she told herself. It's going to be great, she repeated, like a mantra, building a positive mindset. Without needing to park a car, Jennifer went straight for the back gate and, using her backside, pushed it open. Head down and arms straining, she hauled her luggage through into the yard, making sure she didn't veer off track and plough into a garden bed, but soon noticed there were no garden beds left to speak of.

She looked up. 'God Almighty!' A rubbish skip overflowing with broken wires, old pipes, horsehair plaster, and empty bags sat beside the fence. The entire backyard was a trampled mess of broken, unrecognisable scrap scattered everywhere. She'd need to get it cleared before Sofie came to work her magic and turn it into a garden.

Desperate to see how her restaurant plans had turned out, she heaved her suitcases all the way to the back door. A wheelbarrow would have been handy right now—or better still, a muscleman. There was little hope of that. She'd timed her arrival so any tradespeople would have left for the day. She had mixed feelings about Calum: she wanted him to be there, yet she also wanted time to prepare herself for when they saw each other again.

She dragged her suitcases to the bottom of the stairs leading up to the living quarters. The interior was spotless, with no grit, dirt, or dust anywhere. No wires or pipes. And the smell of fresh paint and fabrics made her smile.

Overjoyed and bursting with excitement at being able to call this amazing place hers, Sofie's and Claudia's, gave Jennifer a deep sense of satisfaction. This beautiful building, their home, was more than she could have ever imagined.

There was no sign of any workers… no Calum, so bursting with happiness, she let it all out, and with her arms in the air, Jennifer spun around, shouting, 'Yes-yes-yesss!'

Chapter 13

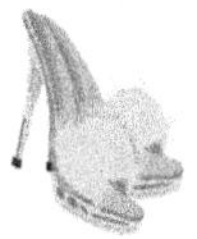

She's here, mate. She's here.

Calum gripped the railing at the top of the stairs; if he didn't, he'd race down, fling his arms around her, wrap her up tightly and hold on…for a long, long time.

From the moment Jennifer left Tumble Creek, Calum had planned to fly to London. It took forever to arrange his passport, but as soon as it arrived by registered mail, he'd bought tickets to London. Two days later, Jennifer called, and he was the happiest bloke in the country. He'd worked hard, sometimes late into the night, to finish the restaurant. He wanted it to be as close to perfect as possible when she arrived.

'G'day, Twinkles,' Calum murmured from the top of the stairs. He couldn't stop the grin that spread across his face or his body that trembled if he tried.

Jennifer screamed and spun around. She was standing in a pool of late afternoon sunlight coming through an upstairs window.

Man, she looked absolutely stunning. His body longed to hold her close, smell her skin, and bury his face in her wild hair. The things she did to him without even trying had to be illegal.

'Shit!' she called up, looking at him and slapped a hand over her heart. 'You scared me.'

'Wouldn't have mattered what I'd done, I would've scared you.' He paused, holding his breath. He had to savour this moment, had to let it sink in.

'Hi,' Jennifer said. 'I almost didn't recognise you without your overalls and covered in plaster dust. You scrub up well.'

Was she panting? He hadn't scared her that much. Nah, she was panting for him, or so he wanted to believe…had to believe, otherwise all this waiting was for nothing.

'Blame Michelle,' he shrugged. He'd have to increase his sister's pocket money.

Michelle had insisted he wear stonewashed jeans and a white shirt with the sleeves rolled up just below the elbow. He asked her, 'Why wear a shirt if you're going to do that?' But she mumbled something about strong forearms, saying, 'It's a woman's thing—just shut up and do it.' Then she kissed him on the cheek and said, 'Go get her, tiger.' Calum didn't care what he wore as long as it worked. 'Sounds like you approve,' he said, and kicked himself because he didn't sound confident, and normally he was.

'Approve? No, I mean yes, you look very…Oh, never mind. It's just that I wasn't expecting…'

'You seem a bit prickly?' *Damn…easy there, tiger.*

'I am not! I thought I'd timed it exactly so I wouldn't have to see…' She shook her head. 'Oh crap, I sound ungrateful, and I'm not, truly. Sofie told me how hard you've worked. It can't have been easy for you via FaceTime and emails.'

'Knowing it was for you made it the most rewarding job I've ever done.' Had he said the wrong thing? She looked stunned. Quickly, he headed down the stairs, his sneakers squeaking on the wooden treads. He stopped one tread above her, and without thinking, raised his hand to cup her face. His thumb slipped across her cheek, feeling the silkiness of her warm skin, as he studied the sparkle and deep emotions in her eyes. He leaned closer, searching for nervous anticipation and hope in her gaze. Jennifer didn't move, and Calum, worried, wondered if he'd got it wrong. She inclined her head, resting in his hand. Yes, she wanted him, and seeing that made him shake inside. He needed to get a grip, slow things down, or he'd rush, and neither would have time to savour the moment, make it special. He softened his gaze and, with superhuman effort, withdrew his hand; voice husky, he said, 'I'll take those,' and grabbed her suitcases.

'W-wait a sec, please show me what you've done…for me, Sofie and Claud.'

'Sure,' he said with a heavy sigh, hoping with every fibre in him that she liked the result. Quickly dropping the cases, they thudded to the floor. 'Hold my hand and close your eyes.'

Her soft palm rested comfortably in his rugged, calloused hand. Slowly, Jennifer closed her eyes. Without thinking, and heart thumping, Calum lifted her hand to his chest, longing to kiss each delicate eyelid.

'We're not moving,' Jennifer murmured.

'Sorry, you distracted me,' he said, chuckling, and led her down the hall. 'Okay, you can open them now.'

Jennifer gasped in awe. Calum grinned.

'Oh my God—fireplaces. Never in my wildest dreams. You never mentioned fireplaces.'

'We wanted to surprise you.'

Her hand slipped from his as she moved in to look at them more closely. 'Well, you certainly have. They're gorgeous.'

'When we pulled the plaster off the columns on either side of the shop, there they were: two original black marble fireplaces. Sofie chose the colours throughout the room. What do you think, look okay?'

'Colour changes when sent via email. But I knew there was nothing to worry about with Sofie choosing the palette. And I was right. The deep red looks stunning, and the matching velvet drapes are perfect.'

'We've made sure the shop and house upstairs have plenty of security. You'll never need it.' No, because his plans were to be here every night with Jennifer for the rest of his life. His body itched to make her his. 'Because the drapes are so high up, you've got a remote control that slides them back and forth. There's an intercom from upstairs to the restaurant's kitchen. And a list of all the gadgetry and how they work in Bob's office.'

Taking her time, Jennifer scanned the room. 'How did you get the mosaic floor to come up so beautifully?'

'Sofie and I had a restorer check the floor. The tiles are stone, and his advice was to polish off the grime and reseal them. That way, the floors would last another hundred years or more.'

'It's magnificent.' She wiped at her wet cheeks. 'You must have worked like a madman to get so much done.' She leaned in and kissed him on the cheek.

His hand moved to her waist, and he couldn't resist flexing his fingers. When she stepped back, he nearly followed.

She studied him, her eyes fixed on his, and they were greener than he'd ever seen. 'Thank you,' she whispered.

'You're welcome,' his voice rumbled deep with emotion, and there wasn't a damn thing he could do about it. 'Go explore.'

Calum leant back against Bob's refurbished curved glass and brass-framed display case. Enjoying the sway of Jennifer's hips as she rounded a table setting, her fingers sliding over chairs and down drapes, and her breasts that rose and fell as she marvelled at her new surroundings.

'This is the best thing that's ever happened to me. The photos Sofie sent of the tables and padded chairs didn't do them justice. It's all stunning and absolutely brilliant! I love it all and I can't wait to see the kitchen.'

'This way, and tell me if you need anything changed.' He held the swinging doors open for her.

'Wow, it's a chef's dream! It's my dream. The steampunk cappuccino machine is a brilliant choice,' she laughed softly. 'I can't wait to turn on the gas burners and create something. You'll be the first to enjoy a meal out of this, *your* kitchen.'

'You're on,' he said. 'And it's your kitchen now.' Arms crossed, he leaned back against the kitchen bench, finally able to unwind. 'I'll get the courtyard sorted before Sofie gets here.'

'She can't wait to start on the garden.' Jennifer ran her hands over the sparkling new appliances. She turned to face him, a tender look in her eyes.

Damn, he was eager to reach out, hold her, kiss her soft mouth, carry her upstairs, and make love to her on the bed covered in flowers, preferably naked as the day they were born. But he didn't dare, not yet. He shoved his hands in the back pocket of his jeans. After a long pause, she stepped closer. Her expression shifted from one moment to the next, grateful, happy, awestruck, and a few others he couldn't quite grasp.

'I'm so happy I decided to start a restaurant here. And you made it all so easy for me.'

'I'm glad to have been part of it,' he said. Jeez, is that all he could come up with? Tell her you couldn't eat for weeks. Tell her you went to the mountains to scream. Tell her your dick doesn't work anymore unless she's around. Tell her it's a package deal that you come with the kitchen. 'C'mon,' he managed to say. 'I'll take your bags up.'

Calum grabbed two cases, while Jennifer struggled with the smaller one, plus her handbag, the size of a small hippo.

'Same room?' he asked.

'Yes, please.'

He could feel Jennifer behind him. Her nearness sparked a warmth that spread through his chest. As long as it stayed there and didn't ignite a trail south, he'd be safe. He placed her suitcases at the end of the bed and briefly looked at the flowery quilt with longing.

'Are there any more bags outside?' He was out of breath, and it had nothing to do with the cases.

'No, that's it. The rest will arrive by crate on a container ship.'

'This is it, you're staying for good?'

'I've just spent thousands transforming this place; I intend to stay—forever.'

He nodded. 'Nice idea, and a bit longer than last time.' *Ouch! Fuck*. He could've kicked himself again.

'It's not just an idea.'

'Uh huh.' Calum studied her eyes. They remained steadfast.

'I'm staying,' she said emphatically.

He shoved his hands into the back pocket of his jeans. Otherwise, he might lose the bet with himself that he'd play it cool.

'I've seen countless city people come and go in this town. Few can hack it long-term; they miss the city and all it has to offer.' Calum moved closer, leaving only inches between them. The impulse to throw her onto the bed and kiss her senseless until they both got hot, naked, and sweaty was overwhelming.

Jennifer's wide green eyes spoke volumes; right now he didn't know what they were saying. It could be that his one-track mind assumed she wanted what he wanted. On the phone to her in London, he'd said that he'd never sleep in without her…never, but she hadn't shown enough of her feelings for him to go and throw himself at her. Calum leant in slightly, on the verge of kissing her. She gave a little gasp. The air between them hummed hot with promises.

He zeroed in on her mouth. She closed her eyes, or was that a slow blink? Mate, what are you doing? He hesitated and pulled back. Did he see disappointment? Last time he kissed her and made love to her, she'd left the country. Better slow down. Rushing Jen wouldn't help.

'Are you hungry?' he asked. Her wide-eyed look could have meant anything, but Calum decided it meant yes—safer that way. 'Thought as much.' He took her hand and led her to Bob's kitchen. 'Sit,' he said, pointing to a chair. He made coffee and brought out a plate of massive, wholemeal sandwiches from the fridge. The crusts were crunchy and nearly an inch thick.

'Good God, are those for me?'

He chuckled. 'It's okay, just eat as much as you want.'

'Did you make them yourself?'

'Yeah, straight after I crutched four hundred sheep.'

'Oh, lovely, a little extra flavour for that country taste,' she threw back dryly.

Calum winked and moved the plate closer to her. He poured steaming coffee into two large mugs and sat opposite Jennifer, who was squishing the sandwich down with her palm.

She turned to him with a look that said *Help me.* 'I can't get my mouth around it.'

Don't even go there, pal. 'Sure you can,' he said, and couldn't stop the grin.

Jennifer managed to bite off a chunk and chewed, closing her eyes. 'This is delicious,' she mumbled through a mouthful. 'The silverside is cooked to perfection, and pickle…Hmm!'

'Gran's homemade pickles. Don't ask me what's in it.'

'Do you think she'd give me her recipe?'

'As long as you didn't enter it into any of the local fairs, she probably would. If you're not too tired after this, I need to show you something else.'

'I'm fine. I had a lovely week's rest in Sydney with Sofie and Claudia. Got rid of all my jetlag.' She tilted her head. 'What do you want me to see?'

'It's hard to explain, easier if I show you.'

'It wouldn't have anything to do with the singing drunk, would it?'

' 'Fraid not…' he trailed off as a vague thought crossed his mind, something about Parrot Rock, but it disappeared in a flash. 'Hmm, strange.'

'What's strange?'

'I don't know, it's one of those things you can't quite get a handle on. Doesn't matter. If it's important, it'll come back to me.'

She washed her sandwich down with a gulp of coffee. Calum went back to the fridge and brought out two small bowls of lemon sorbet.

Handing her a spoon, he said, 'Gran insisted. She made so much of it yesterday that everyone she cares about is getting a helping.'

'Oh,' she breathed. Looking a bit stunned, she took a spoonful. 'Hmm…this is delicious, so refreshing. Your gran knows a thing or two. But then, most people of that era do…my gran could turn her hand to just about anything.'

She licked her lips, and Calum couldn't help but let out a throaty rumble. 'That good, huh?' he grinned as, sadly, Jennifer's tongue popped back into her mouth. 'Come on,' he took her spoon and set it on the table. 'You can lick the bowl out later. I want to show you what's been bothering me about your uncle's rooms.' He ushered Jennifer down the hall and into the pink bedroom. He could feel warmth as she stood beside him, staring at the roses and swirling vine wallpaper that even his grandmother might reject—maybe.

'Okay, here we are. What am I supposed to see?' Jennifer wrinkled her nose and squinted. 'Have to change that God-awful wallpaper…sorry Uncle Bob.'

'I know it's hard, but forget about the paper. There's something odd about this room and the bathroom. Come with me,' he said, leading her into the en-suite. 'See this corner here?' He pointed to the right of the door.

'Oh, good Lord!' Jennifer ignored him and, eyes wide, took in the luxurious new bathroom. 'The old claw-foot bath looks as good as new. My God, the shower.' She spread her arms wide and hugged the curved glass door. 'Six people could fit in here.'

'Not with you they won't.' He gave her a look. When he saw her slightly stunned expression, he couldn't help but smile. *Oh well,* he thought. 'I know, I know, that was a silly statement.'

'Um…yeah.' And she let go of the door.

'Okay, Jen. Hopefully one day soon, we'll get to know the shower.' Pink flushed her cheeks. Part of him felt good that he had this effect on her; another part told him he should stop making her feel uncomfortable, but man, she was making it bloody difficult. His eyes slowly drifted down to her open mouth.

'Um…Jen? I want you to focus now.'

'I am,' she blurted out. 'But you're not.'

One corner of his mouth twitched up. 'Okay.' He raised his hands. 'I promise to behave.'

'Oh, that's no fun, you've been digging so many potholes, I wondered how far you'd go.'

Calum started with a chuckle that gradually turned into a full-bellied laugh bouncing around the bathroom. Pulling himself together, he said, 'I love your humour, your fun.'

Shaking her head, Jennifer giggled, 'That's because you leave yourself wide open. You were trying to show me something?'

'Okay, I'm on it. See where this wall ends here?' Calum stepped back into the bedroom. 'It stops about here, at the left side of this wardrobe. By rights, it should connect with the hall, but obviously it doesn't.' He took her hand. Wanted to take hold of a lot more. Concentrate, he told himself. He guided her out to the hall and started banging on the wall with his fist, pointing out where the deep, hollow sound ended, about two metres along.

Jennifer gasped.

'You catch on quick,' he told her.

'That would mean—'

'Don't look so worried. Yes, it's a hidden room, but it could be as simple as a boxed-in stairwell. Whatever it is, I need to find out. If there's wiring in there, it'd be like the rest of the house,' he said, tapping the wall for emphasis. 'And there's no way of knowing if it's live.'

Calum pressed his fingers into his tight neck muscles, hoping to massage the tension out as he watched Jennifer work through the new problem.

* * *

Jennifer felt sick with anxiety. She couldn't find a way to access a hidden space the size of a large walk-in closet. She covered her mouth as dark thoughts flooded her mind. Some of the kindest people did the strangest things. Her mind told her, leave well enough alone and pretend this didn't exist. She and her sister had been kept in the dark about significant parts of their uncle's life, like his vineyards and wine collection, all very innocent, but to take such lengths to hide something from them and everyone else? What could it possibly be?

She felt Calum's strong hand warming the small of her back as he carefully guided her through the door back into the pink room. She moved to the edge of the bed, which gave her a reassuring buffer of about three metres. Standing with her arms folded, Jennifer eyed the enormous wardrobe with trepidation, feeling the weight of her family's secrets pressing down on her shoulders.

'Mother knew something.' Jennifer said quietly, knowing this to be true.

Did she make Uncle Bob feel so ashamed that he had to hide whatever it was? And what if it changed everything she knew and loved about her Uncle Bob?

'No one knows about this but you and me,' Calum assured her, giving her a gentle nudge. 'When Dwaine worked on the plumbing up here, he focused on the bathrooms and kitchen. I did all the wiring and found some of it goes off into this space somewhere here. The first time I walked into this bathroom, I thought it was odd.'

'Sofie and I weren't checking for wires or trying to work out where they went, so unless someone pointed out the weirdness of it, we wouldn't have noticed, not yet anyway. But you're saying the plumber worked here for about a week, and he didn't notice?'

'It's cleverly disguised, but yeah, Dwaine,' Calum nodded for emphasis, 'is a great plumber, the best.'

'Taking a shower is such a pleasure now. I will never forget, Dwaine, the plumber.'

'Yeah,' Calum chuckled, 'You should see his business card, Dwaine Pipes.'

Jennifer burst out laughing. 'Oh, that's brilliant. Dwaine sounds like a great bloke. There isn't a business card around that can top Dwaine Pipes.'

'Yeah, and he's always ready to help anyone.' Calum lowered his chin; his steady gaze made Jennifer uneasy. And sure enough, 'Ready for more surprises?'

'Yes. No, what am I saying? No, no, I'm not sure.'

'Hey, there's nothing to worry about, have a little faith. Okay, let's shove this closet aside and see what's behind it.'

Negative energy surrounded Jennifer, pressing heavily on her chest. She didn't want to face what was behind the closet right now…or maybe ever.

She should stop him.

Putting his shoulder into it, Calum pushed hard, but the closet wouldn't budge. 'This must weigh a ton,' he grunted with effort. 'Can't do it on my own.'

'I know it's big, but you should've been able to slide it a bit,' Jennifer said, peering down the side nearest the wall, partly hoping it was never going to shift. 'It's probably bolted to the floor or the wall. Oh well,' she shrugged.

Confused about what to do next, Jennifer sat on the edge of the bed. Gazing at the looming wardrobe, her thoughts drifted to the dark side. What if there was something horrible buried behind these walls—like the dead bodies of women he'd lured into the pink bedroom? She loved and trusted her uncle; he was a kind and gentle man. But even decent men did strange things. How many times had she seen on the seven o'clock news bemused friends and neighbours saying, 'We just don't understand it; he was such a lovely family man. Wouldn't hurt a fly. Pity about all the bodies buried in his backyard.'

Stomach churning, Jennifer turned to Calum. 'I don't think I want to know.'

Calum chuckled. 'Aren't you curious? It might have nothing to do with Bob. It could have been the people who owned it before your uncle. Maybe they built it to stash their money. It might still be in there. Want to look for an opening?'

Jennifer tugged at a lock of her curly hair. 'I don't know anymore.'

Calum stepped back and, using careful judgment, assessed size against area and weight, plus electrical wiring, then told her, 'Sorry, Jen, but it has to be done.'

'Well, it's obvious,' she said, 'the only way in is through the closet.'

'Yep.' Calum nodded, hands resting on his hips.

'Okay,' Jennifer said, and with a reluctant sigh, she gave in. 'Let's look. Otherwise, I won't be able to sleep in this room, I'll have one eye fixed on the damn doors, all four of them.'

'Your house, your closet,' Calum said, hand out. 'Or would you rather I went in first?'

'No, but thank you. I'm being a wuss.' Jennifer mentally apologised to her Uncle Bob— for what, she didn't know. 'Okay, here we go.' She reached for the doorknobs and hesitated.

'Come on, Jen, nothing's so bad that you can't check it out with a good friend. It's not like whatever's in there has anything to do with you personally.'

Jennifer knew it had nothing to do with her, but mud sticks, especially if it belongs to a relative.

'Okay, but if it's—you know, unsavoury—no one else must find out about it.' She frowned, remembering the cryptic note Bob had left for her and Sofie. She repeated his words aloud: 'Forgive me. Leave it alone—don't search. I meant no harm; what I did was for me, no one else.'

'What?' Callum asked, frowning.

'That was in a note Uncle Bob left us.'

'Look, I won't tell a soul, Scout's honour.'

Jennifer arched a warning brow as she glanced at his oh-so-innocent face. She removed her shoes and suggested that Calum do the same. 'Okay, here goes. If we're transported to another time and place, I want you to promise to get me home in one piece.'

'Stop procrastinating, Jen, and do it.'

She stepped inside and whispered an apology, 'Sorry, Uncle Bob, but this needs to get sorted.' Her uncle's clothes hung from a central rod. Smaller items, such as belts and ties, hung from rails attached to the back wall. She pushed his clothes aside, reached out, and felt the old timber beneath her hands. 'This is a bit like Doctor Who's Tardis.'

'I'm coming in,' Calum announced. There was a rustle of plastic and hangers sliding as he moved closer. 'Found anything?'

A second later, she heard a faint click, and suddenly, total darkness closed in around them.

A strangled cry escaped Jennifer's throat. 'What happened?' Jennifer spun around, causing hangers and plastic to crinkle and rattle. Fingers outstretched, she grabbed hold of Calum's arm and held on. 'Why is it so dark?' she asked, sounding panicky.

'The door swung shut behind us.'

'Well, go open it!'

'Okay, don't panic. Are you claustrophobic?'

'Not as a rule, but this could change things. You don't want a hysterical woman with you in a closet.'

'It's not a problem, Jen.'

The sound of clicks and scrapes only made Jennifer feel edgier.

'There, it's open.'

'Why is it still so dark in here?'

'I had to slip a piece of paper in between the lock and catch. I could wedge it with a kitchen chair.'

'No! As long as I know it's not locked, I'll be fine.' Jennifer carefully turned and ran her hands down the side and back wall. 'Nothing's happening here.'

'Move over a bit,' Calum said, leaning forward, his arm brushing against her chest. 'Sorry.'

If it hadn't been so dark, he would have seen her smile. They fumbled and bumped into each other, laughter and nervous energy filling the cramped space.

They edged down to the floor while Jennifer told herself to relax…right, like that was going to happen. Then she collided with his chin.

'Shit-ouch!' Calum cried out.

'Sorry.' She rubbed her head and felt his breath against her cheek. His mouth was near her ear, which sent goose bumps down her side, as he asked, 'Are you okay?'

'I can't take much more of this. It's hot and stuffy, and sweat's beginning to trickle—'

'Really?' Calum's amused voice sounded hopeful.

Oh, not fair. Can I bite him? A nibble maybe…No? Bugger.

'Let me just get over this side,' he said, crawling over the top of her.

Oh, now I'm definitely going to nibble him.

Her fingers tingled as she grabbed him and pulled him down. They fumbled for each other's lips and only missed once. She slid her fingers into his hair, delighting in the silken strands. Her breath came short and fast. His mouth was delicious, soft, yet firm—hungry, eager to please.

'Jen,' he whispered, voice rough, 'I've missed you more than…damn it, I can't find a word that can explain how much it hurt not seeing you, talking with you, laughing with you, just being with you—hell, you make everything right.'

The desire to feel his skin overwhelmed all rational thought. Jennifer slipped her hands inside his shirt and pulled it off. She gripped his broad, bare shoulders and leaned in to nuzzle his skin. 'You smell so good, like citrus honeysuckle and pine.'

Suddenly, Calum toppled backwards and disappeared.

'Where'd you go!'

'Crap!' he grumbled, lost among the hanging coats and suits.

She could hear him scrambling; seconds later, hangers went flying.

Jennifer couldn't see, thankfully, her knees brushed past what she assumed was his nose.

'Don't help—please!' he said breathlessly. Then he pulled her close, his body all firm muscle and warm skin. She ran her hands over every part of him; all her senses heightened. Knees and elbows knocked and thudded against the floor and walls as Jennifer pressed closer. Before she said too much, like *be with me now and forever*, she kissed him.

Their kiss continued, shifting from wild and hungry to tender and sensuous.

'You're amazing,' Calum murmured with feeling.

'Oh?' She kissed along his jaw. Her body glowing and tingling so intensely that even a gentle touch made her giggle with pleasure.

Their shared gift would last a lifetime. Neither moved, holding each other close, savouring the moment.

Jennifer wrapped her arms around Calum and thought, he was right where he should be. And she was right where she should be…perfect.

He murmured, 'I want to see you.' He lifted her up, which Jennifer found impressive. She buried her face in his neck and held on tight. Then he moved back towards the door. 'I just have to…' With a regretful sigh, he set Jennifer down on the floor and thumped the door a couple of times with his hip.

'I thought it was open.'

'That might have been a little white lie.'

Her fingers dug into his shoulders. 'You mean we're locked in?'

'Not for long. I didn't want to say anything earlier in case you panicked; I can get us out of here, no worries.' Calum's hands patted her body until he found her face. He cupped her face, then kissed her softly on the mouth. 'We have two options.' He kissed his way to her forehead. 'I can break the lock, which might splinter the door.' He kissed his way down to her nose. 'Or I could grab my phone and ring a locksmith.' He kissed her mouth again.

'I don't fancy the last one. The two of us stuck in the closet together, it would blow through town before he's down the stairs. So go ahead and force the door open, slowly. Please.'

'Okay.' Calum leaned his shoulder against the door, and with his foot pressed against the opposite wall, he pushed. The door popped open with nothing more than a bent lock.

He swept her up and, cradling her, headed for the bathroom where he set her down on the bathmat. He gave her one of his sexy, quirky grins and held out his hand. She took it. Calum turned her palm up and kissed her there. Stripping off, he led her into the new, modern shower cubicle. Warm water washed over her like gentle rain. He took his time to lather and slide his hands all over her body. Calum wrapped his fingers around her wrists and slid his hands down to her forearms, then back up. Jennifer moved with pleasure under his touch. Then, like a dancer, with feet splayed, he slowly slid his tanned, athletic body over hers. Jennifer followed his lead and found that wet, naked dancing in the shower was breathtaking, magnificent, and spectacular.

Blissfully, Jennifer closed her eyes and hummed with pleasure.

'Jen…Jen, I love seeing your eyes. I want to see your beautiful face,' Calum murmured low. His words drew her closer to the edge. Her expression softened, her mouth parting as her body responded to his sweet caresses.

It was her turn to admire the beauty of his loving face.

His strong hands held her at the hips. Tilting his head, he locked eyes with her, then slowly closed his lids as he leaned in for a long, deep, meaningful kiss. Calum came up for air, gave her another quick kiss, and, breathing heavily, rested his forehead against hers.

Catching his breath, he straightened and looked at her, really looked with an intense gaze that made her heart swell. 'You have to be the most beautiful woman I've ever met.' He shook his head. 'And that just doesn't cover it. You drive me crazy.'

'Oh,' Jennifer said, 'that makes us even. You drive me nuts. But keep talking.'

Holding her at the waist and keeping contact with her skin sliding against his, he cupped her face, and with warm eyes meeting hers, he gently asked, 'You okay?'

She rose up onto her toes and answered, 'I'm the best I've ever been.'

Calum wrapped his arms around her, holding her tight as the warm water flowed over them. 'Fuck, I'm glad you're back.'

'Me too.' She pulled back enough to look at his face. 'Can I ask what all this "fuck" stuff's about?'

He let out a deep, infectious chuckle, and with a gravelly voice for emphasis, he said, 'Because if I don't swear, I'll explode. Seeing you, holding you, it's…it's intense.'

'Oh,' she breathed, eyes wide as she nodded in understanding.

'Good to know I'm not alone in this.' His expression was dead-set, serious. 'Fuck!' Calum chuckled. 'Looking at you like this makes me want to…'

'What does it make you want to do?' Jennifer breathed.

'Makes me *not* want to miss a second of you.' His hand curled around her neck, thumb sweeping across her jaw, he said, 'I'm staying the night.'

'Okay,' she said calmly, while inwardly she was doing a major happy dance.

'Good, not that I was taking no for an answer anyway, not with weird stuff happening here.' He swept a hand across her waist, turned the water off, and wrapped her in a towel.

Warm and dry, Jennifer tilted her head and, with a contented smile, watched Calum dress. The best part was how his jocks slipped over his firm backside. Head bent, and a quick dip of the knees, he adjusted himself for comfort, then turned and grinned at her. He didn't need to say a word; his eyes spoke volumes.

She told herself to focus, girl; think about the dessert menu! Put undies on. Chocolate mousse…yum, lick it off his flat, hard stomach. Oh my God, I did not think that. Put bra on. She shook her head to clear her thoughts, but Calum's powerful physique kept intruding. He was all muscle; she guessed it was because he climbed ladders and hauled cables, not to mention all the farm work as well. And he'd refitted her shop. It was a wonder he'd had the energy left to do the wild thing in the closet and shower. And from now on, she knew, when she looked in his eyes, there'd be that knowing, cheeky, sexy thought exchange. Like just then, when he was adjusting his jocks. A private look that even in public said, if we weren't here, we'd be in the closet, the shower, or some other part of the house, touching, holding, loving.

Calum moved, slowly and with purpose, towards her. He took her hand, brought it to his mouth, and leisurely kissed her palm. A tingle travelled up her arm into her chest, down past her belly, and straight down, making her legs feel tingly and weak. Oh, what this man can do. Head dipped close to hers, he placed her hand on his chest; she could feel the thud of his heart.

He smiled at her, the look in his eyes tender and warm. 'All good?' he asked softly.

Do you reckon she could talk? 'Huh?' she paused, gathered her thoughts and said, 'I'm ever so good!'

Jennifer loved watching him laugh with pure, unrestrained happiness. 'Ever so good?' he mimicked.

'Was that a bit naff?' She could easily call up a few more UK idioms.

'Stop it, you're killing me,' he kissed her warmly and asked, 'Can we do this all again?' He cupped her chin and lightly brushed the cushion of his thumb over her lips.

'Are you kidding? I'm not letting you out of my sight,' she nodded. 'I'll have a lot more of the same, please.' She nibbled his thumb and played her tongue around the pad.

Calum let out a soft gasp, held his breath, then let it go with a chuckle. 'Stop that or I won't be responsible.'

Jennifer smiled and let his thumb slip from her mouth. He tilted his head and moved in until his warm, soft lips touched hers. The tenderness in his kiss almost made her cry. He pulled back just enough to speak. His eyes brimming with passion—and more, so much more. Love so deep and strong it turned her bones to jelly, and yet at the same time, the unknown that lay ahead scared the pants off her.

'Ready to see what's behind the closet? Come on, Jen, let's do it.'

Calum stepped into the closet wearing nothing more than his jocks and a wink.

Jennifer gulped, quickly jiggled into her bra, and followed.

Chapter 14

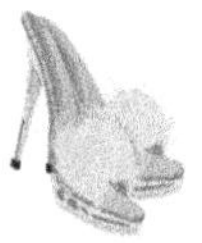

Loud banging echoed through the house. Calum poked his head out of the closet.

'What the hell was that? Did you drop something?'

Jennifer grabbed her jeans and pulled them on. 'Not me. Someone's at the door. Don't explore without me. I'll get rid of them, back in a sec.' She snatched up a T-shirt and threw it on as she hurried down the long hallway and then down the stairs.

Heavy thundering continued through the shop.

'Okay-okay! Keep your shirt on, I'm coming!'

Jennifer hurried through the restaurant and suddenly stopped at the door when she saw the silhouette of a man behind the frosted glass panel. She hesitated for a moment before yanking the door open, ready to give the person an earful about having patience.

'Bret!'

White-faced terror etched her brother's face. 'I'm being followed,' he rasped urgently.

Jennifer glanced up and down the street, grabbed his arm, and hauled him inside. 'Thank God you're all right.' She slammed the door, wrapped her arms around him, and hugged him tightly.

'Jen, Jen, I can't breathe.'

She pushed him back to arm's length and looked him over from head to toe. 'What the hell are you doing here? Why haven't you called anyone—anyone at all? Last we heard, you were heading for Broome.'

'I was never in Broome. I just said that to throw the idiots off my trail.'

'What!' Jennifer, furious yet relieved, was lost for words as she grabbed his shoulders. 'I could happily strangle you!'

'Okay-okay. I tried ringing Sofie a few times, but I kept getting a snooty woman's voice saying this number is unavailable.

'But I gave you Sofie's *new* number.'

'I didn't get a chance to recharge my phone, and when I tried to, it wouldn't.'

'You know, you could've dropped by the school where she works, and left her a note.'

'JEN!'

'Okay!' Jennifer cried out, exasperated. 'What made you come here? I've only just arrived myself.'

Bret's slim shoulders lifted in a shrug. 'I didn't know you'd be here. I was planning to hide in the garage for a while. I saw the lights were on and took a chance. I was hoping it wasn't Sofie. She's lovely, but when it comes to something like this, she's custard.'

'Why not go straight to the police? At least you'd save everyone from an anxiety attack.' Bret looked at her, eyes haunted with troubled thoughts. 'Oh, for God's sake.' She pulled him in for another hug. 'I know you don't mean to, but you make us crazy.'

'Sorry, Jen. The police can't do anything. I owe these blokes. I didn't know where else to go.' Bret blew out a lungful of air. 'All that running made no difference.'

'Did you drop by your old haunts—your Sydney flat?'

'Yes, but only for a few days to rest.'

Jennifer shot him the older sister, don't-bullshit-me look.

Alright, you win. I might have stayed a couple of weeks. I only went out at night. Anyway, I haven't got a friggin' clue why they're still chasing me; I only borrowed five grand. That's peanuts for blokes like that.

'Oh really? Well, they told me to hand over ten grand, or they'd break both your legs—slowly.' Jennifer jabbed him in the chest.

'That's extortion!' Bret yelled, looking rattled.

'Interest is a bitch. From now on, no more lies!' she snapped at him. 'Or half-truths.'

Bret's face showed genuine remorse. He nodded, 'Sorry, sis.'

'Okay, one thing at a time. They could be barging through this door any minute.'

Footsteps approached from behind. Heart thumping, Jennifer spun around.

Brow furrowed, Calum extended his hand. 'G'day, Bret. Couldn't help but overhear. Your, erm, let's say discussion echoed up the stairs.'

'Calum,' Jennifer whispered, relieved. She thrust Bret at him. 'Take him upstairs and hide him somewhere—quickly, please!'

'No chance. You hide him.' Calum shoved Bret back at Jennifer. 'How've you been, Bret?' Calum glanced at his hand still extended, waiting. 'You know, here, and in all country towns, we greet with a handshake. I repeat, how've you been?'

'Been better.' Chin lowered, Bret shook Calum's hand.

'Still travelling?' Calum asked in his easy-going manner. 'S'pose you could murder a steak?'

'Yeah, got any?'

Hands on her hips, Jennifer glanced from one to the other, her face showing disbelief.

'What?' they asked in unison.

'You two don't even know each other!' They looked at her, puzzled. 'Must be a man thing,' Jennifer muttered. 'Bret, this is Calum McGregor.'

'Why do you need to hide?' Calum asked.

'Spill it, Bret,' Jennifer said. 'I'm your sister, and Calum is a close friend.' Had she blinked, Jennifer would've missed Calum's hurt expression. She gave him a what-was-I-supposed-to-say shrug. He raised a what-the…eyebrow back at her.

Bret started pacing. 'I saw this fantastic horse online.'

'Here we go,' Jennifer groaned.

'He looked like a real winner,' Bret enthused, eyes wide. 'The odds were unbelievable! Turns out I knew a friend of the horse's trainer. He said he was a winner for sure. I didn't have the cash, so I borrowed five grand.'

'And the horse came in last.' Hands on hips, Jennifer glared at him.

'Second last. I tried to bargain with them. I said I'd work it off, but they weren't interested,' he shrugged. 'And now they're saying I owe them ten grand. They're a bunch of sharks and the interest just keeps piling up.'

'You idiot!' Jennifer snapped. 'There's only one way to make money, and that's to work hard for it like the rest of us. When will you get it into your thick skull that you don't need approval from mother and father? You think they'll love you more just because you've got money?'

'I dunno, sis—yeah?' Bret shrugged again.

Calum looked puzzled and rubbed the back of his neck.

'What am I gonna do?' Bret nervously chewed on his lip.

Jennifer gave a worried, sideways nod towards the shadowy movement behind the frosted glass door. 'Your business partners and investment bankers are here.'

'What?' Bret squeaked, confused.

'That, little brother, is what mother uses, because a bank teller isn't upper class.'

'Jen, I don't care, do something,' Bret whispered shakily.

'Why should I? They're your idiots?' she hissed back at him.

'Sure, but they're bloody big, dangerous idiots.'

Jennifer rolled her eyes and sighed. 'I'm calling the police.'

'Please, Jen, don't,' Bret pleaded. 'You'll only make it worse.'

'Brock's a top cop,' Calum told them quietly, 'but unless they break the law, there's nothing he can do except scare them. In the end, Bret owes these blokes money. Take him upstairs. I'll get the door.'

'Are you out of your mind?' Jennifer rounded on Calum. 'This is our problem. *I'm* going out there—Bret, you're coming with me!'

Bret turned pale and had wild eyes like a trapped cat.

'Okay, I'll do it alone,' Jennifer announced and headed for the door.

'Bret—disappear,' Calum ordered, pointing to the stairs.

Loud banging rattled the glass panels in the door. Jennifer yanked it open, fire in her eyes and a burning desire to bash a couple of thugs around the head.

On second thoughts, maybe not.

* * *

Calum pushed past Jennifer and grinned at a couple of thugs. Muscles bulged under black T-shirts and black dress pants; they waited on the footpath like extras from a gangster movie.

'Gentlemen,' he said, 'the restaurant's not open yet.'

'We're lookin' for Bret The Pigeon,' the taller one said. 'We saw 'im come in 'ere. There's no point denyin' it.' The guy's rough accent was out of keeping with his fine clothes.

Calum swung an arm across, stopping Jennifer from leaving the doorway. He stepped outside just as the streetlights flicked on. Much to his annoyance, she didn't take the hint and followed. Calum dared not take his eyes off the blokes to give her a get-back-inside glare.

'And you are?' he asked calmly.

'This here's Stef,' the taller one said, pointing to his mate. 'And I'm Fry. We're businessmen, runnin' a business.'

Calum pulled a what-the-face. 'Fry?' he asked.

'Use your imagination,' Fry said. 'Or is that too difficult for ya?' Fry shifted his bulk and leant in close. 'I'm losin' me patience. The money?'

'Bret doesn't have any!' Jennifer's enraged tone made even Calum turn to look. 'Threatening to break his legs won't change a thing.'

'I couldn't give a fuck what you say!' Fry cut in. 'I'd wanna break his legs for the irritation.'

'Gentlemen, I'm sure we can do a deal.' Calum shot them a steely glare. It worked on the bulls back home, so why not here? All Fry did was roll his toned shoulders and neck. Maybe it was a sign he was feeling the strain.

'This is legit, alright?' Fry said. 'The kid owes us ten grand.'

'What a bunch of lazy-arsed bloody sharks!' Jennifer took a deep breath, getting ready to give them more.

Calum gave her a shut-up glare, but she stiffened and shot one back. Man, she had guts. He had to hold back a grin, despite the situation they were in.

'If you'se two have finished makin' love eyes...?' Fry growled.

'That's a hefty amount.' Calum was hedging for time, hoping the pressure of doing business out on the footpath would build and they'd cave...Or maybe not.

'Okay,' Fry began, shifting from one foot to the other, his aggravation obvious. 'I reckon you're a fair bloke—how about nine Gs?'

'That's outrageous,' Jennifer hissed. 'We don't carry that sort of money around, and it's Friday night, you idiots. Banks don't open until ten Monday morning.'

'You'd better have a word with your missus,' Fry said, slapping a fist into his cupped hand.

'Don't threaten my missus,' Calum said, glaring down past his nose at Fry. He felt his lip twitch and hoped it added weight to his message.

Fry stared back, flexed his neck and said nothing.

Calum turned and moved closer to Jennifer. A whisper of air separated his face from hers. 'They're a couple of uglies, and you're naive. Don't say another word unless you want to see blood.' Slowly, Jennifer nodded. 'Theirs, of course.' He winked. 'Stay put. And I mean it this time.' He turned back, sensing a deal was imminent.

'Boys,' Calum said with a sideways nod, 'come with me.' He headed towards his parked Range Rover. Arms crossed, he casually rested his butt on the bonnet. 'We're country folk. We provide you with steak and veg. There has to be a way around this problem.'

'I'm a vegetarian,' Stefan informed him loftily.

'Shut the fuck up, you idiot,' Fry barked.

Calum, all casual-like, spoke to the thugs. Resting his foot on the bumper, he told them in a tone that brooked no argument, 'It's this or nothing. I'm willing to meet you halfway, five grand.'

Stefan looked as if he were in pain. Muscles bulging, Fry hardened, balled his fists, and took a deep breath. 'How's this? Five grand, plus two for expenses?'

'What sort of expenses are we talking here?' Calum wanted to know.

'Oh, for fuck's sake!' Fry lost his cool. 'Petrol money, motels, nervous tension, I don't care—whatever you want to call it—but that little fucker is gonna pay.' Fry leaned forward, chin out. He jabbed the air inches from Calum's chest. 'That friggin' little aggravation owes us. It's the principle. Part of good business practice. No one owes us—no one!'

'I'll give you six.' Calum stated firmly.

Stefan grumbled. Fry paused long and hard and rolled his shoulders again.

'Okay. For fuck's sake,' Fry spat out, 'so we can get the fuck outta this fucking hole.'

'To make a digital transfer, I need your details.' Calum waited while they fumbled with their phones.

Arm extended, Fry shoved his phone under Calum's nose. He made the transfer, and Fry stepped back to show Stefan, saying, 'The minute we get out of this shithole, we change our password.'

Fry and Stefan jumped into their black Mazda Sports. Tyres squealing, Fry made a U-turn and flicked them the bird as he drove past.

'Oh, very nice.' Jennifer's tone crackled with sarcasm.

Calum ushered her inside. 'Don't look at me like that. Go tell Bret it's done.'

He was about to close the door when he saw Bruce casually clomping towards him in his farm co-op overalls, T-shirt stretched over burly man-muscles. Calum wondered how much Bruce had seen, and did it matter anyway?

'Evening, Cal.' Bruce gave a slight nod. He had a perpetual puppy face that made women want to mother him.

'Hey, Bruce, how's married life?'

'Bloody brilliant, mate. Bloody brilliant. Mum's come around; she's knitting a layette, whatever that is.' Bruce extended his left hand. 'You got a moment?'

'What's all this?' Calum nodded towards Bruce's leftie handshake.

Bruce brought his right hand out from behind his back and held up a middle finger, firmly wrapped in white bandages. 'I squashed it in the extendable ladder, dislocated the last knuckle.'

'Shit, Bruce, that would've hurt.'

'Shit, yeah!' Bruce grunted and wriggled his bandaged finger. 'Ooh bugger,' he cursed, sucking in air through his teeth.

'When'd you do a stupid thing like that?'

'This arvo, during a drill, the fire chief wanted to make sure we were ready for the wine festival.'

A thought crossed Calum's mind. He knew what was coming and steadfastly eyed Bruce.

'Definitely not. No way!'

'But Cal, there's no one else. You've got to.'

'No, I don't,' Calum pointed out emphatically. 'And anyway, last time I practised, the cattle freaked.'

'Jeez, Cal, it's not so much for me, but what about the rest of the town? Our reputation will be shot.'

'You can't use guilt tactics, Bruce. You're hopeless at it.' The desperate look on Bruce's face was another thing. 'Christ!' Calum sighed. 'You owe me, big time. Fuck, I don't believe I've agreed to this—shit!'

'You'll be fine.' Bruce laid his good hand on Calum's shoulder. 'I've got bucketloads of confidence in you.'

'You'll need more than that. You'd better have a word with the universal dudes. Or whoever thinks this is some sort of twisted payback for leaving.' Calum turned to go.

'There's something else,' Bruce said. 'The heritage committee wants to know if you've got extinguishers in the restaurant kitchen. It's not mandatory, but it probably wouldn't hurt to have one upstairs as well.'

'Yep, there's two in the restaurant and one in the pantry upstairs. Mightn't be a bad idea to come by and show Jen how they work.'

'I can do that.' Bruce's face wrinkled up. He seemed full of misgivings as he scratched his head.

'Now what?' Calum asked.

'Well, I kinda scared the pants off her—hey, not literally. Jeez, that came out all wrong.'

Calum grinned, admiring the big bloke. 'Yeah, no wonder Jennifer squealed when you took Jen down the ladder after she threw the toaster out the window. What've you been eating?'

'Nothin',' Bruce said with wide-eyed innocence. He peered down at his ample belly. 'Free doughnuts at the station, and Kathleen's an amazing cook.'

'Listen mate, Jennifer has never mentioned that she was scared,' Calum stated with a grin. 'I think she's very proud of herself. But for her sake and her guests, you'd better give her instructions on how to use extinguishers. While you're at it, tell her anything else she needs to know—like what to do with a full restaurant in case of fire.'

'Okay, will do. Hey, I didn't interrupt anything earlier? Those two blokes you were talkin' to left in an awful hurry.'

'Yeah, just lost idiots. Hope Brock catches up with them. A couple of speeding tickets would do the trick, say a thousand dollars' worth would be good.'

'Yep, that'd hurt,' Bruce said. 'Not friends then?'

'No. I'll tell you all about it one day.' Calum turned to go back inside. 'Don't forget Jen and her fire drills.'

'I won't. I'll drop in as soon as I can. And don't forget to practise.'

'Yeah, right, wonder where I'm supposed to do that,' Calum felt a grin forming and said, 'I know. I'll come to your place.' He left Bruce standing on the footpath, mouth open.

*   *   *

Upstairs, Jennifer paced the hall, and each time she walked past the kitchen door, Bret looked up from twisting a piece of cotton he'd plucked from his hoodie. She was angry, yet her heart went out to him.

Finally, familiar footsteps echoed up the stairs. A few seconds later, Calum stepped through the door.

'What kept you?' she asked, relieved to see him unharmed. 'I saw them take off.'

'Got to talking with Bruce.'

'What did he want? Did Bruce see anything—did anyone?' *Damn*, Jennifer thought, *I sound like my mother.*

'Yeah, he asked. I told him they weren't friends and hoped Brock would book them for speeding.' Calum studied her face.

'What were you doing over by your car?'

Calum gave her a knowing look. 'Let's get Bret. Then I don't have to repeat myself.'

'Don't go getting all—thingy on me,' Jennifer protested, and instantly regretted her uppity tone.

'Thingy?' Calum couldn't hide his amusement.

'The hero who looks after the little woman and is taking control—thingy, like you did outside.'

'Wait a sec, I get it. You were worried about me,' he said, giving her one of his quirky half-smiles and placing a hand on his chest. 'I'm touched.'

Jennifer strode down the hall, with Calum close behind, his amusement almost like a feathery tickle up her back.

'You're a farmer from a country town. They're nasties from the city. And now you're caught up in my brother's dodgy dealings. And probably the whole town's involved as well— bloody hell.'

'Hey, I can look after myself. I've got brawn.' His eyes smouldered, then he whispered in her ear, 'And I can make you pant for more.'

Jennifer couldn't deny it. 'And that makes everything okay?'

'Lots of things should make it okay.' He leaned in and kissed her cheek.

Jennifer thumped his shoulder. 'Bret's in the kitchen.' She glared at the grin he tried to hide.

Bret looked up from the table, worry lines aging his weary face.

'Let's talk.' Calum swung a chair around, straddled it, and rested his arms on the back.

Bret rubbed his face. The ceiling light made the dark circles under his eyes more noticeable. 'Are they gone?' he mumbled.

'Yep,' Calum replied.

'I think it's time you took responsibility for your actions,' Jennifer told her brother. 'Get a job like a normal person. Learn a trade. I'll show you how to julienne carrots.'

Bret's face screwed up in distaste. 'No thanks. I'd rather do something outdoors.'

'You what?' Jennifer slammed her hands on the table in front of him, leaned forward, and closed in on his face. 'Listen, you don't have a say anymore, got that?' She straightened and gave him a clip, an upward swipe to his head.

Calum cut in. 'You can help on the farm. Since the renovations here, I've got a truckload of chores.'

'Um…' Bret mumbled, his worried eyes flicking from one to the other.

Jennifer was ready to throttle both of them, one for hesitating at a great opportunity, the other for offering it.

'Wait just a minute, Calum. My brother's a schemer. He uses people, even his own sisters.'

'Fair go, sis.'

'It's true. You're constantly looking for ways to make a quick buck to impress Mother and Father, and along the way, you leave a trail of destruction. The goons won't give up; they'll be...' A thought struck Jennifer. She spun around to face Calum. 'Just what did happen out there? Don't tell me you paid them off?'

'Yep, six grand flew out of my account to save Bret's legs. To my way of thinking, he can work it off on the farm, one leg at a time.'

It took a moment for Calum's bombshell to sink in. 'You what!' Jennifer yelled.

'Six?' Bret asked. 'I've just been sweating over ten for nothing! How?'

'I negotiated,' Calum replied with a smile. 'And I enjoyed it. It was great fun.'

He was relishing this cat-and-mouse game; Jennifer could see it in his eyes. She glanced at her brother, who gazed in wonder at his saviour.

'I realised I'd made a mistake the moment you mentioned blood, and I listened. What makes you think they won't come back for the rest?'

Calum eyed her as if to say, give me *some* credit. 'They won't be back. Asking for ten was a tactic they hoped would work. What better way to make another five grand, which you would have given them unnecessarily.'

'You heard him, sis.' Bret looked at Calum in awe.

'Who says I would've? Don't assume you know everything about me, because you don't,' Jennifer clenched her fists, desperately trying to keep her cool. 'This is our affair. We could've sorted it out. But oh no, Mr Hero had to stick his nose in, and now you've probably put yourself, your grandma, and your sister in danger. Crap seems to follow my brother, and anyone near him will get caught up in his dodgy, messed-up life!' She paused for breath, then added, 'I'll go to the bank Monday morning, and you'll have the money back.'

Calum pursed his lips against a smile. 'I don't want it.'

'Well, you're getting it. And what's so funny?' she demanded.

'You look hot when you're angry, and it makes me want to laugh. I can't help it. You're gorgeous, I love seeing you fiery. If Bret weren't here, I'd…'

'Oh really?' Jennifer said, chin up, but melting inside.

'Anyway, despite all your objections, this is just between Bret and me, man to man.' Calum's tone was final.

'Man to man? Now I've heard it all. You think treating him like an adult will change anything? He's twenty-two, but he acts like a reckless kid! When it suits him, he'll just walk off— disappear. And gossip would spread all over town. You know that girl who's opening a restaurant? Well, her brother…' Jennifer cringed inside.

Calum asked Bret, 'Do I have your word that you'll stay and work off your debt?' Hand extended, Calum waited for Bret to shake on it.

Bret's eyes darted everywhere except at Calum. 'I don't know anything about farming.'

'You see?' Jennifer said. 'He's already making excuses. He's allergic to hard work.'

Calum glanced her way with a cut-the-crap expression.

'Don't you dare give me that *look*.' She glared back. 'I've seen worse, and they had knives.'

Calum turned back to Bret, eyebrows raised in question.

'Chefs,' Bret explained. 'Big ones, even bigger knives.'

Calum grinned. 'You're one hell of a woman.'

'You can say that again.' Jennifer stepped closer, her body tense and determined. 'This is not funny. You're interfering. Everyone will find out I have a brother who brings thugs to their town. How will that look? I'm about to open a classy restaurant. Some townspeople will thank you for giving them juicy gossip, all because you stuck your nose into something that doesn't concern you. You wanted to play the big man, the hero.' Her words rang in her ears. She regretted every word the moment they left her mouth, but it was too late. Not only did she sound like her mother, she sounded ungrateful. Oh God, what had she done? Jennifer wished a hole in the floor would swallow her up and spit her out somewhere far away. Maybe she'd land back in the past so she could start afresh. She felt embarrassment burn her face.

All humour drained from Calum's eyes. 'I'll be back for Bret in the morning.' Without another word, he turned and walked out the door.

Jennifer could almost feel her heart breaking. She stood in the ruins of the evening, blinking back her emotions as the door closed quietly. Like a heavy cloak, silence settled around her.

She glanced back at Bret and saw the same sad expression she'd seen on his face so many times over the years. Every time their mother had accused him of yet another mistake, and now she'd done it to him as well. She'd also lost Calum and his respect. Damn, she'd been such a bloody idiot.

She knew exactly why her mouth trembled.

Chapter 15

Jennifer kept an eye on Bret as, droopy-eyed, he devoured a ham and cheese sandwich. Hands resting on his chin, he could barely keep his eyes open. Jennifer took hold of his arm and guided him into their uncle's bedroom.

'Night, sis,' he said wearily. He flopped fully clothed onto the bed. 'Gee, it's good to see you again.' He gave her a sad smile. 'Even if you do growl a lot.'

Remorse burned inside Jennifer. She understood why Bret behaved the way he did, and couldn't justify what she'd said. Wiping the tears from her face, she took off his shoes, covered him with a blanket, and kissed his forehead.

'You deserve an apology for what I said earlier.' So he wouldn't look away, she held his chin with her thumb and forefinger. 'Yes, you're a little shit, and you need to change how you live for your own sake and for those who love you. And so far, I haven't shown you that I love you. I've done a lot of complaining, but not much else. What I said was horrible. It's what Mother did all the time. It won't happen again, Bret, I promise. Sofie, Claudia, and I, we all love you. And Calum's a good bloke; you can trust him.'

Bret nodded and rolled onto his side, curling up in a foetal position. Seeing her brother like this transported Jennifer back to their childhood home. She remembered how Bret would retreat the same way after yet another razor-sharp dressing down from their parents for not befriending the wealthy kids and inviting them over. Their parents believed that if Bret could climb the social ladder, some of that status would rub off on the family.

Emotion welled up, and Jennifer did her best to hold back a sob. But she couldn't stop the tears from slipping down her cheeks. 'Go to sleep,' she whispered, kissing him again before heading back to the kitchen. She brewed a cup of tea and rang her sister. When Sofie answered, her sister sounded strained.

'Just ignore my tone,' Sofie said. 'And the background commentary of our menopausal mother, who's given up waxing and taken up yoga.'

'Hi Sofe,' Jennifer said through sniffles. 'About Mother, you're joking, right?'

'Nope, but ignore me; what's wrong?' Sofie quickly added, 'And don't polish it for my sake! Give!'

How could she explain her behaviour? She wished a hole had swallowed her up. 'I've just alienated the best man I've ever known, that's all,' Jennifer replied. 'Bret turned up.'

'Thank goodness,' Sofie sighed.

Jennifer could almost see her sister's relieved slump.

'Hang on a sec,' Sofie added. 'He's not in hospital with broken legs?'

'No, he showed up at the restaurant door, scared and exhausted but otherwise fine. He's sleeping in Bob's bed.' Emotionally overwhelmed, Jennifer fell silent.

'Hey Jen, where does Calum fit into this? Why are you blubbering? Don't hide it, I can hear it, for fuck's sake, Jen! Are you alright? Did they do anything to you? Did something happen to Calum? Talk to me, Jen, I'm hyperventilating here.'

'I-I'm fine, Calum took care of the thugs,' Jennifer replied, feeling devastated and guilty.

Sofie gasped. 'You met the thugs. Did they break in?'

Jennifer wished she could reach down the line and grab her sister by the hair. She took a deep breath. 'Calum gave them six thousand dollars.'

'But that's fantastic! Once probate clears, we can pay him back, no worries. What an absolutely lovely bloke. I'm so grateful, I want to throw my arms around him and thank him for helping Bret and us out.'

'Yes…we could do that. He won't take the money, though. He's done a deal with Bret, on a handshake. I more or less said this mess with the goons will blow through town faster than a blink and reflect on us; we'll be tarred with the same brush. I cared more about my image and how it would affect my life than our brother's well-being.' Jennifer wedged the phone to her ear while she blew her nose.

'I don't believe that for a minute,' Sofie insisted.

'All my life I've fought *not* to be like our parents, then when it counts most, it all blows up like sour vomit, *bluuugh!*'

'*Eeewh,* Jen! That's gross. Are you purged now?' Sofie giggled.

'Is that our Jen?' their mother cut in, her shrill voice capable of shattering glass.

'She doesn't give me a moment's peace,' Sofie whispered.

'I live in hope, but you were kidding about the waxing and yoga?'

'Yes, of course. Can you imagine Mum with a hair somewhere it shouldn't be?'

'She's just trying to ingratiate herself so she can get her hands on some of Uncle Bob's money. For our uncle's sake, we can't let that happen. Don't let her get to you, Sofe.' Jennifer poured boiling water into a mug and jiggled the teabag.

'Who are you talking to, Sofie luv?' their mother called out from a nearby room.

'Don't tell Mother it's me,' Jennifer whispered.

'It's another teacher,' Sofie yelled without bothering to cover the mouthpiece.

'If you're going to keep interrupting, Gran,' Claudia hollered, 'Mum's going outside!'

Give me strength, Jennifer thought, heaping an extra spoon of sugar into her mug.

'So, when are you seeing Calum again?' Sofie sounded out of breath.

'What's wrong with you? You sound weird,' Jennifer asked.

'I'm walking outside and talking to an idiot at the same time,' Sofie said.

'Okay, but listen, there's so much I should've done…' Jennifer trailed off.

'What're you on about now? Come on, give.'

Jennifer did her best to keep her emotions in check. 'I'm feeling horrible because I should've been there for Bret. If I'd taken up the reins after Gran died, he mightn't have resorted to this kind of life. And I should've been there for you and Claudia.'

'Hang on a minute there,' Sofie cut in.

'Shut up, Sofe, this is my moment. I'm making a huge leap forward with a confession. Don't interrupt. I should've been there for you both when whatsisname, Jett, took off with Ms Wannabe and had twins. Offering you a trip to Italy was just a cop-out. I'm so sorry, Sofie. I hope you can forgive me.'

'Stop it,' Sofie cried out. 'I love you. I mean, jeez, you had a career to think about. I understand, I really do. Honestly, Jen, will you stop now?'

'I think so,' Jennifer muttered miserably.

'If Calum loves you, Jen, you'll sort it out. So, what happens now?'

'Calum's taking Bret to his farm early tomorrow morning to work off his debt.'

'Brilliant, ingenious. Maybe Bret will learn something.'

'I'll have a quick word with Calum when he drops by.'

'The only word you should use is "sorry".'

'I will. Night, sis.' Jennifer closed her phone and crawled into bed.

*　　*　　*

Jennifer gazed out of the upstairs kitchen window, wrestling with the weight of her past. She knew that to stay true to herself, she needed only to follow her principles and her innate empathy. She loved her brother, and Calum's steadfast kindness only made her more aware of all she'd said and done. Now, with her mind in turmoil, the right words escaped her. Fearful, Jennifer gripped her mug, the coffee trembling as she wondered, was it possible to mend the hurt she caused? She lost herself in the vista of beautiful vine-covered slopes, rich with autumn colours, until the sound of the back door opening pulled her from her thoughts. Turning away from the peaceful scene, heart pounding, she walked to the landing. Looking over the railing, she saw him. Calum looked up, freshly showered and shaved. She could almost smell the soap.

'Morning, Jen,' he said, but the warmth was gone, his smile too, and that hurt.

'G-good morning,' Jennifer stammered, feeling embarrassed about how she'd mishandled the night before. To make matters worse, she missed cuddling into Calum's warm body, his broad shoulders protectively curling around her while his strong hands held her close; instead, she lay awake all night berating herself.

Calum took the stairs two at a time. He stopped in front of Jennifer, eyes levelled on her with a steady gaze. She saw in their hazel depths a glint of anger and disappointment, yet his face remained expressionless.

She stopped her hand from reaching for her hair. You look fine, she told herself, and slid her hands into the pockets of her jeans, just in case she felt the urge to fidget. A thought struck her. So what if she wanted to fidget with her curls? It had nothing to do with the mother thing about hair, clothes, and keeping your knees together on the bus. Oh God, she groaned inwardly.

'I'm here for Bret,' Calum said firmly.

'So soon? He's barely had a good night's sleep.'

He studied her face. 'Have any of us?'

It felt like a fist slammed into her chest, gripping her heart, lungs, and stomach, crushing everything inside into a small, miserable ball.

His gaze stayed fixed, brows furrowed as if searching her face for something he'd lost. The silence and heavy atmosphere surrounded them.

'I was just having coffee and toast,' she ventured. 'Want some?'

'No thanks, not hungry. Anything else?'

'I want to apologise for everything I said last night. I sounded like an ungrateful bitch; I'm truly sorry.' It took an enormous effort to control her emotions, but her eyes welled up anyway. Hands at her sides, she stood waiting.

'I did it for you,' he said, his voice strong and steady. 'This is yours.' He handed over a small black purse, gave her a quick nod, then strode down the hall to Bob's old room.

Jennifer turned the purse over in her hands. It was the one he'd shoved in his jeans pocket the first time they'd kissed outside the door of her uncle's shop. Holding it to her chest, she waited.

Calum came out of Bob's bedroom and strode back towards her. 'Bret's…' He stopped short, studied her eyes with a look she'd never seen before: dismay, determination, acceptance—all rolled into one emotion. His expression softened, then he cupped her face and, using his thumb, tenderly wiped away her tears. 'I don't give a fuck what anyone thinks in this town. The people who know me understand me. I respect them, and in return, they respect me and what I stand for. I shouldn't and won't justify my actions, and that's not going to change—ever. I love you, Jennifer Dove, so you'd better get used to it, because that's me, that's the way I'm made. I said that I did it for you. The thugs are gone. But seeing Bret in there, he hitched a thumb over his shoulder, I did for Bret as well, he deserves a fair go.' He kissed her on the mouth, gave her one last meaningful look, then turned and headed down the stairs.

She had no time to collect her thoughts. Bret came striding down the hall; when he saw her face, his head jerked back, chin tucked in, and his brow furrowed. She probably looked unhinged, but there wasn't much she could do about that either.

'Get a grip, sis, I've got farm work to do. See ya.' He patted her on the head and took off after Calum.

Snapped out of her stupor, thankfully, Bret paused at the back door, looked up at her and smiled.

Hanging over the landing, Jennifer smiled back, 'You can do this, Bret, I know you can.'

Shoulders shaking, Bret dropped his head, his chin nearly touching his chest, then lifted it again and, eyes glistening, he said, 'Thanks, Sis.' Wiping his face with his sleeves, he turned and stepped out the door.

If anyone could, Calum and the farm would change Bret. Since he was now out of their parents' reach, there was hope and a purpose for their little brother. He was her and Sofie's kid brother, and Jennifer was excited for him. She rang her sister to keep her up to date as promised.

After a few rings, Sofie's croaky voice answered. 'Hi, Jen, you're up bloody early.'

Jennifer smiled to herself. 'I'm ringing to let you know Bret's left with Calum. He's off to learn farm stuff.'

'This is going to be really good for Bret,' Sofie yawned. 'I can feel it in my bones.' More noises came down the line. Jennifer imagined Sofie stretching like a cat. 'You should wake me up more often. Did you apologise to Calum like I said?'

'Of course. He was pissed off and disappointed, and I can't blame him, but then he kissed me and...' Jennifer lost it and started bawling.

'Good grief, Jen, pull yourself together. And he, what?'

'He said he loves me, and that I should get used to it.'

'*Oh...oh.*' Strange crinkly noises drifted down the line.

'What are you doing?'

'I'm fanning myself with a magazine. That's so beautiful, Jen. You'll have me crying next. When are you seeing him again?'

'I have no idea,' Jennifer sniffed. 'I shouldn't intrude while Bret's settling in. Besides, there's so much I need to get ready for the opening.'

'Good, get on with it,' Sofie ordered.

'There's something else,' Jennifer began cautiously. 'There's a missing room, a space we can't get into between the en-suite and the bedroom I'm staying in.'

'What?' Sofie gasped.

'It's true. Calum pointed it out. We think the way in is through that massive closet.'

'God…are you worried?'

'Um…nah. Uncle Bob was a sweetie.'

'Okay, let me know if you find anything; I'll be up soon. When's the big day?'

'I was thinking Easter Saturday. It'll give us time to post flyers and advertise.'

'I like that idea. I'll be on school holidays. You'll have to come up with some egg recipes. We can get the kids to look for eggs in the courtyard garden—I'll tidy it up and it'll look stunning,' Sofie said, full of enthusiasm. 'This is so exciting, Jen, I'll go dream up some more ideas and see if I can dream up a man like Calum. You're very lucky…and so is he. I'll see you soon.' She hung up.

*   *   *

Jennifer sat in the kitchen, chin resting in her hand, the other holding a pen ready to jot down anything that came to mind, but Calum's last words, 'I love you, Jennifer Dove', kept intruding on her thoughts. She wished she'd said something, anything; even 'Really' would've been better than nothing at all. She was so in love with him, her body ached; she couldn't eat—couldn't sleep. She'd gone through the closet several times to take her mind off Calum and look for the hidden door. That was a mistake: it only served to remind her how she'd thrown caution to the wind in there and how good it had felt. It was so easy to be herself in the dark, free of the childhood baggage that weighed her down. She promised herself she would enjoy the rest of her life with Calum, without that baggage.

It had been a week since Calum took Bret to the farm. A week she spent trying to work herself out... well, trying to anyway. Bruce had visited to teach her how to operate the fire extinguishers. Then he helped her put together a plan using the exit signs Calum installed. She'd been through fire drills at the London restaurant where she used to work, but this lesson on how to carry out a safe and calm escape was personal. An important day well spent. Other than that, Jennifer continued with the restaurant business. By Saturday morning, she had just one task left before the big opening: writing a 'Help Wanted' notice to put in the window. She slid behind the desk into the den's chair and opened her uncle's laptop. It whirred into life and asked for a password. 'Bugger,' Jennifer muttered softly. The old chair creaked as she leant back and intertwined her fingers behind her head. Was this like an ATM—three strikes and you're out? She tried to think of a password her uncle might use. She grabbed a pen and pad from the top drawer and started jotting down possibilities, like their birthdates and names. She could toss their initials into a hat and pick them out one by one; that might work, but the combinations were endless.

She listed pharmacy, potions, perfume, frock, and glamour.
Marilyn.
Veronica!
She keyed in Veronica and the screen lit up.
'Of course, he'd use his girlfriend's name.' Her fingers hovered over the keyboard, worried but telling herself this wasn't snooping and she should check her uncle's emails in case they needed a reply. She should at least cancel his account and send a message to everyone in his address book. 'So sorry, but Bob is no longer with us…'

She opened Microsoft Outlook and found it empty: there were no folders, nothing—very strange. Unless her uncle had cleared everything in his usual impeccable manner. No, he couldn't have. She'd been in touch with him until the week before he died. They'd chatted via Skype. When they first started contacting each other that way, he'd asked whether she'd mind if he saved the conversations on a disc. He'd explained he wanted to look back and have a good laugh, much like the days when families had slide nights. And of course she hadn't minded.

Jennifer looked around the room: so where were all those discs? Maybe they were stored somewhere in the computer's files.

Jennifer did a search but couldn't find anything. It was as if the computer had never been used, but she knew it had. She needed help from a computer nerd if she wanted answers.

Something didn't sit right about this; she could almost taste it. She shut down the laptop, pushed herself out of the chair, and started taking books off the shelves. Maybe her uncle had stored the discs away neatly, like a book with its own title and cover.

Lost in her search, Jennifer jumped, her heart jolting at the sudden buzz in her back pocket. She quickly fumbled for her phone.

'Hi, Jen,' Calum's deep voice murmured.

Her breath caught in surprise, and hearing his voice made her heart race.

'How're you going for time?'

'I'm good, done everything I needed to. Why?'

'Sorry, it's short notice, but Gran's decided to organise a special afternoon tea,' he said. 'Around three. I need to drop by Armidale for a distributor cap, but I'll be back well before then. Would you be able to make it?'

Absolutely, yes. Thank you.

'See you then. Can't wait.' And he was gone.

Staring at her phone, Jennifer took a deep breath and exhaled slowly, hoping her anxiety would ease. 'Okay, I can do this—keep it together, Jennifer.'

She started to pace. What should she wear? Would jeans be okay? It was warm out there. Maybe something lighter? 'Aggh! Jen, stop second-guessing.' She lectured herself, knowing it was total nonsense and a waste of time. Better to be productive and write the Help Wanted ad. After nearly an hour, she had a clear notice but couldn't get the printer to work. Jennifer gave up; bugger the Help Wanted sign—she'd never seen a sign in any of the fancy restaurants in London, anyway.

*   *   *

Every morning for the past week, Cassius the rooster had woken Bret at dawn. At least he was getting used to the bird's cock-a-doodle-dooing, which sounded less like a rooster and more like screeching tyres. Bret thought he was either getting on in years or had a throat issue. As if that wasn't enough, Priscilla, the sulphur-crested cockatoo and Uncle Bob's old troublemaker, would join in, mimicking Cassius and adding her own flair. Priscilla would follow anyone around, squawking, 'What a lovely frock, darling,' or 'Nice arse, nice arse!' even if there wasn't a frock or arse in sight. She also mimicked the phone and doorbell.

Priscilla was a bloody nightmare. Still, Bret had to admit, she was pretty cool.

Working on the farm was awesome; he woke up excited about what the day might bring.

Connie had insisted Bret have breakfast before mucking out the stalls in the barn. 'You can't possibly enjoy bacon and eggs after shovelling dung,' she'd said.

Bret grabbed a pitchfork and shoved it into the soiled hay. At that same instant, a bloody awful sound echoed through the valley. It can't have been the cockatoo. Bret stopped and listened, but now there was total silence, which also felt creepy. Goose bumps crept up his spine, making him shiver, but he kept mucking out the stables, not minding the smell of steaming horse dung and hay. His muscles strained as he heaved a full wheelbarrow, then headed for the steaming compost heap set up away from the house. As he stepped into the sunlight, Connie caught his eye, her rose-flowered apron fluttering as she hurried towards him on her long, spindly legs. Her face lined with worry, and her frantic waving made Bret wonder what the hell he was doing wrong, especially since Connie still had her house slippers on. Normally, they came off before she steps out the door.

Another agonising bellow ripped through the air and echoed around the hills. Bret cringed. 'What the friggin' hell? Oops, sorry Connie, didn't mean to swear, but that was—*insane!*'

Connie's wrinkles furrowed with worry as her thin arms flapped, vaguely pointing towards the house.

'That,' she paused to catch her breath, 'is George. He's in terrible strife.'

Bret nodded. 'Yeah, and George is letting the world know.'

'The poor pet needs help,' Connie's strong, bony fingers gripped his arm. 'Come on.'

'I've only seen George from a distance. I think he's out of my league. Where's Calum or Michelle?'

'Michelle's at school. We've got to do whatever we can.' Connie gave Bret a warm smile. 'I've seen you with the animals, you'll be fine.'

'Of course they love me. I've got food!'

'It's more than that, dear.' Connie blinked, bright eyes shining with innocence. 'You do have a certain affinity.'

'Yeah, right,' Bret muttered, not entirely convinced he could trust Connie. She was a shrewd old lady, and he liked her a lot, but this was beyond his capabilities.

'Really, dear, I've lived long enough to know you're wonderful with the animals. Believe me.'

Agonising bellows, the sort that tug at your heart, tore through the air again.

Bret stepped back and broke out in a cold sweat. He shot Connie a sideways look. 'Oh no, I'd like to help, but Calum can deal with George.'

Connie slipped her arm through his and led him back to the house. 'I've called him, he's in Armidale getting a new distributor cap for the tractor. It's going to take him over an hour to get back.'

As if on cue, George let go another thunderous roar.

'You don't really want to listen to that poor creature suffering in pain all morning, do you? I would never put you or any of my loved ones in danger. I have no doubt at all that you can do this, Bret…'

Loved ones? Bret's heart swelled, and, with his head in the clouds, he tripped over his own feet.

Connie didn't notice and continued, '…I have every faith in you.'

Bret rallied. 'Small animals like me, but that doesn't sound like one of them.' It was a mistake to glance at Connie's smiling, hazel eyes. His resolve melted. *Shit!* He looked to the skies for mercy.

'Stay right there,' Connie said. She hurried into the house, returning moments later, wearing gumboots and carrying a loaf of sliced wholemeal bread. 'Follow me,' she ordered, walking ahead of him.

'What's the bread for?'

Connie eased her pace so Bret could walk alongside her. 'It's for Killer George.'

Bret grabbed Connie's arm. 'Killer!'

'That's his nickname, because he isn't. You see? Or KG, as Michelle calls him.'

Bret rubbed the stubble on his chin. 'Oh, I think you're having fun at my expense.'

'Not at all, dear,' Connie giggled.

The sun reflected off a partially hidden object in her hand. 'What else have you got there? A gun?'

Connie stopped suddenly, nearly tripping over her own feet. 'A gun? What in heavens' name would I do with a gun?'

'Shoot George out of his misery? Shoot me out of mine?'

Hand to her chest, Connie turned to face him, horrified. 'George is like a member of the family, and you're definitely family, we would never.' Connie gasped. 'This,' she held up a heavy-duty clip on a chain, 'is George's lead.'

Shit! Connie should just stop talking; Bret wanted to believe he was part of this—a family that cared —but he doubted it was that easy. 'We're not talking dog here, Connie,' Bret said quietly.

'Oh, I know, dear. George is much sweeter. Almost sweeter than his namesake, my late husband.'

They rounded the corner of the house and, standing in the autumn sun, his warm breath fogging out of flaring nostrils, was George. He looked like a mythical beast, a hybrid from the future—where genetic doctoring had gone either horribly wrong or magnificently right.

'F-f-far out! What is that?'

'Don't be offensive, young man. He's not a that; he's George, he's a Black Angus. One of the biggest in the country. We've had him since he was a baby.'

'Connie, he's a friggin' giant,' Bret squealed. 'He's got his tongue up his nose.'

'Don't pull that face, dear; you look like you've eaten a lemon. Poor George.'

Bret forced a poker face. For her safety, he held Connie back with his arm across her chest.

'Come on,' Connie soothed. 'He's harmless, or he would've tried to…um…he would've given us the look by now.' She placed a hand on his arm and gently moved it out of her way.

'I've only ever seen George in a distant paddock. What's he doing here anyway? And tried to what, Connie? Given us what?' Bret whispered.

'Did I say that?' Connie asked innocently.

'That's it—we're going inside to call the RSPCA, a vet, or the fire brigade. Let's get all three—we'll need 'em.'

'Don't be silly, dear,' Connie said firmly. 'We've got the bread and his lead.' She pushed Bret closer.

George sniffed the air. He pawed the ground and snorted, frustrated that he couldn't move.

Adrenalin rushed through Bret, and more cold sweat broke out all over his body.

'Poor George.' Connie held out a slice of bread. A long, pale blue tongue gently hooked the slice out of her hand.

Bret squatted at a safe distance and peered under the beast. He grimaced: the massive bull had managed to get its legs tangled in some fencing wire. 'His leg looks awful—not much blood, but a couple of nasty gashes. Friggin' hell, I can almost see the bone.'

'You see what I mean now.' Connie rested her hand on Bret's shoulder and leaned closer for a better look.

'That's gotta hurt, mate.' Bret stood. 'Okay, let's think carefully about this.'

Connie gave him a reassuring smile. 'I knew you could help him.'

'What the hell.' Bret heaved a sigh. 'So he breaks every bone in my body; it's not like I'm busy right now.' He put both hands on his head and stopped to think it through.

'We're insured, you know,' Connie winked. 'We'll look after you, feed you.'

'That really puts my mind at ease. Okay,' Bret nodded. 'Make sure to tell Jennifer I love her, and that I'm sorry for all the trouble I've caused. And if I end up in a coma, she has my okay to pull the plug.'

Connie blinked at him. 'Nothing will happen to you, dear. You must have more confidence in yourself. Just cut the wire with the cutters I left on the fence post.'

'What I need is a rope to secure his horns. That way, he can't swing his head around and stick one in me—or you. Then I can tie the rope to the tree trunk here,' he said, slapping the spotted gum that stood nearby. 'Then I can tie up his rear end to the other tree and pull both nice and tight so he's got nowhere to go.'

Connie stood quietly, considering his plan. 'How are you going to get the ropes on him?'

'Lasso, of course. It can't be difficult, seen it on the telly plenty of times.'

'No-no-no, what *I'm* going to do is feed him slices of bread and clip the lead onto his nose ring,' Connie said. 'While *you* cut the wire.'

Bret shook his head in disbelief. 'Yeah, right.'

Connie dangled a slice of bread. George raised his massive head. His eyes bulged. The whites were showing—he looked insane. He sniffed the air and bellowed, dribbling saliva.

Bret stumbled backwards, losing his footing, and fell flat on his arse.

'Stop teasing him, dear,' Connie called out. 'He won't like that.'

Bret slipped the wire-cutters into his pocket and forced himself to step up to the enormous bull. George's massive, blue tongue curled out, took another slice of bread, and lazily chewed; his trapped leg forgotten for the moment.

Bret hunkered down at the rear end of the beast. 'Shit, they are the biggest pair of gonads I've ever seen.'

Connie giggled. 'They do the job all right. George is famous—aren't you, George? You're just a beautiful big boy,' she cooed, handing him more bread. 'You'd better get a wriggle on. I'm running out of slices fast.'

Bret rolled his eyes and turned back to the task. He grabbed hold of the trapped leg above the injuries, but it was like trying to lift a tree trunk out of the ground. George swung his head around, and Bret caught his eye. 'Don't you look at me like that, I'm trying to help you.'

Drool hung in glistening strings from George's mouth. He turned his head, and his tongue snaked out to lazily lick at an itch on his flank.

'Sorry, Bret. The chain simply ran through my fingers. Besides, I don't think it's a bad idea to let him see you're trying to help.'

Bret sent Connie a pissed-off, narrow-eyed glare. He pulled out the wire-cutters, extended his arm and, with his face turned away, one eye on the job and the other shut tight, he did what he had to do to free George.

Connie fed the bull another slice. 'Won't be long, George.'

Bret sidled up next to Connie. 'It's done.'

Connie squeezed him tight in a bear hug. Bret stiffened, arms and hands flat at his sides. 'Oh, you did it, you did it! I'm so proud of you—but how?' She stepped back, grinning up at him, glistening hazel eyes almost vanishing into the crinkly folds.

A warm glow spread through Bret. No one had praised him like that, no one had included him as part of a family, and no one had ever been this nice to him in a long time—if ever.

'I couldn't lift his foot, so…' Bret's eyes flicked all over the countryside. He didn't want to look at Connie. He could feel a sting behind his eyes and heat rise to his cheeks. 'So I tickled him,' he eventually mumbled.

'You tickled him? Where?'

Bret stepped back and, with his hands up, shook his head. 'Don't ask.'

Connie peered underneath the bull, and suddenly the penny dropped. 'Ingenious!'

'Don't you dare breathe a word to anyone,' Bret pleaded.

'I have to tell Calum, this could be revolutionary.'

'Yeah, right, Connie,' Bret nodded incredulously.

'You can do the honours and take him up to the barn. We'll have to fix his leg as best we can until Calum comes home.'

'What's happened to Killer George?'

'Did I say that?' Connie looked at him, all innocence. 'I could've sworn I said lady-killer.'

'Don't give me that look, I'm onto you, Connie. Yeah, not happy. Let's get the city dude with the killer bull thing.'

'Oh, but he can be dangerous to strangers who get in his way—on his turf—without bread and a lead.'

George took his time lumbering up the hard, dirt drive with a slow-motion swagger and a heavy clump-thump every time a hoof hit the ground. For some reason, Bret found himself comforted by the warmth and massive, steady strength this beast radiated. He felt the most relaxed he'd been in ages, and he was proud of himself—yeah, definitely proud.

Once Bret had spread a thick layer of fresh hay, he led George into the stall and tethered his lead to a post. Connie handed Bret the first aid kit; he opened it, and she pointed to a pot of salve for him to use. He scooped out a lump of the salve and, carefully, he gently spread the antiseptic cream on George's cuts. The bull stomped his leg a couple of times and turned his massive head to see what was happening. Perhaps Connie was right—the old bull knew they were helping him. Bret shook his head in wonder, then securely wrapped the leg with gauze and a crepe bandage.

'I hear a car. Must be Calum,' Connie said.

Footsteps hurried towards them. Calum peered into the stall. George had settled down on the hay to chew his cud.

'Got your message, Gran. Drove here as fast as I could, but doesn't look like I'm needed after all. Crikey! Look at him,' Calum said, grinning. 'Hey Bret, brilliant piece of work, mate.'

'Yeah, turns out *Killer* George is a pushover,' Bret said dryly. 'But you knew that already.'

Calum laughed. 'Ah, but when he's among the cows— watch out.'

'So I've been told,' Bret said.

'How'd you get the wire off him?' Calum asked.

Connie glanced at Bret, then turned to her grandson, smiling. 'He tickled him, and that's all I'm going to say on the matter. No amount of pressure will have me spill the beans.'

There was a long pause as all three looked at each other. Bret knew the moment he caught sight of the bull's gonads squished out between his hind legs that he'd given himself away.

'I get the picture,' Calum chuckled. 'Brilliant, looks like you've made a lifelong friend.'

'Don't go getting smart,' Bret said, pointing at them. 'If I hear about this from anyone else, you're both in deep trouble.'

Connie and Calum stood back smiling as Bret approached George. He hunkered down and tentatively scratched the patch of hair between the old bull's horns.

George closed his eyes and relaxed into Bret's hand.

'I think you like me,' Bret smiled down at the enormous animal.

Chapter 16

'Two-thirty!' Jennifer didn't want to be late for afternoon tea with Calum—and everyone else. She gulped down a glass of water, made a quick call to Brock, and hurried to her room. She changed into jeans, a white tank top, a pale blue cotton shirt, and a padded vest to keep warm in the autumn chill. Lastly, her favourite boots.

She ran to the police station, pushed the door open, and rushed inside. Brock, with a big grin on his face, waited behind the desk, keys hanging from his outstretched hand. 'I agree, a gleaming yellow Cadillac up Calum's drive will definitely cause a stir.' His deep voice almost made the windows rattle. 'It's the old dual-cab in the parking lot.'

'Thanks, you're a legend.' She grabbed the keys, swung around, and was out the door before it had a chance to shut.

Jennifer tried to decipher Calum's directions he'd sent to her phone. She passed the turnip-shaped boulder the size of a house and knew she was close. After another two kilometres, she saw the sign: Merandoora, Black Angus Stud. Approaching the driveway, she turned the car straight in over a bone-jarring cattle grid. She stopped to admire the long, winding driveway and craned her neck towards the windscreen for a better look at the magnificent, gnarled old eucalypts. Their branches arched over, creating a cathedral effect. She leant back and moved the car forward, loving the dappled sunlight gliding over the bonnet and windscreen as she headed towards the farmhouse.

A kilometre further on, a two-storey Edwardian sandstone farmhouse with white trim came into view. A white picket fence surrounded lush garden beds bursting with a riot of colourful asters and dahlias, lining the pathway. What caught her eye most was the gorgeous pink climbing roses that wound over a pergola. Jennifer parked under a gnarly old gum tree. She took a deep breath, and before nerves could get the better of her, she shoved open the door and stepped out of the car. A gentle breeze ruffled her hair and cooled her flushed face. Not sure where to go, she looked at the house then back to the barn, anxiously wondering where Calum might be—was he even back from Armidale yet? She heard water running and splashing from the barn and headed that way. Walking through the enormous barn doorway was like stepping back in time to a horse-and-buggy era. It took a moment for her eyes to adjust, but she could tell there were stalls lining the walls on either side. The smell of fresh hay, waxed leather, and animal dung filled the air, and dust motes danced in a beam of sunlight.

She sensed rather than saw Calum stride towards her from deep within the shadows.

An adrenaline surge filled her chest, and her cheeks flushed. She knew what she had to do, and he deserved nothing less.

She watched him approach; he grinned and, considering how she'd treated him a week ago, he looked very pleased to see her. Her breath caught at the casual way he moved towards her. Jennifer loved the way he walked, the way he looked in his worn jeans that sat low on his narrow hips. She loved his thigh muscles flexing with every step, his hands swinging easily at his sides. His tartan, flannel shirt hung open, revealing his pecs and firm abs under a tight white T-shirt.

Her heart skipped.

Rugged He-Man. Calendar Man, came to mind. Now that was a thought.

Her belly melted, and there was no controlling the heat spiralling through her body. God, she'd missed him.

'G'day,' his deep voice rumbled softly, 'I've missed you.'

Not saying another word, he bent down; one arm went around her back, the other behind her knees. He scooped her up and carried her to an empty stall where he set her down. Using his full length, he pressed her against a wall.

Okay, he wasn't pissed off with her for acting like a bitch—at all. There was no mistake; he was happy to see her.

His hands curled around her jaw, his thumbs gently caressed her cheeks, and his warm, tender eyes searched hers.

'You smell like soap,' Jennifer whispered.

He gave her one of his sexy, quirky smiles. 'Saw you coming and washed up.'

'Oh,' she said softly, and without thinking, she wrapped her hand around his wrist, buried her face in his palm and breathed him in.

She heard him suck in a breath and murmur, 'Fuck.'

Jennifer released his wrist. Calum moved his hands over her shoulders and down her arms until his fingers intertwined with hers. He lifted her hands and held them up, placing them on either side of her shoulders. What was he doing? Her stomach fluttered, sending a sensual thrill through her body.

'How are you?' she asked, trying to keep the wobble out of her voice, as he pressed his body against hers.

'I'm good now,' he murmured, as his deep, gentle gaze, with a hint of a smile, studied her face.

She licked her lips, and his eyes shifted to her mouth. 'Man,' he murmured, 'I've missed you.' His lips pressed softly against hers, slowly deepening their kiss with tenderness and emotion. Then, with a slight nip to her lips, he pulled away.

'I've missed you too,' she whispered, her body craving more of him. She looked around the barn, which had a distinct aroma of horses, cattle, and hay, and giggled as she pressed against him. 'What've you been up to?' she asked, her voice breathy and sultry.

'Farm stuff—hmm, I love kissing you. I love how you taste.' His mouth touched hers, murmuring, 'What've you been up to?'

'Girl stuff… and thinking… a lot.' Jennifer tilted her head, taking in every feature of his face. Calum kissed and nibble her exposed neck. Jennifer let out a soft little moan that seemed to come from a deep and until now undiscovered place.

'Thinking?' he mouthed against her skin.

'Yes,' she breathed, 'so much thinking and…and I kept coming back to the same thing.'

'Yeah, what thing?' he said and sucked her earlobe.

'Stuff…'

Calum stopped and pulled back to look at her face; his eyes held hers captive as he quietly said, 'You should stop overthinking and follow your instincts and feelings. Like you did a moment ago when you pushed your face into my hand. Fuck, you have no idea what you do to me,' he said, voice husky.

She didn't know what to say to that; all she could do right now was stay on her feet and breathe.

'Feel, Jen,' he rumbled, his hot hazel eyes fixed on hers. 'That's all you need to do.'

She nodded. 'Okay, but where is everyone?'

Understanding her reluctance, he grinned. 'Making scones. Stuff happened, and afternoon tea will be late. Right now, it's just you and me.'

Then he kissed and nipped her jaw. His fingers slipped out of hers and trailed down her palms, wrists, and the soft inner skin of her forearms. 'Feel how beautiful you are.' Then, using the backs of his hands, he swept them up again, pausing to caress her palms. All the while, he was kissing and nuzzling her neck, her ear, and her temple. 'Your skin's like silk and I love the smell of your hair.' Jennifer's body sang with pleasure; Calum's hands on hers, keeping them on the wall, made his ambush all the more erotic. Her bones had turned liquid. If his body hadn't been pressed hard against hers, she'd fall in a heap at his feet, but she'd make damn sure he'd come down with her. She gasped as he trailed his fingers down again, further this time to her sides, skimming past the swell of her breasts, her waist, and around her hips to cup the cheeks of her bottom. His strong fingers squeezed and tugged her in tight against his hips. Jennifer pulled her arms away from the wall and moved them around his neck, her fingers slipping into his hair. Eyes on hers, Calum angled his head and, with teasing, painstaking slowness, he closed in, then his hungry mouth was on hers again.

God, he could kiss. She moaned into his mouth. He pressed his body into hers and groaned in return as their kiss deepened.

A bird fluttering into the barn startled Jennifer out of Calum's sexy against-the-wall ambush. Breathing heavily, she tapped him on the shoulder.

'Wait a mo…' Jennifer panted against his mouth. He pulled back, his eyes intense as he focused on her face. She took a deep breath. 'I need…'

'Privacy?' He raised a questioning eyebrow. 'I wouldn't have started unless I knew we had it.' Eyes on hers, and tender with understanding, he added, 'I can give you more privacy.'

Jennifer battled her doubts and her upbringing, which insisted that image was everything, and chose to trust her feelings. 'Um…good.'

He kissed her again, deep, warm, and reassuring, and the moment his warm mouth gave her that, Jennifer felt her body and mind relax.

With a final kiss, Calum stepped back, grinning as he murmured, 'How about you, me and the haystack?'

'Hmm—who cares if I'm allergic to hay.'

'That's okay, I can always find us a big enough closet.'

'I was kidding about the hay,' Jennifer giggled, feeling sexy *and* bold.

'I knew that,' he said. 'I'll never forget that closet and—'

'Shut up, where's this haystack?' Jennifer asked, pulling him in for a quick hot kiss, grabbed his hand and started to make a move out of the stall. She'd go anywhere—behind a tree, over a hill—as long as they weren't within sight of the house.

She didn't get far. Calum stood his ground. She turned back to him, his hands went around her waist, held her close, and he murmured, 'I love you, Jennifer Dove, and that's got nothing to do with the hay, the closet or anywhere else.'

'I love you too,' Jennifer blurted. Okay, it wasn't a dream; she hadn't misheard what he'd said last Saturday.

She could no longer ignore her all-encompassing connection of body, mind, and soul with this beautiful man.

Brow furrowed, his intense, almost fierce, hazel eyes studied hers. 'You can't take that back, you know,' he said.

'Oh, I'm not aiming to, ever. I've had a whole week to think about…us.'

Slowly, his face lost its intense look and softened, becoming tender. 'Good, because it's hell not having you close.' Calum's hands slid up her back, over her shoulders to her neck, eyes on his thumbs sliding across her jaw. His head dipped, forehead touching hers, and his fingers gave her shoulders a little squeeze as if trying to help her understand. 'I fell in love with you the moment you sat up in Sofie's car with your hair all mussed up. Sleepy-faced, confused and bewildered. I love the way you fight for what you want.' His fingers pressed gently into her back, massaging the knots away. She gripped his arms. 'I love you dressed or naked,' he growled. She put a finger to his lips, but he kept going. 'I love how you make me feel,' he said against her finger. 'Nothing works unless you're around; without you, my dick's a useless appendage. Marry me, Jen.'

Jennifer lost her breath. She threw her arms around his neck. 'Make me,' she purred.

He followed her gaze towards the ladder that led up to the loft and smiled.

* * *

Jennifer chewed on a piece of straw, her head resting on Calum's arm.

'We need to organise a wedding,' he said with a wink. 'Have you done weddings?'

'You're my first wedding.' She laughed softly.

'I'm glad to hear it.' He tickled her ear with his mouth. 'Are you okay with having it here?'

'I'd love to have our wedding here, the gardens are stunning, it'd be beautiful.'

'My next question is—gold, white gold, or platinum? What's your preference?

'Gold with lots of bling.'

'What's bling?'

'Diamonds as big as a sugar cube.' Jennifer turned to get a better look at his face. He didn't seem at all worried. 'I'm kidding about the sugar cube.'

'I knew that,' he said, chuckling.

A loud clanging interrupted them. Jennifer sat up, hay in her dark curls and clothes.

'Good grief! What was that?'

'My phone.' Calum laughed, dug it out of his pocket, peered at the caller ID, and answered. 'Yeah, Gran?' he asked, while tugging bits of hay out of Jennifer's hair. 'No, just been showing Jen… Sure, we're on our way.' He slipped the phone back into his pocket. 'Afternoon tea's ready. Hot scones, jam, and cream.' He caressed her face with the back of his hand. 'You hungry?'

'Am I ever. Must be the country air—and hay.'

Calum stood and held out his hand for Jennifer. 'I'll go down first, you come directly after me,' he said.

'You just want to look at my arse,' she said, eyebrow raised.

'Love your arse. I could spend all day…Truth is, if I go first and you happen to slip, your lovely arse would have a soft landing.'

'Okay, my arse on your soft head,' she laughed.

'Yeah,' he chuckled, 'I fell into that one.'

Back on the barn floor, Jennifer brushed hay, seeds, and grassy bits off Calum's back while he tried to do the same for her. Satisfied there was little evidence, he took her hand, and they headed for the house.

'Jen, I can't wait. I want to tell everyone right now, you're mine, I'm yours.'

A rush of adrenaline caught her breath. 'Okay,' she whispered.

Calum toed off his boots and showed Jennifer where she could wash up. Mouth-watering aromas of freshly baked scones and cake filled the air.

The moment Jennifer walked into the large sunny country kitchen, Connie called out, 'There you are. I saw your car drive up ages ago. What have you two been doing all this time?'

Michelle and Bret looked up from the battered timber table, faces beaming, shoulders shaking as they fought to keep from laughing out loud.

'Hi,' Jennifer said, ignoring Connie's awkward question as she held the older woman's arm and kissed her cheek in greeting. 'How are you, Connie?'

'Couldn't be better,' Connie giggled.

Calum came up beside Jennifer. 'Why is everyone looking weird?'

'Could be the bits of hay and crap in both your hair,' Michelle said dryly, pointing at them.

'We were looking for a needle,' Jennifer grinned.

Everyone laughed, and the awkward moment vanished.

'I think you've finally met your match, Calum.' Approval lit Connie's face.

Bret pushed his chair back. Arms out, he headed for Jennifer. 'Jen's pretty quick. Sofie's the dippy one.'

Jennifer hugged him. He still felt skinny under her hands, but stronger, if that were possible in just a few days. 'I'm very proud of you, bro,' she whispered.

On the opposite side of the table, Connie pulled a handkerchief out from the depths of her blouse and dabbed her eyes. 'Come on, everyone, sit.' Her voice broke a little. 'Have a scone before I get any older.'

Calum pulled out a chair for Jennifer.

'Thank you,' Jennifer said, trying to stay calm. She fidgeted with her napkin. Calum covered her hands with one of his and gave hers a gentle squeeze.

He leant into her side and whispered, 'Relax.'

Sure, but he could announce their engagement at any moment. To ease her nerves, she turned to Michelle. 'How's school these days?'

'Too much homework,' Michelle wrinkled her nose. 'Too much of everything.'

'I sympathise, it's tough. Do you know anyone not studying? I'm after a waiter or waitress to help with the restaurant's opening.'

'I'd love to do that, it'd be a terrific experience. I'm your woman—waitress-person,' Michelle said, enthusiastically slathering jam and cream on her scone.

'Do you need to check that it's okay?'

'Of course it is.' Showing determination, Michelle sat up straighter in her chair. 'And Cal's happy to take me into town any time. Just let me know when.'

As there were no objections, Jennifer carried on. 'Michelle?' She waited until she had eye contact. 'Claudia will be up this weekend with her mum. Drop by sometime and we'll go through presentation and waitressing.'

'Sure, it'll be great catching up with Claudia. What're your plans?'

'I want to build a reputation for the restaurant,' Jennifer told everyone. 'Have it known in Sydney as *the* place to dine when they're on weekend getaways.'

'That's a brilliant idea. It'll do wonders for the town,' Connie said.

Bret helped himself to another scone. 'Hmm, these are good.'

'Make it happen, Jen,' Michelle grinned.

'I'll do my best.' It was hard to keep her mind on the topic. Every time Calum moved or opened his mouth, she wondered if he was about to make the big announcement.

'You could start off with a package deal,' Michelle said, full of youthful enthusiasm. 'Motel or B&B, plus winery tours and dinner.'

'Yeah, Jen,' Calum began, grabbing a scone, 'you can show me around and feed me that candlelit dinner you owe me, and then we can f...'

Calum bit into a scone smothered in jam and cream, just as Connie smacked him up the back of the head. Cream splattered his face. Calum didn't blink, scooped the mess with a finger, put the lot into his mouth, and carried on as if nothing had happened. 'Yeah, I've seen how an order comes, and there's this pretty little pile in the middle of your plate with a bit of sauce dribbled over it, a sprig of this and that, and you know someone should've gone to art class instead. But I've heard Bob rave about your amazing meals. The town is going to line up outside your door, Jen.'

Jennifer stifled a grin and tried not to blush. 'A lot of hard work goes into making a meal taste great and look even better. But you wouldn't know; you're probably a meat-pie-and-tomato-sauce man.'

'Not if I can help it,' Connie said.

'I'm your pie man,' Bret announced, reaching for another scone. 'Especially Jen's pies,' he laughed. Weeks of deprivation, while missing and desperate, had slipped away, disappeared.

Bright-eyed and excited, Connie told everyone how Bret had saved the day. 'He was amazing,' she told Jennifer. 'I can see he's going to be a great help on the farm. I told him he had a calming influence and wonderful hands with the animals. And you know what he did? He blushed. My goodness, anyone would think he'd never heard praise before.'

'He probably hasn't,' Jennifer mumbled. She felt the heat rise to her cheeks. 'My parents weren't into praising, not for the right reasons anyway. And I wasn't much help.'

'Yes, you were,' Bret piped up. 'You and Sofe were always protecting me.'

'Yes, Bret, I'm sure they were too,' Connie reassured. 'So what you said, Jen, is nonsense, dear. It's the parents' job to raise their children. You were busy growing up yourself. Bret thinks very highly of you and Sofie. He talks about you both all the time.' She leant across and kissed Jennifer's cheek.

'Jen, as soon as the vet sees George and his leg's okay, I'll come and help out.'

'You can help my fiancée out any time,' Calum announced.

Right at that very moment, Jennifer had a cup of tea to her mouth: she choked, coughed, and tea gushed everywhere. *I have a fiancé. I am a fiancée.*

Silence. Three sets of eyes widened as they looked from Jennifer to Calum. Jennifer could hear her heart pounding. Or was that her fiancé's?

Connie gasped and covered her mouth with both hands in surprise. She gathered her wits. 'This is wonderful news, wonderful!' she laughed. She pushed her chair back and hugged them both. 'I'm so happy for you.'

'Sis, you're gonna marry my boss!'

'And it's about time,' Michelle said.

'Okay, that's enough hugging.' Calum slapped Bret on the back and pushed him off.

'You'd better make me a bridesmaid,' Michelle said, holding onto Jennifer's arm.

'Bridesmaid? Sure,' Jennifer said, suddenly feeling overwhelmed.

'I'd crack open a bottle, but Jen needs to drive home.' Calum brought her hand to his mouth and kissed her palm.

'Perhaps we can organise something just for the family,' Jennifer suggested. 'It might have to be after the opening.'

'Good idea,' Calum nodded, 'And we can have a family reunion when Mum and Dad get back. Meanwhile, FaceTime is great.' He turned to Jennifer.

She could feel him watching her as she admired the homely kitchen. The aroma of fresh scones lingered in the air. The afternoon sun hit the dresser, shining on the vintage crockery where framed family photos stood, some with sports ribbons draped over them. She quickly averted her eyes to the table, now a mess with crumbs and the odd blob of jam and cream, which was, in Jennifer's view, perfect. The family gathered around it, so relaxed, warm, and welcoming, also perfect—and something she'd never experienced in her life. Best of all, Bret had found his place, his home. Seeing him among these wonderful people who had taken him in made her eyes well up, and she didn't try to hide her emotions, no bugger that, not hiding from life ever again. Using her serviette, she dabbed her eyes and took a sip of water.

She felt Calum's warm presence beside her, his reassuring hand resting on her thigh as he quietly asked, 'Are you okay? I'm getting conflicting vibes. What are you smiling at?'

'Are you alright, dear?' Connie asked, concerned.

Jennifer managed a tentative smile. 'Yes, thank you, I'm very alright.' She turned to look at Bret and could see that he knew what she was thinking. His eyes glistened, and he gave her a knowing, but deeply worried, gentle smile, then reached across the table to squeeze her hand.

'Will someone please tell me what's going on here?' Michelle's tone made it clear that platitudes wouldn't be tolerated.

Jennifer took a deep breath and collected her thoughts. 'There are three of us in our family. Sofie, Bret, and me. Growing up, we never experienced unconditional love; there was always a catch, a warning. Appearance was everything.' Feeling old traumas flood her mind and heart, she took a slow breath in and out. 'It's long and unpleasant, so I won't bother you with the details. What you have here around this incredible table is what a family meal should be like—not the sterile, perfect setting our parents always insisted on. Perfection was especially enforced when we were out among their "people."'

'We're nothing special, this is just how we are, dear.' Connie, hand on her chest and mouth trembling, turned to look at Bret, and she didn't speak until she had eye contact. 'You're both part of us now. That will never change…never-ever.'

'Yeah, I'm with you, Gran!'

Jennifer didn't miss the emotion flickering across Bret's face. Heartbreaking, she watched him hold back his tears by sheer will, then a quick, private nod told her everything. In that instant, she knew her sweet brother was finally determined to take control of his life. And that said it all before he ducked his head, and, shoulders trembling, cupped his face. Despite his trauma, Bret was going to be okay, and that made her heart sing.

'Bret,' Jennifer prompted with care. 'It's okay. You're only ever expected to be you.' She leaned across the table and held his arm. 'That's all anyone here wants. If Sofie and Claudia were here, they'd feel the same…Bret?'

He looked up, eyes shining with emotion, but managed a shaky smile. For the first time ever, Jennifer saw her brother not as a boy always striving for approval, but as someone finally beginning to believe he belonged.

But before he could say anything, Michelle—sitting beside him—leaned closer, gave him a cheeky look and, with the biggest grin, wrapped her arms around his shoulders in a spontaneous, honest hug, saying, 'I've always wanted another brother, to hang shit on.' She declared, giggling.

Jennifer caught the look that passed between them—surprise, relief, and a flicker of hope. She smiled, knowing Bret could never deny the moment, not that she thought he would.

Bret startled at first, let out a strangled laugh, and awkwardly patted Michelle's arm. His tentative grin transformed into a genuine smile that lit up his whole face.

The warmth and emotions around the table were palpable as Jennifer held back tears, grateful beyond words that her brother was finally home.

They were a family, imperfectly perfect.

Calum wrapped an arm around her back and, leaning in, whispered, 'Want me to drive you home?'

'No, but thanks for offering.' She kissed his cheek then pushed back her chair. 'Thank you for this…' she stopped to take a deep breath, 'this extraordinary, fabulous afternoon tea. So much has happened and so much has changed for the better.' She smiled and looked at Bret. 'You'll be fine. You've always been amazing.'

Jennifer kissed her brother and Michelle goodbye, then headed for the door, with Calum and Connie following.

'Before I go, Connie, have you seen Calum's amazing work?'

'Not finished, I haven't.'

You and Shirley should pop in for a coffee or tea before the opening next Saturday week.

'That would be lovely, dear. What day suits you?'

'Any time is fine,' Jennifer gave a little shrug. 'Whenever you like. Drop by next time you're in town.'

'Thank you, dear, I look forward to it.' Connie patted Jennifer's hand. 'Please don't worry about Bret,' Coonie's eyes welled up. 'He's a wonderful young man and a joy to have around.'

Thank you, Connie. He needed this change. I could easily stay here all afternoon. I've really enjoyed this, especially seeing Bret and how, with your help and trust, he's come into his own. She reached over and kissed her cheek. But I'd better head off; my sister and niece are due back any moment. Thanks for the scones and tea, and for the love and warmth you've shared. But especially for the positive change in Bret, which is priceless.

Calum's hand gave her waist a gentle squeeze.

*　　*　　*

Calum escorted Jennifer to her car and opened the door. But before letting her go, he pulled her to him, and gave her the wildest kiss. Her knees buckled, she fell back against the door with Calum plastered to her.

'This time you taste like jam and cream,' he murmured.

'You still taste like hay.' Jennifer wrinkled her nose. 'Probably something you ate,' she said dryly, and couldn't hold back the laugh, which echoed around the quiet valley.

'Stop it, you'll scare the animals,' he grinned, hands caressing her waist.

She took a breath and wriggled against him, loving the feel of his big hands. 'You'd better stop that, I need my wits about me when I drive home.'

His grin broadened into a wide, satisfied smile. He stepped back enough to give her some breathing space. 'You'd better drive to the conditions.'

She gave him a wry look and said, 'Excuse me a moment.' She slipped out of his grasp, ducked across the driver's seat to the passenger side, grabbed her wallet, and turned to see Calum looking amused.

'You don't want to go doing that in town,' he said, sounding amused. 'There'd be a pile-up in Grey Street.'

'Huh?' Jennifer didn't know what he was on about.

'You bending over, arse wriggling while you rummage to get whatever it is,' he explained.

She looked over her shoulder and gave him a provocative smile. He deserved nothing less. 'As I have no car, it won't be happening in a hurry.'

'Brock's twin-cab?' Calum nodded towards the car.

'Yep.' Jennifer straightened, opened her wallet, and took out a bank cheque for six thousand dollars. 'Here, I hope this is the correct amount.'

Calum glanced at the cheque, plucked it from her fingers, and tore it up.

'You can't do that!' Jennifer cried out.

'Well, I just did. I don't want your money, Jen. This is between Bret and me. You've seen the change; he's doing great. He grinned, 'I'll be family soon.'

Jennifer studied his face. 'You already are. As for Bret, thanks to you, Connie, and Michelle, I've never seen him this happy and confident.'

He nodded. 'I like what I'm seeing. Bret's a good man.'

'Yeah, he was there all along,' Jennifer pushed him away. 'I've got to go now before I blubber all over the place. It's not a pretty sight.'

'Woman, you amaze me. I couldn't give a rat's arse if you came dripping after me.' He pulled an 'Oops' face. 'Maybe I should rephrase that,' he said, laughing at himself. Jennifer rolled her eyes. 'Jen, you're beautiful anytime, anyway, anyhow,' he said and tucked her in close.

She kissed his ear and nibbled the lobe. Stepping back, she asked, 'When will you be in town again?'

'Tonight, I'm sleeping with you,' he said, as if her question was weird.

'Um…' It was her turn to pull a face. 'My sister and niece will be at the house. I want a little alone time with Sofe, tell her our news and get silly-tipsy.'

'Really?' His eyes lit up. 'I'm not missing out on seeing my woman behaving cute and happy-sloppy-drunk.'

'I'm not cute, seriously.'

'Yes, you are. I'll get there later, around ten; you should be well and truly primed by then.' He grinned his sexy grin, and she couldn't say no. Besides, she was actually looking forward to it and grinned back at him. 'You're a fox,' he said, pulling her into him. 'You, me, and the closet, soon. Or did you go in without me?'

'I tried…it's not nearly as much fun. And I didn't find anything.' Jennifer hopped into the dual-cab. 'Anyway, you, me, and the closet have a thing going. Any time suits.' She gave him a sultry smile and took off.

*　*　*

'I'll just be in my sewing room.' Connie dried her hands after washing the afternoon tea dishes.

'Sure, Gran, I'll get on with my homework,' Michelle said and put the last of the cups away. 'Hope Calum stays far enough away, especially since Bret has gone to check on KG.'

An eerie wail echoed from a distant hill. Connie pushed the lace curtains aside just as George bellowed. 'Come quick, Michelle,' she beckoned.

Michelle reached her side just as Bret bolted out of the barn like a man possessed. He sprinted, wild-eyed, straight for the back door.

Tears of laughter ran down Connie's face.

Michelle clutched her grandmother's arm, 'Crikey, he's the funniest dude!'

The screen door slammed shut, and Bret came charging into the kitchen, barely able to speak.

'What the f-f…hell was t-that?' he said through heavy panting.

'Do you mean the noise or George?' Connie giggled, struggling not to laugh.

'The noise—the ugly noise!' he yelled, eyes wide, pointing towards the hills.

'Sorry, Bret,' Michelle snort-giggled, hand over her mouth. 'Didn't Cal warn you?'

All Cal said was he's heading up the south paddock hill to practise. I didn't think to ask, practise what? It was horrible, and it scared the absolute crap out of George and me. You should've seen his eyes.

'You should've seen yours. And what about us having to put up with your practising?' Connie handed Bret a few slices of bread. 'Here, go and soothe poor George before he breaks something.'

'At least I do it quietly. And don't let Jennifer and Sofie know what I'm practising, it's a surprise.' Bret sauntered off back to the barn. Before he disappeared into the shadows, he turned and yelled, 'Not a word!'

'I'll go and help him,' Michelle said, still giggling.

Connie kissed her cheek and headed for her sewing room. She closed the door, picked up her phone and called Shirley.

'Hi, Shirl, you know how Jennifer's back, well, guess what. My plan worked.'

*　　*　　*

After dropping Brock's car off at the police station, Jennifer walked back to the restaurant, basking in the new feeling that she was a fiancée, Calum's fiancée.

The setting sun cast a deep, golden glow over the countryside, enriching the autumn tones and making them stand out in stunning relief. God, it was beautiful. Her life was beautiful. Calum was beautiful, and she was on a high as she strolled back to the restaurant. She knew the moment she told Sofie her exciting news, her sister was going to cry.

Happiness hummed through her as she hurried inside and called out, 'Sofie!'

'I'm up here! Did you see the posters?' Sofie exclaimed, waiting on the landing, arms wide, ready for a hug. 'Hi, Jen, bet you're excited about the opening?'

'Excited? Are you kidding? I'm ecstatic. The posters look fantastic, thanks for handing them out so quickly,' Jennifer said into her sister's sweet-smelling curls. 'Boy, I'm so glad you're here to help.'

'Only because I'm pathetically dateless.' Sofie stepped back and eyed Jennifer. 'You know I'm kidding, right? Even Adonis on a white horse couldn't keep me away.'

Jennifer gave her sister a squeeze. 'I know that.'

'Come on, I'll make us a coffee. What have you been up to? You look all rosy and you smell like a barn,' Sofie paused to study Jennifer. A soft light grew until it shone like a knowing beacon in her eyes. She grabbed Jennifer by the shoulders.

'Why are you giving me that weird look?' Jennifer asked. Sofie dropped her chin and raised an eyebrow. 'Alright, you win. Calum and I made wild love in a haystack.' Jennifer's grin bubbled into a belly laugh. 'Well, not a haystack, more like a pile of hay up a ladder in a loft, which was in the barn, above George.'

The gob-smacked look on her sister's face was priceless. Hand to her chest, Sofie gasped. 'You had sex with Calum!'

'Twice, actually.'

'In the haystack?' Sofie asked with a wide-eyed stare. 'Tell me you had safe sex?'

'*Well*, it was hot and spontaneous, and safe didn't really get a look in.'

'There'll be a shotgun wedding. I'm so jealous,' Sofie pretended to pout. 'Was it good? Did he make you scream?'

'I believe, Oh God, was mentioned a few times.'

'Does he have a brother, an uncle, a friend? Hang on, who's George?'

'George is an enormous bull.' Jennifer wrapped an arm around her sister's shoulder and led her through to the kitchen. 'And sorry, no brothers, but I can introduce you to a few firemen.'

'Forget the coffee, this calls for a glass of wine—or two—I want all the details.'

'Where's Claudia? I'll go say hello first.'

'Don't bother, Claud, she's in the den finishing off an important essay. I'll give her a censored version. She's earned it after we filled her head with men's crap. First, tell me all about Bret, and then I'll take the spicy stuff, thanks.'

'I'll get the nibblies, you get the wine.'

Jennifer was ready to burst with the wonderful news of Calum's proposal, but wanted to make the moment special. She found nuts and crackers in the pantry and placed them on the kitchen table. Sofie poured them each a glass of red. Jennifer took a sip and let the fruity liquid roll over her tongue.

'Hmm…lovely.'

'So, apart from a frolic in the hay, what else did you get up to?' Sofie studied her face for a clue. 'C'mon, I know there's something.'

Jennifer reached across and held her sister's hands. She tried a mysterious smile and, for a moment, thought she'd pulled it off, because Sofie simply gazed back.

'This better be good,' Sofie said. 'Because despite the look on your face, you're scaring me now.'

'It's good, very good,' Jennifer leant closer. 'Calum asked me to marry him.'

Sofie squealed and lunged across the table, hugging Jennifer. 'Was it only the second day we were here that I said, you'd be married soon?' she asked.

'Probably. I nearly pulled over on my way home to yell down the phone—we're getting married! But I'd have missed that look on your face then.'

'I'm so happy for you both. He's divine.' Sofie dabbed her eyes. 'Where are you having the ceremony? You've got to find a gown, organise flowers and catering, there's so much to do.'

'Keep your undies on. We haven't set a date yet, let us get engaged first.'

'You'll be looking for an engagement ring together,' Sofie said wistfully.

'Let's get off the subject of weddings. You're turning into a mother of the bride.'

After half a glass, she relayed what had happened on the farm. 'Killer George is Bret's pet bull.'

Sofie blinked away her tears. 'Bret's going to be all right, I can feel it in my bones.'

Jennifer raised her glass. 'Here's to you and your bones— and Calum's too.'

'Chin-chin,' Sofie said. 'And now more of the spicy stuff, please.'

The bottle of red was nearly empty when Jennifer finished. She kept the more intimate details to herself. 'Calum tore up the bank cheque. He said it was strictly between him and Bret. Remind me to go to the bank and cancel it.'

'What's happening with the opening?' Sofie asked.

'Michelle's favourite subject at school is art. Last term, they had to design a brochure for a local business of their choice. She got an A plus for her work. She's coming past one day this week to help, and we'll talk about designing invitations. I thought a lovely photo of the dining room, all set out with candles, linen, and tableware, would look good. We can use the same photo on the flyers, with "Everyone Welcome" written across the top. It'll be a great experience for both Claudia and Michelle.'

'Yes, it will.' Sofie waved a hand towards the window. 'The courtyard looks spotless.'

'What?' Jennifer cut in. 'I left not long after lunch and it was still a workman's dumping ground.' She pushed her chair back, went to the landing, and switched on the outside lights. Hurrying to the window, she opened it and hung out for a good look. 'Crikey, they even laid a patio!' she yelled.

'Six burly blokes made short work of cleaning up the mess and laying tiles. All I have to do is plant the beds out, easy-peasy. Can't wait to get my hands dirty,' Sofie said, full of excitement.

Jennifer took a sip of wine and, eyes squinting with concentration, peered into her sister's face over the rim of her glass. 'You're well over your usual bubbly self. What's going on?' Sofie's eyes widened and blinked a little too often as she tried to maintain an innocent expression. Jennifer wasn't convinced. 'Hmm?'

'Okay,' Sofie raised her hands, palms out. 'One of the rubble removers was police officer Brock. Did you know he owns a garden centre?' Jennifer shook her head. 'Well, he's helping me with plants tomorrow. He's gorgeous!' she said on a breath and a grin.

'Go for it,' Jennifer lifted her glass to Sofies. 'And a big fat Cheers to that.'

'Uh-huh, all right for you to say… maybe I'm reading more into this than I should. I mean, he's… he's,' Sofie stammered, then continued in a rush, 'he's one hell of a big bloke.'

'Yes, and?'

'What would he want with me?' Sofie's shoulders lifted in question. 'I'm a single mum, with a teenage daughter. When Claudie's not moody, then I am. Who in their right mind would want that?'

'An ex-SAS guy,' Jennifer nodded, smiling.

'Yeah right,' Sofie shook her head and changed the subject, which Jennifer thought was a shame, because she was *so* enjoying this. 'If Calum has time, the whole back area needs decking out with fairy lights.'

'Sure, I'll run it by him. He'll know which ones we should use.'

'Cool. By the way, Claudie and I had a look at the wardrobe. It's more like a standalone walk-in closet. We tried really hard to move it, but the bloody thing wouldn't budge, so we went inside. Couldn't find a way to get into the space you mentioned. You know, it might not have anything to do with Uncle Bob.'

It was a miracle Jennifer kept a straight face; she was so glad she hadn't mentioned having sex with Calum in the closet and went on calmly, 'That's what Calum suggested. One way or another, we'll work it out.'

An hour and another bottle of wine later, Jennifer was laughing at anything Sofie said. And Sofie was laughing at anything Jennifer said. When Claudia walked into the kitchen, Jennifer's forehead was resting on the table; she brushed her curls aside and looked up at her beautiful niece, free of Goth make-up.

'Great—my mum and aunt are shitfaced. *Niiice* role models.' She pulled a face, shook her head, turned and left, muttering, 'I'm going to bed.'

'Me too,' Jennifer sighed. Steadying herself by holding onto the table, she shuffled around to her sister, helped her up, and took her to their uncle's renovated old room. 'Help your mum, Claudie.' She left them and wobbled and giggled all the way down the hall to the pink bedroom, stripped off her clothes, and flopped into bed.

Sometime during the night, Jennifer felt the touch of Calum's big, warm hand as he gently wrapped it around her waist and pulled her close to his chest and hips.

'Hmm,' she hummed sleepily, snuggling closer.

He kissed her neck and whispered, 'Sleep.'

'Can't,' she murmured lazily, 'something's poking my bum.'

Jennifer heard a quiet chuckle and felt his body shake. She smiled and drifted off.

Chapter 17

Jennifer woke up with a dry mouth and a dull ache behind her eyes. She reached across the bed, disappointed there wasn't a hot Calum to cuddle up to, but he'd left a note on his pillow, which said: 'Panadol, coffee's ready, fry-up good for hangover. Later, Cal, 8.' But what did the eight mean? She placed the note on her bedside table and smiled at his thoughtfulness, even though the thought of food made her stomach churn. Perhaps coffee and toast would be enough.

After breakfast alone, she made her way downstairs to her restaurant, armed with a stack of serviettes. It gave her a buzz to see the stunning Edwardian dining room. Soft furnishings in deep red, crisp white linen tablecloths, sparkling tableware, and lampshades for romantic lighting perfectly complemented the look she was after. Jennifer sighed, breathing in the room's new smell. It wouldn't take long for the aroma of herbs and spices to fill the air. Content, she headed for the buffet with her serviettes, intending to fold them into fan shapes.

A long, mournful wail pierced the air.

Jennifer screeched and jumped in fright, her knee knocking the table and rattling a few glasses. Panicked, she scanned the room and the road outside. The sound took off again, closer this time. And she realised the howling was definitely coming from somewhere out back.

Sofie and Claudia were yelling from their bedroom. Jennifer raced upstairs to join them.

Her sister and niece burst out of their uncle's old bedroom. Hand on her heart, eyes wide, Sofie asked, 'What the hell was that?'

Face pale, Claudia clung to her mum. 'Yeah, what the fuck, that's insane?!'

'Don't look at me,' Jennifer said. 'I didn't do it, and I swear I didn't touch anything. And it's not the smoke alarms either.'

The dreadful wail echoed through the air again, and the hair on Jennifer's arms stood up as a shiver ran up her spine. The wailing went on, then suddenly…blessed silence. Something told Jennifer this was just a lull that would soon end—but when?

She cringed as more discordant notes rattled the windows.

'Whatever that is,' Claudia yelled over the noise, 'it's out of tune!'

Jennifer grinned as realisation slowly dawned. 'It's a piper, and there's only one making all that noise. Can you imagine a whole bunch doing that?' A questioning frown crossed Jennifer's face as she glanced at her sister and niece. 'Do bagpipes need tuning?'

'I don't think so, you don't tune a recorder,' Sofie told them. 'Aren't they kinda the same thing, but without an airbag?'

Jennifer held her finger to her lips for the other two to shush as the noise persisted. 'It sounds like he's getting the hang of it.'

Claudia wrapped her arms around herself to keep warm. Then sweet niece made a face and said, 'You're nuts, Aunt Jen. It sounds like someone's murdering an animal.'

Sofie held out one side of her dressing gown for Claudia to huddle under. 'No, sweetie, that would be violins.'

'Whatever. If it doesn't stop soon, I'm gonna throw a shoe at him or her. And if I can get hold of the bag, I'll personally cut it up into tiny little pieces.' Claudia slipped out from under her mother's dressing gown and hurried back to Bob's bedroom on tiptoes, her fingers in her ears.

'Go have a lie-in, Sofe,' Jennifer yelled over the noise. 'I'll go out the back and ask them nicely to move on.'

'Don't be ridiculous, Jen. Find him and chuck a bucket of ice water over him. It's freezing, I'm having a hot shower. And a lie-in? Of all the crazy…' The bagpipe squealed again, and Sofie took off running.

'I really think he's getting better at it,' Jennifer called out to Sofie and Claudia.

'Bullshit!' was their united reply

Jennifer hurried over to the kitchen window for a better look.

A piper stood below in full dress uniform of red blazer and red and black tartan. His silver buttons sparkled, and braids glistened, a truly magnificent sight. He also looked familiar. He sounded pretty good, even with the odd off note. She could see about forty heads, caps tilted, milling about in the lane behind the fence. Jennifer wondered what the hell they were doing when, as if by magic, they formed up four abreast, in perfect lines.

'Hey, you down there! *HEY!*' she yelled louder. Deafened by his own screeching and blaring, all her waving and yelling had no effect on the piper.

Jennifer hurried outside and immediately recognised the player's legs. Eyes closed, deep in concentration, she needed to get his attention. 'Hey!' she yelled and squeezed the airbag. A bunch of off notes hit the air, making her flinch and shudder. 'Calum!'

He peered out from under his cap and gave her a wicked grin. 'G'day,' he said, voice rumbling sexily from around the mouthpiece.

'G'day?' she said, trying to sound casual, which was pretty much impossible. The allure of his strong, Scottish brawn, a turn-on. Or was it the kilt? 'Take that tubey-thing out of your mouth.' He did, and she pressed her lips to his. He reached for her and drew her close, accompanied by a clatter of pipes.

The airbag whined, *Wheeeaaaeeerh!* until it died.

She ended the kiss and said, 'We just crushed your friend. Your purse is digging into my belly, and those pipey things are putting dents in my boobs. I have to say, Sofe and Claudie will be most pleased that we killed your friend, your pet.' She stepped back to get a better look at him. It wouldn't matter what he wore, but this uniform had a wickedly sinful effect on her.

He grinned. 'Should I wear this more often?'

'Hmm, love the knees,' Jennifer looked down. 'Nice purse. Love the red tartan. What's under the kilt?'

'Secret men's business.' Keeping eye contact with Jennifer, he winked and slowly put the mouthpiece between his lips, blew air into the bag, squeezed, and played a few notes.

Jennifer grimaced. 'You should warn a girl before you blow that thing.'

'Won't do it again until we're coming down Grey Street. You might want to find a good vantage point in case you want another look at the knees. And there's something else you should see.' He performed a perfect about-turn; his kilt whirled tantalisingly high, but not quite high enough, then Calum marched out the gate to join the rest of the band.

Jennifer wondered whether to warn her sister and niece. She went upstairs, found Claudia snoring with her mouth open and her earbuds stuck in, listening to music. Should she bother? Nuh.

She heard the shower running and popped her head in the door. 'Sofe!'

Yeah, Jen. Thanks for finally stopping that bloody awful racket.

'Quick, put something on,' Jennifer grabbed a towel and handed it to her. 'Or you'll miss seeing it!'

'Seeing what?' But Sofie hadn't missed Jennifer's urgency. In a flash, she was dry and pulling on underwear, jeans and a warm jumper. She shoved her feet into her socks and sneakers, ruffled her hair, and headed downstairs.

Jennifer opened the front door and squinted into the early morning sunlight. Eyes adjusting, she took in the colourful scene of people milling about on either side of the street.

'What's going on?' Sofie asked, shading her eyes.

'I'm not sure. Calum mumbled something about a sausage sizzle fund-raiser, but he never mentioned this.'

'Aw, he wanted to surprise you. And us.'

'Here they come.' Jennifer stood on tiptoe to see down Grey Street. She forgot all about her hangover watching the magnificent, glorious colours and pageantry marching towards them. The marshal, dressed in full splendour, twirled his silver mace, followed by Calum leading the band of kilted men marching to Scotland the Brave.

Jennifer's heart swelled and her smile widened as Calum drew closer.

The heart-wrenching music and the men looking so masculine and proud brought a lump to Jennifer's throat. Calum was a mere few metres away when his eyes flicked in her direction. She held her breath and felt the heat of their unspoken connection. Calum's wink proved he felt it too, and her breath quickened. She could hardly believe it. It only took a few seconds, but in that brief moment, amidst hundreds of people, she shared a private, tender connection with Calum. The feeling lingered with her. Somehow, she knew their bond would be eternal. She barely noticed the rest of the band as they marched past.

Claudia, wearing Sofie's dressing gown, peered over her shoulder. 'Hectic!'

Sofie gasped. 'I want one! Can I choose?'

'Mum!' Claudia complained.

'Oh-my-God—oh-my-God!' Jennifer exclaimed. 'Is that…it can't be. He doesn't know the first thing about drums.'

'It's him, right!' Sofie gripped Jennifer's arm, her fingers digging in hard, and gasped. 'He's marching beside the gardener bloke who's helping me fix the courtyard!'

'I don't believe it. Uncle Bret!'

Broad, white straps held a small drum at Bret's hip. He was marching and playing in the middle of a row of drummers, doing his best to keep pace. He might not have been an expert, but he looked brilliant in Calum's red and black clan colours. Back straight and proud as anyone could be, head not moving, his eyes slid to the crowd at his sister and cousin, his mouth working hard against a smile, but he finally let it rip. Tears of pride and happiness shimmered in his eyes.

'Anyone got a tissue—better still, a box?' Jennifer asked, dabbing at her eyes with her sleeve. She wanted to cry and sob for her younger brother. She wanted to run through the marching men and hug him until he yelled, *enough!*

'That's epic.' Claudia clapped with lively enthusiasm.

'Uncle Bob would've been so proud of him,' Sofie sniffled.

'Calum and his family did this. Bret has finally found joy,' Jennifer whispered to herself.

Sofie sighed contentedly and tugged at Jennifer's sleeve, but Jennifer didn't move. She watched the men until they turned the corner and were out of sight.

'Come on, Jen, we need a double shot latté—with a twist.'

* * *

Jennifer took a deep breath and stepped into their restaurant, heading straight for the buffet. She grabbed a serviette, dabbed her eyes, and blew her nose.

'I don't reckon you need to worry about Uncle Bret anymore,' Claudia said with feeling.

'No, he's fine.' Jennifer grabbed the handful of tissues that appeared under her nose. 'Do I look like I've been crying?'

'Hell no.' Sofie performed an exaggerated eye roll.

'I'm gonna make some toast,' Claudia said. 'Anyone want any?'

Sofie swung around to stare at her daughter's back, then spun back, eyes wide and questioning, to Jennifer.

'No thanks, Claudia.' Jennifer shrugged at her sister. 'I've had breakfast.'

'Mum?'

'Love some. Thanks, sweetheart.' Looking bewildered, Sofie blinked at Jennifer, her expression frozen on, I don't have a clue, what just happened?

'Don't look at me, sis,' Jennifer whispered. 'Take Claud's newfound family care and manners and fly with it.

The espresso coffee maker burbled. 'I'll get the coffee—you want one, Claud?' Sofie asked, opening the cupboard for some cups.

'Sure. Thanks, Mum.'

'You think Claudia is old enough for coffee?' Jennifer asked.

'The moment Claudie offered to make toast, she matured ten years,' Sofie said, all misty-eyed.

Toast and coffee in hand, Claudia said, 'I'll take mine in the den and get back to the crap.'

Sofie watched her daughter walk with purpose down the hall to work on her essays. 'It won't be long and she'll drop the Goth make-up. Lately she only slaps it on when she goes out.'

'The Goth make-up really doesn't matter,' Jennifer said. 'Do you think she wears it more as a shield to hide behind?'

'Sadly, yes.'

'Mum—Mum!' Claudia sang out, hurrying down the long hall and charging into the kitchen. 'I'm having a break. I promise I'll finish the essays. Michelle asked me to the Highland band picnic! It's a small fundraiser at Centennial Park. Can I have twenty for the sausage sizzle and dunking the math teacher in the tub—twice?'

'I'll meet you halfway. Ten dollars should do fine,' Sofie said.

'Done.' Claudia took off. 'Gonna get dressed.'

'You look surprised.' Jennifer pursed her lips against a smile.

'That was so easy,' Sofie said in wonder.

'That's because she wanted ten in the first place.' Jennifer smiled and crossed her arms. 'We used that trick all the time, remember?'

Sofie frowned. *Oh.* No more coffees for Claudie.'

Why don't you go have a look around, and spend the other ten?

'I think I will—you coming?'

Maybe later. Calum's coming past to check out that weird space behind the closet. I can't leave; what if he drops by wearing his kilt?

'Good point,' Sofie nodded, then shook her head,

'Stop that or you'll fall over.' Moments later, Jennifer waved her sister off outside the restaurant, calling out, 'And leave the men in kilts alone.'

'Hell no!' Sofie yelled, then stopped and turned to give Jennifer a cheeky look. 'I wonder if Brock's in a kilt. That'd be something.' With a hand to her mouth, Sofie's eyes widened, then, giggling, she said, 'He is so beautiful! Ooh, I might even get to see his legs…' Sofie shivered and melted into the crowd.

Quietly giggling to herself, Jennifer shook her head and silently hoped that big, muscled, kilted Brock would sweep Sofie off her feet. She closed the door, and immediately, the bright morning sun softened through the frosted glass, while the happy crowd noises were muffled. Smiling, she moved around the tables and started setting them up in preparation for the opening. Creating in her own space had been a dream. Jennifer sent a silent thank you to her Uncle Bob.

The restaurant and everything inside it belonged to her and her family. They were in control, and they would make it happen.

'G'day, Twinkles.' Calum kissed the back of her neck.

Jennifer screamed. 'You can't do that! I might be holding a knife.' She threw her arms around his neck.

'Sorry, I thought you heard me. I'll make more noise next time.'

'Thanks for that amazing surprise this morning. We'll never forget how Bret played the drums in a marching band.'

'Bret's a reluctant kilt wearer; says they're scratchy. But, hey, he did really well.'

She looked him up and down, and a slow grin eased into her face. 'I see you've still got yours on?'

'Stop it, you'll make me blush.' Calum reached for her and snuck in a welcome kiss.

'Ooh, that was nice,' she said, pointing to his arm. 'What've you got there?'

'I brought a change of clothes.'

'I like what you've got on, you look dapper, sexy-dapper.' Jennifer slowly licked her lips.

His gaze turned wicked. 'I'll race you to the closet.' He took off and was on the stairs in a flash, Jennifer at his heels.

She looked up just in time to see Calum's kilt swing out. 'You have a great arse.'

In a flash, he was down the hall and in the bedroom stripping off his piper's jacket and toeing off his shoes.

'Anything else coming off?'

'Not yet.' Then he was in the closet. 'You coming?' he asked, voice muffled.

'Just a sec.' Jennifer kicked off her sneakers, and when she caught up, he was checking out the wall behind the belts and ties. She sidled past him, her hands sliding over the old timber from the top to the base.

Calum edged towards Jennifer and climbed over her legs to straddle her hips. 'Sorry.' He squeezed past her.

'No, you're not,' she quipped.

He flipped Jennifer onto her back and almost fell on top of her. 'This closet is insane,' he murmured, hot and hungry.

Jennifer wriggled underneath and kissed him. She cupped his face and gently pushed him back. 'Okay, let's face it. This could go on all afternoon.' She may not have seen him properly, but she felt his grin beneath her palms.

'You're right, got to find the secret tunnel that leads to the treasure.'

Jennifer laughed. 'I thought you'd already done that the other night.'

'I love it when you talk dirty,' he said, and nuzzled her neck.

Her hands grabbed his backside and gave it a squeeze. 'Nice skirt.'

'Kilt, it's a kilt. Tough Scottish Highlanders would be deeply wounded in a very profound way to hear you say skirt.'

'Okay, kilt then. C'mon, Superman, if you can't hover, get off me.'

'I can't until you let go of my arse.' Jennifer gave it a final squeeze, and he lifted himself up. 'Later then,' he murmured, with a knowing smile.

Jennifer giggled. She flipped onto her stomach, knees up and hands out, shifting closer where the back panel met the side. Her fingers brushed against something other than smooth timber. 'Don't move, I think I've found it.'

'Where?'

She gripped his forearm and led him to a tiny hole, just wide enough for a man's finger, halfway between the floor and ceiling of the closet.

'What will happen if we pull it across?' Jennifer whispered, sounding anxious.

'The world as we know it will end?'

She found his shoulder and smacked him on the arm. 'Don't be daft.'

'Let's see,' Calum said quietly, concentrating as he pressed the metal clip with his finger. A wall panel slid across to reveal a door-sized opening.

Excitement, mixed with a generous dose of anxiety, prickled her skin. Jennifer took a deep breath to steady her nerves and stared at the inky-black entrance in front of her. She moved a little closer, reached out, and felt around for something—anything.

'Jen?' Calum was right behind her.

'All I can feel is… is air. It smells stale, but not in a bad way; it's mingled with perfume and lavender, I think?' All sorts of scenarios bounced around in her mind, some scary and some not. The hairs on the back of her neck prickled, sending goosebumps down her arms. She groped around in the dark, hoping to find a light switch, mumbling affirmations, Uncle Bob was a wonderful, caring man, wouldn't hurt a fly.' Jennifer froze, 'Did you hear that? Something rustled, I'm sure of it.'

'Hold on, I'll go first,' Calum offered. 'Can you scoot over?'

'Sure.' Jennifer stepped back, her hands searching for the doorway. But she accidentally stood on his feet. 'Oops, sorry.'

A low rumble escaped Calum's throat. 'Jen, don't rush; whatever's here isn't going anywhere… in case you're wondering. And, just letting you know, in this community, Bob was the best human being around.'

'Yes, he was the best. And I'm glad you're here. I'd hate to do this alone. But, and it's a really big but, there are amazing and helpful people out there who do strange things. And the one person I hope we don't need later is Brock.' A shudder rippled down her spine.

'Have a little faith in your uncle. There's nothing scary in here. Hang on, there's got to be a light switch.'

Jennifer heard a click-click, but nothing happened.

'I'll grab a torch,' Calum said.

'You're not leaving me here alone. I'll grab the torch because I know exactly where they are,' Jennifer hurried to the upstairs kitchen and back. 'You ready?' she asked.

Jennifer sought his hand in the dark, holding it tight. She took a deep breath, turned on the torch, and gasped: its light reflected and sparkled in a stunning array of colours. This was not what she had expected, and the art nouveau lampshade hanging from the ceiling completed the scene.

'Oh. My. God,' she breathed as she gazed at all the beautiful things.

Calum's face lit up as he scanned the room. 'This is it—this is what we're so worried about?'

'They may not have been Uncle Bob's,' Jennifer whispered. 'Like you said, they could belong to the previous owners of this house.'

Calum pointed out a photo hanging on the wall of Bob dressed in a soft pink, sequined gown and a long, wavy blonde wig, with her uncle's signature at the bottom.

It read…*Veronica.*

'Oh my God! Veronica! I wore her—his—nightie. Good heavens, Connie and Shirley saw me wearing it and the stilettos. They went as white as a sheet and behaved strangely.' She shone the torch at Calum. Instantly, his eyes screwed up against the light, and he gently turned her hand away. 'They know something, there's no doubt.'

Calum's smile widened. He held back a chuckle.

'What's so funny?'

'This is,' Calum said, lifting a frock. Sequins shimmered before he put it back.

'Obviously, my uncle felt the need to hide his secret other life.' Taking offence on his behalf, Jennifer's voice rose, 'He meant for no one to see it or find it, even after he was dead!'

'You don't get me, it's amusing, but I wouldn't have laughed at him. Though some in town would have, there's no doubt about that. As I said, I won't say anything to anyone—okay? What Bob did in his private life was his business.' He shrugged and looked around. 'At least I know why Gran loved sewing.'

'Connie made these?'

Yep, Gran has a sewing room. We hardly ever go in there. If we ask who it's for, her answer is always the same: for a friend who loved dressing up for cocktail parties in Sydney and Canberra. She loved making them.

'They're stunning, Connie's got quite a talent.'

'It's a pity they're hidden in a closet. It's all so, I don't know—armless?' He scratched his head, bemused. 'Mind you, I don't understand it.'

'He loved all pretty things.' Jennifer opened a small drawer, peered inside, and found a folded bundle of papers tied with a red ribbon. 'He had a beautiful soul. I wish I'd told him that, and more.'

Calum moved closer to Jennifer, gently cupped her face, and wiped away her tears. 'The way he talked about you, Sofie, Claudia, and Bret… he knew how much you loved him, without a doubt. That's probably why he kept his failing heart a secret. He knew you would've dropped everything to be here with him, and he loved you too much to burden you and your sister with that.'

A smile wavered on Jennifer's face. 'Have you been talking to Father Thomas?'

Calum made a face. 'Nice bloke, but nuh.' He felt for his shirt pocket. 'Got a hanky in here somewhere.'

'In your purse?' Jennifer giggled.

'This is a sporran, lassie,' Calum tried for a Scottish brogue.

'Still looks like a purse to me, and when you think about it, this room is you; you're wearing a skirt as well.'

'Don't knock the skirt, you like what's under there.' He grinned, took her hand in his, and kissed her palm. 'So all this is going to stay right here?'

'I don't know. Maybe I'll use the gowns in the restaurant to give it a 1940s theme.'

'How are you going to explain where they come from?'

'Do I have to?'

Jennifer kissed him and stepped out of the secret room and the closet. Calum followed. Away from the enclosed space and the lavender, her mind cleared, and she started pacing in front of him.

'Do you know how sad this is, how heartbreaking? It's shocking that a gentle man, like my uncle, couldn't be himself in a community that loved and respected him.'

Calum rubbed his jaw and frowned. 'I understand it all too well.'

Chapter 18

'Oh my God!' Jennifer asked, 'Are you saying that you do this as well?'

'Hell no!' Calum's eyebrows shot up, eyes fixed on hers to drive his point. 'But look closely at what you've suggested I might be—and how I've just denied it. What does that make us?'

'Christ! Uncle Bob, I'm so sorry. I would've accepted all of this. I would've helped him choose fabrics.' Tears rolled down her cheeks, and she quickly buried her face in her hands, mumbling, 'He must've suffered terribly. Why didn't he say something?'

She felt his warm fingers under her chin. She pulled her hands away, and Calum dabbed her eyes with a handkerchief. 'Found it in my purse,' he said with a lopsided grin.

'Thanks,' she sniffed and took his handkerchief to blow her nose. 'A hanky. I thought these were a thing of the past?'

'Not with Gran,' a smile spread across Calum's face.

'That's true,' Jennifer said through her tears. 'The first time I met Connie, she pulled one out of her bra.'

Calum's phone rang. He grabbed his jeans off the floor and tugged his mobile out of a pocket. 'Yeah.' Frustrated, he ran his fingers through his hair. 'You've checked everything? I'll be right there.' He turned to Jennifer. 'Sorry, the pub staff are freaking out because the beer fridge is on the fritz. The cleaner probably went behind it with his mop, blindfolded, and accidentally knocked the plug. I'll be back in half an hour, an hour tops.' He undid his kilt and stripped off his shirt. He stood in front of her, naked.

Jennifer struggled to keep a straight face.

'What are you grinning at?' Calum asked, eyes twinkling with humour. In a flash, he became tender, sweet, and honest. 'You know what? I reckon, you should go back to Bob's safe room and get to know your uncle's special secret.'

'Yes, and I will, but right now you're standing naked in front of me, being very tender and caring, and telling me that everything's okay.'

'Yeah, pretty much,' he kissed her forehead. 'Enjoy what Bob's left here for you. And think carefully about how you approach Sofie.' He said, getting dressed, lastly his socks, and boots.

'You think Sofie won't cope?' Jennifer asked absently, while watching, fascinated by his masculine ways of pulling on his clothes

'Your sister can be a little dramatic, in a well-meaning theatrical way. Don't get me wrong, she's a caring, big-hearted person.' His lips covered hers with a sweet kiss. After a heart-thudding smile, he hurried out, yelling, 'Nearly forgot. Gran and Shirl are coming past pretty soon!'

Jennifer yelled back, 'Lovely, I look forward to it.'

She stepped back into the closet and her uncle's secret room. Was she planning to keep his other life a secret?

No, definitely not.

She shone the torch around the racks. Glittering evening gowns of all colours and styles hung neatly, covered in plastic to keep the damaging dust off.

Jennifer felt the blood drain from her face as a shocking realisation hit. It was their mother who continued her father's vicious obsession, despite Polly insisting she leave us alone.

And it was their mother who discovered that her brother, Bob, was cross-dressing. He was immediately cut off and denied existence all those years ago.

She'd heard about her grandfather and his strict, disciplinarian ways. Now, those stories about him flooded back. No wonder he was cut out of his own wedding photo. She realised the outward image had started with his ugly obsession. The slightest mistake by his kids would send him into a rage. Jennifer recalled snippets her uncle had said in passing. 'If I ever came to the dining table without a long-sleeved shirt on, I was sent to my room without dinner, but not without a thrashing.' And their sweet Uncle would try and laugh it off. Did Bob's father discover his son enjoyed dressing up, and that's why Gran was alone in the wedding photo? If Jennifer remembered correctly, their Gran often tried to get him and their daughter, Jennifer and Sophie's mother, to stop their archaic way of disciplining them. But sadly, it didn't help.

Jennifer sank to the floor, her back pressed against the wall. She covered her face and wept for the years of pain and loneliness her uncle had endured.

They were so thankful that once they had their driver's licenses, she and Sofie could see him whenever they liked, even if it meant lying to get out of the house.

Jennifer slowly pulled herself together. She blew her nose on Calum's handkerchief and began searching around. In a large chest of drawers, she found underwear, corsets, bras, and fake boobs. Chiffon scarves and lace shawls. The shoe rack was full of gorgeous stilettos in various styles and colours. Neatly arranged on shelves were boxes of wigs—bobs, curls, long and straight, or wavy.

She recognised a gown from one of the black-and-white glamour photos hanging in the hall. It appeared to be a replica of the one Ginger Rogers wore in the 1934 movie The Gay Divorcee. The heavy velvet gown had a deep green hem slowly fading to a pale green at the waist. It had a sweetheart bodice, and from the shoulders hung narrow lengths of the same deep green velvet as the hem.

A large makeup case sat on top of a chest. Jennifer opened one of the drawers and discovered beautiful costume jewellery that sparkled on a red velvet tray.

'Everything's here to turn Bob into the perfect glamour queen, Veronica.'

Jennifer crouched down to gaze longingly at the variety of stilettos, some lavishly decorated with sequins and beading. A carved wooden box behind the shoe rack caught her eye. She leaned over and picked it up.

'Marilyn?' She breathed the name written on the lid in gold leaf. Jennifer guessed her uncle probably had a few stars he liked dressing up as. Maybe Veronica was his favourite.

She had to talk to Sofie. Searching for her at the picnic could take hours. She decided to keep it a surprise until everyone got home.

Jennifer picked up Veronica's photo. 'I want to bring all these beautiful things out into the daylight. There's no need for shame. I am proud of you, Uncle Bob—Veronica.'

A noise startled Jennifer; she stepped out of the closet and called, 'Hello, is anyone there?'

'Jen, it's me, Sofe. I've got Connie and Shirley with me.'

There was so much to show them, Jennifer's heart skipped as she made her way down the hall and waited for them on the landing.

'We met Sofie at the sausage sizzle and Calum at the front door,' Connie said, sounding a little breathless from climbing the stairs. As she reached the last step, Jennifer held out her hand.

'I wouldn't do that if I were you,' Shirley warned, 'or she'll get really shirty.'

'Only with you, Shirl.' Connie turned to Jennifer. 'Thank you, dear. Calum let us in, and Sofie showed us the restaurant dining room. It looks wonderful, breathtaking and a credit to all of you.'

'There's nothing in town that can top it,' Shirley added.

'Thank you. Sofie and Calum did a brilliant job while I was settling things in London.'

'Yeah, it was such a burden,' Sofie said, running the back of her hand dramatically across her brow.

Connie searched Jennifer's face. 'Are you all right, dear? Have you been crying? It's not something Calum said, is it?'

'Heavens no. He's been my rock.' Jennifer patted Connie's arm. 'You'll have to come with me so I can show you why. Or would you rather have tea first?'

'No, dear, tea can wait.'

'Yeah,' Sofie put in. 'Show us what you found.'

'After you've seen what I have to show you, you might want something stronger.'

'Jeez, is it that bad?' Sofie peered into Jennifer's face.

'It's not like that, Sofe.' Jennifer crooked her arms and invited Connie and Shirley to hook in. 'Since you're all here, I need to ask Connie: did you send me a photo of Calum in the local paper and write on the back, He's missing you?'

'Oops, I've been caught out,' Connie said. 'Did you mind very much?'

Jennifer shook her head. 'Don't worry about it, Connie. The paper and the photo you sent were a lovely surprise on an otherwise dismal day. I was missing everyone, and your parcel was the push I needed to get moving. I wasn't happy in London anymore.'

'Before I forget,' Connie dug into her handbag. 'Calum mentioned you wanted my pickle recipe,' she said, handing it over. 'But until I'm gone, you can't enter any of the local agricultural shows.'

'Connie! You're not going to die and I wouldn't dream…'

But Connie gave her a wise, old-lady look.

'Thank you, I'll treasure it always.'

Jennifer asked everyone to follow her into the pink bedroom. She stopped in front of the closet and nervously wondered where to go from here.

'I've always loved this room,' Shirley said, admiring the decor. 'And you haven't changed it a bit. You must love it too, Jennifer. I especially like the wallpaper—you can't get paper like that anymore.'

'Did you help Uncle Bob decorate?' Jennifer asked for future reference.

'Yes, he needed it, otherwise the room would've…would've…' Shirley faltered and looked at Connie.

Sofie decided to lend a hand. 'Looked too glamorous for a couple of young women?'

'That's exactly right.' Shirley nodded.

Connie gave Jennifer a knowing wink.

'Right,' Jennifer began, 'no more delays, it's time to set Uncle Bob's spirit free. This might sound strange, but just humour me and come into the closet.'

'Ah-ha,' Sofie exclaimed. 'The mysterious space.'

Connie and Shirley seemed surprised, but no one showed the slightest hesitation.

'Is this a secret passage or something?' Connie giggled.

'No, but you're close,' Jennifer said as she guided them through and switched on the torch in Bob's secret room.

'Holy shit!' Sofie cried out. 'Sorry, ladies, but holy shit!'

'It's all right, dear,' Connie laughed softly. 'I think it's worth a holy shit or two. So this is where they all are—except for one.'

'Let me guess,' Jennifer said. 'Uncle Bob went to the hereafter in a gown.'

'Yes dear, he did.' Connie inclined her head, resembling a wise old fairy godmother. 'When he realised time was running out, he jokingly said, 'I would love to go dressed up as Veronica.' Without thinking about how we'd do this, Shirley and I offered.'

So, these two lovely, dear friends had dressed her uncle after he passed away. Jennifer worked hard to keep her chin and mouth from trembling. 'That's quite something; I don't think I would've been able to. Thank you so much. It would have eased his mind knowing he was dressed in his favourite frock.'

Sofie shook her head. 'I wouldn't have been able to do that.'

'I'd like to say it was a pleasure,' Connie said. 'And I guess, in a way, it was—once we were finished.'

Shirley leaned in close. 'He did look wonderful, so glamorous. I said…'

'What is it, Shirley?' Jennifer asked.

Eyes wide, Shirley and Connie exchanged glances before turning to Jennifer.

'What Shirley said was that Bob looked like a movie star and could've attended any embassy function. The reason we're here now is that we met two Polish embassy men today. I saw them at the funeral. Gerek and Antonin would very much like to meet Bob's family.'

'Antonin! I'm stunned, it has to be the same Antonin I met at a Polish embassy cocktail party when Uncle Bob came to Paris,' Jennifer told them. 'And they're here—in town?'

'Amazing,' Sofie said. 'I've got goose bumps. But surely, they didn't come all this way from Paris.'

'They're at the Canberra embassy now,' Shirley said.

Jennifer's thoughts hurtled from one incident to the next. 'They didn't happen to mention a bloke called Dobry, did they?'

Sofie gasped.

Connie shook her head. 'No, never heard of him.' She reached forward and gathered a frock, feeling the fabric. 'I loved making these. Bob was so much fun.'

'Connie, I have an idea, but I'd like your and Shirley's approval.'

*   *   *

By mid-morning the next day, Jennifer found time to take out a couple of tall glasses of refreshing homemade lemonade with crushed ice to the courtyard. Brock, who had helped tidy up the courtyard of builder's rubble, was now helping Sofie prepare the garden beds for planting. He stepped forward, thanking her with a nod and a warm, tentative smile. She moved into the shadows, admiring the plants, and was about to go inside when she saw Brock set his glass down on a nearby table. He extended the other glass towards Sofie. Jennifer watched, fascinated, as Brock took one of Sofie's hands and wrapped her fingers around the sweating glass. He took her other hand and placed it underneath, making sure it wouldn't slip and crash to the pavers. Once she had a firm grip on her lemonade, he slowly slid his fingers along her cupped hand, let her go, picked up his own glass, and drank at least half.

Eyes wide, Sofie looked at the big, powerful man, too stunned to drink her lemonade.

Brock tore his eyes away from Sofie, turned to face Jennifer, and, with a sweet smile, drained his glass and said, 'The best,' his deep voice seeming to bounce off the courtyard walls.

'You're welcome,' Jennifer smiled. 'In a couple of hours, Calum will show you where you can shower and change for dinner.' He gave her a quick nod, emptied his glass, and handed it back to Jennifer. She took it, winked at her sister, and walked back inside wearing the biggest grin. With Claudia and Michelle's help, she organised a delicious smorgasbord lunch. Normally, this wouldn't be a problem, but now her head spun with thoughts of Sofie, Brock, and exciting possibilities.

Bret, Claudia, and Michelle followed Jennifer's instructions exactly so the restaurant would look its very best, with white tablecloths, sparkling wine glasses, cutlery, and, of course, candles and a posy of flowers in the centre. The three adorable teenagers were doing a superb job.

An hour before the guests arrived, Jennifer called out to everyone, telling them it was time to freshen up.

Now that everything was sorted, Jennifer waited nervously outside her restaurant door, with Calum beside her, his comforting arm around her waist.

She spotted her guests near the town hall. As they slowly made their way towards them, her body tensed; this was it.

Bending down, Calum whispered in her ear, 'Relax, it'll be fine.' Then gave her a reassuring kiss on the temple.

Connie, Shirley, a lady she didn't know, and two men all came striding up the footpath.

Jennifer took a deep breath to calm a rush of anxiety, hoping her plan wouldn't backfire.

Connie's big smile and tight hug helped a little, before she stepped back to introduce the strangers. 'Jennifer, Calum, I'd like you to meet Bob's Canberra friends, Antonin, Gerek and Anna, Gerek's wife.'

Anna, whose photo they'd found in the cellar, meant Gerek was the singing drunk.

After big smiles and handshakes all around, Jennifer ushered everyone inside to meet the rest of the family. She noticed Antonin admiring the large black and white photos of her uncle's favourite movie stars that she'd taken down to hang in the restaurant for everyone to enjoy.

With lunch over Jennifer finally had a moment to study the eleven people sitting around the living room chatting and drinking coffee. Brock handed Gerek the photo of his wife, Anna, that she'd found in the cellar. Antonin looked over his friend's shoulder, grinning. Bret, Michelle, and Claudia were talking and laughing. Connie, Shirley, and Anna were discussing fabrics. Brock stood next to Sofie, his big hands around a beer. He tried to keep his expression blank, but his stance gave everything away. Jennifer smiled at the magnetism between her sister and the local police officer.

She sighed, hoping what she saw was real, and turned away to speak to her guests. 'Where do I start?' she began.

Antonin looked up. She caught his smiling eyes and, with a backward nod, beckoned for him to join her. He excused himself to the guests and headed over to her.

'Calum, can you and Sofe look after this lot?'

'Not a problem.' He looked at the tall, debonair Antonin and smiled. 'Don't look so worried, mate.'

Jennifer kissed Calum on the cheek. 'Come with me, Antonin.'

He offered his arm and said, 'Please, take.'

Jennifer slipped her arm through his, and together they climbed the stairs and walked down the long hallway into the pink, girly bedroom. Antonin faltered; she tightened her grip on his arm and saw a look of shock cross his face.

'I know. It's over the top. I learnt yesterday it wasn't Uncle Bob's idea of decor.'

'No, no, not his taste.' Antonin shook his head, eyes wide.

'I have something to show you that was his taste, and I'm pretty sure this won't shock you…I hope.' She took his hand. 'Come with me.' She opened the closet, pulled him in, and slid back the panel. 'It's all easy once you know where everything is.'

'I feel strange,' Antonin said. 'I smell my dear friend Bob. But what is this place? It's so dark.' His voice trembled with sadness.

'I'm sorry, Antonin.' Jennifer reached down for the torch left in its usual spot on the floor. 'I didn't mean for you to grieve all over again. Before I switch on the torch, think of this room as a celebration of Bob's life. Are you ready?'

'Yes, light please.'

'Voila!' and the room sparkled.

Antonin gasped. His hands came up to cup his face. 'Veronica's beautiful gowns…*Choodnee*. Beautiful.'

'You've seen all these before, haven't you, Antonin?'

He smiled through his tears. 'Yes,' he said. He took a couple of steps closer to touch the frocks. 'Some, not all.'

'Antonin, do you have another name as well? Like Bob, who became Veronica?'

'No one knows, but yes, I am Marilyn. I gave Bob a Marilyn Monroe key-ring, a little gift from me,' Antonin said, hand on his chest.

'Oh Antonin, that's so beautiful. Bob has left something for you.' Jennifer turned to get the small, carved wooden box and handed it to him. She ran her hand over the name printed there: *Marilyn*. 'I haven't opened it. I thought Marilyn was another favourite Hollywood star my uncle loved to dress up as, but now I know the box is yours.'

Antonin gazed at it and smiled. He set it aside and opened his arms for Jennifer. She stood on tiptoes, wrapped her arms around his neck, and hugged him back.

'We are a pair, yes? Both weeping like old ladies.' Antonin gave a deep, throaty chuckle. 'I am all right now.' He opened the box and seemed relieved. Inside were photos of Antonin and Bob, some letters, and neatly labelled discs bundled together with a rubber band. 'Thank you for everything. In the wrong hands, this information would ruin my career and my life.'

Horrified, Jennifer wasn't sure what to say. 'Um…that's dreadful, but I do understand. Obviously, Uncle Bob felt he couldn't come out either. Otherwise, there wouldn't have been any need for this room. I wish the world were more accepting. By the way, I happened to try his laptop, and I'm sure it's been wiped. So, I think, you don't have to worry about that either.'

'I must apologise, Gerek did look around a bit. He may have cleaned laptop.'

'*Oh.*' Jennifer nodded slowly as all the little, and not so little, incidents suddenly made perfect sense. 'So, he was the one holed up in the cellar that night—obviously drunk and singing.'

'So sorry, but yes, was Gerek.' He dipped his head as if a little abashed. 'So sorry about your apartment too,' he said, looking remorseful.

'Under the circumstances, I accept your apology, but if I ever come across Dobry again, I think I might have to smack him around. Seeing my personal belongings tossed all over my flat angered me. I felt violated.'

'Dobry was, how you say, pissed off because you kicked him out. Best idea.' Antonin gave her a steady gaze and tapped the side of his nose.

'Was Dobry a plant—a spy?' Her breath caught, flabbergasted at the idea she'd had a spy in her life, in her home…Shit! In her bed! 'Did Dobry make reports on me?'

'Do not worry. He had nothing to report.'

'Really?' Jennifer asked, not certain she wanted to know. 'Our affair must've been terribly boring.'

'No-no, you not boring, ask Gerek. You are chef, very good chef,' he added, peering into her eyes to make sure she understood. 'But not rocket scientist.' His laugh was more like a low thunder-rumble. Imagining this man in a gown was becoming more and more difficult. 'Dobry did other jobs, spying. He, as you say, is not the smartest tool in the shed.' He laughed, adding, 'Is good saying.

He should not have made a mess at your home. He got into big trouble.'

'Hang on, how come you knew he made a mess?'

'He told us he felt like big man to trash your home.'

'Oh!—*Oh!*' If he'd bragged about ransacking her home, he would've bragged about their sex. 'What else did he say about me, my home?' *My bedroom!*

Antonin gave her a blank look.

'Come on, he would've said something about how good he was in bed?' She was feeling antsy now.

'Ugh, he did that all the time, and we did not believe him. Everything he did was rubbish.'

Jennifer briefly wondered if that was a dig at her skills and concluded that ignorance was bliss. 'He's a moron.'

'Oh yes, a big idiot.'

Dare she ask? But there was no holding back; she had to find out. 'Are you a spy?'

'Antonin shrugged and gave a short-sharp grunt, 'E! Everyone spies.'

'What do you mean, everyone?'

'We spy, they spy. All a big joke. Whole families in US of A spy.'

'True, I thought at the time how silly it was to send whole families back after being away from Poland for so long.'

'Yes, especially sad for the children who didn't grow up there.'

'So, Antonin, your life as Marilyn, how did you manage with everybody spying on everybody else?'

'I have private apartment,' he smiled. 'Spies think I have girlfriend.' He laughed again. And Jennifer laughed with him.

'Antonin, I have a plan and was hoping you'd join us. Can you come back next Saturday?'

*　*　*

It was late Wednesday afternoon when Jennifer finished the dinner preparations for an intimate thank-you meal for everyone who had worked so hard. Sofie and Brock, who did all the heavy lifting and hadn't stopped helping her sister create a beautiful cottage garden along the courtyard's fence line, were still at it. Bret, Claudia, and Michelle worked diligently to get everything ready and to make the restaurant sparkle, including ensuring the fridges were stocked. Connie and Shirley declined, saying they were entertaining Gerek, Anna, and Antonin, who were thoroughly enjoying themselves on the farm.

Jennifer poured herself a glass of wine and stood by the upstairs kitchen window overlooking the courtyard. The transformation from a dump to a romantic garden setting had come together beautifully. Brock was on his knees, his large hand around a tub filled with delicate red petunias; he released the plant from its pot and placed it in the ground, covering the roots with rich soil.

After decorating all the fences with fairy lights and draping more in the neighbour's tree that hung over the six-foot fence, Calum moved away and disappeared from view. Shame, she loved watching his agile body at work.

Jennifer heard footsteps on the stairs and turned to see Calum come into the kitchen. He moved behind her, slid an arm around her waist, and the other across her chest to hold her shoulder. He nuzzled her neck behind her ear and softly said, 'You ready?'

'Hmm, not sure what I should be ready for,' she giggled.

'Nothing scary.'

'That's good. I'm too tired to do scary.'

His arm around her waist gave her a squeeze before reaching his back pocket, then his arm came up and pointed his phone at the courtyard. In a flash, all the courtyard's fairy lights lit up.

Dazzling.

Laughing, Jennifer clapped her hands with joy. The change from a plain space to a sparkling, genuinely romantic setting was stunning. She turned and kissed him.

'I'm guessing you like the result,' his deep voice rumbled behind a smile.

'It's everything I imagined. It's spectacular!'

He dipped his head and found her lips for a light but luscious kiss. Jennifer closed her eyes and rested her forehead in his neck.

'Do you know what's going on down there?' Calum asked.

'Where?' she asked, moving her face away from his warm skin.

'Down there,' he said with a nod to the courtyard.

Jennifer held her breath. Surrounded by the magic of tiny lights, Sofie and Brock stood barely two feet apart, facing each other, not moving, just staring. Sofie dropped her trowel; it clattered on the paving stones, and Brock flinched. It seemed to snap him out of a trance because he took a step forward, picked up the trowel, and offered it back to Sofie. When she didn't move, Brock's big hand went to her shoulder. He slowly let his hand slide down her arm until he gathered her fingers in his. Gently, he took her wrist and carefully placed the trowel back in her hand, curling her fingers around the handle for her. With a soft glance over his shoulder, he moved away to plant another tub of flowers.

As if in a dream, Sofie looked down at her trowel, shuffled over to her garden bed and using a watering can, watered the newly planted flowers.

'Christ,' Calum murmured.

'Yeah,' Jennifer murmured back. 'Dinner is going to be…interesting.'

*   *   *

The Grand Opening.

A rush of adrenaline jolted Jennifer awake. She took a deep breath and lay still for a moment, enjoying the sensation of

Calum's chest rising and falling against her back. She twisted around to look at him, and he slowly opened one eye.

'What?' he asked, with a silly grin on his face, his voice sleepy-warm and inviting.

'I thought I heard something.' She listened, but all was quiet. 'It must've been my imagination.'

'Come here. I want to fool around with your imagination.'

'Aw,' Jennifer giggled. 'You wouldn't be able to keep up.'

'I'll give it my best shot,' he chuckled, deep and husky.

She lifted his comforting arm from around her waist, leant across his chest, and squinted through the dim light at the numbers on her bedside clock. 'But I've only got…six hours.'

He tucked her in close. 'I think we can squeeze something in,' he murmured, nuzzling her ear.

She smiled, remembering the previous night when she'd found a dazzling diamond ring in her pumpkin soup. She flexed her fingers to make it sparkle. When she met his gaze, time became irrelevant.

*　　*　　*

'Food? It's five-thirty, too late for lunch and too early for dinner,' Jennifer complained. 'I'm so nervous I can't eat, and besides, Sofie pulled the ties on the back of this dress so hard, there's no room. And every time I breathe, my boobs pop up like a couple of balloons.'

'I know,' Calum gave her a wicked grin and kissed each soft, voluptuous mound, then he straightened and handed Jennifer a shot glass filled with cognac. 'Have a mouthful of this.'

She eyed him, knocked it back, and coughed. 'That'll do it.' Jennifer grabbed her gown, swung around, and called for everyone's attention.

'Okay, remember our plan: as soon as the Cadillac comes back around and we stop in front of the shop, Antonin, you switch on the outside sign. Gerek, you open the doors, and Anna, you draw the drapes.' Gerek translated for his wife, and Anna's face lit up with a smile. Everyone nodded, understanding the process. Jennifer could only hope, but even if it all went wrong, it didn't matter; to her way of thinking, it would add to the day's fun.

'Okay, ready?' Calum asked. 'I can't believe I'm driving four hot, Hollywood babes around the block. I'll be the envy of every bloke in town. Who are you all supposed to be anyway?'

'I'm Marlene Dietrich,' Sofie sucked in her cheeks, struck a pose, and lowered her voice, saying, 'I just love this silver sequined gown, darling.'

'I'm Elizabeth Taylor, whoever she is, and this gown is…I don't know, but it's pink, and I feel like a princess Barbie.' Claudia fluttered her lashes. 'Apparently, Liz had lilac eyes and oodles of lashes, and they weren't fake like mine.'

'Antonin insisted he make me up as Marilyn Monroe. He told me to pout a lot.' Michelle puckered her lips. 'How's that?'

'Fantastic,' Calum said. 'Don't do that anywhere near a bunch of young blokes.'

'Yeah, right,' she scoffed. 'I'll be pouting every second. And bending over a lot, because this gown barely covers my—'

'I really didn't want to know that, sis,' Calum interrupted with a mischievous grin aimed at Jennifer. 'I know who you are.'

'Uh-huh, big boy. I'm Veronica Lake,' Jennifer purred and flipped her long, blonde wig back to reveal a cutaway, red satin gown and one bare shoulder. 'You look mighty handsome in your liveried chauffeur outfit.'

'Later, Veronica.' Calum took her hand and kissed it. 'Okay, ladies, hop in please.'

This was it. Nerves fluttered in Jennifer's stomach as she slid into the front passenger seat of her uncle's yellow Cadillac Deville. With the top down, they were open to view. She turned to the others in the back seat and reassured them. 'There's no need to be nervous, you all look gorgeous.'

'I'm not nervous,' Claudia said. 'This is what I do most days, lots of make-up and weird clothes. I've not been in a Cadillac before, and I love it.'

'Michelle, are you okay?' Jennifer asked. 'You look a bit stunned.'

'Oh, I'm stunned all right, but loving every minute.'

'Sofe?' Jennifer twisted around to see her sister.

'If I don't get a date out of this, I'm cutting up my lingerie and joining a nunnery. What are we waiting for?'

'Bret's going to honk the horn when he's in the back lane,' Calum said.

As if on cue, a strangled honk sounded, and Calum backed the gleaming, chrome-laden Cadillac with whitewall tyres out of the garage. He drove up behind Bret, who was driving a borrowed Model T Ford.

'It's Connie and Shirley,' Jennifer waved. 'I didn't know they were going to be in the back of the Ford!'

'Hey!' Sofie called out. 'You look gorgeous.'

Connie and Shirley turned as much as their old bodies allowed and waved back. Their wide-brimmed hats, held down by swathes of lilac organza, complemented the vintage car look.

Calum drove slowly down the lane after Bret. Riding in the Cadillac felt like floating on a massive air mattress on the ocean, and they wallowed majestically around the corner into Grey Street.

Sofie cranked up the volume on Jennifer's portable CD player as Liza Minnelli belted out her signature song, Cabaret.

Heads turned, people laughed and some shouted, 'Good on ya, luv!' As Sofie handed out more invitations to the opening.

Someone yelled out, 'So which one of you is Veronica?'

Jennifer waved at the crowd; she could never have imagined anything as wild as this. The flyers posted around town had brought scores of people out to cheer them on. She sent a little prayer to Bob in the sunny, bright blue, autumn sky. She was living a dream, and the most important people in her life were living the dream with her.

Calum slowed down near Centennial Park. Jennifer reached across and took his hand.

'Quick, everybody. Smile,' Michelle said. 'It's Frank, the local journo, and he's pointing his camera at us.'

'Where is he?' Sofie asked, waving.

'Right there on the traffic island with his telephoto lens sticking out half a mile.'

'Ooh—ooh, I'm going to be in the paper.' Sofie, grinning like a maniac, waved at the journo taking photos.

They passed the photographer, who followed them easily enough on foot: Sofie posed and insisted he take a flyer.

They drove back towards the restaurant, with the crowd following and joining the people already waiting outside.

On cue, the drapes were drawn back, the doors opened, and the sign lit up.

Jennifer, Sofie, Claudia and Michelle, in all their finery, stood up in the Cadillac.

Calum climbed over the back of the driver's seat to reach Jennifer.

'What're you doing?' she asked, laughing as he straddled the seats.

He gave her one of his quirky grins, then one hand curled around her waist, while the other moved up to hold the back of her head. He then dipped her back for a long, hot Hollywood kiss in front of everyone. Jennifer raised her arm straight up. As rehearsed, everyone in the car struck a pose and pointed at the crimson neon sign that said,

VERONICA'S

BOOK #2 Sofie and Brock

City girls' country love.

#3 Adelyn Takumi

#4 Ava and Lawson

ABOUT LOUISE FORSTER

Louise, an award-winning author of bestselling novels in the Tumble Creek series, is working on her fifth book, Tumbling Back. She lives on the far north coast of New South Wales, Australia, five minutes from the Pacific Ocean with her family and a menagerie of pets. She loves writing edgy romances with a touch of humour, mystery, and sensual passion. She enjoys writing from a hero's perspective—resilient, straightforward men who love their women unconditionally. They can also fix anything, including a broken heart. Her sassy heroines are strong and stand up for their beliefs, even when they feel vulnerable.

Thank you.

Cheers, Louise ♡

Author Links

www.louiseforster.com

Facebook
https://www.facebook.com/LouiseForster.RomanceAuthor/

Instagram
Louise Forster (@louise.forster.author) • Instagram photos and videos